ACCLAIM FOR KARINA HALLE'S EXPERIMENT IN TERROR SERIES

"*Seductively entertaining...I'm convinced that it has some secret ingredient (like the sauce on a Big Mac or the coffee beans at Starbucks) that makes it immediately addictive.*" – Bitsy Bling Books

"*I don't think, short of being completely ridiculous, I can encourage you more strongly to read this series. It has quickly moved to the top of my favorites list.*" – The Bookish Babes

"*A ghost hunting adventure with original characters guaranteed to please!*" – Romancing the Darkside

"*Loved it, loved it, loved it. I can't say it enough. I've never related to a character as much as I did to Perry Palomino.*" – Pretty Opinionated

"*Halle's first-person narrative is written in a breezy fashion that instantly made me feel like I could hang out with her protagonist.*" - Forever Young Adult

"*Perry and Dex are two charismatic and slightly crazy characters that carry you in kicking and screaming along for the ride.*" – Naughty Between the Stacks

LYING SEASON

BOOK FOUR IN THE EXPERIMENT IN TERROR SERIES

∞KARINA HALLE∞

\m/ Metal Blonde Books \m/

First edition published by Metal Blonde Books DEC 2011

Publisher's Note: This is a work of fiction. Names, characters, places, and incidents either are the product of the author's imagination or are used fictitiously. Any resemblance to actual events, locales, or persons, living or dead, is entirely coincidental.

Copyright © 2011 by Karina Halle
All rights reserved, including the right to reproduce this book or portions thereof in any form whatsoever.

Cover illustration by Karina Halle
Design by Bret Taylor
Author photo by Amanda Sanderson
Edited by Bob Helle

ISBN-13: 978-1467948258
ISBN-10: 146794825X

Metal Blonde Books
P.O. Box 845
Point Roberts, WA
98281 USA

For more information about the series
and author visit: www.experimentinterror.com

For the dogs of my life, Duke, Ellie and Muffin

CHAPTER ONE

"Tell me about the accident, Perry."

I barely heard what the doctor said. I was busy staring out the window of his office, watching the leaves of the oak tree outside waver in the spring breeze. It wasn't quite five o'clock but the sun was already setting, creating a harsh orange glow behind the buildings of downtown Portland. It caught the edges of the tiny symmetrical leaves, making each one look like they were tinged with flames, that slow burn towards the middle.

But they weren't on fire, were they? No, they only looked like it.

"Perry, where are you?"

I tore my eyes away from the window and gave Dr. Freedman the nastiest look I could muster. His skinny, narrow face was aglow with the fiery light, but like usual, I couldn't tell what he was thinking. He had that stupid noncommittal look of a psychiatrist; that patient, patronizing stare that never gave anything away. All of that was scribbled away on his notepad.

"Where the fuck do you think I am?" I sneered at him.

He merely nodded and looked down at his precious notepad. "Just checking, Perry."

"You're always saying my name," I said, and looked back at the window. The sunset's flames had turned each new, green leaf into a burst of crimson. I could figure out why he was always saying my name; I guess shrinks thought they had to constantly remind their patients who they were. Well, I knew who I was. What I didn't understand was why I was there. Why I was *really* there. No pretenses.

"So, tell me about the accident," he said, careful to leave out my name this time.

The accident. The accident. Always this Goddamn "accident."

A strand of my neon blue hair fell down in front of my face and I examined it carefully. It looked dry and brittle; the bleach job I did a few months ago had done nothing but damage the core. That was the first thing my mom had said, "Not only do you look like a punk, but you've ruined your gorgeous hair forever." I was glad it hurt her more than it hurt me. It was her fault that I was here. Not some accident.

I looked through my hair; it created a gauzy blue curtain and I liked the fact that I couldn't see Dr. Freedman clearly through it. It made it easier to deal with him.

"You tell me about the accident, doctor."

He nodded again to himself. I wished he was the one on fire, not the leaves outside.

"Who is Jacob?" he asked.

I flinched. I didn't know why.

"Jacob is a friend of mine. Well, he was a friend of mine."

"Why is he no longer your friend?"

"You know why. He turned creepy. After the party..."

"After the party? Last time you said he got 'creepy' before the party."

"Did I?" I asked absently.

"How did you first meet?" he continued.

The last time I was here, he asked me the same question. I don't know why I always had to repeat myself and I didn't understand his fascination with Jacob. It really wasn't that interesting.

I took in a deep breath, letting him know how annoyed I was with my sharp exhale and told him the story. Again.

"Jacob was..."

Jacob was a skid. Jacob was 18-years old. Jacob failed the 12th grade probably a million times. Jacob had a really tall black Mohawk that was held together by numerous packages of Knox Gelatine. Jacob always wore a studded denim vest with a black D.O.A patch on the back. Jacob was kind of always D.O.A himself. He was always in trouble with the police, with his parents, with his schoolmates or with his friends. And he thrived on this trouble. He'd wear black lipstick to school and try to kiss the jocks. Jacob was always asking to get beat up. He was a martyr to the skids and I'm pretty sure he thought he was a martyr to humankind. But the truth is, even though there were parts of me that admired him, that respected his nature to piss off authority, to be true to himself, and be fearless (there were even parts that found the black lipstick to be sexy), Jacob was just kind of an idiot.

"Were you in love with him?" Dr. Freedman asked, so casually, as if the topic of love was as important as whether I preferred chocolate ice cream or vanilla.

"No," I said adamantly. That was the truth. I barely knew Jacob. Like I said, I admired him a bit and when he talked to me, at first anyway, I would get giddy about it. But I got giddy when any guy looked my way. It was so easy to overlook the fat girl.

"But you liked him enough."

"I guess," I shrugged. I liked him enough when it was from afar. And I guess I liked him enough the first time he really talked to me, away from his friends and the rest of the skids.

I was walking home from the bus stop one day. Normally I would have taken my car to school but my parents had confiscated it from me. Something to do with drugs, I don't know.

Anyway, I was walking home, listening to my MP3 player, when a tall, spiky shadow appeared beside me. It was long because the nights were longer then and it was just getting dark enough to put me on my guard.

I could tell the person was speaking to me but I couldn't hear them above the music. I don't know why people have to talk to you when you've got headphones on; I mean, come on.

Finally I looked over and saw it was Jacob. I stopped, surprised and pulled out my earphones.

He was dressed as he always was. A true skid.

"What are you listening to?" he asked.

"Alice in Chains. *Music Box*," I replied, rather proudly, thinking he might approve.

"They're all right. I mean, they were all right. Kind of a shame about Lane though. That fucker is irreplaceable. But he was too smart for the band anyway."

I wasn't sure what was so smart about Lane considering he died because of drugs, but I hadn't been too smart either. Then I noticed Jacob's wrists. They were wrapped in thick bandages.

"You said Jacob had tried to kill himself?" the shrink asked me, his words cutting through my memory.

"That's what they said. Everyone at school," I told him. "Earlier that week, there were rumors that Jacob had killed himself. Killed himself over some girl. Some even say he burned himself in a car. Lit the fucking car on fire. And I never saw Jacob at all that week, so I believed it. But then there was no news of a funeral or anything, no news anywhere really, so I started to think it was just a rumor. One probably started by himself, another martyr cry or something. He'd often disappear from school for even weeks at a time."

"But the wrists told you otherwise."

"Well, d'uh."

But even though I had proof in front of me that Jacob had tried to commit suicide, I didn't want to bring it up with him. It seemed in bad taste. And even though I liked that he was speaking to me, there was something about him that had me a bit on edge. Maybe it had something to do with the fact that it was getting dark and I was walking alone with only my schoolbooks to protect me. Maybe it was the fact that he seemed a bit on edge himself, more so than usual. Either way, it was enough that I thought I should start taking self-defense classes one day.

"And then what happened, Perry?"

I shrugged. "He walked me home. We talked a bit."

"What about?"

"That day? It was just music. He went on about Lane, then Sid Vicious, then some dude I had never heard of. Then he said goodbye to me about a few houses down from my house."

"Did you know he lived in the area?"

"No. And I still don't think he does. I mean, he never did."

"You think he's still alive?"

I gave the doctor an odd look, confused. Where was he getting that information from? "Of course he's still alive. Why wouldn't he be?"

I could tell the doctor wanted to say something else but he stopped himself and said, "What did you guys talk about the rest of the time?"

I sighed and racked my brain back. I couldn't really remember all that well. I think most of it was nonsense. I mean, the dude had walked with me for three weeks straight, we talked about a lot of things and I still had trouble remembering what happened yesterday. Still, there was something Jacob kept mentioning to me that the doctor would have loved to know. But it would only egg the doctor on and I'd be back for another session. I knew enough about psychiatrists at this point to know how they worked.

I gazed out the window again, letting my thoughts float away. Yes, the leaves were now certainly on fire. In fact, all of Portland looked like it was ablaze. If I looked hard enough, there was a strange shimmer to the horizon, a weird, warpy air that I had seen before. But the shimmer wasn't in the distance, it was close to me. It was like a mirage that stood between me and the window. And beyond that mirage was a raging fire that quickly turned the trees outside to tinder and the buildings into a merciless inferno.

It wasn't real though. I knew that much. It wasn't real *this* time. But when it happened the other day, at Adrianna Gee's house, it had been real. The flames were real that day. And had Jacob not been there when the whole party went up in flames, and those...*things*...came out, I wouldn't have been sitting in Dr. Freedman's office. I wouldn't have been anywhere.

And to think they called it an "accident."

CHAPTER TWO

"Hey! Miss Muffin Top! Anyone home?!" Brock Alma's booming, domineering voice shot across the field like a rocket.

I took my face off the mud and fastened my eyes on Brock with the last ounce of strength I had left.

I opened my mouth to answer him but then thought better of it. The last time I talked back to him, I, well, ended up where I was, doing fifty push-ups in the gooey brown mud. And these weren't girly push-ups either.

I swallowed hard, battling my urge to be a smart aleck, and pushed myself up into the last final movements, my hands slipping beneath me, my chest and arms screaming and shaking.

"I said," Brock continued, satisfied with my non-response, "once you're done the push-ups, I want you to run around the field twice, then you can come back and join the rest of the group."

At that, my arms gave out from under me and I was eating mud again. At least it was on the fiftieth.

What was I, a pariah? I had been doing this stupid bootcamp for two weeks now and from the very first session our trainer/psycho drill sergeant Brock (how perfect of a name is that, by the way – it's like Bastard + Jock = Brock) had it in for me. We had been meeting in the afternoons every other day and every other day I had to do more push-ups than everyone else in the class. Now I know I was paying someone to torture my ass but I definitely wasn't paying someone to single me out.

That said, I did have a hard time controlling my mouth around him. The other trainer, Michelle, was sweet but firm, kind of like a less threatening Jillian Michaels, but Brock knew how to push my buttons and he pushed them good.

I rolled over onto my back, not caring how dirty I was getting and slowly got to my feet, my thighs aching beneath me. We were in a field in eastern Portland, the site of our twisted fitness sessions, rain or shine. Since it was the end of November, the shine thing rarely happened and it was cold. It didn't matter though. Despite Brock picking on me, the cardio circuit drills in sleet and thunder, the days where I couldn't even walk up the stairs to my room, I was almost done with the boot camp. One more day and it would be over and I would be walking away stronger, more confident, and just the tiniest bit slimmer.

And it wasn't just the bootcamp I was doing. See, ever since I returned home from D'Arcy Island in one ragged, bruised heap, I'd decided to take things into my own hands. If I was going to be doing the Experiment in Terror show with my partner Dex and putting myself in dangerous situations, I was going to need to prepare myself for anything and everything and in as many ways as possible. And until recently, I hadn't been prepared at all.

From being thrown through windows to riding bucking broncos to being attacked by wild "animals" to being attacked by potential rapists to being clubbed over the head and locked in a floating coffin...well, these aren't your ordinary work hazards. In fact, if I think about it too much, it really starts to scare me. And sooner or later, my good luck, or whatever it is that's keeping me in one piece, will run out. I know this.

Once upon a time I had taken some training in self-defense and I've had karate and stuntwoman classes but it's just not enough insurance against the unknown.

And so, as soon as Dex dropped me off at my house after the last "adventure" two weeks ago, and after seeing my parents' faces when they saw what an absolute wreck I was, I promised them, and myself, that I was going to "man up." So I signed up for a quick boot camp, I went back to the firing range that I used to frequent a couple of years ago and I took three private, refresher Karate lessons. None of these were cheap, of course, and with my sparse salary coming in only from Shownet, and only sporadically at that, plus the fact that I was now paying rent to my parents, it swallowed the last of my paycheck from my previous receptionist job. But I knew it would be worth it, if not right away then somewhere down the line.

But as I finished up my two laps around the field and felt the fire building up around my heart and the stiffening pinch in my chest, it did seem like a waste of money. Once again, why was I paying someone to put me through pain?

I stopped and caught my breath for a quick second, ready to return to the group of chubby college students, single moms and frail yoga flowers before Brock called me Miss Muffin Top again (such an endearing nickname), when I noticed they were done and everyone was staggering back to their cars. Looks like I wouldn't have to join them on burpees and mountain climbs after all. Class was over.

Relieved as hell, I turned toward my motorbike Putt-Putt, which sat off in the park's parking lot. *One more day*, I thought.

"Muffin Top!" I heard Brock bark.

My shoulders sank and I reluctantly looked in his direction. He was walking over to me, his strong legs rippling in the dying afternoon light. What now? Private after-class torture sessions?

I crossed my arms and gave him my best "you've got to be kidding me" look, feeling the first waves of chilly pre-winter air nipping along my sweaty body. Even with the sweater and jacket I had back at Putt-Putt, it was going to be a cold ride home.

Brock stopped in front of me and smiled uneasily. I wasn't used to seeing him smile; maybe that's why I thought it looked strange on his face. Not that he had a bad face; he was handsome in that broad-necked, tanned way that most fitness buffs were. But whenever he was barking at me, it was accompanied by a grim, overseer look.

"What?" I asked. "Class not dismissed for me?"

He scratched the back of his head, his Adam's apple pulsing in and out. "One more class...," he said and I suddenly got the impression that he was shy, like a boy trying to make conversation in the schoolyard.

"Yeah," I said, eyeing him suspiciously. "Thank God."

He looked embarrassed and said, "Sorry if I've been pushing you too hard."

I narrowed my eyes at him, trying to figure him out. All that was missing was for him to twist his toe into the mud.

"As you said, it's just one more class," I told him, feeling the situation growing strangely awkward. The breeze swept in and I eyed Putt-Putt again, wanting to get warm and go home.

"I watch your show, you know," he said.

I looked back at him, surprised. "You do? My show? Experiment in Terror?"

"Yeah. Seen every episode."

Not that that said a lot since there had only been like five of them. I was always shocked when I found random people who watched it.

"You knew who I was from the start?"

"I sure did. I didn't want to say anything in case it embarrassed you."

I burst out laughing. "You've been calling me Miss Muffin Top for two weeks straight and running me ragged till the cows come home. And you didn't want to embarrass me."

"Hey, you're not Miss Muffin Top anymore, right?" he asked, smiling again as he reached over and grabbed my love handles with one of his strong hands. It was brusque and off-putting and my body tensed up, my instincts greased and ready to go. He was right though. A lot of extra chub I had carried around my waist was now gone. I hadn't been this streamlined in...well, ever.

Still, I stared down at his grabby hand, unimpressed. He took it back and shrugged. "Anyway, I just wanted to say I'm proud of you. You've changed a lot in two weeks and I hope this will go far...in the future. I knew you needed to get on top of your game, I could see it on your face, I could it see in the show, especially that last episode...on the island. It scared me, if you can believe it, and I thought it must have scared you and I figured you could use an extra push."

"I see," I mused. I wasn't sure what to make of that. I looked back and tried to pinpoint if at some moment it seemed like he was trying to convert me into a UFC champion or something. I couldn't see Brock as anything more than just another ego-tripping trainer who liked to make unfit women's lives a living hell. In fact, it sounded like he was trying to sell me on signing up for another class.

"Would you like to go to dinner sometime?" he asked sweetly.

I almost laughed again but I'm glad I didn't. One glance at his face and I could see he was sincere. My 'roid monkey bootcamp sergeant was asking me, Perry Palomino, out on a date. The question caught me so off guard that I didn't even know what to say. I didn't even know how I felt about it.

OK. That's a lie. I did know how I felt about it. It felt wrong. Not because Brock was a bad guy, a bad-looking guy, or because I knew we'd probably have nothing in common. It felt wrong because my heart wasn't in it. My heart wasn't intrigued. My ego, sure, that was poking its head about inside, ears pricked and raised. But my heart...it belonged to someone else. Someone who wasn't mine.

It's funny. Even though it had been two weeks since I last saw Dex, time had done nothing to erase my feelings about him. The island had done something to us. At least, it had done something to me. If I thought I was head over heels for him before, this time I was so far gone it's like I fell into my own grave. Head over heels and down a hole. Bury me with dirt, stick a stake into my heart, and call it a day.

"I'm sorry," Brock said, his expression turning down. "I didn't mean to be so bold."

I shook my head and tried to wipe off the look on my face, which probably looked pained. I certainly felt pained. My heart ached in a different way than it had just minutes before, when it was suffering from cardio onslaught.

"No, don't be sorry," I said, trying to smile.

"You have a boyfriend, of course," he said.

My smile fell slightly. "No. No I don't."

Because, of course, Dex was just my partner. Sure I was in love with him, sure he told me some things on that island that melted my heart, sure I still had tingly images of him with his head between my legs and felt his grip on my hips. But there was always Jennifer Rodriguez, his stupid fucking girlfriend who never seemed to be going anywhere. I had hoped that perhaps after her pregnancy scare, after Dex confronted the fact that he wasn't ready to be a dad, and after, well, he kinda (perhaps regretfully) cheated on her with me, that she'd be on her way out. I still held out for that hope – it's not like that's the kind of thing we'd discuss on the phone anyway – but as far as I knew, she was still in the picture.

"Oh," Brock said, and I realized how awkward I had just made it for him. What was wrong with me, anyway? A cute, buff meathead was asking me out for dinner and all it was doing was making my head spin and my soul hurt. That wasn't right.

Without thinking, I reached over and grabbed his beefy forearm.

"I'd love to go for dinner with you," I said. This wasn't true, but I said it anyway.

He must have seen that on my face because he hesitated and then said, "Really, I can handle rejection, I-"

"I mean it," I said quickly and started feeling like maybe I *did* mean it. "You just caught me off-guard. I'm not used to being asked out."

He gave me a disbelieving look. "Oh, please, I have a hard time with that."

I shrugged, not wanting to get into it. "It's true but anyway, thank you, I'd love to. Just promise me you'll stop with the nicknames."

He agreed. I already had one nickname and that was enough.

~~

"Hey, kiddo."

It was Dex on the phone. We had gone from texting and emailing each other whenever we had something to say, to calling each other every now and then, sometimes just to talk. At least our relationship had progressed in that way.

After I had arrived home from the boot camp and took a hot shower to wash the mud off and ease my aches and pains, I roamed the house looking for my sister, Ada. For once, I was miffed that she wasn't at home. Not that she was home all that often, especially since she started dating this guy Layton, who was two grades older than her (my sister is 15), but I needed to talk to her. I know this sounds stupid coming from a 23-year old, but I wanted her advice on boys. What happened with Brock had simultaneously torn me up and excited me and I needed to vent to someone about it. I had become more and more dependent on Ada as a friend instead of viewing her as just a sister.

Which was great, but on this night it left me feeling fidgety. And talking to Dex wouldn't help either. Though Dex was my friend in every sense of the word, and I trusted my life to him, he was the last person I could vent about this to.

Regardless...

"Hey Dex," I said, cradling my phone against my ear. I didn't just say it though, I *smiled* it. I was sitting cross-legged on my bed, thumbing through an old issue of *Guitar World* magazine, looking for inspiration and an excuse to use my electric guitar that sat forlornly in the corner of my room.

"How was *The Biggest Loser*?" he asked, the amusement flitting along the trough of his deep voice. It was his nickname for the bootcamp, despite the number of times I told him there were no real fat people in the group.

"It was...interesting," I said and suddenly didn't want to say anymore about it.

"That guy still riding you hard?"

I snickered. I couldn't help myself.

"What?" he asked, never one to like being left out of a joke.

"Nothing," I said, trying to hide the smirk in my tone. "Only one more class, then I'll be buff enough to kick anyone's ass."

"You already were buff enough to kick anyone's ass. I don't think my nose will ever be the same."

Oh, that's right. I ended up punching Dex right in the nose while we were on the leper island. I could barely remember what it had been about; there were a lot of things about the island that I had tried to block out (not his head between my legs and his grip on my hips however), but all I knew was that it had been a long time coming. I still felt bad about it, in a vague way, but it wasn't keeping me up at night. Dex liked to bring it up occasionally, just to keep me on my toes.

"What can I say, you're an easy shot. But I don't think the rest will be like you."

"The rest? You're planning on going around and punching more people in the face?"

"People...ghosts."

"From Ghostbusters to Facebusters?"

"Something like that. Anyway, I feel better and that's the point."

He was quiet for a second. Then, softly, he said, "I know, kiddo. Don't think I wasn't thinking about it myself. If you hadn't done it, I would have suggested it. You're right, about what you said before, that we won't always be so lucky."

I didn't like getting into touchy subjects like this on the phone. It made me want him too much.

"Well, perhaps you oughta be taking some sort of self-defense class or something," I suggested lightly.

"I don't need self-defense. I have you," he said. I could almost hear him grinning over the phone. "Anyhoo, I have some good news."

I didn't spend much time wondering what it was before he announced, "We got it."

"Got...it?"

"Permission. From the mental hospital. Riverside. They said next week, Tuesday and possibly Thursday, they'll let us in to film."

Since returning from D'Arcy Island, Dex had been trying nonstop to get one of Seattle's oldest mental institutes to open their doors to us. The Riverside mental hospital was reputed to be one of the most haunted places in Washington State. So far, many ghost hunters, including some with bigwig TV shows, had tried to film the hospital and were turned down. Understandably, considering that the hospital was at least 30% operational. It was a dying, costly breed but it still housed some people who needed the strictest mental care.

"How did you do that?" I asked.

"I can be pretty persuasive," he said. Yeah. Persuasive or pushy and annoying.

"Uh huh."

"And, again, I think because we're small and on the internet we're kind of reputable. They know this isn't the Hollywood treatment; we aren't sensationalists. I'm still not sure what exactly we are allowed to film but it's still great news. I've been going fucking mental over here over this."

It sounded like he was making a pun, but I knew he wasn't. It was a spooky slip of the tongue. Not only was Dex on medication for his so-called mental condition (which I was starting to call "Deximia"), but I recently learned he had been in a mental hospital himself. Ever since he brought up this mission of his to secure us a chance to film in Riverside, I had wanted to bring up the whole mental institute thing. You know, how is this a good idea considering your past (and present) and all that, but I couldn't find the right way to say it. And again, something I didn't want to get into over the phone with him.

But if digging up his past bothered him, for once he wasn't showing it. Perhaps he felt a need to prove something to me, or himself. That he was over it. That it was in the past. I just hoped he knew what we were getting into.

Still, I repeated, "Mental?"

"Yeah," he said without missing a beat. "Fucking mad as fucking madness. Jimmy has been breathing down my neck about what our next plans were but I just felt – no, I just *knew* – that eventually the people at Riverside would cave in and let us. That's why I didn't want to book us anywhere else. Fuck, I didn't look anywhere else."

Jimmy was his boss. Well, our boss. And he was very good at breathing down Dex's neck. Luckily, I never had to deal with the jerk, only through Dex.

"Well, gamble paid off then."

"Paid in spades and worked out perfectly. Next Friday is the Shownet Christmas party and I figured you'd come up to Seattle for that anyway."

That was presumptuous of Dex, as usual. Granted, I still didn't have a full-time job, so it wasn't like I wouldn't be able to take time off or anything. It's just assuming I'd go all the way to Seattle for a Christmas party, one that I hadn't been officially invited to. I still didn't feel part of this whole company, even though they were the ones playing my meager salary.

"Perry?"

"Yeah, sorry. I was just thinking," I said, scrunching up my forehead with my hand. "Are you sure I'm invited?"

"To the party? Don't be a tard, kiddo. Of course you are. I just invited you."

"Yeah, I know. But I don't know, I just don't feel like I belong to your whole work thing. And I haven't gotten an invitation in the mail or anything."

"Ah, jeez. Come on. You do belong to the whole work thing, and if there's any reason that you feel like you don't, it's because you haven't met anyone else but me. And Jimmy that one time. And I swear, the rest of the crew is so much nicer than Jimmy and I put together. We're the rats of the whole bunch."

That was probably true. "But..."

"Also, everyone knew I would be the one inviting you. Everyone expects you. Everyone wants to finally meet the famous Perry Palomino, the reason I have a broken nose."

"Oh, Dex, you didn't," I stammered, feeling my heart drop.

"Didn't tell them you punched me in the nose? I told *everyone* you punched me in the nose. It's a good story."

Oh fuck. My face flushed red with heat. I had already been worried what people at Shownet thought of me and now they thought of me as a partner puncher.

"I bet Jenn wants to kill me," I whispered.

"Uh. Well, no. She laughed and said I must have deserved it. And I did. And everyone is really, really jealous of you, Jimmy especially. And I wouldn't be surprised if you ended up getting some special plaque for it."

I shook my head, despite the fact that he couldn't see it over the phone.

"So, it doesn't matter. You're coming. And it would be better if you could come a few days earlier too. Say, Sunday night."

"Well, how long is Shownet going to cover the motel costs, cuz I can't afford anything right now."

"Motel? No, you'll be staying with us."

My breath froze somewhere in my throat. I had to cough to get it out.

"Us?"

"Yeah. Forget about a motel. We have the spare room. You'll stay with me, Jenn and Fat Rabbit."

"Who the fuck is Fat Rabbit?"

"Fat Rabbit is our dog."

This was all too much. I wasn't sure what to focus on, the fact that I would be staying with Jenn and Dex, or the fact that they had a dog. A dog called Fat Rabbit.

"When in God's name did you get a dog, Dex?"

I heard him scratch his chin scruff over the phone. "Hmmm, maybe a week ago. I sold my old apartment, got a new one. And the new one allows dogs. And now we have a spare bedroom, perfect for guests like you. You'll be our first one."

"I need to lie down," I managed to say, and did just that. I lay back onto my bed with a pillowy thunk, while Dex explained that his old apartment in the Queen Anne district had been for sale for a while. Someone finally bought it and they snapped up one in Belltown, right beneath the monorail. And all this time, Jenn had wanted a dog but they weren't allowed pets. Now that they were, Jenn went and bought some sort of white French Bulldog that apparently looked like, well, a fat rabbit.

I didn't know what was more disturbing. The fact that all this happened and Dex never said a word of it to me or the fact that they got a dog together. Sure, there was no kid on the way, thank God, but a dog was a huge commitment.

And now I had the chance to see it all up close.

Still, I couldn't turn Dex down. If I did, he'd think something was up. And honestly, as much as the idea of living with Jenn and Dex made me want to vomit (for real, the bile was making its way up) and cry, I couldn't afford to be in a motel, not after all the money I'd spent in the last few weeks.

I did have to turn down Sunday night though. Because that was my date with Brock.

"I'm sorry...what?" Dex said after I told him.

"I have a date," I repeated.

He burst out laughing. The anger steamed up inside me.

"What's so funny, asshole?"

"I'm sorry, I'm sorry, kiddo. It's not funny, it's just surprising. Who is it with?"

"Brock. My bootcamp trainer."

He started laughing again. Howling, actually. When he calmed down long enough he sputtered, "The 'roid monkey?"

"He's not a 'roid monkey!" I said defensively, even though I had called him that earlier. Ugh, I definitely talked to Dex too much. "And so what, why can't I go out with him?"

I was hoping Dex would say something that would make me think he was jealous in some way. But no.

"You can go out with whoever the hell you want to, kiddo. But you're a hard rock chick of sorts and he's a jock. And those two types don't mix."

"Dex, this isn't high school. Grow up."

"Some things don't change."

"Oh, were you a fuckface back in high school too?"

Pause. I knew he was taken aback at my ferocity.

"Yes. And a skid and a bit of a punk."

"Well so was I," I reasoned.

"It's too bad we didn't go to high school together," he said. "We would have made a good couple."

I swear, I was this close to hanging up the phone. Or throwing it against the wall.

But Dex continued, smoothly, "Listen, if this date is important to you, Perry, then by all means go on it. Come up on Monday. We'll figure something out."

The weight behind his voice made me reconsider whether the date was worth it or not. What if it was more important for the show for me to be there earlier? What if an opportunity came along? I could always go out with Brock when I got back.

"It's nice to see you have a social life for once," he added.

And that comment made all the difference.
"Monday it is," I growled into the phone.

CHAPTER THREE

When the night rolled around, I still hadn't had a chance to talk to Ada about my boy woes. The night before, she had come home after I had fallen asleep, something she had been doing more and more often now that she was dating Layton, and was off to class in the morning.

I couldn't even catch her after school because she went straight to a friend's house and then jettisoned home before we all went out for our dad's birthday dinner.

My dad is a fellow Scorpio like myself, bringing up the end of the spectrum, which still leaves him full of scorpion sting but with none of the passion. At least, none of the passion that I understand. I'm pretty sure the only thing my father feels passionate about is convincing his wavering theology students of the "truth." That and really good Chianti.

Naturally, his birthday dinner was held at a really old, authentic Italian restaurant just outside Portland, a place he and his brother Al had been coming to since they were young boys. It was no Olive Garden, I can tell you that much.

I half-expected that Ada would have brought Layton with her, but I guess when you were in the tenth grade, bringing your boyfriend to your dad's birthday bash wasn't something you took lightly.

It was for the best. I know nothing would ruin my dad's birthday more than having his teenage daughter's older boyfriend there but from the glances I stole of Ada on the drive over there, I could tell she was a million miles away and already pining for him, her bright blue eyes swimming in the early darkness. I felt pity for her and her young love for exactly three seconds before reality slammed into me and I realized I was no better than she was.

With family being such an important factor to Italians like my father, I knew that my Uncle Al was going to be there, as well as my nephews Matt and Tony. I hadn't seen those three since the whole lighthouse incident in late summer and I had been itching to see them ever since. It felt like years ago when I had first met Dex in that fateful tower, when my life had twisted around on itself and changed its course.

What I didn't expect was that Uncle Al had brought a special guest with him to the dinner party.

"Her name is Marda," my mom told Ada and me as we got out of the car and walked towards the restaurant. Mom looked elegant as always and not the slightest bit cold in her lacey caplet that barely covered her toned arms.

I struggled to keep up in my heels, not used to dressing up for any occasion, plus I was dealing with overused leg muscles.

"Al has a girlfriend!?" I cried out. I was happy for him, of course, Al seemed like such a lonely bachelor since his ex-wife left him, but it was still surprising. He didn't go out much, except to play the occasional poker game, so I wouldn't even know where he could meet any women. It's not like he'd be at the grocery store, pushing his cart around with the bananas facing a certain way (I had read this is what some singles in grocery stores did. A certain type of fruit in one direction meant you were single. I think melons and bananas were probably all you needed).

My mom gave me a funny look, probably because of the very unladylike way I was walking. "Yes, Marda is his new girlfriend. You should ask him how they met; it's mostly your fault."

My fault? I hadn't played matchmaker since my high school days and that was only because I was the fat, helpful girl who had attractive friends, but before I could ponder that any further, we entered the restaurant to cheers and applause from the waiters and kitchen staff (no one does birthdays like an Italian restaurant) and the sight of Al, Matt, Tony, and a petite blonde woman (Marda, I'm guessing) standing around a Chianti-strewn table.

And then my eardrums were blown out. Drunken exaltations (noting at least one bottle of wine was empty), hugs, cries, slaps on the back and loud hellos were exchanged among the Palominos at deafening levels.

I gave Matt and Tony one big hug at once, happier to see them than I originally thought. There was something about those twins, their goofy demeanor with an underlying wholesomeness, that made me miss the person I was when I last saw them. Everything seemed so simple then.

I pulled back and peered at them. They looked different somehow. Cleaned up (I'd say fresh-faced if Matt didn't appear to be suffering from some bad acne) and maybe the slightest bit older.

"You guys are starting to look like men," I said, and grabbed both their biceps for show. There still wasn't much there.

"So are you!" Tony exclaimed with a smile that made him look momentarily younger. He then grabbed my arm, which was now bare after the hostess took our coats away.

I looked down at it and blushed. I know I had lost some weight but it had only been two weeks since I started the sessions, and though my arms were stronger, they certainly didn't look much different. It would be a long time before I looked like Sheryl Crow.

"Thanks, I think," I said to them just as Uncle Al came over and picked me up in a bear hug.

"Perry!" Al exclaimed joyously, his voice muffled into my shoulder.

"Hi Uncle Al!"

He put me down and gave me the once over. A wash of concern came across his wrinkled brow.

"You're looking beautiful, you're as tiny as ever," he said, but I didn't quite believe him.

"But?" I prodded him.

"But nothing." He smiled and put his arm out for Marda, who came slinking under it with a shy expression.

"Perry, meet Marda," he said, squeezing Marda's slight shoulders. She was a very lovely, sweet-looking lady with small, sparkplug eyes and a long porcelain face, roughly my uncle's age (late forties). A good match for Al, who wasn't quite as robust and hard-faced as my father.

We shook hands quickly, her grasp warm.

"Quite the grip you've got there," she commented, taking her fair hand back and looking at it.

I blushed. I was always the person assigned to open any tough pickle jars. My small but durable hands were probably freakishly strong now thanks to the boot camp. Push-ups really did work every part of your body.

"Sorry," I said. "It's nice to meet you."

"She's my lady friend," Al boasted, squeezing Marda closer into him and kissing the top of her head. The relationship couldn't have been more than a month old, so it was extra endearing to see Uncle Al acting like this with someone.

But before I could ask them how they met (after all, I apparently had something to do with it), my father demanded everyone sit down. The birthday boy was starving and thirsty. A deadly combination.

I took my place next to Ada and the twins, with the "adults" on the other side of the table. I gave Ada a quick smile but she was staring dreamily into her glass of water. My sister was still the top of the pops when it came to her fashion blog and an occasion like this was a prime excuse for her to dress like someone who had just fallen ass backwards off the catwalk. My black knee-length dress (the only dress I really had) looked fine on me, I guess, but it wasn't a backless cashmere dress with embroidered details like Ada was wearing. I was actually surprised she hadn't asked me to take a picture of her like she did every other day when she was wearing an outfit "for the blog." But Ada wasn't herself these days, anyway.

While I pondered that over, the conversation around the table turned to pleasantries and news stories. The twins told me about this ATV they bought and I pretended to listen while I picked at my pseudo-healthy chicken Marsala. I was watching Marda and Al with interest. They were sharing bites of their food between each other, pouring each other wine. A bottle of red. A bottle of white. And I was instantly reminded of Billy Joel's "Scenes from an Italian Restaurant." The memory poked at my insides a little bit until I winced it away.

There was no denying it though; there was a lot of love at this table tonight. It didn't take long for my mother to pick up on it and say, "Would you look at this! You won't find dopier, more love struck people than my two daughters and their uncle."

"Me?!" Ada and I both protested at the same time, then consequently glared at each other in that, "yeah, you" look that we did so well.

"Caught red-handed," Al said, squeezing Marda's hand. "And it's all thanks to Perry."

"Yeah, what's the deal with that?" I asked, happy to have the conversation turn over to him.

"Well Marda here works in property insurance. I had to file a claim after you blew up the lighthouse."

I loved how, even though I barely had anything to do with the lighthouse blowing up (what, it's not like *I* set it on fire or anything), everyone still referred to me as the person responsible for its demise. OK, so it would probably be standing today had I not gone poking my nose into its business but then Al wouldn't have met Marda.

"See, something good has come out of it," I pointed out, directing most of that toward my father, who just shook his head to himself and poured himself another large glass of wine from a reedy Chianti bottle.

"Of course," Uncle Al said. "It's not just the good fortune of meeting my lovely Marda here either, the boys have been happier too, haven't you?"

Matt and Tony shrugged but even I could now see they looked a bit...relieved. Maybe it wasn't that they looked older, it was that the ominous, overseeing lighthouse was no longer on the edge of the property, taunting and teasing them with its evil secrets. They looked, well, happier. Al was right.

"And you wouldn't have your little ghost show either," he added. "A lot of good has come out of it."

"You must tell me about this show, Perry," Marda piped up in her soft voice, leaning against Al and fixing her attention on me. "I haven't had a chance to watch it yet. Al says it would keep me up at night."

Matt looked at me. "We've been telling all our friends about it. That shit is fucked up."

"Matthew!" Al admonished.

He shrugged unapologetically and looked back at me.

"That last episode was f...sick. What was the deal with the deer? That scared the shit out of us!"

"Matthew!" Al again.

With the attention now turned to me, my cheeks flared a beet red. I still have trouble coming to terms with having myself on the internet and I was suddenly grateful that Brock hadn't told me about knowing who I was until the very end.

"I honestly don't know," I told him, trying not to look at the rest of my family, who I knew were looking at me with their usual disbelieving eyes (except for Ada but I could tell she wasn't even paying attention to me). "We woke up in the middle of the night and like a whole herd of deer were gathered around our tent. We never even saw them after that."

"Weird," Matt said. "You said on the blog that a lot more happened but that footage was all lost at the bottom of the sea."

"Oh, how convenient," boomed my dad, sounding more drunk by the moment. My eyes flew to him, enraged. *It's his birthday, let him have this*, I thought, trying to bury the urge to yell at him.

"It's true," I said through gritted teeth, trying to keep focused on Matt's curious face.

"Well, what happened?"

Too much for me to tell. After Dex and I returned back home, after I got my wrists patched up because of my altercation with the rose garden, and Dex had his raccoon wound stitched up, we decided to show everything we shot (that still remained with us and not on the Super 8 at the bottom of Haro Straight) and leave the rest up to the viewer's imagination. Normally, I would have written a lengthy blog entry telling the entire story, elaborating on the stuff that the cameras couldn't pick up on. But this time...I just couldn't do it.

I think a part of me was afraid that the more I admitted what happened, the more that this "Anonymous" person would come on the blog and comment on what a liar I was. Yep, I knew the hater I had was still lurking around on the internet somewhere, waiting for me to say the wrong thing. And this time, at least, I knew that others would agree with her (Dex seemed adamant that it was a female).

What happened to Dex and me on D'Arcy Island seemed like more than a bad dream. If I told anyone what actually happened, how a psychotic, cross-eyed midget from a 1900s mission turned me against Dex, how we were hunted down by zombie-like lepers, and how I nearly drowned saving a child who was already dead...well, it sounds so unbelievable even I think it over in my head. There was a reason why I blocked most of it out. Except for that second night, when we awoke to the wails of an insane ghost and my need for Dex overtook everything else. And when I say need, I mean lust. That was purely my fault.

I gave Matt a small smile, knowing the blush was deepening up to my hairline.

"A lot happened that I can't even remember. I'll tell you the rest one day."

I shot a look at my parents, who were exchanging wry glances with each other. Well, let them think what they want. I was happy to know that at least the twins gave me more than the benefit of the doubt.

"Apparently, Perry thinks she needs to work out now to fight ghosts," my mom said after she tore her eyes away from my dad's increasingly red ones.

I bit my lip, not sure how to answer that without sounding like a loon. I knew from my mom's voice that she was treating the whole thing like it was a joke.

"But if that gets your weight down, I'm all the more for it," she had to add.

"So," Al said, shooting my mother a wary look and then smiling at me as if he was apologizing on her behalf. He didn't need to. I was used to that shit from my mom. It's probably why my father and Ada didn't even notice. "If you don't mind me asking, how do you plan to defend yourself from…uh…ghosts?"

I knew Al didn't believe in ghosts per se (though he did believe in "Evil"), hence the gentle yet skeptical tone he was using, but he still seemed sincere in his questioning. Marda was watching me expectantly too.

I tried to answer as diplomatically as possible. "I just think it's good to be prepared. It's not so much the ghosts as it is the situations we are in."

"Is that how you got this?" Matt asked, pointing at the scar on my wrist that sat beneath the purple Silly Bandz bracelet.

"That…was a lively rose bush," I said, knowing how stupid that sounded.

"So you've been going to the firing range so you can shoot gardens?" my dad scoffed. He had never been very supportive of the whole gun use thing. Not that I had a gun or ever planned to get one.

I stared him down. "As I said, dad, it's good to be prepared."

"How do you kill ghosts anyway? You obviously can't shoot them," Marda said, somehow managing not to sound the slightest bit patronizing.

I honestly didn't know. I had always wondered that myself.

"I'm not really sure. I don't think you can; I mean they are already dead and everything. I think you can trick them though."

"How do you mean?" Tony asked, leaning forward past Matt so I could see him.

"Well," I started and wondered how best to explain without sounding crazy. I decided I already sounded crazy and went on, keeping my eyes on the wax that was dripping off the candles in the center of the table.

"When we were on the island we had to escape this ghost named Mary. She had stolen one of Dex's knives and was about to sever the rope that connected the sailboat to the shore."

I looked around me to see how everyone was reacting so far. My dad rolled his eyes and got up, going to the washroom or perhaps outside to get fresh air and wonder where in God's name his daughter came from. My mom was watching me with worried, fearful eyes. The rest, including Ada now, were glued to my every word.

"I didn't know what to do," I continued. "I didn't even think. I just grabbed the flare gun out of Dex's backpack and shot it at her."

The twins hollered simultaneously.

"You're fucking joking!" Matt cried out.

Even Al looked too flabbergasted to get mad at his son's use of language at the dinner table.

"No, I wish I was. I just fired it. She was maybe only ten feet away."

"And did that...kill her?" Marda asked.

"I don't know. I don't think so. She was already dead, so how could it? But what I think it did was trick her. My theory is that most ghosts don't really accept the fact that they are dead. I think they spend most of their time wandering around in another dimension, living in denial. I don't know. Anyway, I think all that did was make Mary think I killed her, at least long enough so that we could get away. It at least knocked her ass off the cliff and that's all we needed."

"Why the hell didn't you write about this?" Matt said, shaking his head and reaching for his glass of wine.

I laughed.

"Why? Because...who the hell would believe me? I sound like a lunatic, I know I do."

"You sound like your grandmother," my mom said in the coldest tone I'd heard from her lips in a very long time.

Al gave her another look, this one fully loaded. Something was going on but I couldn't read into it, not across the table in this busy Italian restaurant. My mother rarely spoke about my grandmother. She died when I was very young and I only saw my grandfather when we went on family trips to Sweden.

"What's that supposed to mean?" I said to her, trying my hardest to not sound defensive.

My mother looked down at her manicured fingers for a second before taking a tepid sip of water. "Your grandmother lied a lot, that's all."

I smiled at her though there was nothing pretty about it.

"I'm not lying."

She didn't say anything else but she didn't need to.

Trying to dissipate the tension, Tony spoke up. "Too bad you don't have one of those boxes from Ghostbusters. You know, some way to contain them."

"Yeah," I agreed absently, still keeping my eyes on Al and my mother. "But we're still trying to figure this whole thing out. Learning as we go."

"You and this Dex fellow," Al said, noticing my gaze, and for once I was glad to talk about Dex.

"Yup. Going up to Seattle on Monday to film the next episode at the Riverside Mental Hospital. Then on Friday there's a Christmas party for work. 'Tis the season."

"And is your work going to be paying for your hotel this whole time or are we going to have to help out?" my dad asked, returning to the table just in time. It's like he has some radar that alerts him when someone mentions anything money related. Or touches the thermostat.

"No." I glared at him despite my promise to play nice because it was his birthday. "I'm staying with Dex and his girlfriend."

It's like a collective breath was held above the table. Everyone froze. Finally Ada started coughing on her water.

"Are you insane!?" she yelled and grabbed my hand. I pulled back, surprised at her outburst. Aside from when Al and Marda had asked her about Layton, she had been silent the entire dinner.

"Possibly?" I answered.

My mom reached over and tapped Marda on the arm gently. "She's in love with her Dexter partner."

Marda nodded knowingly while I exclaimed, "No I'm not!"

I swear everyone at the table rolled their eyes in unison.

"And his name isn't Dexter!" I sat back further in my chair and crossed my arms. "Whatever, I'll be fine. I have a date on Sunday night anyway. With another man. Who isn't Dex."

Another gasp at the table. This was the longest dinner ever.

"Don't act so surprised," I muttered.

"Who with?" Ada asked.

"My bootcamp trainer, Brock," I said, ready for everyone to laugh the way Dex had. Surprisingly, everyone looked impressed.

Finally my mom said, "Now this guy sounds like a keeper. Imagine how skinny you'd get around him! Maybe then you could do a fitness show instead."

There was no use in saying anything. I swallowed my indignation with the last few gulps of my wine and soon the conversation flowed to the local college basketball team and other things, leaving me locked in my head with thoughts that went nowhere.

CHAPTER FOUR

I'd like to say that I escaped my dad's dinner the other night with no other humiliations or poignant conversations, but that wasn't the case.

At the end of the night, when everyone had had too much wine and had stuffed themselves to the gills, I was accosted by Uncle Al as I was heading back from the bathroom.

"Perry," he said, placing a gentle hand on my arm. "Could I have a word with you?"

I nodded quickly, knowing that there was something on Al's mind for most of the dinner but not knowing what it was.

He led me past the kitchen and to the backdoor that let out into the staff parking lot, surrounded by overstuffed garbage cans and a few stray cats hanging around. I crossed my arms against the cold and watched as Al stuck a moldy doorstop into the door so it wouldn't lock behind us.

"Are we allowed to be back here?" I asked, eyeing a tabby warily.

"This place is like a second home to me," Al said jovially.

"Are you planning to off me?, I jokingly asked. "Because this is looking like a Sopranos set-up."

"Nothing like that, I just wanted to give you some advice." He walked forward a few feet and stopped. The yellow light above the door obscured his face, making him look more and more like a mobster. I knew he was just my Uncle Al but it frightened me how overactive my imagination was these days.

"Perry..." he started and then trailed off. I couldn't see his expression in the dark but I could tell his eyes were probably closed and his forehead was scrunched up dramatically. "I worry about you."

Oh, here we go again.

"Not in the way your mother worries about you," he said quickly. "Just...in a fatherly way. I'm sure if Daniel" (my dad) "wasn't tipsy right now, and wasn't so bullheaded about you, he'd be telling you the same thing."

I shivered against the chilly breeze and took a step away from the shadowy garbage bins. "Sorry, it's freaking freezing out here."

"I know, just give me a minute. Just...listen to me. I don't want you to say anything until I'm done and then we can go inside. You can get all defensive in the warmth."

I eyed him suspiciously, totally unsure of what he was going to say.

He reached over and pressed his finger into the space above my heart. I looked down at this finger and looked up at him, confused.

"I think you going to Seattle, you staying with Dex and his girlfriend, I think..."

It's a bad idea, I thought.

"I think it's a good idea," he finished. I looked at him, surprised. He put more pressure on his finger. He continued, his voice grave, "You've got this hole in your heart, Perry. I can see it on your face. You're so beautiful, bella, you really are, but you look so...sad. You've got this hole, I can see it and it is bleeding out slowly.

It's clotted only by hope. This hope, based on maybes and what ifs, is killing you. This pin is small and it moves quietly. You need a knife. Get over it. Face the finality of it all and move on."

I was speechless. I stepped back a foot so his finger was no longer above this so-called hole in my heart.

"Are you saying you want my heart to be broken?" I asked incredulously.

"It will heal. And you'll be stronger for it. Much stronger. If you go, you'll get hurt. But it'll be worth it in the end."

I couldn't believe what I was hearing. I couldn't believe it and I didn't want to believe it. Yeah, I knew that going to Seattle was going to suck in many ways but it was just another thing to "man up" about. I'd get through it. But I didn't see how my heart was going to be broken. I knew Dex was with Jenn. I knew they had their new apartment and their Fat Rabbit. I knew every night he was going to go into their bedroom with her and...

"See," Al said. I didn't want to meet his eyes. I knew the expression on his face.

"Can we go inside now?" I asked meekly.

Al put his arm around me and ushered me toward the door. "You'll be fine. It'll be a learning experience. And when you get back, it'll all be over with. You'll be bled out and all the better for it."

And then we went back into the restaurant and joined the rest of the party in saying our goodbyes.

But I had been unable to stop thinking about what Al had said. Did I really keep on loving Dex because there was always that chance of "what if?" What if he broke up with Jenn or maybe if he fell in love with me anyway, or...so many scenarios to even list.

I was even thinking about it as I got ready for my date with Brock on Sunday night. It didn't help that Ada had brought it up.

"So what are you going to wear to the Christmas party?" Ada asked, watching me apply mascara in our bathroom mirror. Rob Zombie blared from the tinny CD player and a half-drank glass of wine sat on the ledge, my medicine for calming my electric pre-date nerves.

I looked down at my dress, the same black dress I had worn at my dad's birthday dinner. I figured it would look nice for Brock too.

"This one," I said.

She gave me the most unamused look. It caused me to put down my mascara and say "What?"

She shook her head. "You are absolutely hopeless. This dress? You look straight out of a Donna Karan ad."

"Is that bad?"

"It's fine if you're going to work. In 1994," she snarled. "Perry, this pains me to say this but your body is way too good for this. How the hell are you going to win over Brock or Dex in this?"

I had to turn around and face her at that. "Win over Dex?"

"What are you wearing to the Christmas party?" she asked again.

"This!" I yelled, pulling at the skirt of it.

"Hold on," she said and left the bathroom, closing the door behind her.

Hold on? Hold on to what? I looked at myself in the mirror and straightened out the dress. There was nothing wrong with it at all. It was boring, sure, but black was flattering and it matched my hair. It hid my boobs and hips and covered up my thighs. I had a nice face, I knew that, so if that's the only thing Brock noticed, that was fine with me. Besides, he knew what my body looked like' he had been berating me as I ran around in Lululemon pants for weeks. I was Miss Muffin Top. I wasn't fooling anyone.

As for Dex...well, like it or not, Dex had seen me naked, so again, I wasn't about to fool him. And I didn't want to anyway. I had never dressed up for Dex and I wasn't about to start doing it at the Christmas party.

OK, so when I wore that low-cut red top for the shoot at D'Arcy Island, that was a teeny bit for him. But, whatever.

The door opened again and Ada flounced in with something satiny in her hands. She locked the door behind her and thrust a dress in front of my eyes.

"What is this?" I asked.

"It's what you are wearing to the party."

My eyes narrowed at her. It was involuntary. I know my sister often meant well, but there was no way in hell I could ever fit in her clothes and she knew it.

Picking up on that, she sighed with keen exasperation and said, "It's not my dress. I mean, I was sent it as a sample, someone wanted me to wear it on my blog. But it's way too big for me. I was going to hold a giveaway for it, but I thought maybe you'd like it."

I gave it the once over. It was strapless and a satiny, almost iridescent, teal blue. A very lovely color actually. But still. My first instinct told me to distrust it. If it wasn't a statement-making concert tee, it wasn't "Perry."

"At least try it on," Ada said, physically opening my hands and placing the dress in it.

"I don't want to wear this tonight, it won't be appropriate for a first date."

"Fuck tonight," she scoffed. "I know tonight's just a distraction. This is about Friday. Dude, nothing matters. You're going to go to that Christmas party looking like a million bucks and you're going to show that stupid whore who's the boss."

I couldn't help but laugh at Ada getting all jealous and protective. She looked as worked up as anything, her feverish expressions causing her smudgy makeup to settle beneath her eyes. I didn't have the nerve to tell her that it wasn't the point of the trip, that I didn't have a chance in hell, and that I was, according to Uncle Al, heading straight into heartache.

"Don't pretend," she said, coming closer. "Just put the damn dress on and I'll tell you the truth."

I sighed and pointed at the door. "Well at least give me some privacy."

She didn't budge. "You're going to have to get used to people seeing you naked," she teased.

"I'm already used to it," I answered without thinking. Her eyes widened.

"What!?"

"Get out, let me change," I told her, opening the door and pushing her out of it.

"But, but," she protested and I locked the door in her face.

"Perry!" She pounded on the door. "What do you mean? Who has seen you naked!?"

"Ada, shut the fuck up!" I yelled back, knowing that was the last thing my parents needed to hear.

She shushed up as I quickly stripped out of the black dress and shimmied into the teal one. It was too tight for my liking and I couldn't zip it up all the way by myself but...

I reached over and opened the door. Ada's eyes bulged comically.

"Holy shite, where the hell do you get your boobs from?"

I rolled my eyes. "Can you just zip me up?"

She nodded quickly and ran it up the rest of the way. I sucked in my breath and the extra few inches of support made my breasts prop up even more.

Ada was speechless for once. I took a step back from the mirror and tried not to be too critical. The color made my skin glow and my hair seem like rich ebony. The darker edges around my light blue irises looked saturated, like the teal color was leaking into them. It was shorter than I would have liked but at least my waist looked small. My breasts weren't obscene or anything, but there was no mistaking them. I turned to the side and eyed my butt and hips. Again, no mistaking them. They were both out there for the world to see, like it or not.

"You look like Joan Holloway," Ada breathed. She apparently watched *Mad Men* like the rest of the world.

"Thanks. A compliment, right?" Although I found Christina Hendricks sexy, it didn't mean my waifish 15-year old sister did.

"Of course you dummy," she said, now turning her attention to my feet. "Are you wearing those clunky black things you wore the other night?"

"You mean the only heels I have? Yes."

She rolled her eyes again. "Hold on."

I wasn't holding onto anything. I was finding myself not only liking the dress but liking the way I looked in it. Wasn't this what Uncle Al was warning me about, with all the maybes and what ifs?

I shook my head in an attempt to snap out of it. I admit, I did want to go to the Christmas party now looking like a million bucks. It wasn't to win over Dex. I knew him well enough that the way I looked wouldn't change anything. But I did want to show to everyone else that I wasn't some fat, dumpy, stupid ghost show host. I knew Miss Anonymous wouldn't be there but I still knew that everyone would have read those comments and I needed that one extra push that no, I wasn't like that at all. Miss Anonymous, what a stupid, jealous bitch, she doesn't know what she's talking about.

Ada came back in with a computer printout in her hand.

I took it from her and peered at it. "What's this?"

"I got a gift certificate. Fifty bucks at the designer shoe warehouse. I'm sure there's one in Seattle. Go and get yourself a sexy pair of shoes when you're there."

I looked over the printout and it confirmed what she was saying.

"Ada," I began.

"No," she said, closing my hand over the gift certificate. "I have enough shoes."

"You're just too good for discount shoes," I said with a smile.

She smiled back. "You know me too well. Now go break Brock's heart. You'll need it for practice."

And with that, she shut the door behind her, leaving me with the gift certificate in my hand, wondering when my sister had become 23 and myself 15. At least, that's what it felt like.

~~

The date with Brock went better than expected. He picked me up (I wasn't about to ride Putt-Putt in a dress, nevermind the helmet hair) in his Honda Civic and took me to a trendy bar in downtown Portland, with a smashing view of the Willamette River.

He was a perfect gentleman. He laughed at my jokes, paid for the food (despite my insistence), and he looked quite handsome in his grey dress shirt, a nice change from his jock outfit.

We talked about a lot of things, though I tried to keep the conversation focused on him. Only near the end did he start asking more and more about the show and ghosts. He was a believer, which was good. The last thing I wanted was to be with someone who just wanted to pick my beliefs apart. That would be akin to a Catholic going out with an atheist.

No, Brock was fine. And he was a good kisser, too, as I found out on my parents' front stoop. He didn't seem to want anything more and anything less. It felt good to taste someone else's lips, to feel someone else's feelings, especially ones so transparent.

But as I was saying goodbye to him, I had a heavy, sinking feeling in my heart.

For one, there was the fact that he liked country music. The minute he admitted his love for Rascal Flatts, I knew we would never be. And then there was the simple, sad, ugly truth that he wasn't Dex.

I tried my hardest to ignore that feeling the entire date. I tried so hard. But at every awkward pause and every glance at the clock on the wall and every quick slurp of wine, all I could think about was that if this were Dex sitting across from me...everything would just be OK.

And that thought made me sad as hell. It's like that first date you take in order to move on. Full of false promises and lies you tell yourself, the lies that you'll find someone else, someone better. At some point, those lies become truths. But I needed that to happen sooner, rather than later.

So as I was saying good-bye to Brock, and my heart had no real interest in seeing him again, the logical side of my soul kicked in. I asked him if he wanted to go out again when I got back from Seattle, and he said yes. He even looked a bit surprised; maybe he was smarter than I thought and had been picking up on mixed signals from me. I knew I had been sending them.

I watched him get into his car and waved at him as he drove off. Even if I wasn't all that excited about a second date, I knew it needed to happen. I needed to move on. I needed, more than anything, to prove Uncle Al wrong.

CHAPTER FIVE

On Monday morning I strapped my over-stuffed duffel bag (Ada's satiny dress included) onto the back of Putt-Putt and got ready to blow the popsicle stand that I called home.

Ada was already at school and my father was off teaching at the university, so it was just my mother and me, staring at each other uneasily in the crisp, foggy morning. Traces of overnight frost still clung stubbornly to our wide lawn, making our house look like a gingerbread one rising out of white icing.

"Do you know where you're going?" she asked, looking extra skinny under the heavy fur coat she was wearing, probably made out of Swedish wolverines or something.

"Yes mom. I Google-mapped it," I said, my breath coming out in a frozen, hanging cloud. I flashed her my iPhone in one quick motion.

"I don't know what that means," she said, pulling her coat in closer. I eyed her feet. She only had her morning slippers on.

"It means I know where I'm going," I replied patiently and gave a final tug on the bag.

I walked over to her and gave her a quick hug. Her coat smelled like a mist of dated perfume and moth balls. She had that coat for as long as I could remember and wore it almost every day when the winter air hit Portland, yet it still smelled like something out of a 1920's German film.

She embraced me back and pulled away with a worried mother look. Sometimes I want to tell her that the more she frowns and twists her lips to the side, the more the wrinkles will come. But that would be cruel and I know she's aware of it. My mother knows everything about preserving beauty.

"I'll be fine," I said, even though she hadn't spoken.

She just smiled tightly and looked down at the shiny brown/black hairs of the coat. "I know."

She looked up and her expression had changed. Now she was the no-nonsense mother I knew too well.

"How was your date last night?" she asked. "We had gone to sleep and you weren't home yet."

I almost detected a prying naughtiness in her voice, as if she was hoping I'd gotten lucky or something.

I gave her a suspicious look. "It went fine."

"Are you going to go out with him again?"

"Maybe," I said and turned back to my bike, ready to not only leave the popsicle stand behind but this weird, awkward conversation as well. "I'll call you when I get there."

She sighed and I looked back at her one last time. She looked fed up but gave me a quick wave.

"Be safe."

I nodded, slipped on my helmet, took one last look at my Google map directions, and got on the bike. I popped one ear bud in my ear, flicked my iPod to the newest Slayer album and off I went.

~~

I didn't start freaking out until I was a Google map-block away from Dex's apartment. And when I say freaking out, I mean, full-on panic attack. Going up the wrong way on a one-way street didn't help either. I quickly pulled my bike into a small parking lot between a donut shop and a sleazy motel, got off it and put my head between my legs.

My entire body was awash with the sickening pins and needles effects that my panic attacks (or extreme nervousness) produced. I was so focused on not losing my breath or fainting out cold in public, that I barely noticed the freezing rain that fell steadily on my back.

I straightened up, leaned against the donut shop's brick wall and raised my head to the sky, hoping the wetness would bring some sense of reality to me.

Sometimes panic attacks did creep in out of nowhere, but I knew this one was the pure product of the situation. Really, there was nothing to be afraid of. I was going to see Dex. Yes, sometimes things between us were a tad awkward when we'd been apart for a while, but even now I didn't think that would be the case. I had even talked to him the morning before, getting the directions to his apartment.

I guess I just wasn't sure what Jenn would be like. And I didn't know how they would be around each other. What if they were some super-affectionate couple and were kissing every five minutes? The thought of that made my eyes roll back in my head.

"You all right, girlie?"

I blinked hard at the rain and looked over at a young, dreadlocked man who was stopped on the sidewalk near me.

I nodded quickly, not finding the words and feeling embarrassed.

"Least someone here likes the rain," he said, more to himself than to me, and started swaggering down the street until he was out of my sight.

I gathered my thoughts and composed myself. I needed to pull it together here and now or this whole week would be a waste of time. If Jenn and Dex were going to be all coupley and cute, so be it. This was just part of the process and I would just have to deal.

Though I didn't want to, I conjured up an image of them together, lips locked in a passionate embrace. It hurt, boy did it ever, but I kept that image in my mind's eye and forced myself to see every detail, to feel everything I was going to feel. Disgust, shame, embarrassment, jealously, envy, awkwardness, even lust. I felt it all right there in that parking lot beside Top Shop donuts, not seeing the people walking past with their steaming coffees and brightly confectioned donuts in hand. I just saw Dex and Jenn. Jenn and Dex.

And then it was over. I imagined the worst and I was still alive, although my legs were shaking slightly and I was feeling pukey.

I shook it off regardless, put on my favorite Alice in Chains song "Again" in my ear to empower me (yeah, I know, strange choice but I was in Seattle after all) and got back on the bike.

I took Putt-Putt around a few left turns, trying to get on the one-way street heading in the right direction and soon enough I was parked outside of their building. It was located on the corner, across from a convenience store and the monorail tracks and stood out from all the other buildings in the neighborhood thanks to its jaunty French design. It looked like the apartment buildings you'd see in Paris, albeit woefully out of place with the Seattle Space Needle looming nearby.

I looked up at the windows, wondering which apartment was theirs and if they were watching me. I took in a deep breath, clenched and unclenched my fists, and walked over to the front doors.

I entered in their buzzer number on the directory and waited with bated breath. There was a quick click from the speaker and when I went over to go speak into it, the door buzzed loudly.

That was a bit too trusting; I could have been anyone. Unless, of course, he or she really had been watching me come in. That made me feel even more nervy but I shoved down the itchy, hot feeling that was creeping up my throat and entered the pristine, art deco-like lobby. I made my way to the elevator, the wet soles of my boots making squeaking rat-like noises on the black and white tiles. I paused in front of the mirror by the elevator and gave myself the once over.

I was wearing my high, cherry red Doc boots, black leggings, a hip-length grey sweater and my black leather jacket, duffel bag in one hand, my brown messenger bag and helmet in the other. I had a bad case of helmet hair, which, combined with the rain, made me look like a scruffy toy dog. My nose was red and could have done with some powder and concealer but I was afraid the longer I stayed in the lobby primping myself, the more likely that either Dex or Jenn would come down and catch me in the act.

I got in the elevator, went up the one floor, and cautiously stepped out into a red carpeted hallway. Their apartment was at one end of the hall, the door looming like something out of the *Dark Tower*.

I walked carefully down the hall and briefly thought about turning around and running away. But I didn't and I couldn't. I just kept walking, heart in my throat, aware of how *ridiculous* my feelings were. But knowing didn't make them go away.

Time to get this over with, I thought and knocked on the door in three short raps.

The door immediately flung open and I found myself face-to-face with none other than Jennifer Rodriguez.

I lost all feeling in my body. I know my eyes looked frightfully wide. I wasn't even able to fake smile at her.

She was taller in person, maybe 5'9", at least the same height as Dex. She was thinner, too, as was usually the case with TV (or internet) personalities. She was lean and long but had more oomph and bang to her form than my skinny-Minnie sister. She was wearing tight jeans, high heels, and a black sleeveless low-cut top that showcased a pair of smallish but mesmerizingly perky breasts. Her skin was the color of clouded honey, her eyes a fiery hazel, her hair annoyingly shiny and curly and a shade or two darker than her skin tone.

I didn't know how long I had been in my head, taking her in, but suddenly her lips parted and all I saw were ivory veneers against pink lip gloss. And then she was reaching for me. To, like, *hug me*.

"Perry!" she exclaimed in a voice that was annoyingly like Blake Lively's in that low, throaty tone. Damn this sexy-voiced couple!

She wrapped her arms around me in a quick embrace, while I tried desperately to say something or do anything. I couldn't even touch her back. I was dumbfounded.

"It's so nice to finally meet you," she said, pulling away and looking me up and down. "Come in, you must be freezing. It's been raining for fucking days here; it gets right in your bones, you know?"

I think I mumbled, "uh huh" as she led me into the apartment.

"Let me take that," she said, picking my duffel bag from my hands. She took it into a room and disappeared. I watched her tiny butt go.

I stood in the foyer of Dex and Jenn's apartment. Aside from a few boxes in the corner, it looked like they were pretty much all moved in. There was the modern kitchen off to the right with a bar top and stools facing the living room that was lined with bookshelves and a giant entertainment system. Beside it, a rounded balcony faced right onto the suspended monorail tracks. In the corner of the apartment were the doors to what I assumed was their bedroom and a bathroom, and covered French doors led into the room that Jenn had gone into.

It was modern, it was small, and it didn't look very lived in. I couldn't detect any of Dex's personality in the place.

"Perry?" Jenn asked as she stepped out from behind the French doors. I looked over at her, not really seeing her or comprehending anything. It was all so surreal. Was I really here? Where was Dex, anyway?

"Sorry," I said, shaking my head. "It was a long ride. I can barely feel my fingers."

Jenn gave me a sympathetic look, one that seemed completely sincere. I don't know why that surprised me;

it's not like I ever had a reason to think Jenn didn't like me...I mean, just because I didn't like her.

And now I was actually feeling really bad for being such a bitch about her this whole time. She really wasn't the evil whore I was making her out to be. Was she?

She walked over, her heels clicking across the hardwood, and reached out with her hands, "Want me to take the rest of your stuff to your room?"

"No, it's fine, I can manage," I said. I took a step towards her, but the squeak of my wet boots reminded me that it was probably rude of me to tread through her (their) apartment. I stooped down to begin the laborious process of untying them but she told me to not bother.

"We're not fussy here," she added, and beckoned me to come over. I wasn't sure if I believed that. Even though Dex was probably a little bit messy, the apartment was looking spotless and most likely all thanks to Jenn. Oh, well. If I could keep my boots on, I was keeping them on.

"Is this where I'm bunking down?" I asked.

"Yes, sorry it's such a mess," Jenn said, and touched my shoulder gently, guiding me into the room that was tiny and not a mess at all. "It's obviously not a true bedroom since there isn't even a window. Dex uses it as his office."

I put my purse and helmet down on the tiny single bed covered in fancy, pistachio green linen and eyed his desk in the corner, which held up a massive flat screen Mac monitor and a range of other technical equipment. A column of clear boxes containing cameras and photographic stuff were stacked beside it. The shelves above the computer were almost keeling over with a plethora of books that ranged from *Paranormal Normal?* to *The Demise of the Record Industry* to *Fear and Loathing in Las Vegas*. On the other side of the desk were two guitars and one bass propped up in their stands. The walls of the room were covered from floor to ceiling with framed photographs of rock stars and arty concert posters such as Secret Chiefs 3 and The Cars. Aside from the pretty green bedspread, this room was definitely all Dex.

"I hope you don't mind," she added. "Just ignore all his shit in the corner."

At that comment, it occurred to me how little Jenn knew about me and how little I knew about her. I decided it was time for me to suck it up, once again.

I faced her straight on, looking into her bright and seemingly earnest eyes, and said, "Thank you so much for letting me stay with you and Dex this week. I really appreciate it."

She waved me away with a bashful look that seemed more coquettish than anything else. "Oh please, I insisted that you stay with us. Dex wanted to put you up in the shitty hotel down the street."

Before I could even wonder about that, I heard the front door open and the sound of canine nails clacking wildly across the floor, along with wheezy dog breath.

A small white French Bulldog ran past the door, skidded to a stop, and then came back and ran straight for us.

The dog, who I assumed was Fat Rabbit since he did kind of look like a fat rabbit, jumped up on my shins like a wriggly, bug-eyed cylinder of excitement.

"This is Harvey," Jenn said proudly.

I tore my face away from the sloppy doggy kisses and looked up at her. "I thought his name was Fat Rabbit?"

Jenn's eyes rolled straight to heaven and I heard Dex's unmistakable burst of laughter from outside the door.

"Have you been telling everyone his name is Fat Rabbit?!" she exclaimed.

"Well he *looks* like a fat rabbit," Dex said, appearing in the doorway with that smart-ass grin on his face and a wet leash in his hands.

I expected the feeling to go all out of my body again like it had a few minutes ago, but that didn't happen. There was just a tiny prickle of heat at my heart. He looked good, of course, with his neat trace of a 'stache, broad chin, and silky black hair. His nose looked a tiny bit different and I immediately felt a wash of guilt, but other than that he was looking as devilishly handsome as ever. Especially as his dark eyes lit up noticeably when they met with mine.

I looked away before it became a lustful staring contest and I eyed Jenn with nervous humor. "Hey, Harvey was a fat rabbit too."

She looked confused. She looked over at Dex for an explanation.

"It's a film, babe," he explained to her. "*Harvey*. With Jimmy Stewart. Big invisible rabbit. You know..."

She shook her head and I smirked internally, happy that Dex and I both knew something she didn't. I met his eyes again and felt the usual pull towards him. Seeing him in front of me made me feel...well, not whole, I wouldn't go that far, but it made me feel like everything was just right.

Except it wasn't. Because I was suddenly very aware that I couldn't go around staring at him all dopey eyed like I sometimes did, because his girlfriend, the Wine Babe Jenn, was in the same room as us. Fat Rabbit, too.

In fact I had expected that Dex would have come over and given me a hug hello, only he didn't. He just nodded at me, still leaning in the doorway and said, "How was the ride over?"

"Wet," I answered. At that, Fat Rabbit jumped up again and Jenn scooped him up in her arms. They were a lot more buff and toned that I had thought they'd be.

"Harvey, Harvey, Harvey," she said to the dog who was gazing up at her perfect tawny face with googly eyes.

"You girls hungry?" Dex asked while he watched this for a few seconds, looking amused.

I was but I waited for Jenn to say something. She walked over to him with the dog in her arms and paused right in front of him.

"Call him Harvey," she said, holding him out. "You're his dad, call him by his proper name."

Dex smirked, took the dog's ear in one hand and whispered, "Fat Rabbit" into it.

Jenn let out a cry of flirty disgust and slapped Dex on his ass. He jumped a bit, pretending it hurt, and grinned at her. A grin I used to think was reserved solely for me.

OK. This was hell. I know what I had imagined earlier but now that I was actually seeing it, it was causing an involuntary narrowing of the eyes. It wasn't the jealousy so much (OK, it was), it was that feeling that Dex knew how I felt about him and yet, here they were...it was uncomfortable, to say the least.

Jenn and Fat Rabbit left the room and Dex raised his ringed eyebrow at me. "How about you kiddo, you hungry?"

Kiddo. Least I still had that. It was better than "Babe."

"I'm freaking starving," I admitted.

He nodded. "I thought as much. I figured you'd be after the ride and shit and anyway so a bunch of people are going to meet us for lunch. That cool? They are all Shownet peeps, good people, and it will make the party on Friday a lot easier to handle once you know how retarded they are in real life."

I couldn't tell if he was speaking quicker than normal because of his medication or if he was nervous. But I told him that was fine. Secretly, I preferred it. Being around other people would take a lot of the awkwardness out of the situation and as much as I'd like to think it was all in my head, as most things usually were, I knew both Jenn and Dex could feel it too. This was going to be one hell of a long week.

"Good," he said, smiling at me in a calmer, more natural, way. He looked around the room briefly. "How do you like my man cave?"

"It's very you," I admitted and patted the bed. "Though I thought you'd have a Star Wars-themed bedspread."

"Believe me, I wanted to," he said.

"You're thirty-two Dex, not eighteen," Jenn chided him, now with the dog and a bowl of water in hand. She explained to me, "We have to keep Harvey in the bathroom when we're gone or else he runs around and tears up the place."

"And takes a dump in your shoes," Dex added.

I had to laugh at that. Jenn grunted. "It was one time, all right?"

"Easy for you to say. They weren't your shoes," Dex said, heading out of the room. I followed, still giggling.

"I hope you didn't find that out the hard way," I told him. He looked down at me, eyes sparkling.

"More like the soft way."

Even though the topic of dog shit wasn't exactly sexy, I was standing next to him in the doorway and this was the closest I had been to him in weeks. He smelled good as always, and that damn current of electricity was sparking again.

"Don't be disgusting," Jenn said, placing Fat Rabbit down on the floor with the water and quickly shutting the door before he ran out of the room. The closed door was met with barks and the clattering of nails against it.

"He'll stop barking after five minutes," she said, and sashayed her way to the kitchen counter, pausing at a bowl.

"Your car or mine?" she asked him loudly above the doggy protests. In one quick motion she pulled a small bottle of hand sanitizer out of her purse, rubbed it on her dainty hands and put it back.

"It's up to Perry," Dex said, turning to me. "Do you like good music or bad music?"

I opened my mouth to say something, or perhaps to just make a noise, since it felt like a trick question, but Jenn picked up a pair of keys out of the bowl and said, "We'll take my car. You're parked on the street and it'll be hard to find a spot later."

"Oh, how considerate of you," he said sarcastically as we left the apartment.

In the hallway, Jenn shut the door and locked it while Dex stood at her side, leering at her in a weird half annoyed, half playful way. I didn't like it. This bickering seemed to be something natural to them, like an actual living and breathing couple who were in love with each other.

That thought took my breath away.

Jenn stuck her house keys in her purse and gave me a funny look, perhaps catching the expression on my face. I don't know what face I was making, but it couldn't have been a happy one.

"Honestly," she said to me in a confiding tone, "I just don't want to listen to Dex play his Crooked Eagles album for the millionth time this week. I couldn't give a shit about Tom Jones."

"Them Crooked Vultures," he said, exasperated. He put his arm around her and my breath was lost once more. "And it's John Paul Jones. Not Tom Jones."

OK. So the cutesy couple bickering pained me and the fact that, right in front of me, just two feet away, he had his arm around her and was staring at her with a, well, not disgusted look on his face, that absolutely hurt. I mean, hurt like a hot, poison-tinged knife was going through my stomach. But I was going to get through this. I had to. Right? RIGHT?!

I looked away. I had to or else I would have kept staring at them, mouth open, looking lovelorn and stupid. I looked down at the carpet.

"Nice carpet," I remarked. Like an idiot.

There was silence for a moment.

"Perry's very observant," Dex finally said to Jenn and out of the corner of my eye I could see him kiss her on her skinny cheekbone. I wished the carpet would swallow me whole.

CHAPTER SIX

Once we were in Jenn's car, things got a little easier. Mainly because I was sitting in the back seat of her extremely clean Mini Cooper and was able to stare out at the grainy scenes of downtown Seattle that whipped past my window. A foreign city was as good of a distraction as any.

I also understood what Dex meant by whether I liked good music or bad music. I didn't know who the hell we were listening to, but I knew that Jenn knew all the words to this auto-tuned female pop star who "sang" about washing her teeth with whisky or something. If it was grating to my ears, I could only imagine how bad it was to Dex, the man who actually composed music and *could* sing.

After Jenn nearly side-swiped a few parked cars (I noted that Dex kept his eyes closed for most of the drive), we arrived at a cute-looking café in the cobblestoned district of Pioneer Square.

Jenn parked the car beside a nearby meter while tourists outfitted in GORE-TEX jackets shared the sodden brick sidewalks with local riffraff and homeless folks. I waited for Dex to get out of the car before I could climb out between the back two front seats. He grabbed hold of my hand and steadied me until I was on the sidewalk, and gave it a warm, unnecessary squeeze. I quickly yanked my hand out of his. His eyes widened momentarily at my reaction, like a brown-eyed owl.

Not cool, Dex, I thought, but put on my best face as we turned and entered the warm café.

The normal tinges of apprehension swarmed through me as I scanned the unfamiliar restaurant looking for people who probably knew a lot more about me than I knew about them. I hate that feeling but it comes with the territory of being on the internet.

"There are the fuckers," Dex said, pointing at a table in the corner beneath vintage travel posters. I followed, hiding myself behind Jenn (even though that was like trying to hide an apple behind a carrot) until we stopped in front of his friends.

"Well, look who it is," a lanky African-American dude in a purple polo shirt and wire-rimmed glasses announced and got out of his chair. He gave Dex a quick hug. "Where you keeping yourself, Ghost Boy?"

The guy looked at Jenn and gave her nothing more than a polite nod. Then he moved his head over to look at me and raised his eyebrows. I returned the action.

"I've been moving," Dex said. He patted the guy on the back and pointed at me. "Dean, this is Perry."

Dex looked past Dean at the other two people at the table, a ponytailed man-boy who reminded me of too many people I went to high school with, who was wearing a tee shirt that said "Ironic Statement", and a woman who I recognized as the other Wine Babe, Rebecca Sims.

"And this is Seb and Rebecca," he continued. "People, this is the infamous Perry Palomino."

"The face breaker!" Seb cried out with a dorky guffaw and then started slow clapping.

"Easy now, Seb," Dex told him and then shot me a cheeky look.

I sucked in the urge to retort something snarky and just smiled at the three of them. "I'm the face breaker. Nice to meet you all."

I sat down across from Rebecca and Seb and next to Dex. Seb asked the couple how the move had been going. As Dex and Jenn explained, I took stock of Rebecca.

She was quite breathtaking, with an old-fashioned kind of beauty that fifties film stars were famous for. She was dressed in a lacey grey V-neck shirt that was well filled out and added to her classic look. Her hair was as jet-black as mine but cut into a chin-length bob with angled ends. Her eyes were dark and sexily hooded, her nose was long and broad, her lips were angular and made for the maroon lipstick she was wearing. Aside from her skin tone, which was so pale she was almost translucent, she could have passed as Dex's sister.

She hadn't greeted Jenn when we arrived, only Dex and me, which I thought was odd since the two worked together. I mean, they were *the* Wine Babes. If only my cousins knew I was having lunch with them, they'd totally die.

She took her eyes away from whatever Dex was saying (I was doing a pretty good job thus far of drowning out anything that sounded too coupley), and placed them on me. Unlike Dex, though, her eyes weren't mysterious or intrusive. They were just frank and regarded me with a strange sort of respect that I wasn't used to.

"So, Perry," she said in a rich British accent. It took me by surprise but then I realized I had never heard her speak on *Wine Babes* before. To tell you the truth, I hadn't seen more than one minute of the show. To watch it had been like pure torture, though, in retrospect, it would be a piece of cake after this week.

"It's so nice to finally meet you," she continued. "We've all heard so much about you; we've been watching you almost every week, yet for a while there, I think we all thought that perhaps you were a ghost yourself."

"Nope," I said, smiling at her and noticing that the other conversation had stopped and now everyone was looking at me. "I can be scary but I'm definitely no ghost."

"So what was it that Dex said that made you punch him?" Seb asked, leaning low on the table in excitement.

"Sea Bass, shut the fuck up," Dex said, reaching across the table to smack him.

I glanced at Rebecca, catching a sort of *come on, spill* look in her eyes and then looked at Dex, whose attention was now on Jenn on the other side of him.

"It's hard to remember," I said, leaning back in my chair and crossing my arms. "I think it had something to do with the fact that he confiscated my phone because he didn't want me checking my emails while I was 'on the job' or maybe it was that he planned on keeping us on the island on my actual birthday because, to quote/unquote, he didn't think anyone in my family would actually notice if I wasn't around."

Now, though this was all completely true, I said it in a purely jovial tone with just the slightest bit of edge to it. And the way everyone at the table laughed and gasped, I could tell they thought it was shockingly hilarious. But Dex was looking at me in total surprise. I could almost hear his gruff, shocked voice in my head asking, *What are you doing?*

I gave him a quick, unimpressed look and tried to hide my smile.

"Well, Perry, you've done what we've all wanted to," Dean said, flashing his broad smile at us. He was extremely likeable. He leaned across the table and held out his hand for a high five. I attempted to return it but Dex stuck out his own hand and held my arm down.

"OK, OK, so I deserved it. You guys done with the witch hunt now?"

"Are you done being a shithead?" Rebecca asked with a cool smile.

Seb and Dean let out a simultaneous "Oooh" like the audience in a bad sitcom.

"And I thought you guys were my friends," Dex said, and though it was in a flippant voice, I could pick up the strained twitches at the corner of his mouth.

"Friends are allowed to punch friends when they are being a shithead," Rebecca said, leaning across the table and faking an uppercut to his scruffy chin.

He smiled, genuinely at that, and cupped his hand behind my head, his thumb stroking against my hair affectionately.

"Only Perry is allowed to do that."

I closed my eyes briefly at the gentleness of his touch. It was automatic and involuntary. He took his hand away. Rebecca was staring at me in a half-amused, half-knowing way that made her hooded lids take precedence, but only said to Dex, "Well, Perry and Jenn, of course."

"Of course," I heard Jenn pipe up from the other side. "I get first dibs."

Everyone laughed at that, though mine was forced, and the waiter appeared with more menus in hand. Despite the fact that I hadn't eaten since my Weight Watchers English muffin that morning, I wasn't hungry at all. I ordered a cup of coffee and a small bowl of Tuscan tomato soup to ensure I'd survive until dinner time without fainting.

To no one's surprise, Dex ordered a Jack and Coke.

"Isn't it a bit early for that, you lush?" I asked, eyeing it as the waiter plunked it down on the table, sending bubbles to spray out in the air.

"We're on vacation, kiddo."

"Technically, Dex," Seb pointed out. "You and Perry are working this week. The rest of us are on vacation."

Dex ignored him and tilted his head to me. "We're at least on vacation for today. Tomorrow we work."

He took a lengthy sip of his drink and I looked over at Seb and Dean. "So what do you guys do at Shownet?"

Seb looked appalled. "You mean you've never seen Gamer Room?!"

I shrugged, no, obviously not.

"Oh, come on Seb, no one's seen your show," Rebecca teased, pulling on his ponytail.

"Well, excuse me if we don't have two foxy ladies such as yourselves showing the latest video game cheats."

Jenn snickered. "Could you imagine? If I hosted Gamer Room, the entire male population would be locked in their basement playing video games. It would be a country of nerds."

"Is that what I am to you miss Jennifer, a nerd?" Dean asked, folding his hands in front of her, his dark eyes glinting beneath his frames.

"Yes," coughed Dex, with a grin. Before Dean or Seb could protest, he quickly said, "I'm no better than you guys. I'd be online with you playing Call of Duty if I could."

"Instead you're out there hunting fairy tales," Jenn sniped. "I don't know what's better."

Her tone surprised me. I leaned forward to get a better look at her. She was rubbing hand sanitizer on her hands again.

"Fairy tales?" I repeated, trying not to sound defensive but failing miserably.

On cue, Seb and Dean went "Ooooh" again.

I avoided looking at Dex and kept my eyes on her. Surprisingly, Rebecca aligned with me and said, "Yeah, Jenny. What do you mean by fairy tales?"

She shrugged and put her sanitizer away.

"I just mean that ghosts don't exist. And neither do unicorns. Or happily-ever-afters. Fairy tales."

I sat back and finally had to look at Dex. He was smiling, sure, but it was an uneasy smile that didn't reach his eyes. He was looking straight forward at a space on the wall between Rebecca and Seb, obviously feeling stuck in the middle.

"I see," I said slowly. I wanted to argue with her but I had been doing so well so far. We had been getting along and as much as I wanted to, I didn't need to rock the boat.

Finally I said, "Well that's fair enough. There's definitely more unbelievers that there are believers."

"And more smart people than dumb people," she added before stuffing a dainty forkful of salad in her mouth.

Dex tensed beside me; I think he knew I was about to go volcanic on her.

I didn't though. I took in a quick, deep breath, calmed my newly caffeinated nerves, and pasted on a huge smile.

There were so many things I could say. More smart people than dumb people? Did she just dare insinuate that I was dumb and that she, she, who didn't know the difference between "What's New Pussycat" and "Stairway to Heaven", was smart? My brain was on overload.

But I just said, "Very true. Thank god for dumb people though; you need someone to believe that you should drink a 2008 Riesling with a fucking KFC Double Down."

Instead of an "oooh" like I had expected, there was a brief, stagnant pause while everyone collected their thoughts and then Seb and Dean erupted into hoots of laughter. Even Rebecca was snickering, despite the fact that it was her show too that I was insulting.

I looked over at Jenn for her reaction. Her cheeks were a bit pink and her eyes were glazed with a hard, almost icy exterior. But she put on a smile that rivaled my fake one earlier.

"Well played," she admitted breezily, and went back to picking at her "meal."

"For the record, Perry," Rebecca said, reaching across the table and putting her soft white hand on top of mine. Her rounded maroon fingernails were mesmerizingly polished. "We know we cater to idiotic buggers. But *I* think what you and Dex are doing is really cool."

Dex was still staring at that spot on the wall, like he was stuck in some weird freeze frame, so I looked as gracious as possible. "Thanks."

"In fact," she went on, "we were just talking about what a name you two have created for yourselves."

Finally Dex brought himself to reality. "What do you mean?"

"You haven't seen it?" she asked, exchanging a quick look with Dean.

"Seen what?" I asked. Dex looked as puzzled as I felt.

"There's another ghost hunting show, called *Spook Factory*," Dean explained. "Just like you guys. A guy, a girl, only they both claim to be ghost whisperers or whatever, and it's exclusively online as part of that Fantasy Network. I'm surprised you missed that, Dex."

"I've been moving," he said quietly, almost to himself.

"Well, what...what have they done, have you watched it? Is it good?" I asked, feeling more than a bit icky about the whole *Spook Factory* thing. Copycats? Already?

"Yeah, I've watched it and it's, like, OK. It's total bullshit though. Both of them are just uneducated d-bags, but they look good, so people watch it. Their background is obviously in modeling and nothing else. No offense, Jenn."

She looked at him sharply but didn't offer any feedback. It wasn't surprising at all to hear that Jenn got her start in modeling.

"Especially the guy in this case," Rebecca said. "He looks like he should be in an Ed Hardy catalogue, and get this, his name is G.J. Jermaine"

I chuckled. "G.J.? That's the stupidest name I've ever heard."

"It stands for Geoff Jermaine," Dean added.

"His name is Geoff Jermaine Jermaine? I stand corrected."

Dex pulled out his iPhone and pulled up Google.

"What about the girl?" I asked. As if I wasn't feeling competitive enough to begin with.

Rebecca shrugged and put her glossy hair back behind her ears. "Annie something. She looks like a blonde, frazzle-haired witch, so it's fitting. But, you know, the show just started and they've been showing two episodes a week."

"Annie Potterson," Dex mumbled as he scrolled through the internet. He took his phone and placed it in front of me. "Here's our competition."

I looked down at the screen and felt bad for a second. Dex had lost his previous iPhone to the depths of the Haro Straight, along with his camera equipment. He obviously had to buy another one, straight out of his own pocket, and here he was showing me our rival ghost-hunting team, copycats, and apparent douchebags, who were already beating us at our own game. Two episodes a week?

Anyway, I only needed a quick glance to know what we were up against. Sure, Annie was slim with obvious fake boobs, but she had horrid unfeeling, dead eyes and crazy lady hair. A witch indeed. And G.J. looked like a G.J., a cross between Vin Diesel and a sandy-haired frat boy.

"What, does he go around kicking ghosts in the balls or something?" I was trying to make light of it but I could see Dex was deeply troubled by this.

"Ha. It's kind of flattering though, right?" Rebecca said. "This only just started and it's all because of you guys."

"And they're in town right now," Dean put in.

"What?" Dex eked out slowly, his lip curling downward.

"Yeah. Their blog said they were in town to investigate the Harvard Exit Cinema in Capitol Hill."

"What's that?" I asked. Dex shook his head.

"Old news. One of the most haunted places in Seattle, but fuck, there's been a fucking ton of ghost hunters and paranormal experts there. For decades. It's nothing new and nobody finds anything."

"Gee, I wonder why." Jenn snickered to herself. Dex's eyes flared dangerously but he was able to rein them in quickly and ignore her.

"If it makes you feel better, Jenn and I have competition of our own," Rebecca said as she rapidly twirled her linguini around her fork.

"Oh yeah," Dex said, leaning back in his chair. He took a quick sip of his drink and wiped his lips with the back of his hand. He looked at me. "A TV network has started *Vintage Vixens*. It hasn't come out yet, we've just seen the ads for it. But it's basically the same fucking idea."

Ouch. Rebecca didn't seem too bothered by it though.

"It was bound to happen. I don't know what these new girls are like, but the fans that we have know us and like us, so I'm not too worried."

Jenn neglected to put in her two cents. I was watching her expectantly but her face never changed. She just pushed the leaves around on her plate, off in her own little world. What a strange thing for all of us to be going through at the same time. All this competition, all these threats. And I wasn't just thinking about the shows either. For the first time ever, it occurred to me that Jenn might actually be a bit threatened by little ol' Perry.

The rest of the meal went along well. There were a few instances where Dex and I acted like we normally did, he teasing me, me retorting back, but it wasn't until it was on display in front of the hosts of *Gamer Room* and *Wine Babes*, that I realized how inappropriate it was. It was harmless; I knew it was and was trying my hardest to make sure it came across that way, but it still made me worry a bit. Every time I even had the slightest inkling that he was flirting with me, I had to look at Jenn and see what she thought. On her end, though, she didn't seem to think anything. She was very quiet, her mind elsewhere, gazing at people in the restaurant, and when she wasn't, she was in a texting frenzy with someone. It was enough that Seb noticed.

"Your fingers are going to fall off, Jenn," he said.

She looked up from her phone and smiled, perfect and easy as always.

"I've got magic fingers. Just ask Dex."

The way she said it, in her throaty, low Scarlett Johansson purr, made me sick. I felt like slinking down into my chair and slithering down to the floor in a sad little puddle.

"She's not kidding." That was his sly response.

I was *this* close to flipping the table over. Ugh. I hated him. I hated her. And I hated Uncle Al for thinking that my heart needed to be broken. Well fuck t-

I felt a slight kick against my shin and looked up. Rebecca was looking at me, her eye in a half wink, seeming like she had something to say. She smiled at me, just a quick shudder on her lined lips, and then turned to Jenn.

"Is that Bradley again?" she asked.

Jenn looked officially annoyed for the first time today. It only lasted a second, but it was enough. That hard glaze reformed and I felt a spiteful energy shooting out from her pupils. But before anyone could pick up on it, her eyes were the pretty, soft hazel again and she was looking like a million, genetically blessed, bucks.

"Yes, you know Bradley. Always harassing me over the shooting schedule," she told Rebecca, and then looked us all in the eye, including me.

"Bradley's your cameraman?" I asked.

"He's the guy who replaced me. The chump, I should say," Dex said.

"It's a dirty job but someone's got to do it," Rebecca said. "Now Bradley is the poor soul who has to fly to exotic locales with us broads."

"And now Dex has to run around with me, with kelpmonsters, skinwalkers and leper zombies," I said. "I think you traded in the wrong job."

"Did I?" he questioned, peering into my eyes, already knowing the answer. His voice was warm and serious. I think he believed he had made the right choice; at least I hoped he did.

"Perry, you're single right?" Rebecca asked, her clipped accent sounding innocent, but the question still made me squirm momentarily.

"Sure am," I said, tearing my eyes away from Dex. I hated that question. It was usually followed by some pitiful look or false empathy, as if being single was a big, huge problem that shouldn't have to befall someone like me. Or, it was followed with an offer of a set-up.

"Because I think you and Bradley would make a great pair."

Bingo.

Dex choked on his drink and started sputtering for air. At the same time, Jenn cried out, "Are you kidding me? No way!"

I was surprised at both their reactions and I think they were too, because once Dex regained control of his throat, a tense, unspoken look went out between the couple.

"What?" Rebecca asked, now playing up an innocent look to match the tone. She turned to me, and said, "He's very good-looking, Perry."

"He's way too old for her," Jenn protested.

"How old is he?" I had to ask.

"Same age as me," Dex said quickly. "And he's a douche." He picked up his straw and angrily chewed on the end. It was a change from his compulsive Nicorette chewing.

"And you know if Dex is calling someone a douche, he must be a real douche," Dean said, grinning at us all.

"He is not a douche," Jenn said with a disgusted grunt.

Rebecca laughed. "Well not to you, dear Jenny, of course not."

I couldn't tell if there was a thread of vindictiveness or something in her voice, since her accent made picking up on subtleties more difficult. But there was an odd, brief hush to the table, as if everyone noticed anyway. There was something weird going on, and because I was the outsider in the group, I didn't know what it was.

"Why do you think we'd make a good pair? Or were you being sarcastic?" I asked, trying to keep the conversation going.

"When isn't she sarcastic?" Seb said.

She yanked on his ponytail one more time. "Be that as it may, I do think Perry should meet Bradley."

"She'll meet him on Friday, at the party," Dex said. "That will be enough." And the way Dex ended that sentence signaled that no one would be talking about Bradley anymore.

~~

After lunch wrapped up, Jenn drove us back to the apartment and dropped us off. She apparently had someplace to be and that was music to my ears. I had needed some time to just be alone with Dex, time to breathe.

"Wanna come for a walk?" he asked me as he opened the bathroom door and Fat Rabbit came bounding out, peppering us with excited woofs. I did, despite the weather.

Outside, the rain had slowed down considerably, making a sporadic patting sound on the roof of my umbrella. Dex pulled up his grey hoodie over his head, having refused an umbrella of his own, and we took off down the street with Fat Rabbit leading the way, straining against the leash.

I observed the apartment buildings and chain hotels around me, the Pink Elephant carwash nearby, the gloomy urban sprawl. Dex was silent and popped a piece of Nicorette in his mouth. With his slouchy walk, eyebrow ring, dark eyes and dark jacket, he looked like an essential piece of the Seattle scenery. I couldn't think of a city that suited him as much as this one did.

"Does the dog need to be taken for a lot of walks?" I asked, avoiding a few puddles hidden beneath a mask of dead leaves.

He chewed a few times, his lips twitching sheepishly.

"Probably not. I'm just used to going out to smoke. Now I just take Fat Rabbit here to clear my head, distract myself. Old habits, you know."

"I'm proud of you," I blurted out.

His eyes shot out to the side, looking down at me quickly, puzzled.

"For quitting smoking," I continued. "I didn't think you'd do it."

"I still don't think it's going to stick."

"But you're trying."

"Yeah. I'm trying," he said, and then sighed, sounding vaguely melancholy. "I've even cut down on this gum a bit. I've found that if I chew more than one piece at a time, I can get quite excitable."

"No kidding," I teased him. We rounded a building and suddenly the Space Needle was right in front of us. We stopped at a set of lights and I craned my neck at the towering icon.

"You been up there?" I asked, even though it was probably a stupid question since he was a Seattle-ite.

"No, actually. That's too fucking high for me."

"You're afraid of heights?" I asked, surprised. Dex didn't strike me as being afraid of anything. After the last couple of times with him, he earned his place as the bravest person I know.

He shrugged. He's also one of the quietest people I know. The light changed and we crossed the road. We walked past a crazy-shaped building that was the Experience Music Project and a Science Fiction museum and I made a mental note to try to check out at least one of them before the week was over. Of course, that all depended on what Dex had planned for us.

"So do we have a work schedule for the week?" I questioned as we walked past an arts theatre and stopped and stood at a grassy patch where Fat Rabbit could run around a bit and tire himself out.

He brought out his gold lighter from his pocket. He flickered it on and off a few times, watching the flame as the rain continuously put it out. Old habits.

"Tomorrow we've got a meeting with the head doctor/administrator dude at the hospital. He said we could interview him on camera and he'd take us on a short tour of the place. I'm not sure if he's going to let us film anything on our own but we'll figure that out. We'll find a way."

"I'm surprised you don't have a pile of homework for me to do. Unless that's your plan for tonight, get me to hit the books."

He flicked off the lighter and put in his pocket and pulled sharply on the leash as Fat Rabbit made a dash for a nearby pooch. He choked for a second against the collar, then trotted back to us, tongue hanging out of his mouth.

I adjusted my grip on the umbrella and raised it slightly so I could get a better look at Dex. He hadn't said anything. I didn't even know if he heard me. His eyes looked troubled and were searching the scrawny, depleted trees that lined nearby pathways. He almost looked...afraid.

"Are you OK?" I stepped forward and gently placed my hand on his arm.

He closed his eyes and let out a deep breath. His brows furrowed close to each other, deepening the permanent crease in between them. My grip on his arm tightened. "Dex?"

"Yup," he said, keeping his eyes shut. "I'm...thinking."

Finally he opened his eyes and smiled. It was a sad one. "I'm sorry. What did you say?"

I took my hand off him and gave him a quizzical look, hoping to find out what just went on inside his head. His expression was blasé, his lids sleepy and uncaring. Once again, he was just too inconsistent, too hard to read.

Fat Rabbit stopped in between us, sat back on his white haunches and alternated looking at both at us. *What's the holdup?* he seemed to be saying. *Why aren't we walking?*

"Is it your medication?"

He shook his head. "I'm sorry this is so weird."

"What's weird? This?"

He sucked his lower lip back and forth and stared down at the dog without seeing him. I waited patiently for his answer. I knew not to prod too much or he'd clam up for a long time.

I sighed and put my hand out, palm up, feeling for the rain. Cold, heavy drops fell onto it, ricocheting off. Fat Rabbit stared up at me like I was holding a treat.

Dex suddenly reached out and grabbed my hand, holding it there. He pushed back the sleeve of my leather jacket and peered at the purple Silly Bandz bracelet that he had given me as a makeshift birthday present.

"You're still wearing this," he said, his voice sounding softly amazed.

I let him hold my wrist, my hand quickly growing wet. His grip was gentle and hot against my cold skin.

"It's my anchor," I lowered my voice, feeling just a bit embarrassed. He raised his eyes to mine and I blushed on command, my cheeks filling with hot blood. He let his hand slide down until it was holding mine, our fingers intertwined. The hairs on my neck stood up like cactus needles. This was not good. It felt good. It felt really, sticky good. But that didn't make it right.

I took my hand away and quickly averted my eyes to the wet grass. A totally awkward pause filled the gap between us.

"This is what I mean by weird," he said. "I actually wanted you to stay in a motel; I was going to pay for it and everything. But Jenn insisted that you stay with us and I knew she would get suspicious if I didn't agree."

I didn't want to say it, but I had to. "Why didn't you want me to stay with you?" I tried not to sound hurt.

He burst into a wry grin. "Oh come on, kiddo. I know how awkward this is for you. It's just as awkward for me. And I know it's awkward for Jenn too. Not that she suspects anything. And not that there is anything to suspect, but you know."

"Why is this awkward?"

He paused, almost doing a comic double take, then saw how serious my expression was. I wanted to hear it from him. I wanted to see if he had the balls to talk about it instead of sweeping what happened underneath a rug.

He stepped closer to me. I lifted the umbrella up so that both of our heads were underneath the wide canopy. His face reflected blue in the shade, his hood creating deep shadows on his face. I felt my breath slipping away, pausing in my throat, waiting for what was going to happen next.

"I *want* you to stay with me," he said. "And that's the problem. Every time you leave me, I need you a little bit more."

I didn't know what to say to that or what to think. My heart might have melted just a bit, solidifying around that pin. I just wanted to kiss him. To touch him. To feel him. But it couldn't happen. I wouldn't let that happen. I had to be strong.

"See, it's weird," he said with a sigh and looked away. "I shouldn't be saying these things to you."

"No," I mumbled, trying to focus on Fat Rabbit, who had gotten bored of us and was now sniffing at the wet grass. "You shouldn't."

"I'm going to try and put what happened on the island past us."

"What happened?" I repeated absently.

"Yeah. What happened. With us. That whole trip just seemed like...a dream, didn't it?"

I nodded. It had. Like a terrible yet enthralling dream, or a flashback to a drug trip.

"It was a dream," I said, still avoiding his eyes. "And a mistake."

I didn't really believe that. At least, I never thought it was a mistake. Not until this moment when I realized how weird it had made things between us. The elephant in the room.

"You think it was a mistake?" he asked. The subtle vulnerability in his voice drew my eyes to him. He was still so close to me, the steam from our collective breaths meeting in the small space between us. He was staring at me in all seriousness. No easy leer, no sarcastic smirk, no horndog grin. It was just him, stripped of any defenses for a few rare seconds.

"Don't you think it was wrong?" I challenged quietly, not wanting to raise my voice in our sheltered enclave.

His head twitched in a small side-to-side movement. No. He continued to watch me, sincere yet unreadable.

Do you regularly cheat on your girlfriend?, I wanted to ask. Do you normally harbor desires to go down on your partner? How is it not a mistake to you? Look at us!

But I didn't say any of that. Instead, I said in my breeziest voice, "I agree, anyway. We need to put it past us. What's done is done. That island was a whole lot of cray cray. And for what it's worth, I'm sorry I punched you."

Finally the smirk returned to his wide mouth. "And I'm sorry for being a...what was it? Shithead? Fuckface? There's been so many words to describe me lately that I can't keep track."

"They are all applicable," I said with a smile.

He playfully punched me in the shoulder. It was awkward. Then he stepped away from me and out into the rain and looked down at the dog. "Well, Fat Rabbit."

The dog looked up at him. Poor Jenn. He was never going to be a Harvey.

We turned around and headed back the way we came, both silent, both lost in our own heads for most of the walk back.

His phone beeped and he fished it out of his pocket. *Probably Jenn, checking up on him,* I thought.

"What are you doing on Wednesday?" he asked me, peering at the screen.

"Me? I don't know. You tell me."

"Rebecca just texted. She wants to take you out for lunch."

I raised my brows at him. "What? Why?"

He shook his head at me, wincing a little, his eyes becoming squinty. "Because she wants to get to know you better. She wants to be your friend, kiddo."

Huh. I actually thought Rebecca didn't like me.

"I wish you could see what I see," he added with some weight to his tone.

"What do you mean?"

He stopped abruptly and crossed his arms. Fat Rabbit honked uncomfortably, pulled back at the collar. "I wish you could see what I see in you. What others see in you."

I opened my mouth to protest but he just raised his hand to pause me and said, "And I know you're trying. You're a lot different from the girl I bumped into in the lighthouse. It's just frustrating to me."

"Well, I am trying," I admitted. "You know, that whole 'Anonymous' thing-"

"Don't even start with that," he said angrily. "I told you to forget that stupid shit."

I frowned at his reaction. "I know, but it's hard. But anyway, I have been feeling better, I've been going to the bootcamp and I feel stronger and-"

"You look amazing and you know it."

I did a double-take at him.

"But you don't need me to tell you that," he continued. "And you shouldn't. You shouldn't need to have to lose some weight in order to feel better about yourself."

"Well, OK, Oprah. When did you become a self-help guru for women's self-esteem?" I said testily.

He laughed and started walking. I followed alongside him. "OK, fair enough. I am probably the last person you should listen to. But look, Rebecca likes you and wants to take you out. And I think you should go."

"Well, of course I'll go. I just didn't think she liked me."

"She can be bit...rough...at times. She speaks her mind, she's blunt. And she's a bit of a shit disturber to tell you the truth. But you could use a woman like her in your life. And *everyone* likes you, Perry."

"Seb and Dean?"

"Yeah. They liked you even before they met you. And I know other people will be won over by you too. My friend Todd is dying to meet you. He and his wife are really...just...the best."

"And does Jenn like me?" I asked cautiously.

Dex rubbed his chin quickly and looked down at his phone in the other one. "What should I tell Rebecca? You're on?"

"Yes. We're on. But don't ignore the question."

He lifted a finger to shush me and quickly typed something out on the screen. Then he put the phone away, came out with a piece of Nicorette and popped it in his mouth.

"Jenn likes you," he said between chews. "You're just a lot different. She's probably trying to figure you out. But she likes you, she really does."

I didn't say anything to that. As we walked back to the apartment, all I could think about was that Dex had just lied to my face. Old habits do die hard.

CHAPTER SEVEN

"This is it," Tara said, her face a shiny silver in the moonlight.

I looked at the house at the end of the block, the throngs of people outside, their laughter and drunken cries filling the air. Cars littered the street, all to be driven home drunk later.

"You having second thoughts?" she asked. Her voice was small, telling me how much she was depending on me. If I didn't go into the party with her, she wouldn't go at all. And all her hopes of winning over Angus, Adrianna Gee's boyfriend, would be dashed. Tara was my closest friend and yet I was still nothing but an excuse for her to come here.

I nodded quickly, despite the warnings from Jacob. The warnings that Adrianna couldn't be trusted. That she had some deal with the devil. That all her friends were against me, waiting to eat my soul. Even though I hadn't seen Jacob for a while, his inane ramblings were still fresh in my mind. I hadn't told Tara any of this, of course. I knew she wanted to go to the party, even though we weren't invited.

Luckily, Tara wasn't a fat ugmo like myself. She was freakishly tall for her age, which did garner her a few choice nicknames, but honestly I'd rather be tall than fat. Besides, she was pretty and slim and if she wore dresses and short skirts instead of her tomboy outfit of cargo pants and vintage camp shirts, she would have turned more than a few heads. The point was, she'd be allowed into the party. I wasn't too sure about me.

"Yeah, I'm having second thoughts," I admitted. "But I'm down. I told you'd come and I will. I just…"

"Just what?" Tara said, pulling out a joint and lighting it.

I watched her puff back on the crinkly paper and inhale until she was a shade paler. Then she exhaled, the pot smoke drifting up into starry late winter sky.

She passed the joint to me and I inhaled halfheartedly. It would take the edge off but pot just felt like child's play these days.

"But…" I said slowly, already losing my train of thought. Should I tell her? Oh, fuck it.

I gave her back the joint and said, "I just heard that these people didn't like me."

"Who told you that?"

I shrugged. "I don't know. A boy."

"What boy?" she asked suspiciously.

"You wouldn't know him. His name's Jacob."

She gave me a disbelieving look before coughing her lungs out.

"Jacob? Mohawk dude who killed himself?" she asked between coughs.

"He attempted to kill himself," I explained. "And yeah, so what, it's him. He's been walking me home a lot." Every day for weeks, until the last week when he was acting just a little too crazy for my liking.

"I'm pretty sure he died, Perry," Tara said.

"Oh yeah, so I've been talking to a dead person," I said, laughing. Child's play or not, the pot was strong and I was already becoming more removed from the situation.

Tara laughed too. "Well I dunno. His funeral was in the paper the other week but maybe I was too fucked up."

I let the giggles flow. "Or I'm too fucked up and I'm talking to ghosts."

"Either way, he sounds like a liar. No one hates you Perry. No one even knows who you are."

That would have stung more a few minutes ago but now her words left just a soft pang in my heart. "Hey..."

"Sorry, Palomino. I just meant that no one cares about you."

I raised my brow at her. Still no better.

"I mean, you're harmless, Perry. No one hates you. Seriously. Let's just go inside and you'll see. It'll be cool."

I nodded and we resumed walking down the dark, barely lit suburban street. I was high as a kite for some reason, though it could have been the two-liter of Canadian cider that we shared on the bus earlier.

And then Tara was gone. And I was alone on the street.

I looked around me wildly, seeing only shapely shadows created by the moon and an empty, wide cul-de-sac. Tara was nowhere to be seen and the noise from the party had ceased. It was like time stopped, everyone on earth had left, and only I remained.

"Perry," I heard a whisper.

I turned and looked in the direction of the house. In the blackness, a lone streetlight turned on. It illuminated Jacob's spikey-haired silhouette as he stood there, frozen on the spot, a gas can in his hand.

"Let's go in together," he said. And without rhyme or reason, I found myself moving toward him, a creeping shadow on the lifeless street.

~~

I woke up with an extremely uneasy feeling and for a few seconds I couldn't remember where I was. I wasn't at home. The room was way too dark and windowless.

I slowly sat up and tried to get my eyes to adjust. There were a bunch of blinking lights in the corner coming from Dex's computer and other gadgets.

It was the second night in the last week that I was dreaming about the past. I don't know why. Normally if I dreamed about weird things, they had something to do with the spirits we were about to encounter. I had begun to rely on my dreams as being prophetic, or maybe a quick glimpse into the mind of a dead person (as lovely as that sounds). But I was dreaming about high school and things that I had pushed out of my mind with the help of medication, doctors and therapy sessions. I didn't like how they were suddenly coming up now. I hope they didn't mean anything. They couldn't. It was all the drug use, that's all it ever was.

Not that I could remember all that much about the dreams. I knew my friend Tara had been in it, maybe Dr. Freedman, my old shrink. Nothing scary had happened. Yet there was something so disturbingly realistic about the whole thing that my heart was pounding away and I was sweating profusely. I felt the sheets. They were a damp. Jenn would probably burn them by the time I left.

Earlier that evening, Dex had cooked Jenn and me dinner (his cooking skills were still surprising) and I had a bit too much wine with it. Just to calm the nerves. Actually, we all had imbibed a tad much, which made the conversation easier. Probably helped that we all ate in the living room, watching TV, and didn't have to stare at each other. I had avoided looking at either of them, the conversation I had with Dex still fresh in my head. We were putting it all past us.

Now my head was spinning from the dream and I was thirsty from the night sweats and the wine. I didn't want to get up for a glass of water; the black room was a bit creepy, and it was always weird being in someone else's place in the middle of the night, but if I didn't, I'd never go back to sleep. I carefully eased myself out of the single bed, unsure if I was going to walk into anything in the blackness. I made it to the door, opened it quietly, and poked my head out into the apartment. Their bedroom door was closed. The bathroom wasn't. Fat Rabbit probably slept with them. I hope he messed up their sex life.

I tiptoed to the kitchen, my socks silent on the floor, careful not to wake them or the dog, and plucked a glass from a high cupboard and filled it up at the kitchen tap. The garish, yellow streetlights from outside came in through the balcony doors, filtered by a gauzy curtain that moved slowly, teased by a draft. Even though the apartment was small and beautiful, there was something so...strange about it. Strange and off-putting.

I finished my drink and filled the cup up again, mulling it over. There was no reason for me to be creeped out and yet I was. I listened hard; I could hear the comforting sound of someone's light snoring in the bedroom, the occasional subdued rumble of a car outside, the tick of a clock on the wall. Everything was normal for a middle of the night Monday but that inkling of the unknown was undeniable. The hairs on my arms were rising with each second I stood there.

I gulped down the rest of the water and quietly placed the empty cup in the sink. If I hung around any longer I would just freak myself out.

I started to walk back to the room, wondering if perhaps I needed to go to the washroom, but something made me pause as I passed through the middle of the apartment.

It was *that* feeling.

That nauseating, lung-seizing feeling that someone, or *something*, was standing behind me. I could feel it, feel this solid presence at my back, watching me.

I wasn't alone.

And I couldn't move even if I wanted to. I felt frozen, my legs locked to the hardwood floors.

Then...

A dripping sound. My ears were so fine-tuned that the sound made my heart jump. A steady, slow drip. Had I turned off the tap properly?

But I knew it wasn't the sink. The splatter didn't echo, it fell in small, thick pats and from a greater distance. If it wasn't the tap, what was dripping?

I looked at my door. It was so close. I could run into the room and lock it. I could prop the bed up against the door for security, pull the covers over my head and pray for sleep. Or I could swallow my pride and run into Dex and Jenn's room like a child who has had a bad dream.

Or I could turn around. And see that there was nothing to be afraid of. Then my fears would be put to bed and I would follow.

I tensed up and very, very slowly, turned around on the spot.

I expected that if anyone was behind me, they would be way back in the kitchen.

This was not true.

There was someone...

Right behind me.

I was face to face with a...*being*...covered in graying skin that puckered in the shadows. Their chest had caved into a red abyss. Their neck looked like a piece of fraying string cheese and could barely hold up their head, which was gruesomely flattened, wider than it was long, like it was smashed in by something heavy, leaving part of it open and exposed, a mixture of brain matter, blood and bone. The blood flowed freely off this gaping wound and fell on to the ground in sticky, wet splotches. The sick source of that rhythmic pattering.

The eye closest to the wound was destroyed, only a hole of gray goo remained, and the other eye fixed itself on me sharply. It was a female eye, puffy, with running makeup underneath. She almost looked like she could be crying, but...

She smiled at me. And it sounded like wasps buzzing.

I finally screamed.

Despite taking self-defense classes, Karate, and boot camp, my instinct wasn't to stay and fight. It was to get the fuck away from it. With nothing in my head but absolute horror, I turned and tried to run back to my room. My socks lost traction and slipped out from under me and I was down on the floor with a frightening thud, lying at the feet of a buzzing dead girl.

I scampered up just as Fat Rabbit's barking form came shooting out from the bedroom, followed by Jenn, who was waving around a curling iron like a weapon.

"What the hell is going on?" she asked, looking around in a total panic. I whirled around to see if the demented woman was there but she wasn't. However, the blood on the floor still remained and trailed away toward the kitchen where it stopped.

"Perry!" Dex yelled. I looked to see him coming out of the room, practically naked and barely pulling on his pants in time. I was too freaked out to find that intriguing.

He stopped and grabbed my shoulders as Jenn flicked on the living room lights.

"What happened? What is it, are you OK?!" He looked over me frantically.

"Are you bleeding?" Jenn asked, eyeing the blood on the floor, which Fat Rabbit was sniffing distastefully.

I shook my head, trying to find my breath and my voice again. It felt like I lost most of it with that scream. It was still ringing in my own ears.

"It's not my blood," I finally got out between gulps of air.

Jenn and Dex exchanged a look.

"Whose blood is it?" Jenn asked. Her voice was laden with suspicion. She was not going to like my answer.

I looked at Dex. He tightened his grip on my shoulders and led me over to their white couch.

"Dex, not if she's bleeding!" Jenn cried out, afraid for her upholstery.

He shot her a sharp look. "She said she's not, so she's not. Go get her some water."

She jumped a bit at his brusque tone but hurried off to the kitchen, frowning as she went and careful to avoid the bloody spots.

He placed me on the couch and sat beside me, his body positioned towards mine. He took both of my hands in his and looked me straight in the eyes.

"Tell me what happened, from the beginning."

I did, very conscious of how it sounded in front of Jenn. To her credit, she didn't say anything during this bizarre conversation, just brought over the cup of water and perched her tiny butt on the edge of an armchair.

"And you didn't recognize the ghost?" he asked when I was done.

I stifled a chuckle. "Recognize? No."

"I meant the person before they died. The normal parts of her. They didn't look familiar to you?"

"No."

I looked down at my hands, which were still enveloped in his firm grasp. I could feel from the occasional twitch that if he let go, my fingers would be shaking uncontrollably. He felt it too.

"This is ridiculous," Jenn said. Dex and I both looked at her. We knew it was ridiculous, but it had happened. After what had happened on the island, I knew better than to doubt myself anymore.

"It's the truth, though," I said quietly.

"Sure. The truth in your mind," she said, getting up. She stretched as if it was all boring her, her gray camisole lifting up, which displayed her richly hued, flat stomach.

"Explain the blood then," Dex said defensively, gesturing at it.

Jenn shrugged. "Could be a bunch of things. And none of them say 'ghost.' All I know is that I need to clean this mess up before it stains the floor."

She walked over to a utility closet and brought out cleaning supplies. I watched Dex watching her. He seemed livid, but with an eerie, contained kind of anger. It made his eyes sparkle and fade, his jaw twitch back and forth. Finally he looked away and up at me. Now he just looked sympathetic, maybe even apologetic. It's just us against the world, his gaze seemed to say.

Soon after Jenn had finished cleaning and went back to sleep, Dex came with me into my room to say goodnight.

"Are you tucking me in?" I asked wryly as he flicked on the light and shut the door behind us.

He smiled shyly. "I just want to make sure you're all right."

Well, I wasn't all right. I never was "all right."

I walked over to the bed and got in, pulling the covers around me. Dex followed and sat on the end of it.

"I'd stay with you here if I could," he said, looking around him at his stuff on the walls, absently stroking the bedcover.

"That's OK," I said even though I never wanted anything more. I had the urge to lean over, grab him by the edge of his plaid pajama pants and pull him on top of me. His body in my hands would make the fear go away. I wanted to tug at his shaggy black hair, suck on his bottom lip. I wanted to run my fingers over the tattoo on his chest, "And with madness comes the light" and feel the madness inside of me until it consumed both of us.

I closed my eyes at the thought. I had to stop thinking this way. When did I turn into such a horny teenager?

After a period of silence he asked, "Are you having any dreams?" He approached the question softly, like he was treading on eggshells.

"Yes." I carefully opened my eyes, afraid that I might see that girl again, but it was still Dex. His elbows were propped up on his thighs and he was holding his head in his hands, looking like he was falling asleep. It was 4 a.m. after all.

"But they aren't nightmares. They are just dreams. Weird...flashbacks. Like I'm reliving the past."

"What past?"

"High school."

"When you were a shoplifting, coke-snorting badass?" he asked, now sounding amused.

I paused. "Yes, those were the days."

"And nothing else?"

"No…"

He looked up and twisted his body to face mine.

"Are you sure?"

My brows furrowed. "Yes, I'm sure."

I pulled up the covers even further around me and asked, "What about you? Do you ever have any dreams?"

"Yeah." He smirked. "I'm all alone and I'm rolling this big donut…"

"I'm serious," I said, though I obviously smiled.

"Then no. I don't have those kinds of dreams," he said. He got up and shivered against the chill that was creeping up in the room. That coldest part of the night before dawn.

"I really don't want to leave you." He walked over to me and stopped, peering down. He put out his hand for mine and I grabbed it, giving it a quick shake.

"I'll be OK," I said, more forcefully. He nodded then cried out softly, "Hey what if Fat Rabbit sleeps with you? He snores and farts a lot but he's solid company."

"Takes after his dad, I take it?" I joked. "Actually I'd love it if the dog stayed here."

Within a few minutes, the lights in the room were off, I was snug under the covers, and Fat Rabbit was happily wheezing away at the foot of my bed. I counted down to the cadence of his breath until I fell asleep too.

CHAPTER EIGHT

Tuesday morning was oddly calm and beautiful. The rains that had plagued the city had stopped sometime after we all fell asleep again and the golden, winter morning sun was making the wet branches outside the apartment sparkle and shine.

Jenn didn't mention anything about the incident in the night, but did cook us all up a giant feast of French toast and bacon, which gave off the vibe that she was making up for something. Not that she had anything to make up, but I wouldn't have been surprised if Dex had given her a warning. She did seem to insinuate last night that my mental health wasn't all what it seemed to be.

Which was nothing new. I was used to people thinking that I was crazy and if anyone was going to think anything less of me, I knew it would be someone like Jenn. But it got me thinking, especially as I spent the morning pattering about in the den and flipping through all the books that Dex had.

You see, none of the books that lined his shelves had anything to do with the mental institute we would be investigating later that night, even though there were quite a few library books there. There were some on the paranormal, stuff I would eagerly devour some other time when I wasn't afraid of a dead girl in his living room, but nothing that was remotely related to our case.

Perhaps it didn't mean anything. Dex had been busy moving and dealing with a dog and all that, and it was possible that he forgot about the research part of the show. But normally I had a script, or something to go on, and even if I wrote that script myself, I did it with his help. This time it felt like we were winging it entirely and at a point when we couldn't really afford to. It wasn't just about our wee *Experiment in Terror* show. It was about how our show did up against the bigwigs like *Spook Factory*. Now was not the time to be going into any situation blind, and yet Dex and I hadn't discussed anything about it at all.

I thought about asking him. I knew he was in the living room, reading the paper, sipping on his coffee, occasionally saying something to Jenn. But something told me not to. And it stemmed from the same reason why I thought Dex was keeping me in the dark about things. Frankly, he didn't want to talk about it.

It must have something to do with the fact that Dex had been in a mental institute. What else could it be? We had never discussed what had happened to him or why he was there. I just knew it was true. But I didn't know how to bring the topic up with him, or even if it was any of my business.

Yet, the fact that we were going traipsing into an actual mental hospital later, well...that sort of made it my business. It was like if you were heading off into battle with a shell-shocked veteran. You'd kinda want to make sure that they were OK with it, otherwise they'd flip out at the first gunshot and you could be dead in a second.

I decided I'd try to approach the subject when the time was right. Hopefully that time would come sooner rather than later.

After we spent the morning doing not much of anything, the couple decided to take me out for lunch in the Capitol Hill district. Dex also wanted to take me past the

Harvard Exit Cinema, the allegedly haunted theatre that our dear rivals were investigating.

We got into the car, Dex's black Highlander this time, and drove off along the sunny streets. It was funny how even in the sunlight, the city had this hidden, shadowy quality to it, like it was just being covered up by sunshine-hued fabric.

In the front, Dex flicked the MP3 player until The Beatles *Abbey Road* came on and gave Jenn a playful nudge with his elbow. She looked at him, coyly peering over the edge of her designer shades, and smiled in return. It seemed to be some little inside joke or perhaps telepathic couplespeak for something.

I looked away from them and kept my eyes on the road. It wasn't as uncomfortable as it had been the day before but it still made me feel funny inside.

"Something" came on, one of my favorite Beatles songs.

At least it was, until Dex started to sing along with it. I had to look. He was eyeing me in the rearview mirror while carefully crooning to the most poignant parts. I shook my head and looked away.

Dex continued the sing along with the next song, "Maxwell Silver Hammer." He was louder this time and to my horrible surprise, Jenn started to sing along too. They traded off verses like some Paul and John session, and when the chorus kicked in, they both began to act out the hammer hits with their hands, in tune with the rhythm. They were smiling at each other, singing at the top of their lungs, and having the world's most stomach-turning karaoke competition in the front of the car. And to a song that was essentially about a serial killer with a hammer.

I felt sick. My face scrunched up at their cutesy, song-sharing coupleness. *Abbey Road* was now forever ruined for me.

Luckily the song wasn't long and Jenn stopped singing as soon as "Oh Darling" came on. Dex kept going, of course. I mean, he was really letting 'er rip. I tried not to be won over by his vocal prowess but it was hard, especially when he rolled down the window and started howling with Paul at the most passionate, throat-burning parts.

Jenn made an annoyed sigh and smacked him on the shoulder. "What are you doing? Roll up the window. No one wants to hear you."

He ignored her and kept belting it out the window to the bemusement of the cars and pedestrians going past. A few of them gave him the thumbs up for the free performance on wheels.

"I'm serious, you're so fucking embarrassing," she sneered, and for the first time, I didn't find her so pretty anymore.

I quickly eyed Dex to see his reaction. He stopped singing and gave her one hell of a look. Had I mentioned that Dex was the king of looks that could kill? It was one of *those* looks. I waited with bated breath for Jenn to explode into flames and I was glad I was sitting far away in the back seat.

She didn't burst into flames, unfortunately, but she did push her shades further up against her face and brought out her phone. She started texting someone, ignoring the bolts of brimstone that were shooting out from Dex's fiery glare.

Finally, he brought his attention back to the road before we almost rear-ended a van, turned down the volume on the stereo and we rode the rest of the way to Capitol Hill in relative silence. It was fucking weird. They had gone from a sickening, "in love" couple doing a duet to the complete opposite in the span of two songs. Who knew the Beatles were still so controversial.

The lunch, then, was brutal for all of us. Dex and Jenn weren't talking to each other and Jenn wasn't talking to me, which left Dex and me making careful small talk with each other, dancing around subjects like two characters in a play. When Jenn got up to go make a phone call outside, Dex exhaled loudly and comically collapsed across his chicken club sandwich.

I watched him anxiously, rubbing the edges of my fingernails. He eventually lifted his head and a small, tired smile tugged at his lips and the corners of his eyes.

"I'm sorry," he said.

"Don't be," I told him, trying to sound cool, like I was an impartial friend and not at all invested in the decline of his relationship. "Couples fight all the time."

"Yeah," he said slowly. Then sighed, sat back in his chair and rubbed his chin, his eyes unfocused.

"Am I making things worse?" I asked.

"Worse? No, kiddo. Things aren't worse. This is just the way it is sometimes."

What I think he meant to say was that "this is just the way it is all the time" but he was trying to save face. I didn't know why. Why did he bother with her? Why did he bother moving with her? Why did he bother getting a dog with her? I didn't understand any of it. Did he love her? Was that it? Did he actually truly love her and was too afraid to let go?

I could have gone on with these questions, as I often did, but I stopped myself and forced myself to think about something else. This was the only way I was going to get over him. Get over him as he sat across from me. I turned my attention to the other people in the restaurant, trying to focus on something, anything else. I picked up on a group of girls my age who were giggling with each other over a Smartphone they were passing around the table. I envied them. It was working.

Jenn came back to table after her phone call was over. She stopped in front of us, leaned over to Dex, moved his face over to hers and kissed him passionately on the lips. There were tongue and slobbering sounds involved. My eyes widened, watching them, unable to look away.

When she pulled back, he looked dumbstruck, while she gave me a quick, sly wink. It either said, *men are simple* or it said, *oh no you don't*. I'd put bets on the latter.

"Excuse me," I blurted out, quickly getting out of my chair, which rattled loudly against the tiled floor, and hurried my way over to the restaurant's bathroom before I burst into tears.

I entered the washroom, which was thankfully empty, and ran the tap, splashing an endless amount of cold water on my face. I wouldn't cry, I wouldn't cry. I was going to get out of the damn city without a single tear leaving my face.

When I calmed down a bit, I gently patted my face with a paper towel and leaned against the mirror. I needed to get a hold of myself. I was tired of being fine and tough one minute and then losing it the next. What the hell was wrong with me? Jenn, Dex, they both had way too much power over me and my emotions. This had to stop. Now.

I breathed in a few times through my nose until I felt under control and then went into the stall to pee. I thought about this Bradley fellow. Maybe I'd ask Rebecca tomorrow about setting me up with him. Maybe he was just the distraction I needed from this whole Dex and Jenn business. Plus, the fact that both of them seemed totally against it, was finally sounding intriguing.

As I pondered this exciting diversion, I heard the door to the washroom open and a woman enter, her heels slowly making their way down toward the mirrors. She absolutely reeked of gin, the tangy scent of juniper flooding the bathroom. That, coupled with the slight unevenness of her gait, made me think that this girl was pissed off her gourd.

I slowly reached over for the toilet paper, not wanting to make too much noise in case she thought she was alone.

But the person giggled.

I paused, listening. There it was again. A high, strange, sloppy giggle. She had to be wasted.

The giggles continued until it was full-out laughter, her loud, braying laugh echoing in the room.

I quickly finished my business and was about to get up off the toilet seat when the laughter died down and the girl spoke.

"He said he loved me," the mystery drunk said in a mild Minnesotan accent. It reminded me of Frances McDormand's character in *Fargo*. Who was she talking to? Was she on the phone?

I got up, pulling on my jeans and tried to peer through the crack in the stall door. I couldn't see anyone. The sink in front of my closed door looked empty.

"He said he loved me. I love you. And the next time he saw me, he told me, 'I'll kill you.'" She laughed in surprise. "He said he'd kill me. Can you believe that?"

I waited for someone to respond, straining my ears to hear the crackle of a voice on the other end of a line.

"Can you believe that?" she repeated, this time her voice lower, edgier. Perhaps she was talking on a Bluetooth. I had no idea. It didn't matter.

I turned, about to flush the toilet.

"Perry, can you believe that?"

My eyes flew to the door. Did she just say my name? I swallowed my breath and kept still, arm frozen in mid-reach. Was she...talking to *me*?

I didn't know what to say. Who was this person? What did she want?

I heard the shoes move, closer to me now, and I had a terrible flashback to the time I was in the Seattle airport washroom and Creepy Clown Lady appeared. But this wasn't her. Not this time.

"Perry..." The voice now buzzed, like it vibrated on the wings of a bee. It filled my head and tickled the insides of my cheeks.

A slow tide of blood appeared at the bottom of the stall door and crept forward toward my feet, a sticky crimson blanket spreading out on top of the black marble.

I gasped, shocked, aghast, unable to process this. Was this actually happening?

It kept coming, a never-ending flow of shiny blood and it wasn't until I saw several wasps, living, breathing wasps, riding the swells toward me like yellow, wriggling surfers, that I finally moved.

I grabbed the door and tried to unlock it. It was stuck. The latch wouldn't turn. The blood kept flowing and the door wouldn't open. I was stuck in the fucking bathroom stall.

Hopelessly, I rattled it back and forth for a few seconds; then, just before the blood kissed the tips of my Docs, I stepped up onto the toilet seat.

I balanced precariously on the porcelain edge, crouched down briefly and leaped up for the side of the stall. My arms caught the metal edge and I hoisted myself up, kicking at the steel sides for support and momentum, the clanging noise banging out across the room. I pulled myself over to the other side, the edge digging into my ribs, dangling like Agent Starling scaling a wall, and then quickly dropped down onto the toilet in the next stall.

One foot caught the seat while the other went straight in the toilet with a cold splash.

I pulled my foot out in one swift motion, and leaped onto the ground. The stall door here was unlocked. I shoved it open and barreled out into the washroom. I didn't look to see if the Minnesota girl was standing there, didn't bother to see if the endless river of blood still covered the bathroom floor. I just ran straight to the doors of the bathroom, my wet foot sopping as I moved, and ran out into the hallway.

I continued straight out of the restaurant, not caring about leaving Dex or Jenn at the table, and ran onto the busy sidewalk, where I almost collided with an old man carrying Christmas decorations.

"Sorry!" I squeaked out and twirled around in the opposite direction. I ran up to the end of the block, my mind racing, my heart convulsing, and stopped beside Dex's Highlander. I leaned across the hood, hugging it, feeling the solidity of the car, the sunshine on my back, the people passing by who were undoubtedly giving me a strange look or two.

I didn't care how long I stood there, hugging the car. It just felt safe, somehow. Safe and real. Not a bathroom full of blood and gin-soaked words.

"Kiddo?"

I sensed Dex's presence behind me before he even spoke.

I closed my eyes and tried to figure out what I would say. I had nothing.

He gingerly placed his hand on my shoulder. I straightened up and turned to look at him.

"What...?" he trailed off and bit his lip. He was looking at my left leg, which was soaked up to mid-calf with toilet water.

I shook my head. "I can't even..."

"What happened?" he crossed his arms and took a commanding stance even though his voice was gentle.

"I'll tell you later," I said, eyeing Jenn, who came out of the restaurant and was walking toward us, looking put out, with my purse and coat that I had left at the table in hand.

She stopped at the passenger door and looked at both of us distrustfully. "What's going on?"

"Perry was just feeling sick," Dex explained.

She smirked. "I could see that. Trying to skip out on the bill there, honey?"

Honey? Oh no she didn't. It was their treat. But I bit my tongue from saying anything that would damn me. I was too confused and exhausted to argue anyway.

She handed me my stuff.

"Thanks. I was feeling ill. I'll get you guys back next time," I said and jumped in the back seat before my legs gave out from under me. I shut the door on Dex, who still looked puzzled, and stood there for a few good seconds before shaking his head and going around to the driver's side.

Five minutes later we pulled up across the street from the Harvard Exit Theatre. I had hoped Dex would have driven us straight back to the apartment, but no. He still wanted to show me some stupid haunted theatre.

"We can see this some other time," Jenn said from the front seat, looking at the small, brick building with disinterest. For once I agreed with her. I was in no mood for paranormal hijinx after what happened in the bathroom.

"Chill out, babe," he said, leaning forward in his seat and scanning the street. "You don't have to get out of the car if you don't want to."

"Good," Jenn and I both said at the same time. He jumped at that and turned around in his seat to look at me, confused.

"Well, I'll obviously need *you* to come with me. That's why we're here."

I stared back at him, trying to telepathically tell him how scared I was, that I wasn't in the mood for some field trip. His eyes narrowed slightly, becoming balls of coal in the car's interior, but he didn't relent.

"Come on, kiddo. I just want to show you the lobby; it's actually really-"

"Dex!" Jenn called out suddenly, smacking him on the arm.

"What?"

She pointed out the front of the car, at four people who were crossing the street and heading over to the theatre. One of them had a camera on his shoulder, the other had a boom mic. Leading the way was a tall guy and girl.

"Is that them...the Spook Factory?" she asked, waving her finger.

I leaned forward between the seats to get a better look. The guy was actually wearing a Tap-Out shirt or something and looked just like G.J. Jermaine. The female had a rat's nest of blonde hair. It was them. And they actually had a crew, too.

Dex and I exchanged a look, both of our brows raised, mouths agape.

Finally he said, "Now will you come with me?"

Jenn and I both nodded in shared determination and got out.

Dex promptly jaywalked across the street and we hurried behind him, getting dirty looks from the passing cars as we slowed their progress.

Once on the other side, he walked down the leaf-strewn sidewalk toward the *Spook Factory* group, his step deceivingly light, his hands in the pockets of his black cargo jacket.

"What's he going to do?" I said, more to myself than to Jenn. I took a step after him but she put her hand out to stop me.

"I don't know," she said slowly. "Let's just wait here and see."

I examined her face. Her thin brows were creating miniscule lines on her forehead. She was worried and on edge. I wondered if she was used to this confrontation from her boyfriend. Dex isn't a big guy by any means. He's on the short side and toned but still thin. But he has unpredictable pit-bull tactics and one hell of a lippy attitude with strangers. For heaven's sake, never give that man a shovel.

My attention back at Dex, I could see the group pausing in mid-stride and conversation as he approached them. I couldn't tell from behind but I had a feeling Dex was smiling broadly in that unnerving way, a wide, joker grin that wouldn't match his eyes.

He stopped in front of them and they started talking. From where we were, I couldn't really hear what they were saying but the *Factory* crew's faces quickly went from apprehensive to amiable. Dex was winning them over, or at least leading them astray.

I looked back at Jenn. She hadn't relaxed and hadn't removed her arm.

"Girls," Dex shouted. He was waving for us to come over. Jenn relented and we walked down the street, both of us approaching them all nervy and wired, like spooked horses.

Seeing G.J. and Annie up close didn't change my opinion about them. He still looked stereotypically "hot" but charmless, and she still reminded me of an orange witch with too much plastic surgery. The guy with the camera was older, with a heavy beer gut, Megadeth shirt (which normally would have won him points in my book but not now since he was involved with this douche show), buzz cut and braided goatee. The guy holding the boom mic had a white-and-red striped sailor top, a white cap and glasses. He looked exactly like a French, hipster version of Waldo.

"Perry, Jenn," Dex said, gesturing to them with incredibly false sincerity. "I'd like you to meet G.J., Annie, Joe and Douglas."

Joe was the guy in the Megadeth shirt. I wondered if people called him Little Joe as a joke.

I smiled at them all as earnestly as possible and quickly shook their hands. Jenn gave a short nod and flash of her white teeth.

"We're big fans of your show," G.J. said to me, holding onto my hand for a second longer than he should have. His hand was greasy and big and he had too many rings on.

"Oh yeah," I said, swiping my hand away and looking him in the eye. "Is that why you decided to copy us?"

"Perry," Jenn hissed from beside me.

I gave her a look. "What? It's true." I looked back at the crew. "Isn't it?"

G.J. let out a laugh that I wished sounded more nervous. He raised his hands in the air, looking back and forth between Dex and me with a dumbass grin on his face. "Guilty as charged. If I hadn't been a fan, I wouldn't have bothered with the job. It's all Annie here, really."

Annie shrugged, her strange dead eyes looking at my forehead. "We aren't copying you. You're just copying shows like Paranormal State and Ghost Lab. We have our own spin."

I shot Dex a look out of the corner of my eye. Did I dare ask what the spin was?

He did it for me. "And what's that?"

G.J. crossed his overly muscley arms and straightened up. He was a good five inches taller than Dex but my partner didn't seem intimidated in the slightest.

"We're *real* ghost hunters."

Jenn burst out laughing. I would have joined her had I not remembered those fairy tale comments from the day before.

"Excuse me?" I asked. "Real?"

G.J. and Annie exchanged a smug look between them.

"I've gone to school for parapsychology," Annie said with a haughty twitch of her head. "I know how to talk to ghosts. I know how to find them. And they know how to find me."

Jenn put her face in her hands and mumbled, "Oh my God, I can't believe I am standing here listening to this conversation." She looked up at Joe and Douglas with disbelief. "Come on, fellas, you can't possibly believe this shit either?"

Joe was silent but Douglas spoke up, adjusting his hat. "We've seen some pretty freaky stuff. These two know what they are doing."

"And so do we," Dex injected. Another total lie. Dex and I had no idea what we were doing.

"No, dear," Jenn said, walking over to Dex and tugging at his arm. "You're clueless. But I still love you anyway."

"Jenn, what are you doing?" I couldn't help but blurt out, staring at her aghast.

She glared at me momentarily. Then she smiled again, big and fake, and looked at everyone. "I'm sorry, I didn't mean to blow your cover. I think you're all full of shit. There are no such things as ghosts. You're all filming dust particles floating in the air and talking to the walls."

"Well, *they* might be," Dex said pointing at Annie.

Jenn snickered and reached into his pant pocket, bringing out the keys. "I'm going back to the car before I lose my mind. Hope you guys don't scare each other to death."

As she walked away, G.J. asked, "Is that the girl from Wine Babes?"

Dex nodded, frowning.

"No such thing as ghosts?" Annie said to him. "How the hell do you put up with that?"

An involuntary smile spread across my face. Dex shot me a look and I wiped it away just in time.

"So you have a degree or something in parapsychology," he continued, ignoring her. "So what?"

"So plenty," she said. She had a lot more confidence than I had hoped. "It gave me the backing to go into the Fantasy Network and pitch the show. I showed them I knew what I was doing so they gave us a budget, a crew, and the ability to make two episodes a week. I'm assuming Shownet's not giving you any of that."

"It's a small network," I explained meekly.

"It's internet only. *Spook Factory* is attached to a TV network, so we have more range and more reach and I wouldn't be surprised if our show ends up on TV anyway."

"As it should," G.J. shot in, eyeing Annie carefully. "I didn't give up a career in Mixed Martial Arts just so I could fester on the internet."

I tried hard not to laugh but failed.

"So you really are going around and kicking ghosts in the balls. That is your job, right?" I asked.

Dex snorted.

G.J. rolled his eyes. "I'm in charge of all the equipment. And I'm the eye candy."

"What am I, chopped liver?" Annie said to him, scrunching up her beak of a nose. "You only got this job because you fucked over Eddie."

"Who is Eddie?" I had to ask.

Annie crossed her arms and sighed, a frazzle puff of blonde hair flying off her face. "Not that it's any of your business, but Eddie was supposed to be working with me. Not G.J. here."

"But I called Eddie with a fake job offer so he'd forget about this one," G.J. finished. He looked way too proud of himself for something so low. "Annie found out later but hey, by then people expected me to be part of the show." He gave Annie an insincere smile. "Besides, Eddie was a wimp. Sure he knew more about supernatural stuff but come on, he'd be running away like a pussy at the first sign of trouble."

So they were our competition, and they were deceptive douchebags. Great.

Dex popped a piece of Nicorette in his mouth and chewed silently for a few beats.

"So, why are you here?"

Annie made a weird, amused noise and pointed at the brick building. "Why the hell do you think? You ever heard of the Harvard Exit Cinema?"

"Well, being as I live here, yes," Dex answered smartly, not looking at the building. "But there hasn't been any paranormal activity in there since 1987. Figured you would have known that."

I felt like kicking Dex. What was he doing, giving them pointers? Let them film at the building that was a dud. Better for us in the long run.

"I did know that," Annie shot back. "But that doesn't mean anything."

"It means that when Bertha Landes, the former – and only – woman mayor, had an exhibit of her items placed at a museum, the haunting here stopped. You're barking up the wrong tree."

"I'm sorry you're so close-minded, Dex Foray. You see, what I've learned in *school* is that people are haunted and not buildings. If a building is haunted that usually means there is some kind of doorway inside, a place where the walls to the afterlife are thin. And if someone who is more disposed to supernatural contact, such as myself, is in such a place, the ghosts come to them."

I hated to admit it, but what she said made a little bit of sense. It would explain why, no matter where I was, certain things would haunt me.

Like the woman in the bathroom. The woman with the voice of wasps, the sticky red blood tide of endless blood flowing toward me, the fact that she knew my name...

"Are you OK, kiddo?" I heard Dex say.

I looked at him and noticed I had everyone's attention. Had I just said something out loud?

"What?" I asked.

He furrowed his brows, slowing down his chewing, watching me carefully. I gave him an incredulous look and repeated myself. "What, Dex?"

"Nothing," he said slowly and then looked back at the crew. "Well, just trying to help you guys out. Don't want to see you wasting your time."

"Oh yeah," G.J. said sarcastically. "I'm sure that's it. You and Boobs here just don't want us to find anything."

"Boobs?" I cried out and looked down at my chest. I was wearing a Nine Inch Nails tee shirt underneath my jacket. Nothing "boobs" about that.

Dex cocked his head at him, annoyed. "Actually you can find whatever the hell you fucktards want. We've got our own fish to fry tonight and we're going to be the first show that the institute is going to let film inside."

"What institute?" Annie asked suspiciously.

"You're just going to have to watch and see, sweetheart," Dex responded with a handsome grin. He grabbed my hand and started pulling me toward the car. I shot the group one final look and followed Dex, walking rapidly to keep up with him.

When we were out of earshot, I said, "What a bunch of douchebags."

"Douchebuckets," he corrected me.

"Should we be worried?"

He shook his head and spit his gum out into the gutter as we crossed the street to his car. "Fuck me, I could go for a cigarette right now."

"That's not a good sign, Dex," I pointed out.

He gave me a quick smile for reassurance but I didn't feel reassured at all.

"No need to worry, we'll figure this out soon. They've got nothing on us," he said as he opened the rear door for me.

I got in and we drove back home. Though I couldn't quite place my finger on it, I had a bad feeling about all of this. Then again, when didn't I?

CHAPTER NINE

After our confrontation with Spook Factory was over, everyone seemed too aggro and annoyed to be cooped up in the apartment. Jenn decided she was going to go to the gym and invited me to go along with her.

"No thanks," I had told her. Going to a gym, with Jenn...I'd rather have a lobotomy.

"Are you sure? You could use the exercise," she said, stretching in her Lycra gear in front of me.

I narrowed my eyes at her.

"For endorphins," she smiled sweetly. "They'll make you feel better."

Uh huh.

So she went on her merry way to burn whatever fat she had left off of her while Dex did the opposite and had a nap.

"Can you watch Fat Rabbit and make sure he's not shitting in anyone's shoes?" Dex asked as he stood in his bedroom doorway. He looked strangely wane and haggard, a sudden change from earlier. A nap would do him good.

"Of course," I said walking into my room and nervously eyeing Fat Rabbit, who was staring at me with devious bug eyes, like he already had shit in someone's shoes and was just waiting for that person to find out.

He closed his door and I was left to my own devices. I went on the computer for a bit, checking my emails and making sure Miss Anonymous wasn't leaving any more scathing comments on the blog posts. To my surprise and relief, she hadn't said anything lately.

I tweeted a few things about being in Seattle and going on a hunting expedition that evening, even though I wanted to put a few potshots in there about G.J. and Annie. But I wasn't about to start a Twitter war with those people.

When I got bored of the internet, I entertained Fat Rabbit by tossing a chew toy around for him in the room, not wanting his loud nails to go clattering across the apartment and waking up Dex. And when Fat Rabbit got bored of that, I started picking through Dex's bookshelf again.

I started with a coffee table book of Led Zeppelin and skimmed through a few rock biographies before settling on a heavy book called "The Devil's Death Metal," which seemed to be about a female music journalist in the early 1970s and her supernatural involvement with a metal band. At least, that's what the blurb on the back said.

But when I opened the book to read the first few pages, my eyes nearly fell out of my head.

The pages were all glued together and a hollow square was cut out in the middle. There were four half-full bottles of prescription medicine inside.

I took one bottle out and examined it. I had no idea what the gobbledygook medicinal name was, but it was prescribed by a Doctor Anderson for a Mr. Declan Foray.

I looked around me warily. Fat Rabbit was lying down on the bed and looking at me like I was doing something wrong. But I wasn't. Was I? I mean, Dex was storing – or hiding – bottles of medicine in a hollowed-out book.

I remembered back to when we first met; he had mentioned that Jenn never knew he was on medication. I thought that had been a joke but it was now apparent that he had been serious. It boggled my mind. How on earth was Dex able to keep this a secret from her, and for heaven's sake, why? She was his girlfriend, the one person who actually had the right to know if her boyfriend was on medication or not.

And four bottles, too! I examined all of them. Some were horse-pill size, some were tiny yellow tablets. And while two bottles were prescribed by Dr. Anderson, the other two were from a Dr. Houston and a Dr. Bains.

I gently put the bottles back and closed the book cover, holding it in my lap. I didn't know what to think. Why was Dex on so many pills? What else was wrong with him? It couldn't just be this so-called bipolar disorder, could it?

"Perry?" Dex called out. Fat Rabbit leaped off the bed and I leaped to my feet and hid the book behind my back just as he appeared at the door, looking all ruffle-haired and bleary-eyed.

"Dex!" I exclaimed, trying to not look suspicious. It didn't fool him.

"What are you doing?" he asked, moving his head over to get a better look at what I had behind my back.

"Nothing," I replied swiftly and stepped backward. I smiled while adjusting the book behind my back, hiding it better.

But as I did so, my finger caught the edge of the book and the cover opened.

All four pill bottles fell out and bounced onto the carpet behind me.

Oh, *shit*.

Dex's face crumpled in horror first. Then stealthily switched to pure, visceral anger. You wouldn't like Dex when he's angry.

"What the fuck are you doing!?" he cried out and lunged toward me, grabbing my arm roughly and snatching the book out my hands. He pushed me over until I fell butt-first onto the bed and scooped up the pill bottles from the floor.

"I didn't mean to-"

He straightened up, clutching his pills to his dark grey T-shirt, his eyes wild. "What, are you fucking snooping through my stuff?!"

I got off the bed and squared up against him, not about to be intimidated. "I wasn't snooping through your fucking stuff, you idiot! I was looking through your stupid books; how the hell was I supposed to know you've got fucking drugs hidden in them? What the fuck is that about?"

"Never mind," he sneered, and turned to leave the room with his precious cargo. I grabbed his forearm and dug my nails into his bare flesh, my turn to be rough.

He stopped and looked at the arm in surprise, then at me. "Ow! Let go of me, you wench."

"You fucking tell me why you're hiding prescription meds in a book!"

"It's none of your business, Perry!"

"It's totally my business. I'm your partner. We've been through this, Dex, I mean, come on. I need to know what the fuck you're on. I was fine with your whole bipolar thing or whatever the hell is wrong with you, but why the hell do you need four different medicines from three different doctors and why the fuck are you hiding it in a hollowed-out book?!"

He jerked slightly, taken aback. He eyed my arm again, more calmly this time, and I removed my nails from his arm. They left crescent indents but hadn't broken the skin. Finally he looked at me.

"Why are you so mad?"

"Because!" I yelled. I peered at the doorway, where Fat Rabbit was watching us. The dog was shaking. I closed my eyes, took back my hand and let out a deep breath. "Because, I just am. I feel so unprepared about this whole mental institute thing, you haven't given me anything to go on..."

"There's a thing called Google, you know. You could look up Riverside yourself. I don't have to do everything for you."

I opened my eyes and shook my head. "That's not the point. It's because you're being so evasive about this whole thing, about the fact that you were in an institute yourself. And you're not talking to me about it."

Dex threw his head back in exasperation. "Oh my God. Did it ever occur to you, Perry, that maybe, just maybe, I don't want to talk about what happened to me in there? It's a fucking mental institute. You have no fucking idea what that means."

Guilt kicked at me from inside. "OK, you're right, I don't. I just want to…"

"Want to what?" he challenged, looking me deep in the eyes.

"I want you to trust me."

"But I do trust you," he said quietly.

"Then tell me about these," I said, pointing at the pills he was still clutching to his chest with one arm.

"Some other time."

"No, now."

"No," he argued. He put his free hand on my shoulder and squeezed it. "It's a long story and Jenn's going to come back here any minute."

"OK, well at least tell me why you're hiding them in a book. Hiding them from your girlfriend."

He sighed. I was being stubborn, but then again so was he. He picked up the book from the bed, opened the cover and placed the bottles inside. He put the book back on the shelf along with the other books I had been flipping through, sat down on the bed and made me sit down beside him.

"OK," he said quietly, and leaned his head toward mine, our faces close. "I hide them in there because Jenn doesn't know I'm on medication…still."

"Still? So she knew at one point?"

"Yes."

"And she thought you got better, or..?"

"Yes."

"And did you?"

He scratched at his sideburn and gave me a sideways glance before carefully saying, "In a way."

"What does that mean?"

"It's hard to explain. And no, I don't have time to explain it now. But the point is, Jenn doesn't know I'm on meds, certainly doesn't know I'm taking this many different kinds, and to answer your question before you ask it, no, she doesn't know I was in a mental institute."

"How can you just lie to her like that?"

He shrugged. "It's easy. And I'm not lying, I'm just omitting some stuff."

"Would you tell her the truth if she asked?"

I watched him carefully. He pursed his lips, thinking it over. He better not think about lying to me.

"No, I wouldn't," he finally said. "I would lie. Because the past is the past and it doesn't concern her in any way."

"But it concerns you, so by default it should concern her."

"You'd think that..."

I looked down at my hands and started playing with my nails. "It concerns me."

"I know it does," he said gently. "But you're different, Perry. You're very, very different. That's why I..."

He stopped himself.

"What?" I prodded.

His lips twitched. "That's why I'm glad you're my partner."

"Oh."

I looked around the room, at the posters on the walls and the rock photos and the guitars and the weird books. None of this made any sense to me.

"How did you two even start going out?" I asked, thinking out loud, not really wanting an answer.

He shrugged again and wiped his chin quickly. "Honestly? She was hot, good in bed, and a bit of a bitch."

Ouch. I could see he was telling the truth. It was a very guy thing to say, but it still stung. I covered it up, though, and raised my brow at him.

"*Was* a bit of a bitch?"

He smiled, sucked in his lip again, but didn't say anything.

"Sorry," I apologized, though I wasn't really sorry.

"It's deserved, kiddo," he said and patted me lightly on the back. "I'm sorry she's so prickly with you. Don't take anything she says or does seriously, OK?"

That was way easier said than done. But I gave him a small smile back and told him that his secret was safe with me. I was good at keeping them.

~~

At 4 p.m., when the city skyline grew a dark grey with the threat of night and impending rain clouds, Dex and I piled our gear and equipment into his car and piloted off toward the Riverside Mental Institute.

After our discussion in the den, Jenn came back from her workout and I hopped on the computer to Google the shit out of the institute. Though I hated him for saying it, Dex was right, and there was no reason why I couldn't be prepared.

The institute was built at the turn of the century to take care of the Pacific Northwest's finest, most depressed people. I guess they had something to do with the first research into Seasonal Affective Disorder, and if there is any place where SAD affects most of the population, it's probably here. I know I get more moody and have more panic attacks when the sun disappears and the gloomy winter clouds park themselves over Portland.

According to the official website, the institute was spread out over a massive acreage, housed three huge brick buildings and a spattering of cottages where the wealthiest patients would stay and rest until their health improved. The photos online were scans from about 80 years ago, showing patients playing crochet and bridge. Not your average mental hospital. At least, not on the surface.

Of course, like most mental hospitals in the country, only one building is still operational, with funding being cut drastically over the years.

But it wasn't all just about curing the blues for wealthy Seattleites. The smallest brick building had been used as a sort of holding station for some of the most heinous criminals back in the day where they would undergo tests to see whether they could plead insanity or not. Naturally this was the place Dex was interested in exploring. The building, called Block C, had only been officially run for 20 years before a few accidents shut it down. Turns out a mental hospital wasn't always the most high-security place to hold serial killers and the like.

Tonight, though, we probably wouldn't be allowed to wander around the supposedly haunted Block C (and that was fine with me), though there were some weird stories about even the main building, which still housed mild mental cases. Regardless, I felt a bit more prepared than I had earlier, especially since Dex kept saying how we were just going to interview Dr. Hasselback and that was it. It put my mind at ease – as much as that was possible.

Back to the car. *Abbey Road* had picked up from where we last left it and we were treated to the moody, yearning sounds of "I Want You." Though I tried not to listen to the lyrics, I knew they were expressing something I wouldn't dare admit to Dex, and it was making me uncomfortable in my seat. I needed to drown the words out before they melted into that jagged, tumultuous ending.

"So, thanks for always driving us around," I said to Dex after he slammed on his breaks before going through a fast-changing yellow light. I said it to just say something.

"No problem. We don't have much choice, do we?"

"Well I guess I could stick you on the back of Putt-Putt," I teased.

He shook his head and said adamantly, "No way. I'd be off that thing in two seconds."

"Oh come on. I'll give you a lesson while I'm here; you'll pick it up in no time."

"I don't think I'd be good at it."

I smacked him lightly on the arm. "Declan Foray, you are good at absolutely everything. And besides, if a klutz like me can ride a motorbike, then anyone can ride a motorbike. It's more like a scooter anyway. Come on, I'll teach you."

His eyes slinked to the side and he smiled slyly. "We'll see."

The light turned green and we went through the intersection, heading out of the city and into the darkness. Light drizzle began to fall. Dex peered at the signs on the side of the road. "Can you do me a favor and get the map out of the glove compartment?"

I leaned forward and pushed the latch. The compartment was crammed full of junk but I eventually found the map book. And a rectangle box that said Epi-Pen on it.

I took out the map and the box and flashed the latter at Dex. "Is this yours?"

He took a quick look and nodded.

"What are you allergic to?"

"Bees," he said grimly. "Wasps, hornets, et cetera."

The image of the wasps floating on the sea of blood flashed across my mind.

"What happens if you get stung?" I asked carefully.

"If I don't get that EpiPen in 20 minutes, I die."

The way he said it so casually rattled me. "You...die? Is it that bad?"

"Yep."

"Why the hell do you keep it in the car? It should be on you at all times!"

"I keep one in the car and one at home. But it's winter, bee season is over. Can you look up the Issaquah area of the map? Please?"

I did so, but still thought about Dex's allergy. He could die in 20 minutes if this wee injection didn't make it into his system in time. I did not like those odds. Not one bit.

Then I thought about the scorpions we encountered in Rudy's hogan while we were in Red Fox. The image of Rudy made me sad. We still didn't know what happened to him but it was apparent that he was never coming back, and the scorpions confused me.

"What about the scorpions? In Red Fox. They were stinging us. Could they have killed you too?"

He gave me a funny look. "I wasn't sure. I was freaking out a bit there until I realized they weren't real. I don't think scorpion venom is as deadly to me as bees, but then again, I've never asked."

Freaking out a bit. That must have been an understatement.

"When did you find out?"

"The map, Perry," he said, tapping it with his hand. "Need to exit on Chesterman Road."

I sighed at his evasiveness and looked at where we were and where we needed to go. "It's the third exit coming up."

I got that Dex didn't like to get into any situations that made him feel vulnerable, so I wasn't surprised when he switched the subject. I was surprised at the subject matter though.

"So how did your date go the other night?" he asked without a hint of jealousy. A hint of jealousy would have been nice.

"With Brock?"

He snorted. "Yes, Brock. What a fucking name. Of course Brock, have you been on dates with other guys or something?"

"No," I answered shortly, not appreciating how incredulous he sounded. "Just Brock."

"And how did it go?"

"It went well," I said while trying to figure just how much to tell him. I could make the date seem like more than it was, or I could be honest. I knew which way would give me the much-coveted upper hand.

"Did you fuck him?"

My mouth dropped open. I edged my body away from him an inch and gave him a look. His vulgarity took me by surprise for once.

"Excuse me?"

He shrugged and kept his eyes on the road, scanning the sides for exit signs. "I'm just asking."

"Well...God, Dex. That's really none of your business if I did. Or didn't."

"Friends talk about all sorts of things."

"I don't ask you about your sex life."

He looked at me quickly and wiggled one brow, his specialty. "You could. I'd tell you."

I knew he would. I scrunched up my nose and turned my attention to the road we were pulling onto, Chesterman. "No thanks."

"I mean, I figured if you could hear us boning last night, it makes it an open conversation topic."

I couldn't hear them "boning" last night, I was too busy flipping out because of a dead, mutilated girl in his living room. I think I got off easy in the end.

I slowly shook my head, unable to say anything but "Dex. Just...shut up."

That lazy shrug again. "Fine. Just making conversation. Sorry your date didn't work out."

"Didn't work out?" I jeered. "Look, just because I didn't sleep with him-"

"Ah, so you held out! Good girl."

"Just because I didn't sleep with him," I repeated to myself, ignoring him, "doesn't mean the date didn't work out. I'm seeing him again next week. And probably again after that."

OK, I wasn't sure about that, but I had to say it anyway. It was worth it to see the flinch across his brow, creating momentary broodiness. He was shocked, if only for a moment. Shocked and speechless. And the upper hand was mine.

"Yeah," I added. "So, again, shut up."

He chewed on that for a few beats more. Then he said, "That's...good. I guess you deserve to have some fun too."

"Yeah," I said sternly. I attempted to stare him down, which was hard to do when his eyes were on the rainy, dark road ahead. "I do. I deserve to have a lot of fun."

I wanted to add in an extra bit about taking Rebecca up on her offer about Bradley since Dex seemed to have such a problem with that idea, but I decided that would probably make me look like too much of a slut.

Things were a tad awkward, so I reached for his iPod and started scanning through his gigantic playlist, looking for anything other than The Beatles.

"Wait, what are you putting on? You can't turn off The Beatles."

"We're in Seattle. It's dark and rainy and I'm pissed off. Can't we listen to Screaming Trees, Soundgarden, Melvins, anything local?"

"Why are you pissed off?" he asked, sounding genuinely concerned and surprised. Sometimes I wondered if Dex actually had any recollection of 90% of the conversations he was involved with.

I sighed but didn't answer him and flicked Soundgarden on. We rode in silence for the next ten minutes as Chris Cornell's wail drowned out conversation. Unfortunately, the music, combined with the spooky atmosphere and our task at hand, turned me into a little panicky puss by the time we drove up the long, winding driveway lined with rain-laden fir trees that seemed too heavy to stand up straight. We were at Riverside, the mental house of horrors. The sign at the gate said, "Your well being is our well doing." Worst slogan ever.

Dex pulled the car up into a visitor's parking spot in front of a massive, overwhelming brick building that looked extra dense and strangely menacing in the dark. It didn't help that the fluorescent hall lights that shone from all three stories flickered on and off like the light fixtures all had dying bugs in them. Moths, flies, wasps...wasps in blood. Wasps on Dex. Their hard yellow bodies covering him from head to toe.

The image filled my head and I quickly, instinctively, pressed my palm into my forehead. I caught what I was doing and picked up on the strange air in the car. I took my hand away and slowly turned my head to look at Dex. He was leaning against the steering wheel, eyes wide, watching me.

"We're here..." he eked out slowly in a quasi-*Poltergeist* voice.

I gave him a small smile, knowing the question that was to follow. "Just got a sudden headache."

"Oh sure you did," he said in weird mix of good-natured sarcasm. "You know they have pills in there for that."

I looked again at the building as the rain continued to fall, echoing off the roof of the car. I bet they did have pills in there for that. For everything that ailed us.

Which reminded me...see, I had something planned for tonight. Something that Dex didn't – and wouldn't – know about. It would only happen if the circumstances were right but a single feel into the very bottom contents of my bag told me everything was ready. It was a plan that made me feel a bit sick, but it was still a plan.

CHAPTER TEN

"Seriously kiddo, are you OK?" Dex reached for me from the driver's seat and placed the back of his hand against my forehead. His hand felt nice and hot. So I quickly opened the door and stepped into the cool night and faced the mission ahead of us.

"Right as rain," I said, smiling as the fat, icy drops fell on to my raised cheeks. I drew my coat in close around me as Dex got out on his side and brought out only a wireless mic and a small camera. We'd go back to get the EVPs, infrared and the rest of our ghost-busting goodies if we needed them but we didn't want to seem too pushy in front of Dr. Hasselback.

We walked together against the rain and wind to the heavy and strangely ornate doors at the front of the old building. Dex tried to open the beasts but after a few attempts, he discovered that it wasn't that they were too heavy but that they were locked.

He glanced at his phone. "Huh. It's only five."

I craned my neck up to get a better look at the windows above but only got rain in my eyes. I wiped them and then tried the door as well. It *was* locked.

"I told you," Dex said.

"Maybe they all like to go to bed early here," I offered. "Didn't you have a bedtime at your institute? Visiting hours? Curfew?"

I knew by the time I got to "visiting hours" I had gone too far, so I stepped away from the door and looked around again, avoiding Dex's eyes.

"It's early," he said after a minute. He leaned forward and peered through the doors. There was a half-lit desk inside the lobby area with a placard that could have said "Administration" but I wasn't sure. All I was sure of was that for five in the evening, the hospital looked dead empty. The short clip of a hallway that we could see was devoid of movement, except for those flickering lights, and all the doors were closed. I started to imagine all the horrors behind those plain doors, the psychotic blank faces and lost lives, but I stopped myself. I did not need to develop a fear of hospitals. I was sure that would come later.

I eyed the side of the entrance but there wasn't even a buzzer or intercom to let people in. I tapped Dex on the shoulder. He looked at me, perplexed.

"You do have this doctor's number right?" I asked. "Just phone him and be like, dude, what the fuck, we-"

The front doors suddenly rattled back and forth with deafening noise. I grabbed Dex's arm in fright as my heart jumped around inside my chest. Were the doors moving by themselves or...

A small figure appeared in front of us, on the other side of the doors, as if she rose up from beneath the linoleum floor.

I screamed but reined it in quickly as I got a better look at the woman. At first I thought she was Mary, the ghost we encountered on D'Arcy Island. She was the same height, freakishly short, and had the same stupid glasses and mousy face. But this woman also had a pinched nose, a mass of wrinkles that only comes from being a cold-hearted spinster. Plus she was wearing a white nurse uniform and seemed to be from this century, albeit barely. She glared at us from the other side, turning her small weird head back and forth as if she were a horse that couldn't look at you head on.

Satisfied, she unlocked the front door and casually pushed it open with all her might. Which was apparently a lot for this tiny, nasty-faced imp. Dex caught the door with his arm and I could tell he was straining to keep it open with the same amount of ease.

"You Mr. Foray and Miss Palomino?" she asked in a voice that had as much reverb as Katherine Hepburn. Her eyes were quick and spastic as they flew between our faces.

"That's us," Dex said. He smiled broadly, hoping to charm her, but I could tell from the tightness of his cheekbones that he was nervous and uncomfortable. Maybe he was reminded of Mary too.

She looked him up and down – finding his moody good looks ineffective – before saying, "You're late!"

Then she turned on her white heel and strode down the hall. We were quickly ushered in through the giant doors and they sealed us in with a jarring slam.

We hurried after her, our shoes squeaking down the hall. She could move fast, whoever the hell she was.

"Sorry, we thought we had enough time to get here," I called after her, watching her white form wiggle jerkily back and forth with each quick stride. "What's your name, by the way?"

She raised her hand in the air as if to tell me to shut up.

"I'm Mrs. Roundtree," she said without looking behind her.

Dex gave me a look that said, "Mrs? Someone's married to her?" but thankfully he didn't open his big mouth. We just kept squeaking and skidding after her until we were midway through the long half-lit, half-dark hallway. She had come to an abrupt stop and pointed at a plain door that read 'Dr. Lewis Hasselback, Head Administrator.'

"He's waiting for you," she said. She had a funny way of keeping her lips as glued to her teeth as she talked.

And then she was gone, jerking down the hallway until her white uniform was just a blob against the shadowy corridor.

I took in a deep breath and raised my brows at Dex.

"Can't charm them all," he said with a disappointed downturn of his lips and raised his hand to knock on the door. Before he brought it down, it was flung open. A short, balding man with beady eyes and thick frames was looking up at us with an anxious look on his face. I thought that being face to face with a psychologist/psychiatrist/whatever would have brought back some unpleasant memories for both me and Dex. But Dr. Hasselback was so nervy and twitchy that he put me at ease for some reason. None of that calm, condescending demeanor that Dr. Freedman had back when I was a teenager. And judging from Dex's nonplussed expression, he seemed to feel the same.

"Come in, come in," the doctor said, opening the door wide and quickly gesturing with his arm while he poked his tiny, tanned head out into the hall and looked up and down it.

I walked close beside Dex and entered the room, a large office that was more messy than orderly. Two hard-backed chairs faced the big oak table, which was strewn with overflowing file folders and piled comically high with a stack of books that seemed to reach halfway to the ceiling. It was like he was playing Jenga with textbooks.

In the far corner of the room were a couch, an armchair and the weird, Disneyland-like set design of a shrink's office, plus a few storage locker cabinets, which I knew housed some pills, and a sink.

As Dex and I were taking in the scene, the doctor shut the door gently and then scampered over to the desk and took a seat in his rolling chair. He barely looked at us and pointed at the chairs in a rough, careless manner. "Please sit down."

The chair was hard and uncomfortable, a big change from his cushy leather one. But even though that was the case, Dr. Hasselback looked like he couldn't be comfortable anywhere. He was already squirming, as if he couldn't get into an acceptable position.

"Sorry if we're intruding, doctor," Dex said, leaning forward in his seat with his diplomat's face on. "I had mistakenly thought we were on for five."

The doctor let out a nervous giggle, steepled his hands together and leaned back in the chair with a creak. "Oh, no, you were right on time. It was my fault. I hadn't told Mrs. Roundtree that you were dropping by. I'm afraid we close the hospital to visitors at 4:30 p.m. I should have mentioned that, too."

"That's kinda early for a mental hospital, right?" I said.

His eyes turned unkindly for second. At least I thought they did. It was hard to tell when they were so small and weasely and he was wearing such thick glasses. But he smiled, perfect orthodontics from childhood. "It is early. But it is the winter and we go by the light here. It's just easier. And our patients don't get many visitors these days anyway. We don't have many patients in general."

"How many are here?" Dex asked.

"Thirty-three," the doctor said. "And the numbers diminish each year. Technically, we shouldn't even have three over thirty, but families get desperate and I have a soft heart."

I wasn't sure about that.

"Do you mind if we start setting up for the interview?" Dex asked, bring around the camera and placing it on the desk. With his other hand he produced a few waivers out of his camera bag and placed those along with it.

The doctor eyed them suspiciously before picking the papers up and giving them a very thorough read.

"I hope you two realize why I am letting you do this."

Dex and I looked at each other.

Dr. Hasselback continued, eyes on the paper, "It's risky for me to open my doors to a film crew. Too much publicity, the wrong publicity, and I would humiliate myself and my patients."

"I can assure you that won't happen," Dex said.

The doctor looked up at him. "Can you? I hope so. The reason I said OK to this little venture is because you aren't the sensational type. You're honest, I believe. I hope, anyway. Sometimes I can't really believe what it is that you're writing, but I've noticed that even if you are making up every episode, you're doing it for the right reasons."

"Which are?" I asked.

He looked surprised and then looked back down at the papers again. "You're obviously seeing things that aren't there. Things you want to see. But you're not making it up for the wrong reasons. For fame. And money."

I opened my mouth to say something in our defense, but Dex laid his hand on my knee and shot me a subtle, warning look.

"And therefore, I don't mind if you film here. Because I know from personal experience that you aren't going to find anything. And I know you won't embellish on something that isn't there. However, I'm also agreeing to an interview and this is the most important part. Because an interview, right now, would help shine a little bit of light on this dark corner of the world. The country has forgotten we exist. And I can bring that light back, with you both."

So the doctor wanted to use us as much as we wanted to use him. I suppose that was perfectly fair. And we were all being honest about it, a major plus.

"That sounds like a great plan, Dr. Hasselback," Dex said, smiling but uneasily eyeing the papers he had yet to sign. He picked up on that and eventually signed it with a runny pen.

He handed them back to Dex and said, "Shall we begin then? I'm afraid I don't have all night. You two are free to film in this building for tonight. The third floor. It's totally empty. I'll see tomorrow about Thursday and access to Block C."

I presumed that it was all up to him whether we were going to film Thursday or not, but I let him have his power trip instead of questioning him. I knew how much of an accomplishment this was for Dex to get us any access at all. I especially saw it in the face of Annie Potterson when she realized we had access to a mysterious institute. They knew all right.

Dex lifted the camera up to eye level and aimed it at him. I wondered if I should say something or introduce it but Dex had already hit record. I guess we would edit my part in later. Fine with me. My hair was wet and grody and I probably matched it.

Dex did most of the talking. He seemed to know a lot more about the institute than I had garnered from my brief internet session. That didn't surprise me at all. The upper hand changed over, at least in this regard.

Dr. Hasselback was just as jittery on camera as he was off camera, but he was forthcoming and passionate about the questions. He gave a thorough history of the place and the challenges of getting funding for America's struggling mental health victims, before Dex touched on the whole haunted aspect.

"When was the first time you heard Riverside was haunted?" Dex asked.

The doctor laughed, naturally for once, and leaned back in his seat. "I have no idea. Probably the first day for me. I only came on board after medical school. Brought on by my father, who, as I just mentioned, took over the institute after the war. But you must understand, every hospital, every institute…or any place with history, is haunted in some way or another. Every place has stories and a place like this, festered with people who have stories of their own…it's inevitable."

"So you don't believe in ghosts?"

"Heavens, no."

"Then how do you account for what has happened here?"

Hasselback clasped his hands into a steeple again, and for the first time tonight, looked calm. He lowered his brow and looked at Dex head on. "You tell me, Mr. Dex Foray, what you think has happened here. What you've heard."

Dex pursed his lips for a split second before shrugging. The camera moved a bit. "Just what has been reported around the world. That patients have seen apparitions in their rooms. That visitors have been locked in with their relatives when they try to leave. That nurses hear whispers and footsteps when no one is around. That Block C is occasionally riddled with random, decaying body parts."

I shivered at that last sentence. I hadn't read that part. I looked to the doctor for his opinion. His fingers were pressed harder together but his expression hadn't changed.

"That's all?" he asked mildly.

"I'm sure it's not all," Dex answered. "But it's enough for us."

"Well it's not enough for me. All of that can be explained with two simple words: Mental Hospital. Anything a patient sees can't be taken seriously."

"And their families? And your paid staff?"

He managed a quick smile and eased himself out of his chair. He walked over to the window and peered out at the black rain-spattered night. Dex followed him with the camera lens.

"I think it's contagious, you know," Hasselback said. "The nurses, the night staff, the old security guards we used to have. These are people who had no connection to the patients at all. But these...diseases. These plays of the mind. They are contagious. And they catch. If this happens to people of rational thought, what happens to family members, when they see their loved ones strapped down to a chair, muttering nonsense about things that aren't there?"

I wasn't watching the doctor anymore, I was watching Dex. The camera had faltered down just a little bit and his eyes looked glazed and fearful at the same time. Like he was remembering something. I wanted to reach out for him and bring him back in but the doctor beat me to it.

Hasselback turned around from the window and looked squarely at Dex. "Wouldn't you say that apparitions are nothing more than a virus? Spread between two people with nothing more than a sneeze. Or a suggestion?"

"Perhaps," Dex said slowly. We both knew what he was saying. We had thought it before. But we also knew it wasn't true.

"So you see, then. The way the mind works. No, this hospital or any of its buildings aren't haunted."

"Because you personally don't believe in ghosts," I pointed out.

"Not in the way that you believe in them. But there are ghosts, oh yes, there are ghosts and they all live here. Because people with mental illness are haunted by ghosts every day. But these are ghosts inside their heads. Ghosts created by chemical imbalances and strengthened through memory. Everyone has ghosts that follow them throughout their lives. Ghosts of the past they wish they'd left behind, ghosts of love they once turned down, ghosts of regret and ghosts of loss. Ghosts of guilt. We all have them. I do. Roundtree does. You both do. And if you don't deal with your demons, they will haunt you for the rest of your life."

Dex and I both fell silent, stiffened and awkward. Hasselback's words hit me hard and I knew they hit Dex hard too. It all made sense. Our personal demons, the ghosts of our past, the things we hid in the closet or under the rug, or inside a hollowed-out book, would eventually find us. Maybe they'd find us in ways that only our mind could imagine and interpret as something supernatural.

But at the same time...that was impossible. Not because it couldn't happen, but that it wasn't the case with us. Not with Dex and me. Certainly not me. I wasn't seeing a dead girl in his living room because I had a hard time letting go of my love for him. I didn't see Mary because I felt unappreciated by my parents. And I didn't see Ol' Roddy because kids teased me when I was young. I saw those things because they were people once and they were haunted by their own pasts and just wanted someone to finally notice. I don't know why they chose me, but to pretend they were a figment of my imagination was wrong. Evil or not, they were people and deserved at least a bit of recognition, even if they couldn't have my compassion.

I looked over at Dex. He still had the camera rolling on the doctor during this long pause but his mind was elsewhere. I reached into my purse again and grasped my iPhone in my hand. I gave it a squeeze and let go. I would need it tonight, I knew this much.

"Did that answer your question, Mr. Foray?"

Dex slowly nodded and looked down at the camera. "I think we've got enough here." His voice was lower than usual and as thick as soup.

Hasselback nodded then peered with his rodent eyes at Dex's arm. He was just in a plain black tee shirt, his jacket on the back of the chair. It was a trifle warm in the room.

"What's your tattoo of?" Hasselback asked.

Dex looked up at him, brows raised. "On my arm?"

"Yes," he said patiently and walked over to him to get a better look.

Dex rolled up his sleeve to show him the black, simple-looking fleur-de-lis on his bicep. His bicep instinctively flexed and looked very nice indeed.

The doctor nodded and stood up straight. "The mark of a criminal."

Dex didn't move. I flinched.

"What?" I asked, leaning closer to Dex's arm. Mark of a criminal?

"I assume Dex knows this. That's why he chose it. The fleur-de-lis is the mark of French nobility, and also the mark of a criminal. They were branded with it, usually on the shoulder or on the back. It showed that they were owned by the monarchy. Are you French, Dex?"

"Yes," he said, sounding plain. He rolled down his sleeve. The movement was very robotic. I watched them both carefully, not wanting to interrupt.

"There you go. Not that that was hard to deduce. I can see it in your coloring. Dark eyes. Dark hair. Olive skin. You have all the French in you. But not all. You're a half-breed."

Dex gave the doctor an annoyed scowl. But the doctor continued, "Sorry. No disrespect. People's ethnicities say a lot more about them than the people themselves. It's part of the past and the past is what molds us."

"We really don't have time for amateur psychology, doctor," Dex sneered. I imagined his sneer was as polite as I've ever heard it.

"I'm hardly amateur. And I apologize for being curious. I can tell this is all news to her and she wants to know more."

He pointed his steepled fingers at me. Dex didn't meet my eyes but kept his focused on the doctor.

"Half French...half Scottish?" he asked.

I expected Dex not to say anything. But he eventually said "Irish" out of curiosity to see where the doctor was going with all this. It was like going to a palm reader. I was more than glad that the attention wasn't on me but I kind of wanted to know if he could guess my background.

"Ah. Irish and French. How perfect that is."

"Oh yeah? How so?"

"You look it. And I bet your mother was the French one, am I right?"

Dex didn't say anything.

I spoke up, "Is this all relevant?"

I knew Dex didn't like to speak about either of his parents. I didn't know anything about his mom except for the fact that she was dead, and his father ran out on him when he was a young boy, forcing him and his family into poverty. Dex had a hard enough time telling me all of that – though it was really nothing in the grand scheme of things – and I knew he wasn't about to do it with some random doctor. Besides, Dex had enough damn doctors already.

"No, not really," the doctor said. "I think we are done here. You may go."

Gee thanks. I got out of my chair and grabbed onto Dex's arm, pulling him up. He followed in a weird sort of daze, his eyes still avoiding mine, looking utterly lost.

We headed toward the door but the doctor called after us, "Sorry for being intrusive. This sort of thing still fascinates me. And it's a nice change to be able to discuss it with people who still have level heads on their shoulders."

Level-headed. That was a new one. I smiled, short and tense, at the doctor and waved, opening the door for us with my other hand.

He waved at us and went back to his Jenga pile of books, calling out, "Don't forget, third floor only and you have one hour. One hour and that's it."

CHAPTER ELEVEN

Dex and I stepped into the half-lit hallway and I closed Dr. Hasselback's door behind us. I moved my hand down Dex's arm to his hand and shook it gently, peering at him.

"You OK there, Frenchie?"

His glare was very unamused, which, luckily, meant he was OK. I dropped his hand and patted him on the shoulder. "Shrinks, huh?"

He sighed and rolled his shoulders back. "Are you ready for the third floor?"

It sounded spooky and creepy already. I much preferred to deal with the doctor's strange questions than to actually continue on with our little ghostcapade. But we had a job to do and in the event that Thursday and Block C wouldn't happen, we had to do with what he had.

"Sure am," I said. We started down the hallway back to the front doors. I wondered if Roundtree would be around to let us back in to get the equipment.

I voiced this to Dex and added, "I'll just stay in here and hold the door for you. You can handle all the stuff by yourself, right? I saw you flexing earlier for the doctor."

Dex let out a chuckle, which pleased me. "That was for you, kiddo."

"Oh, I'm very flattered," I teased and stopped in front of the doors.

He looked around the foyer, then opened the door. "I'll be right back."

"You better," I said. I didn't feel too good about waiting alone in the hospital. But it gave me a chance to attempt my plan. The car wasn't far away, but there was a lot of stuff to gather. I had enough time.

As soon as the heavy door slammed shut and Dex disappeared from my sight, I turned on a dime and raced off down the darkened hallway, back toward the doctor's office.

I knocked on the door as quietly as possible, catching my breath. And waited.

The door opened and Dr. Hasselback gave me a weary look. "Yes? Is there a problem?"

"Sort of. Can I come in? I'll be two seconds. I just need your opinion on something."

He wiggled his mouth and then opened the door. I shuffled in and walked over to his desk. He sat down, gestured to the chair again but I didn't take it.

"This will only really take a moment." I plopped my bag on the tiny patch of clear desk and rifled through it until I found my iPhone. I flicked through the apps to the camera one, knowing the doctor was watching me anxiously.

I found the application. I had secretly taken photos of each pill bottle earlier on the hunch that I would never find out what they were for. I displayed the phone for the doctor.

"I have a friend who is taking this medication. I took pictures of each label, if you just scroll around there."

"Dex Foray?" The doctor looked at me.

"Maybe."

"It says so on the label."

"Oh. OK, yes. But please don't tell him. He's really sensitive about this and I just wanted to know why he was taking medication."

"He's your boyfriend?"

I shook my head adamantly. "Oh, no. No. He's just my partner. For this show. But he's my friend, too, and I'm worried about him."

"Why?"

"I don't know. Can you just tell me what the meds are for?"

The doctor exhaled and brought the screen closer to his eyes. "Well, these yellow pills here are for severe hallucinations. The white long ones are also for hallucinations and also anxiety. The red and blue ones are antipsychotics. All of them are usually prescribed for schizophrenia. But Dex doesn't seem schizophrenic in the slightest. And I have no idea what the little white ones are."

"What? Really?"

He shook his head. "No. This Doctor Bains would know, I would hope, but this name makes no sense to me. I could look it up for you if you wish."

I nervously eyed the door, knowing Dex would try to come back in the building at any minute.

"No that's OK. So...hallucinations. Why...why would he be taking them?"

"You'd have to ask him," he said, handing me back my phone.

I nodded, knowing I couldn't after this. I had gone behind his back. I felt like I couldn't get any lower.

"But I can tell you," he continued, "whatever is wrong with him is nothing to sneeze at. All of these pills combined...I'm surprised he's acting as normal as he is. Though there is something off about him. About both of you."

"Me?" I asked, sticking the phone back in my purse, feeling dirty about everything.

He leaned on his messy stacks of papers. "You know this. You're ghost hunters. You see things that aren't there."

I heard what could have been a car door slam from outside.

"I have to go," I said, turning for the door. "Please don't tell Dex about this. I just needed to know."

He took one look at my face and nodded. "I won't. You just need to watch yourselves. And try to communicate. Most ghosts come up when we can't express ourselves."

I nodded and gave him a quick smile. I left the room and quickly scampered down the hallway toward the doors. He wasn't there yet.

I breathed a sigh of relief and leaned against the glass. I was shaking slightly from the overall icky feeling of going behind Dex's back like that. And the fact that the answers didn't help. Severe hallucinations? What had Dex been seeing? And a mystery pill? What was going on?

As gross and immoral as I felt, I still had one more part of the plan that I was going to try to squeak through. It would also take a bit of luck and timing, but I felt I had both on my side tonight. As well as a touch of evil, which was certainly helping me follow through.

Soon, Dex appeared at the door like a drowned rat, gear in both hands. He looked so helpless in the rain, waiting for me, his dark, shaggy hair wet and flat against his head, the water dripping off the edge of his nose. I walked to the door and laid my hands against the cold glass. He watched me, expectantly, maybe a bit curious as to why I was watching him and not immediately letting him in.

I'm doing this because I love you, I thought. *And that makes it OK.*

I stared at him, through the pane, deep into his eyes, which were even darker in the night, with the brazen glare of the outside lights casting shadows on his handsome face. I loved him and I needed to know the truth.

Finally I opened the door with two hands, pushing hard against it, and Dex stepped in, sopping wet and dripping on the floor.

"Weren't going to let me in?" he asked, sounding mock hurt. "Second thoughts? Gonna stay here overnight instead?"

I laughed, small and a bit forced, and shut the door behind him. "Thought I would take over Roundtree's job. It looked fulfilling."

I took some equipment into my hands and we made our way to the third floor through the nearest stairwell. It was lit, but with a weak, cheap light that made us both look green.

We reached the third floor and pushed the stairwell door open. The floor was completely dark except for the light coming through the stairwell windows at both ends. I immediately wanted to turn and leave but the door shut behind us with an ominous click that echoed down the empty hall.

"OK, this is fucking creepy," I said.

"Agreed. Which is why it's perfect."

I gave Dex a look. He smiled at me and popped a piece of Nicorette in his mouth with his free hand. "Shall we get set up?"

I nodded and he brought out a tiny lantern from his pocket to provide a bit more light for our faint area. The only problem with that was that it made the rest of the floor look even darker than it was. Uneasy shadows danced down the corridor, tricks of the eye.

Out of his pack he brought out the EVP gadget, the first time I had ever really seen it. He had gotten it over the last week. It was supposed to pick up Electronic Voice Phenomenon, you know, like the hidden voices and sounds that we couldn't hear properly with our own ears. The whole idea of using the EVP freaked the hell out of me, but holding the walkie talkie-sized gadget in my hands (it was really nothing more than a gimmicky tape recorder) made the unknown at least a bit familiar.

"Want to try that out tonight?" he asked, noting the way I was cradling it like some alien baby.

"I guess," I said reluctantly. "Though I'm not sure what we could pick up. This is like the quietest mental hospital ever."

He paused as he fiddled with the large camera on the ground, rocking slightly on his haunches.

"And how many mental hospitals have you been in?" he asked. Though his voice was low, he sounded a bit defensive and I couldn't blame him for that.

I didn't answer. He didn't look too annoyed, though it was hard to tell from the light source.

"Besides, we're on the third floor," he continued, voice softer. "There's nothing up here. And even if there were patients up here...you know, it's not like the movies."

I shrugged. "I know. Sorry. I just thought there would be screaming people or..."

"Like I said. It's not like the movies."

"Sorry Dex," I mumbled, feeling ashamed.

"Don't be. I'm not mad, I'm just saying. Not all mental hospitals mean the people behind the doors are all raving loons and wrapped up in straightjackets. I'm pretty sure that the second floor is just a bunch of rooms where you'll find some pretty sad but fairly normal people going about their nightly business."

"And the first floor?"

"I could smell the cafeteria was at the end of the hall, beyond the doctor's office. Probably the communal rec room too. This isn't a horrible place, Perry. And the people here have probably been here for a long time. Time obliterates the screams. Medication and time."

"How long did it take for you?" I asked him, knowing full-well he wouldn't tell me.

He got to his feet with his camera firmly in hand and looked me square in the face with a peculiarly blank expression.

"It took six months."

I was surprised at that. At the swiftness of time, at his blunt admission. Oh, how I wanted to keep asking him, to keep peeling back the layers and find out more. I chanced it.

"And how long did you have to stay there in total?"

He sighed and rubbed his chin with his free hand, chewing his gum slowly, his eyes staring off into the blackness. "Two years."

My mouth dropped open. Two years. In a mental institute for two whole years? A place like this one? It made my heart cave in. "Why...why were you there so long? If you were better in six months?"

He kept his eyes focused on the dark. I could see they were shiny and reflective, bouncing back what little light we had. "It's not so easy to just leave. They have to make sure you won't endanger yourself."

"Did you...endanger yourself?" I asked quietly. It was so personal, so fragile of a question, I was afraid he was going to bolt and run like an unbroken horse.

"That's how I got there," he said calmly, finally turning his head to look at me. "I had my reasons. As I'm sure you did too."

"Me?" I repeated. "I never tried to kill myself. What are you talking about?"

"I didn't say you tried to kill yourself. I never really did, either. It was just...a misunderstanding. As I'm sure your accident was too."

He used quote marks around "accident." I frowned at him, trying to figure out what he was getting at and what he knew about this accident I had.

"What do you know about this accident? I haven't talked to you about it."

He raised one brow, which created a spear of a shadow across his face.

"I guess you haven't. My bad."

I didn't trust that. I wracked my brain to see if I had said anything in the last few days...or even ever. Aside from my cousins mentioning some accident to him once, and telling him I had dreams about my high school days, I hadn't said anything to him. I know I hadn't because it was something I rarely let myself think about.

"And anyway, after a while, the hospital was the only home I had. The friends I had before eventually stopped coming to visit. I had no family. There was nothing left out there for me. Everything I had come to know and rely on was in the institute. So even when I could tell they were thinking of releasing me one year in, I did what I could to stay longer."

"I'm sorry," I said, feeling stupid.

He tilted his head at me and smiled. "It's in the past."

Was it? My past had been coming to haunt me lately. Was it the same for him?

"I don't know about you," he said while coming over to me and taking the EVP device out of my hands. "But I think we need to get a move on. We've already wasted time talking about stuff that we could discuss any other time."

I nearly laughed at that but I managed to stifle it in my throat. Any other time always meant never with Dex. I doubted I'd ever hear any more about his time in the hospital. But in a way, that was OK with me. Because I had a feeling he had told me more than he had ever told anyone else. And that made me feel...well...special.

We got the rest of the equipment ready as quickly as we could, while Dex plotted out how we were going to use what precious time we had.

He pointed down the hall. "If you go just a few feet in front of me..."

I did as he asked and stopped just where the lantern light failed to reach.

"I'll have you introduce us. Keep your voice lower than normal, just in case; this mic should pick it up here, no problem. And just walk slowly down the hall. I'll turn on the infrared."

"And if I walk into something?" I asked.

He picked the lantern off the ground and gave it to me. "You won't. There's nothing here."

I took it from him and looked behind me at the darkness. The faded light of the stairwell at the other end looked so far away.

"So I walk to the end, you follow me. That's it?"

"No. We'll go to the end, then come back up the hallway and I want you to try every door. Even if it's locked. You do know how to pick locks, right?"

Actually I did. I did very well. I had great practice on my parents' liquor cabinet growing up, practice I had hoped would come in handy tonight, hence why I had a pair of bobby pins, a credit card and tweezers in my right pants pocket.

"I can try," I said, trying to sound surprised. "You want me to try every room here?" Will we have enough time?"

He shrugged and the recording light of the camera went up and down. He was already filming. That figured.

"Hopefully we'll come across something interesting. If we don't, we don't. Fuck if we overstay our welcome, though you know the gold is in Block C anyway."

We got started. I held the wind-up lantern in one hand, vaguely reminded of our first episode on the Oregon Coast, and gave a short spiel about the institute and what we were doing there. No point in getting into the details when Dr. Hasselback covered that thoroughly and far better than I ever could.

I walked down the hallway when I was done, taking small steps and shining the lantern on the walls. It was creepy in the dark but there was nothing fantastically off-putting about the third floor. It looked old and empty but it wasn't decaying or anything. There weren't even any cobwebs or dust bunnies about, which gave the impression that a cleaning crew still cleaned it every night. That put me more at ease.

We reached the end of the hallway without incident. Dex would pause every so often and hold the EVP thing still so it could pick up on something, but we wouldn't know whether it did or not until later. We certainly didn't hear anything except our own breathing and footsteps.

At the end of the hall, where the weak light from the other stairwell shone in, Dex discovered a blip with the camera.

"Can you fix it?" I asked, standing on my toes and trying to get a better look at the screen. It was black, even though the light said it was on and recording.

He shook his head. "I don't know. It could be the battery, I had a feeling I should have charged it before we left. I'll just switch it with the other camera. Won't make much of a difference."

He put the big camera down and started to pull the smaller, handheld one out of his pack.

It was time.

"I'm just going to go find the washroom," I said, starting toward the door.

"Now?"

"Better now than never. I really have to pee. I'll be right back."

"OK. But if you're not back in five minutes, I am coming down to get you."

"Awww, you're worried about me?" I asked sweetly.

"No, I'm worried about me! You think I want to be up here alone?"

I rolled my eyes. "I'll be right back."

I patted him on the arm and then opened the stairwell door with a heavy, echoing creak. I scampered down the stairs and paused at the second floor, waiting until I heard the door shut from above. Then I looked into the hallway of the second floor. It was lit but empty. So strange to know people were in their rooms, hiding, at 5:30 p.m. It didn't make any sense to me but I wasn't about to think about it too much either. I had a devious job to do and this floor was probably where I had the best chance of doing it.

I cautiously opened the door and stepped onto the hallway. I closed it behind me with as much care as I could muster, not wanting to alert anyone. I was glad for my Chucks on my feet. Though they squeaked when wet, they were dry now and if I walked extra slowly, like, 'we're hunting wabbits' kind of slow; I would be as silent as air.

I wasn't really sure what I was looking for. All the doors looked the same; they just had different numbers on them. I needed something that stood out and looked like it belonged to the staff.

A wild laugh broke out from one of the rooms and I froze in my tracks. The room was in front of me and to the right. The laugh continued, sounding more manic, then sad. And then the sobbing started.

"Please let me die," the voice said. "Please let me die."

My eyes widened. My heart froze. The voice, sounding clear yet still muffled, continued, repeating the phrase. I couldn't tell if it was a man or a woman. It was unearthly. Inhuman. Haunting.

And then it broke out into laughter again. I gathered up enough breath from the fright to keep going, cautiously passing the door, which simply read "13."

Then silence. Like it never happened. I held my fingers to my throat, trying to steady the madness of my pulse and kept my eyes focused on what I had come here to do. I kept walking.

I was near the other end of the hall when I saw what I was looking for. A door that said, "Staff Only."

I looked around me before I quietly laid my hand on the knob and turned it. Of course it was locked. It wouldn't budge either way. There could even be nurses on the other side. Just because the hospital was closed, surely that didn't mean the staff was sent home. These patients needed care around the clock. Didn't they?

I laid my head against the door and listened. After a few seconds, I still couldn't hear anything and I got my credit card out of my pants pocket. I would try that first.

I slipped it between the door and the lock but after a few attempts, I decided that was not the way to go. It was an old lock but it wasn't succumbing.

I brought out the bobby pin next and bent it straight. I hunched down, peered at the entrance of the keyhole and stuck the pin in, feeling for the catch inside. I looked around again as I continued to fiddle, expecting Roundtree, Dex or a mental patient to come running toward me at any moment.

But they didn't. And the pin pushed against something light and a giant click told me to turn the knob. The door opened and thankfully it was silent on its hinges.

I looked around me once more for reassurance and then stepped inside. I didn't want to hit the lights in case someone outside, like a security guard, was watching, so I brought out my iPhone and aimed the useless flashlight app around the room. There was enough light from the streetlights outside the window that I wasn't going to trip over anything.

It was an empty office with just a desk and chair. There were a few picture frames on the table of a woman, perhaps Roundtree, and children. I didn't have time to explore. In the corner was a tall industrial chest. That was the thing I was looking for.

I opened it. It creaked. Loudly. I froze and hung onto my breath, poised and ready to run out of the room if I heard anyone coming. But after a few seconds, everything else stayed silent.

I aimed the iPhone into the cabinet and shone it over the various shelves inside. There were pill bottles on every shelf, but whether they contained what I was looking for was another story.

The first shelf had some innocent looking white pills that matched the ones that Dex had, but when I got a better look at the name, it seemed too dangerous and risky to take. I had to stick with what I knew. What I wanted were placebos.

I went to the next shelf. Here I found tiny yellow pills. I picked up the bottle and looked at it closely. It said diazepam on the label. I knew this wasn't the best thing to be taking, but at least I knew what it was. I had spent half of my life on Valium. Plus they looked exactly like the pills that Dex had been taking for his hallucinations or whatever apparently ailed him.

I quickly opened the pill bottle and poured half of the contents into my hand and shoved it into my pocket. Then I continued searching. I didn't find the placebos until the very end, but at least they matched Dex's pills with their round, Aspirin-like body and there were a lot of them. I took a generous helping of those out of the bottle and shoved them in my other pocket.

I didn't want to waste any more time. Two different pills were enough for my experiment to go through. I closed the cabinet door, slowly this time, and crept over to the door. I poked my head out into the hallway and breathed a sigh of relief when I saw it was still empty. I was shaking all over. My body, and my subconscious.

I closed the door behind me with nothing more than a gentle click and started walking down the hall back the way I came.

A loud POP came from behind me while the hall in front of me became a smidge darker. The loud and unexpected noise caught my breath and made me jump mid-stride. I stopped and stood still.

Another quick POP followed by another level of dimness. I turned around expecting to see someone but what I saw was the overhead lights at the very end slowly going off.

Pop. Pop. Pop. They were fizzling out and leaving the once-bright hallway in darkness, as if some invisible being was going along and removing the bulbs. I knew enough that the scenario wasn't all that crazy.

The dark was catching up with me. I turned and started to run as quietly as possible, chalking it all up to faulty wiring on a stormy night. But as I neared the stairwell at the end, the stairwell lights went off and so did every other light in the hallway.

The darkness engulfed me. I paused, disoriented and scared out of my wits.

Thump, thump, thump.

The sound of footsteps raced toward me from the far end of the hallway. They didn't sound quick but they were coming.

For me.

I ran blindly for the door and felt around for it until my hands connected with the handle. I yanked it. It wouldn't open. The door had locked behind me. There was blackness outside and in. I whirled around, hearing the footsteps still coming, this strange, slow and sloppy run.

They stopped somewhere in front of me, maybe a few inches away. I held my breath. All I could feel was that terrifying notion that something was standing in the dark and watching me. Wanting me.

"Please let me die." The voice from earlier came from down the hall.

"Yes, please let me die," another voice came, this one closer to me and from the left.

"He let me die," said one more. This one sounded familiar. This one wasn't a human being, a patient in a room with no hope or normal life left. This one had an accent. This one was dead. It was coming from right in front of me.

I slowly stuck my arm straight out in front of me. I wanted to see how close it was. I waved it around but hit nothing.

Raucous laughter erupted from the rooms. It caught on like a wave, crashing down the hall until it was all I could hear. Insane, unforgiving, unrelenting laughter, the type that you'd hear being howled at the moon. It reverberated through the hallway until it forced me to cover my ears.

I thought about calling Dex. He could come down and let me out. I could tell him I went to look for the bathroom on this floor. I took one hand away from my ear and took out my phone, conscious of not crushing the vulnerable, secret meds in my pocket.

BANG!

The lights above me suddenly came on with the sound of snapping wires and the low hum of a generator kicking in. The area just in front of me was illuminated, hurting my eyes. I could see again.

And there was nothing there.

The same went for the rest of the hallway. As each light went back on, it showed how empty the place was. And the laughter stopped along with it.

Until the end.

The last light went on.

There was a woman standing beneath the waxy light bulb. In the middle of the hall. Facing me. She was far enough away that I couldn't make out her face. But I knew from the snakelike angle of her head that I didn't want to.

She stood as still as night, not moving. Just facing me like a gunslinger during a standoff.

This...wasn't good.

I slowly lifted up my hand that had the phone and dialed Dex while keeping my eyes on her.

She still hadn't moved. But I knew it was misleading.

I put the phone to my ear and after a few rings (I could almost hear it ringing on the floor above) he answered.

"Perry? You OK?"

"I'm locked on the second floor," I whispered. "Please come and let me out right now."

"OK, one sec," he said. I heard him hang up, a few footsteps from above and then the sound of the third-level door opening onto the stairwell. I breathed a sigh of relief, not taking my eyes off the figure at the end.

Which was good. Because she twitched. And now, she was moving, walking toward me, twice as fast as a normal person, almost gliding down the hall as if she were on skates.

Her arms were outstretched, her head wobbled back and forth with each quick stride, and a thick flow of blood flowed off of her, falling to the floor behind her like a red bridal train.

It happened so fast.

She was there.

And then she was in my face.

Her grey, decaying hands around my neck. Her hands felt ice cold. She smelled like gin. She buzzed like bees. And her mouth opened wide, wider than any mouth should ever open, like a steel trap on loose hinges, with brown, rotting teeth as a horrific frame. A single wasp crawled to the edge of her bloated, black tongue. The whole hallway vibrated with an incredibly loud drone that was deafening and debilitating. I couldn't move. Couldn't think. Couldn't live.

"Perry!"

The door swung open and before Dex could enter, the girl was suddenly gone. Vanished into thin air and taking her dead hands, split face and infernal noise with her.

Dex looked around the empty hallway wildly and then focused on me. "What just happened to you?"

I shook my head, placing my fingers at my throat where the icy feeling wasn't going away. I pointed at the floor above. "Need to get out of here," I croaked.

He nodded, got me through the door and up the steps. Halfway up, I stopped on the landing and motioned for him to stay. I leaned over on my knees and tried to get my breath and my bearings.

Dex had the small camera on him and brought it up to my level, aiming it on me. "What happened?"

He was filming but I didn't care. I was having a hard time gathering my thoughts, almost like someone else was sucking them out of my head.

I raised my finger in the air for him to give me a second and slowly breathed in through my nose. I felt at my neck again and gestured for him to touch it.

He did. His hand was hot.

"It's freezing. You're ice cold, Perry," he said. He removed his hand and put it up to my forehead. "You're hot here though. What happened? Did you see something? Did something...hurt you?"

He stammered through those last words in a way I would have normally found touching except I didn't know how I felt.

I nodded. "I went...I went to use the bathroom here. I got halfway down the hall and all the lights started going out...one by one. Then there was this laughter. I think it was the patients. From behind their doors. They were all laughing. And then they stopped. The lights slowly came back on. And when they hit the very end...I saw her."

"Saw...her? The girl you saw in the apartment?"

"Yes. It was her. I saw her earlier today too."

He nodded, not looking very impressed. He nibbled on his lip for a few seconds and then said, "In the bathroom. At the restaurant. I wanted to ask you about that but...I didn't want to pry."

That was an odd thing for him to say. Dex liked to pry about everything and anything, especially when it had something to do with me. It was almost like a hobby to him, just as bugging him for information was a hobby to me. But I let it slide. For now.

"Yeah. It was her. And her again now. She ran after me. And suddenly she was right here." I waved my hand in front of my face. "I could smell her...the gin."

Dex turned a wicked shade of pale. All expression left his face and the camera lowered an inch. I watched him carefully, not expecting that reaction.

"What is it? Dex? Have you seen her too?"

He shook his head, blinking hard, seeming to come out of what mini-episode he just had. "No. It just...reminded me of something."

"What?"

"Did she hurt you?" he peered at my cold neck inquisitively.

"She wanted to kill me. I don't know if she hurt me. But she would have if you had not shown up. Then she just..." I snapped my fingers.

I put my hands back to my throat and felt around again. My skin temperature was returning to normal but my heart was still racing, the beat popping out my jugular like a drum. "I'm OK."

He nodded, not looking too convinced, and then turned off the camera. "We've got 20 minutes left. Care to do the rest of the third floor with me? I'll understand if you say no."

I didn't actually want to do anything but go back in the car and return to their apartment with Jenn and Fat Rabbit, as funny as that sounded. But at the same time, I felt like as long as I was with Dex, I would be OK. For whatever reasons, this ghost was not showing herself to Dex. Only to me. As long as I was with him, I would be safe. At least, that's what I was counting on.

"That's OK, let's do it," I said and stepped onto the first step.

Dex reached out and put his arm around my shoulder and gave me a squeeze. "Are you sure, kiddo? You're my most precious equipment here."

I gave him a brief smile. "Yeah, I'm fine. At least if she comes back now, maybe we can get her on film."

"Now we're cooking with gas," Dex said with a smile. He was pleased to keep going; lord knows how important the show was to him, but I could tell he was the tiniest bit torn up about leading me up there and inviting the same kind of torment.

I was torn, too, but I determined to go through with it. One of those instances where turning back wouldn't really make much difference. This ghost was appearing in his apartment for crying out loud. It was wherever I went. That thought sunk my chest like a heavy rock through water.

We walked up to the third floor and entered the hallway, which was still barely lit by the lantern on the ground. Some of his equipment lay scattered about, including the EVP gadget, which was propped up against the wall, lights blinking, obviously recording.

Dex held up the camera and motioned down the hall. "Now we'll just try each door and see what happens."

I nodded and walked forward into the darkness, the lantern now swinging from my arm. The only sounds were our footsteps and my heart in my head. We stopped at the first door. It had no numbers on it. I paused before I tried the handle and looked at Dex and the camera.

"Where is everyone, anyway?" I asked him in nothing more than a whisper.

"What do you mean?" his voice automatically lowered to match mine.

"When I was downstairs. I heard people in their rooms. But I never saw any nurses. Do they really leave people alone like that? Is that normal?"

He shrugged. "It could be. If they operate by different hours here and they control those hours, this might be their bedtime. I'm sure Roundtree is flitting about in her bat-like way, but that's probably it. The place I was in had over 100 patients but I'm sure one head nurse could handle them all when they are supposed to be sleeping."

"But how can they sleep now?" It was so fucking early.

"Kiddo, I don't know. We can ask the doctor on Thursday. But for now, we're running out of time, OK. Just...try the door."

I sighed and turned to it. I placed my hand on the handle and it shocked me with a giant bolt of static electricity that left me speechless for a few seconds and unable to move. It was like I had been poking around a live light bulb.

"Jesus Christ, that was some shock!" Dex exclaimed. "I could see that as clear as lightening. Are you OK?"

I nodded when I found my nerves again but was a bit iffy about touching the knob. I stepped back and said, "You try it."

Dex grimaced in the low light but he stepped forward, hand extended. He placed it on the knob....

...and shook back and forth violently, his teeth chattering loudly with his spasms.

"Dex!" I yelled and came forward, unsure of whether I should touch him or not.

But he stopped abruptly and took his hand away from the door. "Just kidding."

He smiled at me. Enraged, I punched him on the shoulder. Hard. "That wasn't fucking funny, you asshole!"

"It was kind of funny," he said, still smiling, though it was disappearing slowly.

I crossed my arms and shook my head. "No, it wasn't. And you're opening all the doors from now on."

He pouted but his lips reversed when he realized how angry I was. How dare he just make light of that, considering everything that had been happening to me.

After everything I had just told him. What a fucking chump.

"Sorry kiddo, I was just-"

"Just open the fucking door," I said.

He nodded quickly and tried. The knob actually turned and the door opened with a tiny push from his shoulder.

We stood in the doorway and I brought the lantern light forward. At first we could only see the swirling dust catching in the beam, but after it settled and our eyes learned to look past it, we could see a narrow room comprised of a single bed, a sink with a cloudy mirror above it, an armoire, a door to either a bathroom or a closet, and a side table. The window was covered by a heavy shade that blocked out most of the light from outside.

"So this is what they look like on the inside," I said while breathing out. "This is terrible. To live like this..."

Dex didn't say anything. He pushed the door open wider, pushing in the lock on the knob as he did so, and stepped in. I wasn't too eager to follow him. I stood where I was in the doorway.

"Was it like this for you?" I asked. I couldn't help but relate everything we were going through to him. It was hard not to. We were in a mental hospital, who better to know what was going on than someone who had lived in one. For two whole years. It still boggled my mind.

"A bit," he answered hesitantly. "A bit bigger. It was New York. And I did have some inheritance at the time. But the same idea."

And there I was, feeling sorry for him again while seconds earlier he had acted like the biggest jerk in the world. I breathed out a puff of angry air, annoyed at my stupid feelings.

"What is it?" he asked, his head turning toward me in the dark.

"Nothing," I said quickly. "Now what? Film the room? There's not much in here. I'm not sure what you were hoping to find."

"Can you come in and close the door?"

I could. But I didn't want to. "Why?"

"Just...do it."

I looked back at the empty, black hall behind me and wondered if something was watching us play it all out. I shivered. I wouldn't be safe anywhere.

I stepped in the room, still careful not to make any excess noise, and slowly shut the door.

"OK," I said.

"Turn off the lantern."

"Are you serious?"

He walked over to the sink and placed the camera on the edge of it. Then he walked across to the bed, which only consisted of a moldy-looking mattress, and sat down. He patted the space beside him.

"Sit down and turn it off."

I didn't know what his plan was but I knew I didn't like it. I still did what he said, though. Mainly because Dex had an uncanny ability of being right when things seemed overly wrong.

I sat beside him, immediately feeling the cold seep in through my pant bottoms. I shivered from the thought of rampant mold on my ass.

Dex took the lantern from me, turned it off and placed it on the floor. Then he put his arm around me and pressed me up against him, shoulder to shoulder.

"Um, what are you doing?" I asked suspiciously.

"Trying to comfort you."

Was he? I couldn't tell in the dark, in this small claustrophobic room on the abandoned floor of a mental hospital. There could be no comfort here.

"I'm OK, Dex," I said and lifted his arm off me. He took it back and didn't say anything. I could tell his attention was already somewhere else.

"What are we-"

"Shhhh," he hissed.

I shut my mouth, stopped my breath, and listened. At first I couldn't hear anything except the rain outside and the occasional blast of winter wind.

Then I heard it. Footsteps coming out from the hallway. Not like the ones I had heard earlier, the ones that belonged to the girl. These footsteps were slower, more discreet and even gaited.

I suddenly wanted Dex's strong arm back around my shoulders.

"Wha-" I opened my mouth to speak again but he pressed his finger against my lips and held it there. Despite the circumstances and my rising fear, there was still a tiny part of me that was sorely tempted to put his finger in my mouth and suck on it.

We both listened, as still and quiet as statues. The footsteps came closer.

And closer.

Closer still.

Then they stopped, right outside the door. Dex took his finger away from my lips and put his arm back around my shoulder, holding me in such a way as if I was about to bolt. I wanted to, but if I went out the door, I'd run into whatever the hell was out there.

The door knob jiggled. The sound of it turning. Dex had locked it and now I knew why. The jiggling continued.

I nervously eyed the camera on the sink, which was filming the door and understood what Dex had done. But what would we do if the thing came inside?

The knob stopped rattling. It was followed by a few heavy knocks that filled the tiny room and made the window rattle. Then there was a scuffling sound, as if the person (creature?) was leaning against the door, trying to hear us.

Then it stopped. The footsteps picked up again and continued back down the hallway from where they came. We listened to them until they faded away into the night.

We waited for a good five minutes, breathing as quietly as possible. It felt like the longest five minutes of my life. Dex's grip around my shoulder's loosened and eventually he took his arm off me.

I leaned close to him, sensing his face wasn't too far away, and whispered, "What the hell was that? Did you know that was going to happen?"

"Sort of. One of the things people had reported was that back in the day, a security guard had killed himself. Hung himself on this floor in one of the rooms. Apparently he had gotten too close to the patients and one in particular had been...mean. Played mind games with him. He killed himself, and afterward people reported him walking up and the down the halls, making sure everyone was in bed and asleep. I don't think he means any harm but...I would have hated to see what happened if I hadn't locked it."

"But you heard that, right? The footsteps? You heard the doorknob turn?"

"Yes," he said, sounding surprised, almost insulted. "I hope the camera got it too. That's really all we need to make tonight worthwhile."

The reason I had asked was that Dex hadn't seen anything else this whole time. Sometimes I wondered if only I picked up on certain things. And maybe I did. But it was a relief to know what just happened was something shared by both of us.

"Can we go now?" I asked, ready to get the hell out of there, even though I didn't feel like making it down three floors of dead security guard, mutilated bleeding girl, and one already suspicious doctor.

I felt him nod in the dark. "We've outstayed our welcome anyway."

He got up and gathered the camera, turned on the lantern and we left the room. The hallway looked the same as it had earlier. Blissfully unoccupied.

He closed the door quietly behind us. I began to walk away.

"Hey wait," he called out, reaching for my arm.

I stopped. He flicked a few switches on the camera until the infrared came on, the one that picked up heat sources. He aimed it at the door.

Through the viewfinder, I saw two large handprints lit up in a glowing pattern of yellow and red. They were fading fast.

"Are those yours?" I asked.

Dex reached with his hand forward and held it beside the handprint without touching it. The handprint was almost twice the size of Dex's hands. They weren't his and they most definitely were not mine.

"The security guard," Dex whispered excitedly. "I think we've fucking got something here. Fuck G.J. Jermaine and his Douche Factory. We've got this."

We both watched the camera screen until the colors on the handprint faded and the door looked normal again. That was some pretty awesome proof to have. That almost made everything tonight worthwhile.

Dex shut off the camera and looked at me. He was grinning. It lit up his face more than the lantern light did. He looked ridiculously manic and ridiculously handsome. I couldn't help but smile back at him. Then I turned and headed down the hall before I got all mushy-eyed.

We made it down the hallway (Dex pausing briefly to collect the EVP he left recording), made it down the stairs and to the heavy front doors that led outside. This time Roundtree was at her post. She eyed us warily from her short seat.

"I hope you weren't causing trouble up there. This place has no use for troublemakers," she said.

"No way, ma'am. You're probably the biggest troublemaker of them all, ain't that right, sweetheart?" Dex said in his most sincere voice. He opened the door and we bustled out into the cold, wet evening before we could hear her response.

He looked down at me as we walked over to the car, adjusting his pack on his shoulder. "I could never get along with the nurses. Don't know why."

I shook my head. We got back in the car and headed back into the city and civilization, leaving the looming building with its layers of secrets behind us.

For now.

CHAPTER TWELVE

"Perry? Kiddo, you awake?"

Dex's voice entered my dreams and a light knock at the door brought my eyes open. I was on my back, in bed, in the small, dark den, trying to recall the fragments of the dream I just had. Jacob was in it, again. Jacob and Dr. Freedman.

"Perry?"

The door knob turned and Dex entered the room, covering his eyes with one hand, harsh daylight splaying inside. "Hey, sleepyhead, are you decent?"

I groaned and rolled over. I was decent but all I wanted to do was keep on sleeping.

With a click the lights came on and I heard the door close behind him. He came over and sat in his chair at the desk. I turned my head away from the pillow and blinked blindly up at him. He was wearing camouflage cargo pants and a white T-shirt that was on the tight side. This wasn't a bad thing. I could see every curve and sinew of his upper body. The fleur-de-lis peeked out noticeably from under his sleeve.

His face looked good. Curious and amused at the fact I was still in bed. He was clean-shaven, highlighting his high, sharp cheekbones and that olive coloring the doctor mentioned last night, and his moustache was almost faded out of existence. His eyes looked bright and not as broody as usual. Not crazed either. Interesting.

I had a reason for inspecting him like this. A terrible reason, but a reason nonetheless. After we had gotten in last night, I put my plan into action. Once he took Fat Rabbit out for his last walk, I quickly dumped out the contents of two of his prescription pills and refilled them with the Valium and placebo pills. I hid his actual medication in the very bottom of my duffel bag and placed the pill bottles back in the hollowed-out book like nothing had happened.

When Dex came back from the walk, he came in the room, we chatted a bit about the mental hospital footage and watched some of the interview we did with Doctor Hasselback. Then he took his pills with a glass of water. I watched him do this, trying not to be intrusive or overly interested, but it was hard. I didn't know if he'd notice the pills were different. What if they didn't feel the same way going down? What if they tasted strange?

But Dex didn't seem to think anything was off. We said our goodnights and that was it. He left the room and I went to sleep.

Now, though, he was sitting in front of me and looking more or less fine, even though the night had passed and the medicine was coursing around in his system.

I know it's totally wrong to play around with someone's medication. I know that. Don't judge me. At least, don't judge me much. But I needed to know what would happen if Dex wasn't on his meds. Sure he was still on some – I had only switched half – and Valium was no picnic either, but I needed to see why he was on them. When we were in Red Fox, he had forgotten his medication and had gone the entire weekend without any. There were some side effects, but he had professed to me how much different, almost better, he felt without them. Yet, for some reason he was back on medication again, and this time a whole lot more. It made no sense to me and I knew I'd never get any straight answers out of Dex. I was just planning to do this for a few days, then put his real pills back in before I left. My own little experiment.

I guess I was staring at him a tad suspiciously because he furrowed his brows and asked, "What? Something on my face?"

I smiled quickly, trying to bury the guilt deep down and said, "Just your nose."

He rubbed it vigorously. "This old thing? Anyway, time to get up, lazybones."

I sat up slowly and looked around. It was hard to tell the time in this room with no window. "What time is it?"

"Eleven," he said.

"Eleven!" I exclaimed and sat up straighter. "I have a lunch date, don't I?"

It was Wednesday. Time was flying and I was supposed to go out with Wine Babe Rebecca for lunch.

"Yes you do. And I need to start working through the rest of the footage we shot last night. And you're kind of in my office."

I grunted and got out of bed, but not before making sure I was wearing pajama pants underneath. "Why did you let me sleep in so long?"

"Because you needed it after last night. I needed it too. I only got up an hour ago and that's because the Rabbit was licking my face, threatening to piss all over me."

I gathered up my clothes for the day and my toiletries bag and hurried to the bathroom to take a shower and get ready. The apartment was empty and cold and Fat Rabbit was spread out on the couch like a floppy doll and snoring loudly. The skies outside the windows were grey, wet and wild as the Monorail rumbled past the balcony.

I had barely gotten ready when Dex pounded on the bathroom door to tell me Rebecca was already waiting outside. I had wanted to look nice today – there was something about Rebecca that had me nervous and wanting to look just as put together as she did – and it took a lot of extra time to blow dry my thick hair straight (even though I used Jenn's super-powered dryer that nearly flattened me against the wall) and put on more makeup than usual.

I opened the door and Dex was right outside, waiting. He gave me a surprised once over.

"Whoa, who are you trying to impress?" he asked with a smirk. "This isn't a date, you know."

I rolled my eyes and hurried into the den, throwing my pajamas on the floor and shoving my boots over my leggings. "I just like to keep you on your toes."

"Well, you do that, all right. One minute the 'who gives a shit' rock and roll tomboy, the next you're all pretty and girly and stuff."

I quickly laced up the boots and straightened up, flipping my hair back over my shoulders. I put my hands on my hips. "And which one do you like better?"

"I like all of you," he said. He smiled, closed-mouthed and strangely sad. I blushed and quickly pushed past him through the doorway.

"I'll text you when I'm coming back," I called over my shoulder as I made my way to the door. Fat Rabbit noticed I was on the way out, flipped right up, and scampered over to me. I shooed him away with my foot.

"Oh wait!" Dex exclaimed and scooted over, digging into his back pocket. He pulled out his wallet and handed me a fifty-dollar bill.

"Are you paying for my lunch?" I took it from him, confused.

He nodded at it as he stuck his wallet back in his pocket. "Just give that to Rebecca. She'll know what it's for. K, kiddo?"

I frowned at him as a way of saying goodbye and left the apartment.

Once I reached the lobby and saw how wet it was outside, I thought about going back upstairs to get an umbrella but I could already see Rebecca's hazy form through the fogged up doors, sitting in a running hatchback parked at the curb.

I stepped outside, not giving myself enough time to get nervous about my lunch date with one of Dex's friends (and a Wine Babe, let's not forget) and quickly opened the door to the car as the rain poured down on my newly straightened hair.

"Hi!" I said, waving at her.

I stepped in the car and shut the door, which shut in the inevitable awkwardness with us.

I turned in my seat to look at her and was met with a giant puff of pot smoke.

I coughed, my lungs seizing from something they hadn't been exposed to in a very long time.

"I'm sorry," she said in her proper English accent and blew the rest of the smoke out to the left of her and out the window, which was open a crack, the rain coming inside and saturating the rim of the door.

"That's OK," I said, getting a hold of the spasms.

"Do you want any?" she asked, offering me the joint in her pale, delicate fingers.

I shook my head, not wanting to explain that I wasn't eager to go down that path again. I didn't have a problem with anyone smoking pot, it's just that there was a reason they called it a gateway drug. And even though 90% of the population can smoke it and call it a day, it was just the starting point for me. It was better if I avoided it entirely. On that note, it was probably better that I never drank again, either, but we can't do everything that's right for us. I was allowed at least one vice.

"More for me then," she said with a smile. I noticed how much softer her face looked when she smiled, almost girlish. She was dressed impeccably, wearing a modest grey linen shift dress that was structured and tailored to her body. The sleeves went out into little pointy corners that combined a 40s look and a futuristic style, like something out of Blade Runner. She had a thin black patent belt at her waist, her hair was perfectly in place and a maroon felt hat sat on her head at a nice angle and perfectly matched her lips and nails.

Even though I put in the extra effort that morning, I felt like a giant slob next to her.

"So where do you want to eat?" she asked and brought the car out onto the street. It felt like the beginning of awkward small talk.

"Oh, I'm easy," I said. "I don't know Seattle that well so I couldn't really suggest any place."

We paused at the corner and she craned her head around, looking out at the street. "Which one's your car?"

"They let me park in the apartment parkade. I have a motorbike so you can just rest it in the corner and no one says anything."

Rebecca laughed, rich and amused. "A motorbike?"

She gave me a quick look before she brought the car onto the main road and roared along beneath the Monorail tracks, one hand on the shift, the other holding the joint and the wheel. "No offense Perry, but you do not look cool enough to ride a motorbike."

I'd actually heard the opposite. That I looked cool enough, but didn't act cool enough. Same difference, I guess.

"None taken," I said as nonchalantly as possible and looked out the window. Dex had been right about Rebecca being rough around the edges. I wondered if agreeing to lunch was a mistake. If she was going to end up being someone just like Jenn, I was in for a hellish time.

"I know just the place, anyway, and it's close by," she said.

Whatever, I thought. Then I remembered Dex slipping me the fifty note.

"Oh," I said and pulled it out of my pocket. I waved it in the air. "Dex said for me to give this to you; he said you'd know what it was for."

She eyed it without turning her head. She had unnaturally thick and long lashes. She laughed. "Oh, he's run out all ready? I suppose he's not taking quitting too lightly."

I squinted at her, not understanding.

"Just hold onto it for now," she said and flipped on the radio with her hand. "Come Together" was on. I rolled my eyes. This album was freaking following me everywhere.

I stuck the bill back in my pocket and soon we were pulling up into a metered parking space in the middle of downtown.

"Look at this luck," she said. When she had finished parking, she pulled out the ashtray and put the joint out in it. I was relieved we didn't have to go far. It always made me nervous when people smoked pot and drove at the same time. Probably because when I was a teenager that's why my parents took my old car away. Had a little mishap with the cherry tree in our front lawn.

We got out of the car and she pointed up at what looked like a downtown mall. We were on the corner of Pike and 5th, amongst office workers out on their lunch break, shielding themselves from the rain with a multitude of overused umbrellas. There were retail stores everywhere, from Anthropologie to All Saints. My sister would have gone nuts here.

"Hey," I said to Rebecca as she locked the car and we quickly walked down to the lights to cross the street. "I've got a gift certificate for this Designer Shoe House or something, is there one around here?"

She nodded and pointed down the block. "Just down there. Want to do some shoe shopping after lunch?"

I nodded. "I don't have any nice shoes for the Christmas party. I mean, I thought I did but my sister said they looked Amish."

I looked down at Rebecca's shoes as they stood poised in the falling rain. Of course they were as high as hell, as shiny as her belt and as maroon as her hat, lips and nails.

"Not a problem," she smiled and she looked soft again. I could also see she was being sincere, which started to put me at ease. That was the one thing missing from all of Jenn's perfect smiles: Sincerity.

We went up a few floors in an office building cum mall and ended up at a spread-out restaurant and bar that was named after me. Or my last name at least.

I chuckled as the perky waitress led us to our table. "Have you been here before?" I asked Rebecca, thinking it was just for me.

"Actually, yes," she said as we took our seats and took the menus from the waitress. "Work isn't too far from here so we sometimes come here after meetings. Best happy hours ever and we all need one or five after dealing with Jimmy."

I leaned forward on my elbows and looked at her. I couldn't help but smile like a goof. It finally occurred to me that I actually had a job with co-workers who were interesting and seemed somewhat interested in me. I didn't know much about Shownet, obviously, due to geographic restrictions, but I couldn't get over the fact how nice it was to be able to talk to someone about it, someone who wasn't Dex. Sometimes I got the impression that Dex was trying to keep me separate from that world, even though it was the world that gave me a meager paycheck every two weeks and broadcasted my fat, scared face to the entire planet.

Sensing this, maybe, Rebecca put her hand out on mine and held it there. "This is my treat. Don't worry about what to eat and what not to eat. I'm really glad you decided to come out today."

I straightened up in my seat and blushed again. "Well, thank you. I was nervous...I thought maybe you didn't like me."

"Oh, I know," she said, patting my hand and then returning her attention to the menu. "Dex told me you felt that way."

I sighed. It figured. She lowered the menu and peered at me. "I knew if Dex liked you, I mean seriously liked you as he does, then I would like you too. We don't disagree on too many things."

There was way too much in that sentence. What did "seriously liked you" mean and what else could she tell me? Having Rebecca here reminded me of having Maximus at my disposal in Red Fox, except Rebecca didn't seem to have a hidden agenda and would just tell me whatever I needed to know.

I took in a deep breath and brought my attention to the drink menu. Part of me wanted to just enjoy the company and the free food and learn something about my partner if it came up. The other part wanted to spend the next hour asking Rebecca question upon question about the man I was in love with, even though I was desperately trying not to.

"They do a really good dirty martini here," she said. "It's strong."

"It's lunchtime," I said, noting how early it was for martinis.

She raised her threaded brow. "You need it."

Did I? She was the one who was high. Maybe she needed me to catch up. But I nodded anyway, and soon we had two of them coming, along with hearty salads.

When our martinis came, we clinked over the table. I avoided her eyes even though I could feel hers boring into mine, trying to figure me out or work through my secrets in a telepathic way. Her cold, dark eyes were so unnerving at times that I wouldn't have put it past her. In some other lifetime, she could have been a vampire or a witch. But one of the sexy ones.

"So how do you like working on the Dex Files?" she asked after taking a small sip of her martini, her lips leaving a red mark on the glass.

I laughed at the 'Dex Files'. "That's a good one. I like it just fine."

"Just fine? Oh darling, this isn't a job interview here. Look, Dex is a dear. I love him very much, as much as anyone can, perhaps, but you can be honest with me. I'm not here because of Dex. I'm here because I just wanted to know you better. You seem familiar to me in some strange way."

I felt the same way about her but I didn't voice it. It wasn't that I knew her, I knew I didn't, but there was something strangely comforting underneath the slightly awkward situation. It was hard to explain and if I did try to explain it to myself, the best I would come up with was again how much like Dex she was. Only she was honest.

I took a gulp of my drink for courage, enjoying the salty brine as it slipped down my throat while fiddling with the stack of olives in the glass.

"I like working on the show," I admitted. "I mean, I love it. Sometimes. I love feeling like I'm doing something that I'm good at...even though it's not really a skill anyone would acknowledge. I don't know. It's hard to explain. But I'm grateful that I have this. It's so much better than working reception, what I was doing before. I'm happier now."

She was watching me, chin resting on her hands. "And you and Dex?"

"What about us?" I asked, trying not to sound suspicious. I started stabbing the olives with the stick, spearing them and re-spearing them.

"What's the deal with you?"

"There is no deal. We're just partners."

"Are you sure? Because we all have bets on whether you guys are banging each other or not."

My jaw dropped and my stick missed the last olive, causing it to ricochet out of the glass and onto the table.

She quickly reached over and plopped the renegade olive into her mouth. She smiled at me between chews, breezy and innocent.

"We aren't...banging," I protested.

"I know darling, I'm just teasing," she said and raised her glass at me.

My eyes shot to the heavens again. "You are just like him."

"Oh we've heard that before. You know he asked me out before he asked Jenn out."

"Oh?" I said. I didn't want to sound too interested but it was really hard.

"Well, I shouldn't say 'ask out', that sounds terribly stodgy. He did ask me out but he and Jenn were just a sweaty, shagging mess before anything serious came-"

"That's OK, I got it," I said, raising my hand briefly.

A smile twitched on her lips and she cocked her head to the side. She was silent for a few moments, watching me, nothing but sympathy on her face. It wasn't pity, which I appreciated.

She put one of her olives in her mouth and used the end of the stick to twirl the thick liquid in the glass. "Three...maybe four years ago, when we first started the show...Dex asked me out. He was strangely arrogant and shy at the same time. He'd been flirting with me and I suppose I had given him the impression I was flirting with him. I wasn't. I mean, I was, yes, but not to mean anything. We all do that. Dex does. All the time."

My heart creaked a bit at the thought that perhaps that's all it was with me. It must have shown on my face, I knew my brow was tight, because Rebecca leaned in closer to get my attention.

"I know you know this, but just listen," she said in a confiding tone. "He asked me out. I turned him down. He wasn't my type."

"Really?" I said, surprised. She seemed like a female version of him, to a tee.

"I'm not into men, Perry," she said matter-of-factly.

"Oh," I replied stupidly. A louder one followed when I realized what she was saying. She was a lesbian. My God, I hadn't picked up on that at all.

"It's because I don't fit the stereotype," she continued. "And I'm fine with it but so many people expect you to be a Butch. That's so not the way it is. But then again, I get flack for being the way I am, even within the gay community, so whatever, fuck them."

I nodded, intrigued, and more at ease. Sounds dumb, but it helped to know she wasn't interested in Dex. Jenn I could handle in a way, but Rebecca and Dex would be too much.

"Then he went after Jenn. I think because I was his first choice, Jenn had it in for me ever since."

"Had it in for you?" I repeated.

"Jenn's a cunt," she said.

I choked on the martini and half of it threatened to come up my nose. The waitress chose that time to come by with our salads and stared at me curiously. I waved at her to let her know I was OK, while Rebecca ordered us more drinks.

When I recovered, I wiped my mouth and turned to her. "I'm sorry. Jenn's a...you don't like Jenn?"

She looked at me as if I was crazy. "I fucking hate her. Everyone hates her. She's not as innocent and docile as you might think."

Actually I never thought Jenn was any of those things. It was just so surprising to hear. The *Wine Babes* didn't get along.

"I'm just...wow," I said, putting the napkin back down.

"Oh, I know. Anyway. This is why we all have bets on you guys."

"Bets? On Dex and me? What happened to wanting to set me up with this Bradley fellow?"

"Oh, I lied. Bradley is an asshole. I had a theory."

We all seemed to have theories these days. Theories based on lies. "What theory?"

She stuck the final olive in her mouth and held it between her teeth for a few moments before biting it in half. "Just a theory. Anyway, Dean and Seb and I have a bet as to whether you guys have shagged yet. But I can tell now that you haven't."

"Is that why you invited me out for lunch?"

"Oh, Perry. Why are you so paranoid? Of course not."

I shrugged and downed the rest of my drink, more than ready for another one.

"Look, we are all on your side here."

"What makes you think I want Dex...in that way," I said, looking her straight in the eyes.

Her forehead rose, the top of her hat lifting a bit from the movement. "Oh...well, it's obvious, dear."

I sighed again, long and hard and wished the waitress would hurry back. "How obvious?"

"It's obvious to me. And that's because I'm intuitive and can...see a lot. It's obvious if you know what you are looking for. It's in the glances you give each other, and the glances you don't give each other. It's in how you speak to each other and what you don't say."

"Oh, great, so I'm screwed no matter what I do."

"You're not screwed, Perry. You're just in love with him."

"There's a difference?"

I sat back in my chair and nodded politely to the waitress when she brought my next drink. I ignored the salad and went straight to drinking it. Noon or not, these were going down fast and I didn't care anymore.

Rebecca watched me carefully. She opened her mouth to say something but then thought against it and started to eat her salad. I felt tears rushing forward. Another reason why I shouldn't drink so early in the day, and on an empty stomach.

But I controlled them and sucked in my pride. I started to pick at my salad and owned up to the fact that there was no real shame in being in love with someone who wasn't in love with you.

"Do you think I should tell him?" I asked.

She paused, fork halfway to her mouth, and then lowered it. "Tell him you're in love with him?"

"Do you think he knows?"

She thought about it and then said, "No. I don't think he does."

"Do you think he might love me?"

The words hung above our table like a heavy net waiting to drop. I couldn't believe I just said them. It was just all coming out now. I wondered if I got a contact high from being in the car earlier.

"Perry. I honestly don't know. I've known Dex for a long time now and I still can't claim to know him. If anyone would know that question, it would probably be you. You know him better than Jenn, I can tell you that much."

I shoved lettuce in my mouth and chewed, not tasting the dressing or the ahi tuna.

She continued, "He wants to shag you, I can tell you that much."

I raised my head and looked at her sharply.

She smiled. "Well, that part is obvious. If you could see the way his face lights up when he talks about you, when he looks at you, and compare that to Jenn. Oh, darling, no comparison. But Dex's heart? I don't know about that. And I would never lead you on."

"But...he has a heart..."

"Yes," she said. She reached over and brushed a piece of hair behind my ear, much like he would have. It felt nice. "Dex has a heart. I just don't think he knows how to use it."

She looked sad at that and it was a sadness I understood. A feeling of wastefulness and hopelessness. He had it in him, but whether it would ever be used was another thing.

"You know, he never talks about his past," she said, eyeing me watchfully.

I nodded, knowing this all too well.

"I know he went to high school in Washington. Went to college in New York. I don't know anything else. Nothing about his family. About what he used to do. We don't know anything about him and we're used to it. But...you know things, don't you?"

"I know some things. Just the tip of the iceberg. I might be an old woman before I get to the bottom,"

"Jenn's in the same boat. And for some reason, I think you have the upper hand. And that makes me very, very happy."

I shook my head at her, still disbelieving it all. "So you really don't get along with Jenn..."

"Or Bradley. They are a perfect pair of superficial fucks. If you ask me. The pitiful thing is, I don't even know if Jenn can tell I can't stand her bony arse. She's not very smart."

"Why the hell is Dex with her?" I blurted out.

"Have you been in a long-term relationship?"

I had, I just wasn't sure if it counted. "Sort of. For a year. Then he cheated on me."

"Uh-huh. Well that happens. We all know. I was with a guy for two years back in England."

"A guy?"

"Yes. That's how in denial I was. But not just about my sexuality. I was in denial about...life. Changes. It was so much easier to ignore the truth and pretend. I cared about my boyfriend, even respected him, but I wasn't in love with him. I was in love with my best friend, Alyson. But I never got to be with her, or tell her how I felt, because it was easier to go on and pretend everything was fine. Change is scary and it can be scarier to some people more than others. Dex needs stability, that much I can see. You wonder why overweight people say they want to lose weight but they keep going on getting fat on lollies and burgers. It's the same thing."

"Do you think he loves Jenn?" I asked.

"I think...I think he loves her as much as he can. As much as he lets himself and as much as he wants to. But I think if you compared that to, say, the way I feel about my partner Emily, it would amount to nothing. Not that we have some Romeo and Juliet love. But it's close. The free, can't live without each other, passion consumes you kind of love. Sure, Dex and Jenn have been together for three years or something now and Emily and I are still more or less new, but I never saw what we have in them. And really, how could that ever be? Look at Dex. And look at Jenn. They might look good but there isn't an ounce of respect between them. And if you don't have respect, what do you have?"

My shoulders deflated and I stared down at my plate. I felt dumb and hopeless. What Rebecca said made perfect sense and it's that reality that hurt. I could see Dex staying with Jenn forever out of fear. They survived a pregnancy scare, they got Fat Rabbit, they moved to another apartment together. All these things could have been a catalyst for Dex to break it off. Or for Jenn, when you think about it. But they hadn't. They were still together and would probably be for as long as I was in the picture.

That hot, wet feeling of tears appeared again at the corners of my eyes and I immediately looked up to the high ceiling and the lights.

"I'm sorry," she said quietly. She scooted her chair closer to me and put a slender arm around my shoulder. "It sucks. It's stupid. I wish more than anything that you were with him, not her. He may be like an overgrown child at times, but there's just something about you both that just...you belong together. That's just what I think."

"I think so too," I mumbled, and finished the rest of the martini in one go. She did the same and then grinned broadly, her face becoming aglow.

"Hey, now that we're all sappy and drunk, how about we do some shoe shopping? Let's see if we can get something the Amish would spit on."

A tiny smile tugged at my mouth. Despite the feeling of sorrow, the touch of truth I was trying to bury away, I still felt a layer of warmth around my heart, knowing there was someone who was on both our sides.

CHAPTER THIRTEEN

Rebecca pulled the car up to the apartment after our successful outing to the shoe store. It had taken me quite a while to settle on a pair of shoes for the Christmas party, especially since the shoe was a madhouse with sales and early shoppers beating the season's rush, plus the amount of gorgeous shoes in that place was staggering, at least to someone like me.

Eventually I settled on a pair of shoes that would have made Ada proud. At least Rebecca looked impressed. They were stilettos but with a 1.5-inch platform so the angle wasn't too unbearable. They were raspberry red, almost magenta, and a smooth suede. I knew they didn't match the teal dress but I found the color combination intriguing. Plus they took me from 5'2" to 5'7" and the feel of that height was intoxicating. The only problem was they were slightly too big but Rebecca got me to buy toe pads to stick at the bottom so I wouldn't fall out as easily.

I gathered up the shiny bag and glanced up at the apartment. I had texted Dex to let him know I was on my way but he hadn't responded.

"Well, thank you so much for lunch," I told Rebecca.

"No hugs goodbye?" she asked, looking hurt, her maroon-lined lips pouting.

I blushed, not used to random hugging, and leaned over in the car to hug her. As I did so, I caught of whiff of heady wildflowers and Jasmine in her hair.

"Oh, before I forget!" she cried out and flipped open the console between us. She brought out a clear baggie of marijuana and put it on my lap.

"That's for Dex," she said simply.

I eyed the bag of weed in my lap. There was at least a quarter pound of it. "Um, what?"

"That's what the money was for," she said.

"Um..."

"He goes through stages. I guess because he's quitting smoking that he's doing this now. I don't know. We used to hang out a lot of Dean's place and smoke but Jenn got suspicious and uppity about it. So don't show that to her. You'll get him in deep shit."

"Okaaaay," I said and placed the drugs in my purse, feeling paranoid and sketchy as I stepped out of the car and onto the rainy street.

I waved goodbye and was about to shut the door when she leaned forward.

"Wait, what are you doing before the Christmas party on Friday?"

I shrugged impatiently, wanting to get inside. A young couple with a baby walked past and they gave me a funny look. Oh, they could totally tell I was packing.

"How about I drop by before and we can get ready together. I'll bring Emily. It'll be fun."

It did sound fun. I never really got to experience the whole "girls night out" primping ritual, even in college.

I smiled at her, feeling oddly touched and said, "That would be awesome."

"Perfect," she said and wiggled her ivory fingers at me. "See you then!"

I shut the door and then she was off.

I checked my phone to see if Dex had texted back but there was nothing. They had better be home; otherwise, I was shit out of luck.

But when I buzzed their apartment, I was let in with another anonymous click.

Turns out they were both home. Jenn let me in, giving me a strange look.

"I heard you went out for lunch with Becky," she said. Her voice didn't sound pleasant. It was almost jealous, if you could believe that. Then she spied the shoes.

"And you went shopping! What did you get?"

I decided to indulge Jenn. I placed the bag on the kitchen counter and took out the shoes. While she oohed and aahed over them, I looked around for Dex. He was nowhere to be seen but the door to the den was closed. I wondered how he was doing. The fact that I had messed with his meds hadn't left my mind all afternoon.

"Where's Dex?" I asked innocently.

She nodded at the room while rolling her eyes. "In there, working."

She put the shoes back in the box and then looked me over, as if she couldn't believe that I would be wearing them. Well, to be honest, I couldn't really believe it either.

"Are you going to break them in?" she asked.

I frowned. "Break them in?"

"Yeah. You can't just wear those straight out of the box, honey," she said with an amused laugh and a hair toss. "You better start wearing them around the house. Today."

I looked at the shoes like I was sizing up a new enemy. Who knew shoes came with so much responsibility?

"Actually I have a great idea," she said, smiling and taking a step closer to me. My instinct was to step back, away from her, but I held my ground and tried to match her grin, which was predatory in nature. "You and I should go out tonight."

Now Jenn wanted to go out with me? What the hell was going on today?

"Go out?" I repeated. "Like just us two?"

"Yeah. There's a new club that opened near Pioneer Square. I think it would be fun. We haven't had a chance to get to know each other yet."

Oh, God, this was the worst idea on earth. Clubbing with Jenn? I couldn't imagine a greater hell.

"I'm not really much of a club girl," I admitted as politely as possible, hoping she got the hint.

"Neither am I. I mean, look at me. I'm thirty-one. I'm way too old for that shit, but that's why it'll be fun. And then you get to break in your shoes too."

I'd rather break in my shoes by standing in a pile of Fat Rabbit's shit, but I didn't say that. I had to wonder what the hell was in it for her.

She put her tawny hand on my shoulder and gave it a firm squeeze. She looked me straight in the eyes. Hers were all glittery and emerald and doe-eyed. Damn her, was she trying to glam me or something?

"I think it would make our man really happy if we did this," she added.

I flinched. Our man? This was getting to be too much.

"I'll think about it," I said and turned away from her, picking up my bag and heading over to the den before she said something else that made me want to punch her lights out.

I hesitated at the door and listened. I couldn't hear Dex working away inside. I looked sideways at Jenn, who was watching me, her arms crossed, then I knocked.

No answer. I knocked again.

"Dex?" I said loudly. Suddenly I had an image of him passed out on the floor, blood streaming from his nose, a tragic consequence of having played God with his medication. I pounded harder at that thought, the door rattling.

"Dex!" I yelled.

Finally it swung open and Dex was looking at me, worried as anything, but alive.

"What, what is it?" he said. He looked at me and then over at Jenn, who just shrugged at him and turned her attention to the fridge.

My heart was still beating fast but I gave him a look as nonchalant as possible. "Sorry, I didn't think you could hear me."

"I had my earphones on," he explained and opened the door wider for me.

I walked in and he took his seat at the computer. He was in the middle of editing the footage we took. I paused and gestured to the door.

"Do you mind if I close the door?" I asked.

He was puzzled but didn't protest when I did so. I was sure Jenn wasn't going to be too happy about that.

I sat down on the bed as he turned in his chair to face me, leaning forward, elbows on his thighs, hands clasped.

"What's the problem? Are you OK?" he asked. His eyes roamed my face inquisitively.

"Are you OK?" I blurted out.

"I'm...OK. A bit dizzy, actually, and tired, but I've been staring at this fucking screen for the last few hours. Why? Do I look wonky?"

His eyes were a bit droopy, now that he mentioned it. But I was relieved to see that he seemed to be functioning relatively normally. And I knew that the dizziness was just the Valium working through him. He would have had to take another dose of his pills while I was gone.

"You look fine. But I have something for you."

I reached into my purse and pulled out the baggie of weed. I held it in the air without giving it to him. His eyes lit up.

"Ah, my sweet Rebecca," he said and reached for it.

I held it back. "No. First, tell me why you're buying a quarter pound of pot."

His mouth twisted into a confused smirk. "For the same reason I buy 26 ounces of Jack Daniels?"

"So you quit smoking but you're smoking pot instead now. How does that work?"

"I don't know, Perry Mason. It's something to smoke. Since when did you become a narc?"

"I'm not a narc," I said, looking down at my feet, but couldn't find anything to add to that. The truth was, I didn't really have a problem with him smoking pot. It was the fact that he would be doing so while on Valium, missing meds and taking the rest of his mystery pills. But I couldn't say anything about that without blowing my cover.

"Perry?"

I looked up at him. He leaned in closer to me.

"What's wrong?" He reached over with his hand for my knee. I moved it out of the way.

"Nothing, sorry. I guess I'm just weird about drugs now."

"As you should be. Just don't worry about me, OK, kiddo?"

I nodded and then gave him his weed. I wondered if he was going to place it in yet another hollowed-out book but instead he just stuck it in the top drawer of his desk. Interesting how it wasn't as secret as his meds.

"So how was the lunch?" he asked.

"Great. Rebecca is...really cool."

"I knew you guys would hit it off," he said with a knowing grin and turned the chair to face the computer. "I've been going through our stuff and it's looking fucking rad so far. Still waiting to hear back from Dr. Hasselback about tomorrow night, though. We don't have quite enough here for an episode but what we do have is fucked up. Take a look at the handprint."

I got up and peered over Dex's shoulder at the screen. His black, shiny hair smelled like shampoo and some natural musk of his. I'm ashamed to admit that I closed my eyes for a split second and breathed it in deeply like a love-struck weirdo.

I turned my attention to the screen before Dex caught on. The handprint that we saw through the screen last night looked really good and bright on the computer. Clear as day, almost.

Then Dex zipped the edits back and showed me the shots that the camera got from being propped up on the sink inside the room. You could clearly see the doorknob turning back and forth. Of course, even though we knew we were the only ones there, it was one of those shots where the audience would probably assume it was faked.

Hence why we would need to get more footage. We just didn't have enough to go on.

"What about the EVP, have you listened to that yet?" I asked, my mouth close to his ear. He shivered slightly at my breath and I took a little bit of pleasure in that.

"Not yet," he said. He turned his head to look at me out of the corner of his eye. Our faces were so close that I could count the pores on his nose. "I'd say we could give it a listen now, but we don't have enough time."

I stood back. "Why, where are we going?"

"I've got some errands to run and then we've got dinner plans tonight with some friends." He pushed pause on the footage and saved all of his work before shutting off the monitor.

"Am I included in these dinner plans?" I asked wearily, sitting back on the bed. The thought of having to go out for dinner with more strangers was tiring. I just wanted to hang out here and keep an eye on Dex.

"Of course you are. You're my prisoner this week, don't you remember? Personally, there are a million other people I'd rather introduce you to. Sarah and Jorge are really Jenn's friends more than mine, but, you know, compromise and all that bullshit."

"Dex Foray knows how to compromise?" I said. "You learn something new every day."

"Yes, you do," he said, and got up. He saw the shoes in the bag. "You went shopping with Rebecca?"

"Yep," I said, pulling the shoes out of the box.

His brows went to the heavens. "Wow. Those are like...Jenn shoes."

"These are not hooker shoes," I said defensively.

"Well played," he said. "You going to wear those to dinner?"

I told him no. I wasn't even going to change since I already looked nicer than usual for the lunch date. But I didn't mention the whole clubbing thing with Jenn. I was afraid there was a small chance he might think the whole thing was a good idea.

Unfortunately, Jenn didn't keep her mouth shut about it. She was in the middle of parking the Mini near the restaurant when she brought it up to Dex.

"Did you see Perry's shoes?" she asked him as she ran the back wheel onto the curb. Worst driver ever.

"I did. Dangerous looking things."

"I want her to wear them clubbing later. She needs to break them in."

Dex's hand flew out and caught Jenn's arm as she straightened the wheel and attempted parallel parking for the second time. "Hold up. What? Clubbing?"

He looked behind him at me. I tried to shake my head as subtly as possible but Jenn said, "Yes, I thought some girl time would be great for us."

"Is Rebecca going?"

"No," Jenn said, scrunching up her nose in distaste. "Why would she? It's just Perry and me. I thought it would be great to let our hair down and get to know each other. Isn't that right, Perry?"

Now she had turned in her seat to look at me. Both of them were waiting for some sort of reaction. I could see that Dex knew how uncomfortable I felt but he didn't say anything. A "oh, let Perry stay home tonight" would have been a sufficient touch from him, but no.

"Yes," I said monotonously. "Girl time."

Dex shook his head, "You girls are fucking nuts. It's a Wednesday night. Who goes clubbing on a Wednesday?"

"Aww, Dexy Poo, are you jealous that we are leaving you out?"

Dexy Poo? Excuse me while I vomit.

"Ha!" he said, slapping his knee. "I sure wish I could get hit on by douchebags all night, dance to asinine monkey beats and drink $20 beers... Jesus Christ, woman, you want me to park the car for you?"

Jenn was now going back in for a third attempt at parallel parking. She glared at Dex but managed to do it this time. Third time's a charm.

I got out of the car, squeezing out between the seats and looked around me. I had no idea what part of Seattle we were in, maybe Bellevue? It was quite a smart-looking area with lots of little cozy-looking cafes and posh boutiques that were done up in twinkling Christmas decorations. It was another reminder that the season was upon us and Christmas would be here before we knew it. I just couldn't get into the spirit for the life of me. It seemed like my whole life had boiled down to just this one week in Seattle. Looking beyond this trip seemed impossible.

It had stopped raining, too, which was good, but the wind was picking up and for once the air was fraught with winter chill. The kind of chill that smells like snow, like a massive breeze had stormed down a snowy mountainside and danced in and out between the city buildings. I held my coat close around me, stuck my hands deep in the pockets and joined Dex and Jenn on the sidewalk.

"We're a few blocks away, but at least it's not raining," Jenn said as we walked down the street together.

"Heaven forbid you try to find a parking spot close to where we need to be," Dex sniped from behind us.

Both Jenn and I turned and gave him a look that probably matched. Maybe mine looked more concerned than Jenn's.

"What the hell is up your ass tonight?" she asked.

"Nothing," he shot back but as he did so, he winced considerably.

I stopped and made him stop, too, by placing my hand on his chest briefly. I was starting to worry again. "What's wrong?"

"Nothing," he said, calmer now. He avoided Jenn's eyes but once he saw mine, he relented and said, "Just a sudden migraine or something."

Uh oh. The guilt took hold of my heart and squeezed it.

Jenn sighed and gave him the keys to the Mini. "There's some Excedrin in the glove compartment."

He nodded thanks, wincing at the movement, and took off down the road back to the car. Jenn pulled at my arm, turning me around and led me on our way to the restaurant, walking slow enough for Dex to catch up.

"Does he get headaches often?" I asked, hoping that he did. He never seemed to when he was around me. Maybe Jenn brought them on. That wouldn't have surprised me at all.

"Sometimes," she said casually. "He used to when we first started dating. Not so much in the last year or so. I don't know, I don't really pay attention."

No kidding, I thought.

She caught the look on my face and explained, "You know Dex, it's always something."

That was true but he was still her boyfriend. Speaking of which...

I stopped and looked behind us expecting to see Dex heading back from the car. Only I couldn't see him anywhere on the dark street.

I glanced at Jenn. "Where did he go?"

She shook her head and then had a quick look at her diamante watch.

"I have no idea but we're already running late."

Yeah, cuz you can't park worth shit.

And then she turned around again and started back on her way. I couldn't believe it. I stood my ground and said, "I'm going to go find him."

She sighed, long and exasperated, but it made her stop. She came back to me and said, "Fine."

We hurried down the sidewalk, looking for him. Maybe he was back at the car. Maybe he popped into a store.

But the car was empty and the closest store was a linen shop. Not exactly Dex territory.

"Dex?" I called out. A few passersby turned at the sound of my voice but kept walking.

"Arghh," Jenn growled, and pulled out her phone. "I'll just call him."

We waited for a few seconds. I could hear the phone ring through her phone. And then I heard Dex's suddenly ironic "Final Countdown" ringtone ring out into the air. Jenn and I looked at each other and then took off down the street toward the sound, which was actually past the car in the opposite direction.

"Dex?" she called as we looked around us.

We followed the sound, the ringtone that kept repeating, sounding more ominous with each tinny ring.

We turned a slight corner and found ourselves looking down a dirty, narrow alley. Halfway down, beside a Dumpster, Dex was sitting on the ground, his head between his legs, his hands covering his ears.

The sight shocked my heart. It apparently shocked Jenn, too, because she just stood there at the entrance to the alley, looking more annoyed and afraid then concerned. I gave her a crazy look and ran over to Dex as fast as I could go.

"Dex!" I cried out softly and dropped to my knees in front of him, the cold wet ground immediately soaking me.

I placed my hands gently on his shoulders but he didn't look up. I looked wildly at Jenn and couldn't believe she was still standing there.

"Jenn!" I yelled at her. I turned back to Dex and scooched in closer. I took a quick look at his body; he seemed fine, but was behaving like a little boy in the middle of a nightmare. I couldn't see his face at all and it was unnerving.

I put my hands on his and lifted them off his ears. They were cold. I squeezed them and slowly tried to rub some life back into them.

"Dex?" I whispered. "It's Perry. Dex, are you OK? I'm here. You're safe. Please just let me know you're OK."

I felt Jenn come behind me and stop.

"He's fine," she said.

My jaw dropped and I whipped my head around to give her a vicious look. "How the hell do you know he's fine?"

"Because he used to do this. Didn't you, Dex? I thought he was done with the panic attacks."

"Panic attacks?" I repeated and looked back at him. He slowly raised his head and looked at us. Me first, then Jenn. His eyes were red like he had been crying.

"I am fine," he said, emotionless.

"See," she said. "Now I'm going to the restaurant before Sarah and Jorge think we've ditched them."

And then she just turned on her heel and walked down the alley, disappearing around the corner.

I wiped her behavior out of my head and turned my attention back to Dex. How could he be fine? He was sitting on the wet ground in a city alley, in the dark. He was the furthest thing from fine and even if it was just a panic attack, that was nothing to brush off.

He wasn't looking at me anymore. His eyes were closed shut. I touched his cheek and laid my palm against his icy face.

"What happened?"

He shook his head slightly.

"Please, Dex," I implored and leaned in closer. I put my other hand on his face and raised his head somewhat. He opened his eyes and looked into mine. My insides crumbled at how lost and scared he looked. Seeing him like this made brought the threat of tears to my eyes.

"What happened? You can tell me. You can trust me. You know you can. Is it...your medication?"

I don't know why I asked this since I was pretty sure that's what it was, but I needed to hear it from him. This was turning out to be one terrible idea.

But he did that slight shake of the head again. It actually didn't make me feel any better.

"Perry," he whispered, his eyes flitting to the right, toward the Dumpster. "Can you go look down the alley? And tell me if someone is there?"

"Someone?" I asked. He just nodded and closed his eyes tightly again. "OK, no problem."

I got up and peered down the alley. I couldn't see anyone. It was a dead end, after all.

I even took a few steps toward the Dumpster. I looked around the edge of it but there was no one there either.

I turned around to go back to Dex.

And then I did see someone.

Standing at the other end of the alley, where the people were passing by. It was just a silhouette, but one that I had seen far too often these past two days.

She wasn't moving, but against the grainy streetlights I could see the blood slowly falling off of her.

Splat. Splat. Splat.

Then she turned, her broken neck at that unnatural angle, and was gone.

I walked over to Dex. He looked up at me. I stared down at him. We both saw it. And now I knew the problem.

I held out my hand for him and told him to get up. After a moment of hesitation he did so, and I steadied him with my hands as he got used to his feet.

"You saw her too," I told him.

He breathed in deeply but didn't exhale. I stepped closer to him, close enough so that he had to back into the damp alley wall. I ran my hands through his thick hair and held them there, holding his head steady.

"You saw her," I pressed. "You saw her, you saw what I've been seeing this whole time."

"Yeah. I saw her."

He exhaled and tried to look at the ground but I held his head tightly. Headache be damned. He was going to look at me.

"What is the problem? She's a dead girl. She's a ghost. This is what we do, Dex. We see ghosts. We see things others can't. Why is this any different?"

"Because I shouldn't be seeing her!" he said through gritted teeth.

"Why not?" I asked. "Why not? Why not for you? Why do I have to?!"

"You don't understand," he said, trying to move his head out of my grasp. I grabbed his hair tighter and held him in place.

"Tell me then!"

His eyes darted around, trying desperately to not meet with mine. He was going to lie, I knew it.

"I...I know her."

I wasn't expecting that. I let my hands drop off of his head.

"What?"

"This is not a good sign, Perry. This is not a good sign," he said. His eyes were watering. His low voice quavered. He looked so lost, so small, so helpless and afraid.

I stepped closer again and brought my hands around his shoulders and brought his head down into the nook of my neck. I held him for a few moments, feeling his cold skin against mine, his breath as he exhaled slowly. Eventually he took his arms and wrapped them around me, holding me so tight it almost took my own breath away. My insides felt like they were mourning, for him and for whatever pain he was going through. And if I had anything to do with it.

"It's Abby," he said after a few minutes, speaking the words into my neck in wet bursts.

"Your...ex...your old girlfriend Abby?"

He nodded.

Oh boy. That was a fucking doozey. It explained so much. His ex had died in college after a fight with Dex. She had been cheating on him, Dex went over and they fought. Then she locked herself in the bathroom with a bottle of gin, escaped through the window and drove away. And then ended up being another victim of drunk driving.

And here she was, suddenly haunting Dex. But why now? Why now that I was in the picture?

"Dex...why do you think this is happening now? Has it happened before?"

He relaxed a bit in his grip but still held me in an embrace. I wasn't about to let him go, so this was fine with me.

"No. I mean..." He brought his head away from my neck so he could talk properly. Our mouths were still only a few inches apart. He rested his forehead against me and kept his eyes closed. "Last time I saw her...was after she had died. She...well, she was everywhere I was. And it drove me insane. And I guess with my past...it was too much. And that's how I got in the institute."

"She literally drove you insane?" I asked, voice low, conscious of how close our mouths were.

"Yeah," he breathed out. "Just the straw that broke the camel's back."

I thought about that and tried to figure out what to do next. What was there to do? She was a ghost and like it or not, we were both seeing her.

"Did she try to harm you before?" I asked.

He sighed and straightened up, breaking up the closeness of our embrace. He looked around him at the dark alley.

"Not exactly," he said. "But I never gave her the chance."

"How did you get rid of her?"

"Medication," he said. "Therapy. Whatever they did to me."

At the mention of his medication, I swallowed hard and looked straight forward at his chest.

I debated on saying anything for a while. I didn't want to make him suspicious. I already had a feeling he'd go home and check his meds, which meant I could easily be busted if I wasn't fast and careful. In the end I couldn't figure out what to say. So I just gave him a small smile.

"You'll be OK, Dex," I said. I was so close to leaning in an inch and kissing him delicately on the lips. Very close.

"Will I?" he breathed back, his frantic eyes powering down with a wash of passion.

I was starting to feel competing feelings of lust rise up throughout my body. It frightened me enough that I had to pull back. I let go of his back and looked away, back up at the end of the alley. Abby was still gone.

"Look, I know this is hard for you," I said, finding my breath hard to control. "But at least we both see her. We're not crazy. You shouldn't have even been on any of those medications anyway, or in therapy. You can't cure ghosts with doctors and pills."

"Can't you?" he asked.

I looked at him sharply, expecting him to be vindictive. But he still looked alone and cold, which melted my heart again. I reached for his hand and held it in mine.

Dex, I love you. That's what I wanted to say. I wanted to tell him that and confess my sins of what I did to him.

But of course, I didn't do either of those things. I just gave his hand a squeeze and said, "I'm in this with you, you know that."

He nodded and fished a piece of Nicorette out of his pocket. "I really wish we could just go back home and be alone."

Be alone? I was unable to hide the shocked look on my face.

He caught the expression and shot me a sly grin as he popped the gum in his mouth.

"Don't worry, kiddo. I just meant I'd rather be with you and not with any of these fucks that Jenn wants us to eat with."

"I thought they were your mutual friends," I said, crossing my arms.

"I said this was a compromise, didn't I?" he said.

"So what do we do? Go eat or go home?"

He sighed and stepped away from the wall, shooting an anxious glance up and down the alley.

"Am I fit enough to go for dinner?" he asked.

I looked him over with a discerning eye. Of course everyone looked garish under streetlights in a dirty alley, but he looked OK. Eyes were less bloodshot and his hair was sexily messy thanks to my handiwork.

"Show me your ass," I said to him, turning him around with my hands.

"Perry," he admonished in fake shock but he let me twirl him. The back of his pants were all wet from sitting on the ground but luckily his black cargo jacket was long enough to cover most of it. He had quite the perky butt, which helped.

"I think you'll pass," I admitted. "I don't know what Jenn's going to think…"

"Who cares," he said with a shrug and straightened up his collar.

"As long as you don't," I said sternly.

"I'll be OK," he said. He took a step forward, trying to walk away but I grabbed him and brought him closer to me. He was taken aback at my gruffness.

"You're not allowed to lie to me anymore, you got it?" I said. "You tell me everything that's going on. The next time you see Abby, you tell me, just as I would tell you. Just as I have told you. We're in the same boat now. I don't know what the fuck she's doing here or what she wants, but it's something and I don't think she's going to go away until she gets it. You…me, we both have to be prepared for this. Got it?"

He blinked hard and then eyed my Kung-Fu grip on his arm. "I've got it. Wow. Perry…when did you…"

"When did I what?" I challenged.

He smiled. It started off small and then spread across his face until the corners of his mouth cracked. "When did you start acting like me?"

I paused at that. But just for a second. Then I hoisted him forward (which was really just a foot) like I was throwing him against the wall. He laughed and trotted off toward the street. I joined him and we went to the restaurant, leaving the alley and Abby behind.

CHAPTER FOURTEEN

Dinner was a total chore. The restaurant was absurdly expensive, considering it was just "tapas" and we pretty much had to pay $50 each for a bunch of tiny appetizers and weak drinks. But neither Dex nor I made a peep about it. We had other things on our minds.

Their mutual friends, Sarah and Jorge, were nice enough. A yuppie couple who made it big on the internet back in the 90s. At least Jorge did. Sarah seemed to be his third wife, but she was Jenn's college friend and there was a weird competition between them. Every time Sarah flattered Jorge on how well his stocks were doing, or whatever they were talking about, Jenn bristled all up like a porcupine and then mentioned how well Wine Babes was doing in the ratings. She never once mentioned Dex. I guess because Dex wasn't technically doing all that well for himself, at least not financially. The truth was, *Experiment in Terror* had still yet to make it big, despite the copycats out there.

Dex seemed withdrawn and disinterested in the conversation and his food. Only his drinks got his attention.

I was surprised that after three drinks, he was still as coherent as usual. I thought the Valium would have done more than make him see the ghost of his ex-girlfriend. But I suppose that was probably the worst side effect any medication could ever have.

I couldn't help but think about Abby throughout the whole excursion. It made me think that the reason Dex was on medication was because he was seeing ghosts. But if that was the case, it was wrong, not to mention unfair. I saw ghosts too, but I wasn't carted off to shrinks and prescribed shit. Why were ghosts seen as a mental illness instead of just fact? Or at least a fact that was accepted, if not understood? It seemed like cheating, kind of. Then again, I never knew why he was on his medication. I had Hasselback tell me, but Dex never actually answered that one. I made a mental note to ask him later.

I was also frightened about the whole thing. How long had Abby been trying to terrify him? Was she in his apartment every night for the past five-odd years? Or was she only there because I was there...because I was either weird competition, or because she knew my abilities. Maybe after years of trying to get through to Dex, she finally found someone who listened: Me. But why? What did she have left to say? Did she blame Dex for what happened to her? Was she out for revenge...or worse, whatever worse could be?

Yeah, I was terrible company and so was Dex. Jenn had to spend most of the meal handling the conversation. I didn't feel bad for her, though. She was the one who saw her beloved sitting in an empty alleyway, head between his knees, hiding from a nightmare, and she acted like it wasn't a big deal at all. I didn't understand her one bit and I was liking her less and less by the second. I didn't even think that was possible.

Unfortunately, whatever I thought about Jenn didn't matter because as soon as dinner was over and we were back at the apartment, she scooted me into my room.

"Go put on something sexy, Perry," she said throatily, her voice going all Scarlett Johansson again. She hadn't forgotten about the whole clubbing thing.

I paused in the door, held my stance and looked at Dex fearfully. Not only did I not want to go clubbing, but I especially did not want to leave Dex alone in the apartment with Abby on the prowl.

But to my amazement, Dex said, "Just go, Perry, you'll have fun."

My mouth dropped. "Dex. I am not leaving you here!"

I froze when I realized what I'd said.

"Leave him here? What are you talking about?" Jenn asked, her voice building with each word.

I quickly looked at Dex. He gave me a very quick, poignant look that said "please don't say anything."

I took in a deep breath and somehow found the strength to smile at Jenn. "I mean, it's not really fair to leave him here while we go out and have fun."

"Phhfff," Jenn said, waving her hand at him. She walked over to me and pushed me into my room. "You know he'd hate it. Now quickly get dressed."

She shut the door. I was quickly enveloped in the dark but switched on the light before the terror seized me. Part of me could not leave Dex here, *would not* leave him. But the other part told me I just might have to. He was trying to save face and act like nothing was wrong.

Well, as long as I had time to myself in the room, I had time to switch his pills all back. Even though I was tempted to continue on with the experiment, I didn't want to put him through any more terror or pain. Whatever his pills were for, the fact that I just switched some of them, the pills that had to do with delusions, it couldn't have just been a coincidence. Whether it could be proved or not, I felt partly, if not fully, responsible for what happened in the alley.

I brought out my duffel bag from beside the bed and brought out all of my clothes, strewing them across the pistachio bed. I reached into the bottom of the bag. And found nothing but powder.

I opened the bag wider against the light and peeked in, my chest heaving. All the pills were crushed. There was nothing but a white and yellow powder lining the bottom of the bag. What the fuck?

My hands flew up to my mouth in horror. What happened? How did the pills get crushed? I thought about earlier when I was shoving clothes in my bag. I was rough, but not enough to crush a handful of pills. What the hell could have done that?

Then I looked at the bag again. The outside was covered with a lot of fine white hair. Dog hair. Could Fat Rabbit have stomped all over the bag? He didn't seem big enough to do enough damage, but then again, his name started with the word "Fat" and he was known for pissing people off.

And that was the end of that idea. I couldn't replace Dex's pills with dust. I couldn't do anything now but watch him unravel, watch his nerves fry as Abby came and did her worst.

But that couldn't be it. It couldn't be. It had to be a coincidence. How could pills prevent you from seeing ghosts? If that were true, wouldn't I have been on something similar in high school...

I pushed that thought out of my head. I didn't want to conjure up Jacob at a time like this. There were far more important things to worry about. Like Dex. And going clubbing with Jenn.

I sighed and quickly shoved on the skinny jeans I had, the raspberry heels and a plain white tank top. I didn't bother with my face or my hair. I honestly did not care. In fact, if I could have covered myself with ghoulish makeup, I would have done so.

I opened the door (after shoving the duffel bag and its powdery evidence underneath the bed) and stepped out into the living room. Dex was gone, the door to the bedroom closed. Just Jenn stood in the living room, flipping through the TV stations.

At the sound of me, she turned around and gave me the once over. "Is that what you're wearing?"

I looked down at myself. Suddenly the tune of "Makeover, Makeover" from *Clone High* rang through my head but luckily Jenn wasn't on the same plane. She just nodded and said, "Whatever, it works."

"Where's Dex?" I asked, eyeing their door.

"Sleeping, reading, I don't know," she said and gestured for me to come forward. "Come on, let's get going."

I eyed the clock in the kitchen as I walked over to her. "It's only ten. Are we in a rush?"

"No, no," she said breezily, smiling at me. "Just getting a head start on the fun."

She turned and walked to the door. I followed, suspicious of everything and everyone. I wanted nothing more than to go into Dex's room and make sure he was OK, but I knew that would only get him in trouble. So I steadied my nerves and followed Jenn out the door.

We took a cab to the venue, since Jenn planned to get quite drunk. Those were her actual words on the elevator down: "I hope you know I'm going to get quite drunk, Perry."

That was fine with me. I was curious to see how drunk Jenn would compare to sober Jenn. Maybe she was less bitchy, less selfish and more vulnerable.

Well, 20 minutes into our arrival at the douchiest nightclub in the Pacific Northwest, I found out that drunk Jenn was the same as sober Jenn. Just...amplified.

"I need another drink," she said, trying to wave down the bartender who was doing quite a good job of ignoring us the whole time. The music was on a continuous suck cycle except for the occasional addition of Kylie Minogue or Lady Gaga. We were occasionally getting sized up by guys but neither of us had been hit on at this point.

I wasn't surprised by this when it came to myself (I definitely wasn't slutty enough) but I thought Jenn would have been approached at least a few times already. She was a Wine Babe after all, and she did get recognized quite often. Here, though, that wasn't the case. And the drunker she got, the more she picked up on it.

"You're so lucky, Perry," she said, bringing my head out of another worrying daydream about Dex.

I frowned at her. "How do you mean?"

"Well look at you," she said while chewing on her straw and waving at me up and down. "You could become as thin as I am and you'd still have boobs."

Was that a compliment or...

"OK," I said. I raised my glass to my mouth and shot the rest of the drink back in one go.

"No, I mean it," she said, slapping me lightly on my arm. I raised my brow at her, feeling the tiniest bit of instinct to fight her. Which was not usual, I swear.

"Sure you could stand to lose a few pounds but your boobs are huge so even if you got skinny, you'd still have them. When I lose weight, mine are the first to go."

She stood there, poking at her boobs through her top. I bit my lip and clenched my fist around my drink, trying to push down the angry swell that I felt rising through me.

"Well, just be glad I am the way I am," I managed to answer. "Otherwise, I'd be taking over your job. And that would just be the beginning."

And I smiled at her, big and bright.

Jenn looked shocked. Then she laughed, nervously at first, then just drunk and stupid. "You're pretty funny, Perry. I can see why Dex likes you. He likes to laugh at things."

My smile tightened. My grip froze. There were so many things I wanted to say, but Jenn's head flew around in a whirlwind when the next song came on. It was actually a dance song I didn't mind, LCD Soundsystem's "North American Scum."

She grabbed my arm and said, "Oh we must dance to this."

Oh crap. I put my empty drink on the bar and let her lead me to the floor.

I'm not a good dancer. I know this. I like to either groove slowly or just go all out. I only did the latter with people I knew and trusted. In this case, I was doing the slow, timid white girl bump and grind. But Jenn, she was going all out. First she started by rubbing up all over me like I was the dude, then she started making eyes at me. It was fucking weird, like a total nightmare. I'm not kidding. If I foresaw this scene a month ago, I would have shit myself.

Of course it wasn't for me. It wasn't about having fun with me or making me feel comfortable. It was about teasing the men who were watching, making us look like we were about to make out. No wonder Rebecca hated her so much.

Jenn continued to do this for the entire song (let's add "North American Scum" to "Maxwell Silver Hammer" in the "songs I used to like until Dex and Jenn ruined them for me" pile) but after not being approached by any guys, she slinked off the dance floor, all downtrodden. She took me by the hand and back to the bar, where she tried to get the bartenders attention again.

"I don't get it," she said, looking absolutely defeated. Her eyes were welling up with tears. It scared me. It meant I was going to have to make her feel better and I did not want to do that. She did not deserve it.

"It's cuz I'm old," she sniffed and delicately rubbed the corners of her exotic eyes.

"Um, you're thirty one Jenn. That's nothing."

"Easy for you to say. You're twenty two..."

"Twenty three, actually."

"Whatever," she said and took a bar napkin to her nose. "You're like almost ten years younger than me. You have your whole future ahead of you. All this promise and possibility. What do I have? Nothing. Just a few more years and everyone will move onto someone younger."

She sniffled again. With her curly, sienna hair falling across her face, she looked younger than her age. Her attitude helped bring her down a few pegs too. She was a gorgeous, stunning girl. At least, she was to anyone who didn't know her. She probably wasn't getting approached or hit on because she seemed either too desperate or the opposite, too secure. And the fact was, she *had* a boyfriend. And he was at home, in their room, scared to death and feeling alone. And she was here, with me, complaining about how unattractive she was. I was torn between feeling sorry for her and sympathizing with her, and wanting to punch her lights out for being a stupid, selfish bitch.

Of course, I didn't punch her lights out. I sucked in my pride. "Look, I'll buy you a drink."

I waved at the bartender and for some reason, I was able to get his attention and not her. I ordered us both shots of Jaeger and more vodka sevens.

When the shots came and Jenn gave the bartender the bitchiest look, I raised my glass to her, trying to find hidden reserves of strength deep inside myself. I was cheering my enemy in an attempt to make her feel better. What was wrong with me?

Jenn clinked the shot glass, smiled and downed it. Half of it almost came back up again, but she buried that with the seven. Then her phone beeped.

She fished it out of her bag excitedly. My first thought was that it was Dex, but judging from the subtle way she grinned to herself, I knew it wasn't.

I watched her text back and then put the phone away. She kept smiling and noticed me watching her.

"Oh, that was Bradley," she said. Uh huh. That figured.

"Yeah?"

"He was in the area and he's going to stop by."

I remembered what Rebecca said. They were a pair of fucks. She had a theory. Suddenly, I had that same theory.

"So I finally get to meet this Bradley?" I asked, wondering how to phrase my next sentence. "Wasn't he the guy Rebecca wanted to set me up with?"

"You don't get everyone," Jenn sneered, slamming her drink hard on the counter. It made me jump. It made the people next to us jump. The Latino in Jenn was coming out.

I raised my hands in surrender. "I never said I wanted Bradley. I've got a boyfriend back in Portland anyway."

"Oh?" She seemed floored. "You do? Oh. Well...who is he? Dex never mentioned him."

"His name is Brock. I just started dating him. I don't tell Dex everything," I lied.

She nodded quickly, composing herself. The look of relief flooded across her brow. And for the next bit, Jenn was a lot more relaxed with me. Drunk, but the competition mode was turned off, at least a smidge.

Soon, Bradley showed up. Actually, it was really soon. As if he was in the same club with us this whole time.

"Perry, this is Bradley," Jenn said as a tall, strikingly handsome man gave her a quick hug and turned his sights on me.

He was tall and well built, in a dapper shirt. Longish light brown hair, a stylish five o'clock shadow, sparkling blue eyes and one hell of a devilish grin.

I shook his outstretched hand. He smiled, perfect teeth that matched Jenn's in the veneer category, and cocked his head to the side. "So you're the girl..."

"I'm the girl?"

"Yes. The girl who somehow tore Mr. Foray from the Wine Babes. I'm surprised."

How amusing. "Oh yeah, how is that?"

"You're taller than I thought."

"I'm wearing really high heels," I answered. "Was that it?"

My voice was totally accusatory. I was sure my face was as well. I didn't have to listen to Bradley any more to know Rebecca's assertion was correct.

"Nice to meet you, Perry," Bradley said, and then pointed upstairs. He turned to Jenn. "Jenn, there's a friend of mine I'd like you to meet."

He looked at me quickly, all false charm. "Perry, you don't mind. I'll return her soon. I'm sure you won't be here alone for long."

Before I could open my mouth to say anything, Jenn and Bradley walked off across the club, toward the stairs. I watched them like a hawk the whole time. Just as they were about to disappear from view, I saw him put his arm around Jenn's waist.

I was so angry. Not only was I just ditched in some shitty-assed night club, but it was quite obvious that Jenn and Bradley were having an affair, or something close to it. I felt the frustration fill up my veins and turned my attention to the bar. Once again, I got the bartender's attention pretty quickly, which was a needed ego boost, especially after all of Jenn's comments. I ordered a glass of Jack on the rocks in honor of Dex and sipped it slowly. I gave Jenn and Bradley as long as the drink. If they didn't return by the time I was done, I was leaving.

It took me twenty minutes to drink it. It was the longest-lasting drink of my life. Then I texted Jenn and told her that I was thinking about heading back to the apartment. I waited for a response to that but after ten minutes, there was nothing.

Fuck that.

I marched out of the club, ignoring the gross leers of the grody men in there, and got the first cab that was waiting outside. It took me straight to Dex's apartment.

In the meantime, I got a text from Jenn that said, "Oh, you are? We're just upstairs with friends, are you sure you don't want to wait around?" Again, fuck that.

I got out of the cab and, after tipping the cabbie too much, I looked up at the apartment. Dex was standing on the balcony, looking down at me with a feeling of shock. He was smoking, a cloud of it surrounding his head despite the slight breeze.

"Perry?" he said, sounding scared. "Is Jenn with you?"

I turned and watched the cab drive away. "Obviously not. Can you let me in?"

He nodded and put the smoke out on an ashtray. I went to the door and was buzzed in.

He answered their door in plaid pajama pants and a grey T-shirt. His eyes were red and he reeked of pot. He stuck his head out into the hallway, looking all paranoid.

"I'm not with Jenn," I told him again, and pushed past him into the apartment. I leaned against the kitchen counter and kicked my wretched shoes off. They hurt like hell and almost fell off a bunch of times while dancing.

"What happened? Why are you home so soon?" he asked, sounding panicky.

I leaned against the counter and put my head down on it.

"I don't know. Clubbing sucks," I mumbled. I didn't know what to say. Part of me wanted to tell Dex what I thought about Jenn and Bradley, or at least to mention he was there on our "girls" night and that they ditched me. But the other part felt that if I did that, she would deny it and I would look like his psycho jealous partner.

"Where's Jenn?"

I opened my eyes and stared blankly at the far wall, glad he wasn't in my line of sight.

"She saw some friends and wanted to stay. I didn't. So I came back."

"Oh. Well, did you have fun?"

I turned my head the other way to look at him. "Do you think I had fun, Dex?"

He smiled to himself and let out a funny giggle. "OK then."

He walked over to the couch and plopped down on it. "Want to join me?"

"What are you doing?"

"Watching *Mitchell*. Mystery Science Theatre 3000. I know you love it. We've had drunken conversations about it."

"That works out well then. Cuz I'm drunk right now."

"And I'm high," he said, and patted the space beside him on the couch.

I was drunk, drunk enough to know that sitting next to him wouldn't be a good idea, especially after all I found out tonight. So I sat down on the armchair, splaying my body across it like Fat Rabbit, who was doing a similar pose on the rug in front of the television's blue glow.

Dex pressed play and started laughing away. I'd seen the episode enough that I didn't need to pay attention. I focused my attention on him. He had a stupid look on his face and his eyes were red, but I was guessing it was from the pot and not because he saw Abby again. Perhaps pot wasn't a bad idea for him after all. Anything that kept him smiling and not cowering in an alley in fear was a good thing.

After we watched about half the movie, Dex lowered the volume and said, "How are you kiddo?"

I turned my body over and shrugged. "Tired."

"All danced out?"

I laughed. "No. Not danced out."

"You should learn to dance one day. It's fun."

"Excuse me," I gave him a look. "I know how to dance."

"Oh really," he said, straightening up on the couch, giving me a flirty look.

"What?"

"I'd like to see these dance moves."

"I'm sure you will on Friday."

"Oh, come on baby."

I paused at that. He hadn't called me baby since our time on the island. He didn't seem to notice though. He got up, a bit wobbly, and walked over to the stereo.

"I bet Jenn has some good dance music," he said, flipping through the settings.

"Dex...I'm not dancing. I'm tired. I'm done. I'm going to sleep soon. It's like the middle of the night."

He ignored me and settled on the recognizable synth beats of Lady Gaga's "Poker Face." He cocked his finger at me.

"No, no way," I protested.

But he turned it up. And as soon as the backbeats broke in...Dex started dancing.

I tried not to laugh but it was impossible. My face cracked open and the resulting guffaw scared Fat Rabbit enough that he ran away into the kitchen. Either that scared him, or it was Dex's dancing, which was silly and over the top, yet still skilled. I hadn't forgotten that the boy knew how to dance; he was quite adept at it at the bar in Red Fox.

"Come on," he said, waving his hands at me. He started singing along with the chorus and doing Madonna face moves. The volume went up again.

And so did I.

I got to my feet and started dancing like an idiot. And when I say idiot, I mean doing the hustle, the lawnmower, the skier, the shopper, the sprinkler system.

By the time "Bad Romance" started pumping through the speakers, both Dex and I were helicoptering and jiving in a circle in the living room. Fat Rabbit stopped being afraid of us and tried to get in between us, wiggling his little butt around.

I was just drunk enough to start singing along with this song; all the lyrics were way to applicable to our situation. But he sang them too. It was surprising that he knew them, but then again, how did I?

"Are you sure this is Jenn's CD?" I asked suspiciously, breathing hard between moves.

"It might not be." He didn't hide his sheepish look.

By the time he got to singing the French parts of the song (which he pronounced perfectly) I was starting to feel awkward. Stupid sexy language. But Dex just grinned at me, put his arms around my waist and pulled me closer to him, so we were doing a sort of fast-paced slow dance.

Our bodies were moving, our hips were grinding against each other. Sweat was flying. Our faces were close, mouths grinning, shared intoxication.

And then the song ended.

"What the hell?"

Dex and I immediately took our hands off of each other and turned to the doorway. Jenn was standing there, looking haggard and drunk.

"Perry," she said, shutting the door behind her and stumbling over to us. "Why did you leave like that?"

She turned her attention to Dex, not seeming to find a problem with the way we were dancing, or the humor in finding of us both dancing like idiots to Lady Gaga.

The next song came on, which made us jump, and Dex quickly turned it off. Jenn just watched him with her sloppy eyes until his attention was back on her again. Then she continued, "I went to get some drinks with some people and then Perry just left. Just like that."

Seriously? Was that seriously her version of events? She eyed me so fast it was almost imperceptible, which told me she was afraid I would contradict her. I wanted to. Did I ever. But what would be the point.

Dex didn't even bother looking at me. I think he could tell that it wasn't something I did on purpose. He put his hand on Jenn's head. "It's OK, I'm sure it was a misunderstanding. Time for bed, OK?"

Jenn nodded and stumbled past us toward the bedroom.

The door closed. I looked up at Dex. "I didn't ditch her."

"I know you didn't. I'm surprised you went out with her in the first place. That was really big of you."

"Really?"

He walked over to the kitchen and poured us both a glass of water. "I know you, kiddo. That was one for the team and I appreciate it. I don't think you could ever get out of my good books for that one."

I sipped at the water. I wasn't too sure about that. I looked him over. "How are you? While I was gone...did you...see anything?"

He shook his head. "No, thank God. Maybe the pot helped. Or being distracted. Or just having the dog here. I felt fine enough to dance with you, so I guess I've been doing OK."

"I was worried about you," I admitted.

"I know," he said, placing a hand on my shoulder and slowly leading us back to our rooms. "And knowing that you were, it made me feel...safe."

That warmed me a little.

"Good night, Dex," I said, stepping into my room.

"Good night, Perry," he said in return. I shut the door and climbed into bed. I finished half the glass of water and then closed my eyes. As I drifted off, my thoughts turned to Dex. I wondered what would have happened between us had Jenn not come home so early.

CHAPTER FIFTEEN

"Who's your friend here?"

I turned my head and looked over at Tara, who was sidling up to Angus, her lanky arms hanging at her sides, unsure of what to do with them. The party was absolutely packed with people, some I recognized from class, some a bit older, maybe college-aged. The air in the house was filled with clouds of pot and tobacco smoke, music was blaring from three different rooms and beer and hard liquor was being spilled in all directions.

Tara pointed at me and asked Angus, "Her? That's my friend Perry. I thought you two were in the same math class."

I sighed internally and walked over to them. I gave Angus a shy smile. He was cute but not my type. "No, it's the same biology class."

Angus nodded quickly, thinking it over. A flash of recognition came across his freckled face. "Ah, right, Perry. You sit at the back with the Asian dude."

Actually there were several "Asian dudes" in our class but my partner was Andy Lao.

"Listen, I better go find Adrianna. I think there are some people who shouldn't be here." Angus patted Tara on the shoulder and disappeared into the crowd.

She exhaled all dramatically and threw her hands up in the air. "I can never win."

"Oh come on," I said. "Just forget about him. You know he's with Adrianna. Go find someone else."

Tara shook her head angrily. "Easy for you to say. You don't have anyone and you don't care about anyone."

I was a bit shocked at that. Tara made a disgusted noise and then took off into the crowd, going the same way Angus went.

Well that sucked. What did she mean, I didn't have anyone? I had...well, her. And I had...and what about me not caring about anyone.

I looked around me awkwardly, feeling like I stood out like a sore thumb in this place. Of course, no one was paying attention to me at all. They never did.

I chugged back the rest of my beer that Tara had stolen for me from the fridge and then made my way to the back of the house, squeezing through people, too many of whom couldn't handle their alcohol.

It wasn't any better outside. The air was crisp but a few people were puking here and there. Mrs. Gee's garden was going to be totally obliterated by teenage vomit come morning.

I walked out away from the noise and smell and around the side of the house. I wanted to be alone, needed time to get a hold of my heart, which was racing. I had done a line of coke in the bathroom earlier and it was already wearing off. I didn't have any more, so I brought out another joint and lit that, taking in a deep breath and slowly exhaling it while keeping my cough to a minimum. My lungs were so used to it now, and this strain was surprisingly gentle to me. Potent as hell though, which is why I liked it.

"Perry," I heard someone whisper.

I sprang up from the fence I was leaning against and grabbed at my pounding chest. I couldn't see anyone in the shadows where the motion detector light didn't reach, but eventually I heard a shuffling noise and Jacob stepped out in front of me.

The tips of his inky Mohawk sparkled in the light. He was looking unusually pale. The bandages around his wrists were gone and what remained were two vicious looking red welts. Whatever he had used to attempt suicide with must have been jagged in nature. It made me feel sick.

"I need your help Perry," he said.

"Jacob, what are you doing here?" I asked, trying not to sound frightened. He had been so obsessive with me lately, the way he followed me around when people weren't looking, that it was starting to freak me out. And now, he was here, at this party that he wouldn't have been invited to.

"My girl is in there," he said. His voice sounded strange and metallic. He nodded at the house. "Adrianna. I've come to free her. And help you."

"First of all, Adrianna is not your girl. She's with Angus. I'm sure you can go plan a line of attack with my friend Tara, she'd be happy to take him off your hands, but for now, those two are a couple. Get the net. And, help me...help me with what?"

I took a smaller toke of my joint and offered it to him. He shook his head and pushed my hand away.

"Listen to me, Perry," he said. He stepped closer to me, cornering me up against the fence, and suddenly I was totally afraid. "We have a job to do tonight."

"We?" I asked, my voice stammering. I shrank back as far as I could go.

"I need to show you some things. Because you obviously don't see them, do you?"

I shook my head, not understanding anything at all. It wasn't the pot. What he was saying made no sense.

He raised his arm and pointed over at the back yard. A couple were in the middle of it, making out on the grass.

"Do you see it?"

I squinted. "See what? The couple about to hump each other?"

"No. Beyond them. Do you see that shimmer?"

I squinted again. I didn't see anything.

"Relax your eyes. Like a Magic Eye painting."

He placed one of his cold fingers and laid it on my temple. The temperature jarred me and I was conscious of having his mangled wrist so close to my face. I could almost...smell it. It smelled like death.

"Try again," he continued.

I took in a deep breath and tried to concentrate on the space beyond the couple, on this shimmer. I didn't see anything but a dark lawn and the outline of the wooden fence against the passing clouds.

"No, Jacob, I..."

But I stopped in mid-sentence.

There was something. Something sort of in between where the couple lied and where the fence was. It was a shimmer, like a mirage in the desert, or heat lines. It radiated from the ground straight up into the sky. It didn't take up all of the yard, but it was there, and the more I stared at it, the more it was all I could see. My eyes were locked.

"What is that?" I whispered. Was the house on like a leaking gas line or something? That thought filled me with panic.

"That...is where I come from," Jacob said.

I turned my head and looked at him, unable to process that properly. "What?"

He lowered his head and stared at me with his eyes. I watched them, mesmerized, as they turned from brown to bright red, like unripe cherries. "That's where the rest of them will come from too. Tonight. The demons."

Demons? That's it, I'm quitting drugs first thing in the morning, I thought. Then I slumped to my knees and passed out at Jacob's feet.

~~

A solid tap on my shoulder woke me up. I blinked hard at the bright light and looked around. I was on Dex's couch and he was standing above me, poking me repeatedly. The sound of vomiting filled the air. I had thought perhaps I had been dreaming about someone puking, but no, it was Jenn in the bathroom.

I groaned and sat up uneasily, holding my head.

"You just passed the fuck out," he said, lifting up my legs over and taking a seat beside me. "You all right?"

I nodded gingerly and looked at the clock on the wall. It was 10 a.m. and I had only been up for an hour but my damn hangover was in full swing. I didn't think I was all that drunk last night but I guess mixing all the drinks didn't help either. I had lied down on the couch to watch TV and I guess I fell back asleep right away.

The vomiting noise continued, which turned my own stomach.

"Is Jenn OK?" I asked.

He bit his lip before saying, "She doesn't do hangovers very well. I'm pretty sure this day will be a write-off for her. How much did you guys drink?"

"I didn't drink all that much," I told him. "It was her goal to get loaded."

"Well it worked. Too well. She snored all night long before the snores turned into puke. That God I had the sense to put the wastebasket beside her last night."

I made a disgusted face and wiped the fogginess from my eyes. Despite it being early in the morning, there was a weird creepy vibe in the apartment. I looked at Dex, feeling more than ashamed as the realization of what I had done hit me. He was going to be going down a dark road of mental torture and it was all because of me.

He caught me staring and opened his mouth to say something but I cut him off. "I'm OK, Dex, really. I should be asking about you. Did you sleep OK?"

"Aside from Miss Snore n' Puke? Yes. No...nothing else, if that's what you are hinting at."

"Good," I said. I wanted to ask him about Abby more, and about his medication, to find out if he'd tell me the truth about it, but even though Jenn was occupied, I knew he'd never talk about it here, if he was even going to talk about it at all. "So what's our plan for today?"

"Not too sure." He leaned back against the couch and put his arms back behind his head, legs splayed open. His T-shirt lifted up a bit, displaying a sliver of stomach. I was tempted to lean over and poke his hairy belly. Then I was tempted to follow the trail of hair beneath his boxers. Start by undoing his belt and then unzipping his pants, slip my hand under...

I blushed and looked away. What a freaking mess I was. It was just morning and already I was a horndog.

I got off the couch and walked over to the kitchen, opening the cupboards absently. I wasn't hungry and could barely eat a slice of buttered toast that morning, but it was something to do. Something to distract me from my weird conflicted feelings, all while Jenn was still barfing her head off.

Dex was watching me curiously as I pulled out a box of cereal and started picking at it.

"What do you want to do?" he asked.

"I'd like to take you for a little motorbike lesson," I said, popping some flakes in my mouth and chewing the cereal without tasting it. Taking out the bike would be the perfect opportunity to get him out of the house and away from Jenn.

"Are you serious?"

"I am serious."

He laughed to himself and got up, peering out the balcony doors to the street below. "Well, lucky for you, it's not raining out. I don't know, we should really work on the footage we have and see if Hasselback calls. And we haven't checked out the voice recordings either."

I shuddered and put the cereal back, wiping my hands on my pants. There was no way in hell I wanted to listen to the recordings, at least not right now when I had this weird icky feeling. "We can do that later. The doctor will call you when he calls you. I just...I need to talk to you." I eyed the bathroom door and lowered my voice. "In private."

Dex nodded, understanding and walked over to the front door, slipping on his skate shoes and jacket.

"OK, let's go," he said quickly.

I was surprised at how fast he moved. "Don't you want to tell Jenn?"

He sighed and yelled at the bathroom. "Hey babe, we're going out for a bit. Fat Rabbit might need to be walked later, just so you know."

There was silence. Then she said in a tiny, quavering voice, "Harvey, you moron." And the puking resumed, which thankfully now sounded like dry-heaving.

As soon as we headed down into the parkade and I rolled Putt-Putt out onto the busy street, I felt better. My head seemed to be a bit clearer, thanks to the brisk air, and the hazy winter sunlight was making me feel less creeped out by the second. It was weird how his apartment would take on that feeling from time to time. It made me wonder if it had something to do with Abby. Maybe sometimes she just watched us but didn't make herself known.

I shivered at that thought as we waited to cross the road.

"Cold?" Dex said eyeing me up and down.

I shook my head and pushed the bike across the street. There was a large empty parking lot up ahead, which would be perfect for a few rounds.

"Hold on, I've got to get rollies," Dex said, and quickly ducked into the convenience store beside us. I waited on the sidewalk, avoiding the eyes of the passersby, who were looking at me and my bike and probably assuming I wasn't cool enough to ride it.

I looked up at the apartment, still visible on the other side of the monorail line.

Abby dead, decaying body was at the balcony window. At least, that's what it looked like. I froze but kept my eyes locked on her. I stayed that way until Dex came out of the store.

"Guy keeps trying to sell me cigarettes, won't take no for..." He stopped beside me and followed my gaze across the street to the balcony window.

"Do you see her?" I whispered.

"Yes," he said, swallowing hard.

"Is...Jenn in danger?"

We looked at each other. We hadn't thought of that before. We assumed that because we were the only ones who could see her, that she wouldn't be of harm to anyone else. But what if she was? Jenn was alone in the apartment with her. Jenn was his girlfriend; maybe Abby wanted her all along.

Dex looked like he picked up on that thought. Panic strained through his eyes. "Maybe, just in case, we should go back."

Even though the light was red, he sprinted across the street, narrowly getting hit by a white sedan that had to slam on its brakes.

I watched him run past the corner and disappear. With my bike in my hands, I had to wait for the light to turn before I could cross. I kept my eyes on the balcony, watching Abby.

She watched me for a few seconds, her grey goo of an eye barely visible against the window glare, then turned her head and disappeared from sight, moving farther back into the apartment.

Come on you fucking light, I thought wildly.

Since it was a one-way street and the traffic had let up, I chanced it and rolled my bike across. Of course, now the problem was, how was I going to get back into the building? I didn't have a key and I didn't know if Dex would buzz me in. I didn't even know if he'd be safe in there.

I waited anxiously by the door, sneaking glances up at the other balcony of their corner suite, the one that came from their bedroom. Finally, tired of waiting and on the verge of a heart attack, I rolled my bike down the steps to the buzzer and buzzed him. It rang and rang with no one picking up. Eventually I stopped and looked around me, hoping someone would come either in or out of the building and let me in. I took out my phone and called him at the same time.

There was no answer. I did simultaneous buzzing and ringing until there was movement inside the lobby and Dex, Jenn and Fat Rabbit walked out of the elevator toward me.

Jenn looked like wrecked and extremely put out as they opened the door and stepped outside to join me. Fat Rabbit was straining at the leash that Dex held, oblivious to what was going on.

"OK, OK, I'm outside," Jenn said with a grunt and quickly slid her sunglasses down on her face, covering up her tired and ashen eyes. "What the hell is so important that you have to drag me out here?"

"I don't want to discuss it here," Dex said. He pointed up the street. "Let's head to Seattle Center."

She groaned. "Dex, I just want to go back to bed. I'm not walking anywhere."

"Please babe," he pleaded, putting his arm around her. It didn't help her expression but she relented with a sigh.

We walked off toward Seattle Center and the Space Needle, the same route Dex and I had made on that wet Monday, only now I was awkwardly pushing my bike behind them.

A block into our excursion, near the fountain in the small square, Jenn demanded that we stop. She looked faint and had to lean against Dex. My goodness, she really didn't do hangovers very well. What a princess.

"Just tell me what's going on, Dex. Or should I ask Perry," she said, turning her head to me. I knew her expression despite it being hidden by those glasses.

"OK," Dex said, licking his lips nervously. "OK, but hear me out. Don't say anything till I'm done."

She exhaled and crossed her skinny arms against her, wearing only a thin jacket, but nodded.

I watched a bead of sweat appear on Dex's brow. I knew how hard this was for him. I wondered how much of his story he was going to share.

"The other night, when Perry saw...someone...in the apartment. That wasn't in her head."

Jenn opened her mouth to say something but Dex shushed her.

"I told you. Just listen. I know you won't believe any of this, but if I don't tell you, then I'd blame myself if anything happened to you."

She frowned but kept quiet and he continued. "Perry sees ghosts. You know this. I see them too. You also know this. What you don't know is that I saw this same person last night. That's what triggered the panic attack. Which wasn't a panic attack by the way, it was just me...not being able to handle seeing her again."

"Who again?" Jenn asked suspiciously.

"Abby."

Jenn shrugged. "I don't know who that is."

He took in a deep breath and closed his dark eyes. I wanted to hold his hand for support but I knew how inappropriate that would be. Instead, I propped up my bike against the brick wall, tired from holding it.

"Abby was my ex-girlfriend. She's...dead. She died in a drunk-driving accident back in college."

Jenn put her hand to her mouth. I don't know if it was out of shock or because she felt sick. Could have been both.

"Oh my God," she exclaimed softly. Dex nodded.

"It was...rough. And that's putting it mildly as fuck. It was a long time ago and it really screwed me up. I had tried hard to forget about it, and for the most part it worked, until I saw her in the alley. It was Abby. It was the same girl that Perry saw in the living room and-"

"Oh my God," Jenn exclaimed again. "You think you're actually being haunted by your ex-girlfriend?"

I did not like the patronizing tinge to her voice. I exchanged a worried glance with Dex. He didn't like it either. His face fell.

"I know it sounds crazy," he said in a voice barely above a whisper. "But you have to believe me."

She shook her head, seeming to be at a loss for words. She looked around her at the people occasionally walking past, at the monorail line, at the bare trees that waved slightly in the breeze.

Finally she pointed at me and said, "I'd understand if she was the one saying these things. She's a bit off her rocker, but you, Dex..."

My mouth fell open. I was the one off my rocker, not Dex? Dex, who had been in a mental institute? I was so close to saying something but I bit my lip. Hard.

"Jenn. Please. This is what is going on, like it or not."

"So you rushed into the apartment and pounded on the bathroom door like a fucking maniac, yelling all over the place, because you thought your dead ex-girlfriend was going to harm me? Are you serious?"

Dex's head hung low. It looked like all the fight had gone out of him. That wasn't like him at all. He stared at the ground, keeping his face away from Jenn.

Finally, I had to say something.

"It's true, Jenn. I know you don't believe us and that's fine, but we had to tell you. Like he said, if anything were to happen to you..."

"You'd be the first one dancing on my grave!" she spat out. Fat Rabbit looked up sharply at the tone of her voice.

I sucked in my lips and looked away. An unbelievably stifling silence enveloped the three of us. Even the dog stopped panting and shook ever so slightly.

"What if I told you-" Dex began to say, raising his head to look at Jenn, but I put my hand out and squeezed his arm.

"You don't have to say anything, Dex," I told him, begging him with my eyes to keep his mouth shut. Jennifer wouldn't understand in a million years.

"What could he possibly say to make any of this normal?" she asked incredulously. "You both sound like total fucking nut jobs. You can do whatever you want with your ghost-hunting show; I really, really don't care. But please, don't let it interfere with my life. You fucking dragged me out of the apartment for this?"

"Why are you so mad?" I asked her. It just came out.

Both of the looked surprised at my question.

"What? Because," she stammered, stamping from one foot to the other. "I'm cold. And I want to go to bed. And I don't want to have anything to do with your little ghost club here. This is like an episode of *Goosebumps*."

And at that she took the leash from Dex's hands and stormed back to the apartment.

We watched her go, her mad supermodel strut even when on the urge of vomiting.

"Should we let her go back?" I asked, even though she was halfway there.

"Whatever," Dex said, turning around and leaning against the wall. He stared blankly at the ground in front of him. "We warned her. That's all we can do. Something tells me Abby won't be bothering with her anyway."

"Why is that?"

"Because," he said slowly. He looked at me from the corner of his eye. "You're more of a threat than Jenn is. When it comes to seeing things. And otherwise."

"Otherwise," I repeated.

He nodded, popping a piece of Nicorette in his mouth.

I mulled that over for a second. "What happened when you went back inside?"

"Nothing. Abby wasn't there. The apartment was one big cold spot, though, but Jenn's been complaining about the lack of heat in that place."

"You were going to tell her about the institute, weren't you?"

He smiled to himself. "And then you stopped me, kiddo. Here I thought you were a beacon of honesty but you kept me from telling the truth."

That stung a bit. I knew how far from the truth that actually was. I pushed it aside.

"It wasn't the time. She could barely handle what you said about Abby."

"You're right," he said with a sigh. He looked at the bike.

"Still want to give me a lesson?"

"What will you give me in return?" I asked.

He gave me a funny look. "What, so now I have to pay for a lesson? This was all your idea."

"Tell me what your medication is for."

He jumped a bit at that and almost sneered at me. "What are you harping on about now? I told you."

"No," I said, shaking my head and adjusting my bike handles between my hands. "You didn't. So what are your pills for, Dex? It's no big deal; I just would like to know."

He chewed slowly and raised his face up to the sky. The sunlight hit his face and created a shadowy crevice between his furrowed brows. He raised his shoulders up slowly. "Nothing to worry about. Some are for sleeping, others are just for my mood. You know, to keep me on an even keel. That's it."

My heart pinched. I grimaced in response, a look he didn't catch. "Are you sure? Maybe your medication has something to do with the fact that you see ghosts. Isn't that how they treated you in the hospital?"

"I got better."

"And yet you're seeing Abby again."

"Fine," he said quietly. He straightened up and rubbed his hands against the side of his face, pulling at his eyes and then tugging at his hair. He let out a quick burst of air through his nose and spit out his gum. "I'm jonesing for a smoke so hard, you have no idea."

I didn't say anything, just observed him calmly, feeling like he was going somewhere with all of this.

"The truth is..." he said slowly, carefully, watching me with each word that left his mouth. I stared back at him, as emotionless as possible.

"I'm not bipolar. I mean, I guess I am...a bit moody. But I don't think I'm bipolar. I just explain to my doctors what has been happening to me, my past, and they give me medication. Sometimes it's bipolar stuff. Sometimes they give me meds for schizophrenics. Because it makes things go away. Do you understand?"

I nodded. It was what I thought. It was still shocking to hear him admit it.

"I tell doctors that I see dead people. Just like that kid from *The Sixth Sense*. Whatever happened to him, anyway? Whatever. Sorry. So I tell them that. And they prescribe me antipsychotics. Because they think I'm crazy. And I let them think I am, even though I know I'm not. And sometimes the medication doesn't work. So I go to a new doctor and they give me something else. So far I've got a combination that seems to work…or at least it did."

I looked down at my feet at that, paying extra attention to the cracks in the grainy, damp sidewalk. "That doesn't seem fair, Dex."

"It's perfectly fair," he said, surprised. "I don't want to see them. That's why you're here. To see them for me."

My head jerked up at him.

"Well, it's true," he explained, fumbling for words. "I mean, it *was* true. At the beginning. That's why when I saw you in the lighthouse and you heard the things I heard and seemed to believe what was going on…I thought you could just see everything for me. You could take the brunt of everything and I could walk away, sanity intact."

I glared at him, not able to take everything in at once. Angry heat rushed to my face. "You used me?"

"No!" he cried out and grabbed my hand. "Not at all. We saw everything together…"

"You weren't…you weren't attacked by Roddy, you weren't strangled by kelp and held out of a window, almost killed, you weren't almost raped by-"

"I know! I know, Perry, I know but that was just…what happened. You were there. It could have happened to me too, it was just as likely. It wasn't about you instead of me. You…just don't understand."

"No, I obviously don't," I snarled and whipped my hand out of his.

"This is why I've been lying to you. I knew how pissed off you'd be if you found out. I was just trying to protect you."

"Oh!" I said, throwing my hands up and waving them at the sky. "Look at Dex Foray being all big and noble again, as usual. My knight in shining fucking armor!"

"Perry please," he said and grabbed at me again.

"Don't touch me," I whispered.

He did the opposite and brought me closer to him, his hand around the small of my back, raising my body into his. Though they barely registered in the moment, I could tell the passing people on the street were staring at us, worried.

"Perry," he breathed hard, his brown, fathomless eyes looking deep into mine. "You don't understand. It's not just Abby. I have a past that I can't run away from. Just as you do. I know you do. I can see it on your face, after a bad night's sleep. You're haunted in your dreams. I'm haunted in my everyday life. Now part of it has come back and I would do anything to keep her away. I'm not as strong as you are. I wish I was. I would do anything to have your strength, Perry."

Now would have been the perfect time to tell Dex that I fucked with his meds. He was bound to figure it out on his own anyway. But I couldn't bring myself to say anything. I felt like I had that rare upper hand again. It was a sick, sad thing to want but I couldn't help but grab at it. With Dex, you never knew how long it would be until the rug was pulled out from under you again. As I had just found out.

I hate you, I thought, my eyes turning narrow and bitter.

"Maybe I should go on meds too," I said while trying to get out of his grasp in such a subtle way that it wouldn't cause attention on the street.

He released his grip a bit but kept his head down and close to mine. "Do you remember in Red Fox. When I had been off the meds and I told you how...alive I felt. That I really felt something?"

I nodded, keeping my breath controlled.

"That was the truth. Because the medication does some funny things to you. When it shuts down one part of your brain, it has a ripple effect. It keeps you from seeing with all your eyes. It sucks away your creativity. It hampers your soul. It keeps you from how you really, really feel. Deep, deep inside. For once, I felt everything. And the biggest thing I felt was the way I felt about you. That was like a hammer to the heart."

I was speechless. I looked into his eyes, which were so close to mine. He was sincere. Sincere, worried, ashamed, scared and so many emotions. And I could see he was feeling something, whatever it was. Despite the damage I had done, I had freed him somehow, even if he didn't know it. Even if it came with terrible, terrible consequences.

"What are you saying?" I said softly.

"I'm saying that you're like my best friend," he said. "You are my best friend, and I could never let pills take away what makes you, you. Your heart. And your beautiful soul."

Oh. It was wonderful to hear, because I had come to think of him as my best friend, as twisted as that was. But…

And then his motherfucking phone rang. He kept my gaze for a few more moments before letting go of my waist and fishing out his phone.

I didn't know how many best friends held each other like that.

He glanced at the display and answered it, looking excited. "Hello, Dex speaking."

He smiled at me as the other person talked. It broadened and for the first time that morning, he looked truly happy.

"Thank you so much. We'll see you then."

He hung up and stuck the phone back in his pocket.

"That was Doctor Hasselback."

"I figured."

"He said we're all set to film Block C tonight," he said, clapping his hands together and wiggling his fingers. An entirely crazed look overcame his eyes, which made me think that he was at least, naturally, a bit manic when it came down to it.

I was still mad at him though. And at one glance at my face, he knew this.

"Look. I know you think I'm a pretty shitty guy after what I just told you. But you have to know that I'm constantly looking out for both of us. I care about me. And I care about you. In the end, I care about you a lot more."

Well at least he admitted it wasn't just one way.

"But I'm being honest. I really am. That's all there is. And now you know it."

I did have to commend him for actually coming clean when he didn't have to. It took a lot of guts and a dip in his pride, which I knew didn't happen too often. I could have come clean too. But I didn't.

I just nodded. "So I assume Doctor Hasselback didn't have a problem with us poking around the other night? I was a bit worried about the lights on the second floor, thinking he'd blame it on us."

I was also worried that after I showed him Dex's pills, he'd think twice about letting us in.

"No, he didn't mention it. Doesn't matter, we're in."

He raised his hand to high five me. I returned it halfheartedly. With everything that was going on, returning to the institute kinda seemed like the worst idea on earth.

He clasped my hand in his and gave it a quick shake. "I'm sorry, kiddo. I'm sorry I wasn't honest with you earlier. I really am. I hope we can just...tell the truth with each other from now on."

I gave him a tiny smile. There was nothing I wanted more, I just knew on my side it wasn't going to be too easy. Then again, Dex was here, functioning, and aside from seeing Abby, he seemed to be doing OK. He seemed...alive, as he would put it. Maybe everything would be fine.

We turned and headed back to the apartment. I let that last thought drift behind me and get caught up in a dirty breeze. Of course, things never end up being fine.

CHAPTER SIXTEEN

The rest of the day was uneventful. We passed the hours watching past seasons of *Futurama*, while Jenn slept her hangover away. Every little creak from the apartment, every blast from the monorail, or fart from Fat Rabbit had us both jumping in our seats. To say we were on edge was a bit of an understatement.

Finally, at 6 p.m. (a bit later than we left on Tuesday), we got into the Highlander and headed off toward Riverside. We were both mostly silent during the ride, too tense and overwhelmed to talk. I was scared of what we would find in the building. I knew there was some truth in what that Spook Factory chick had said about certain buildings and people being conduits to the unknown. Wherever I was, I attracted these things and it was bound to intensify in a haunted, historical place with a sordid past.

I eyed Dex occasionally as he drove, making sure he wasn't overly tired from the Valium. So far, he seemed to be making good on my mix. The placebos obviously weren't harming him, and the Valium would have just calmed him down a bit (which was never a bad thing), so all that was left was him dealing with his "visions." But as long as he knew that I could see what he saw, we would be OK.

Still, there was something he had said earlier that I kept running through my thoughts during most of the day, and certainly on the drive over through the mounting darkness and the rain that occasionally splattered our windshield. It was "It's not just Abby. I have a past that I can't run away from."

Not just Abby. What else was he haunted by?

But I couldn't dwell on that forever. I was sure, especially now that he was off the pills, it would rise on its own, during some other time.

I wasn't looking forward to that.

"You nervous, kiddo?" he asked as he pulled the car up the long, tree-lined driveway, past the cheesy Riverside logo and the flickering lamps.

"Yes," I said, letting out a low breath.

"Me too," he admitted. He pulled the car into the parking spot and turned off the car. Even though it was the same building as before (Block C was around the corner and in the woods a bit, naturally), it still looked scary and foreboding. I guess this time we knew exactly what – and who – lurked inside.

We sat in silence for about a minute, listening to the occasional gust of wind or sporadic rain.

"Having second thoughts?" I asked.

"Yes. You?"

I couldn't help but smile. "Yes."

He reached into the front pocket of his black cargo jacket and took out the packet of rolling papers. From the other pocket he took out a small bag of weed.

He started cutting up the weed with a tiny pair of scissors he brought out of yet another pocket and shot me a quick, rather sheepish, look.

"You don't approve."

"I...just don't know if now is the time to light up."

"When was the last time you smoked pot?" he asked curiously, and started to divide the smelly grains into an open piece of rolling paper. I was amazed at how well he could see in the dark.

"I don't know," I started, and thought back. After high school, maybe. After the sessions with Doctor Freedman, after I crashed the car, after my parents freaked out. After the accident. "Long time ago."

"I think this helps me. It at least makes me feel better. Maybe dulls one part of the brain while the other one lies open. My medication is obviously not doing its job anymore and I'll be damned if I'm going into this situation totally unaware."

I could understand that. "I'm not judging."

"Oh, but you get that little Perry twinkle in your eye."

I smirked at that. "I have a twinkle?"

"Oh yeah. It's gorgeous."

I felt embarrassed and looked out the window.

"No really," he said. I looked back, caught by his sincerity. He rolled the smoke up, brought it up to his mouth, and ran his wide tongue along the length of it.

My inner thighs had been that joint at one point.

"Well...as I said, I'm not judging," I told him, pushing that naughty thought out of my mind. "Lord knows I'm no angel."

"So what was your drug background, if you don't mind me asking."

I kinda did mind. I really didn't want to go dragging that back up. And I know I had explained some of it, the Cliff Notes version, to him at some point. But as he rolled down the window and lit up the joint with his gold lighter, it reminded me that I missed that part of my life. Not the drugs, but just being young and stupid. I was too afraid to be young and stupid again. At twenty three, I felt terribly immature and strangely old at the same time.

"I think I already told you."

He inhaled and blew most of it out the window and nodded. "You did. You mentioned you did coke once or twice. Pot. Booze. Pills. Sounded like the normal teenage experience to me."

Normal or not, it sounded heavy coming out of his mouth. But if he could be honest with me about his pills, I could be honest about this. And I really had nothing to hide, not from Dex anyway.

"It was a little bit worse than that."

He turned in his seat to face me, undoing his seat belt and bringing his foot up on his seat.

"What was your accident?"

"My accident," I repeated. Drugs were one thing. The accident was another.

"You always blamed whatever accident you had on the drugs. I just wanted to know what the accident was."

Did I even remember what the accident was half the time? I remembered a fire. A shimmer in the air. I think I was just really high. Jacob was there. He started the fire and I got blamed. That was it, really. But I was having this conversation in my head and not with Dex.

"Someone started a fire at a party I was at. I got blamed. I mean, for the company I kept."

I looked down at my hands, at the pale glow cast on them from the nearby lights.

Dex frowned while he inhaled and shot the smoke out of the corner of his mouth. His brow never relaxed.

"Reason I ask is that this morning, you were muttering something in your sleep. Which is why I woke you up."

I looked over at him, startled. "What was I saying?"

"You were saying something about the drugs. That it was the drugs' fault you saw…the demons."

The word demons hit me like a brick. I felt breathless. Demons? It didn't bring up any memories but it brought about the most disgusting, helpless feeling that crawled through my insides, just underneath the skin.

"What is it?" he asked.

I shook my head, not sure how to even answer that. "I don't know."

He watched me for a few beats, then nodded, satisfied. He put the joint out in the car ashtray and stuck the rest in the baggie with the weed and put it back in his pocket.

"Well, I suppose we should go in," he said, and opened the car door.

We got out into the chilled air and walked over to the building. I kept thinking about the demons. What did it mean? Had I been seeing things back then? Actually seeing things? And what, if anything, did they have to do with the accident? My brain was sluggish and slow, like memories were trapped around certain corners and it would take a lot of poking about to finally discover them. I didn't like that idea. There were some parts of my head I felt were better left undiscovered. Hidden, buried away.

We approached the front doors and were surprised to see Roundtree on the other side of them.

"Looks like Nurse Ratchett was waiting for us," Dex said out of the corner of his mouth. We waved and she opened the heavy doors with a grunt.

"You're back. I was told. I'll go get the doctor."

She turned and scuttled down the hall.

"Still think she likes you?" I asked him, poking him in the side.

He squirmed. "Yes. I'm telling you, I win over everyone, sooner or later."

He pointed his finger at me like a gun and cocked it with his thumb. "You included, kiddo."

I rolled my eyes. As silly as he could be at times, I was grateful for the playfulness dispersed among the other topics. Sometimes I wondered how things would be if it were just Dex and me on some tropical beach somewhere, free from games and ghost hunting and lies and responsibility. I actually thought about it quite often. It was kind of my happy place when the chips were down.

Soon Doctor Hasselback was coming toward us in a heavy overcoat with a fedora on his head, looking like something out of a classic film like *The Lost Weekend*. He waved the keys at us.

"I've got to let you in," he said, stepping out into the cold and nodding at Roundtree. She went back to her post, the door slamming shut behind her. Hasselback gave us a terse smile.

"Nice to see you two again," he said. "I trust that everything went well the other day."

"Yes," Dex said, smiling. "And I'm assuming everything went well on your end."

The doctor shrugged and walked off toward a path that led around the building. We followed him and his coat that billowed behind him.

"So what did you find?" he said, yelling over his shoulder at us.

"We're pretty sure we found the dead security guard who killed himself," Dex spoke up.

"Which one?"

Dex and I exchanged a look.

Hasselback continued his way past manicured gardens and hedge animals that looked straight out of *The Shining*. Everything looked extra eerie in the dark of night and the unpredictable rain that hit the ground added to the effect.

After a few minutes of walking, we came across a building nestled among tall, swaying cedar trees.

Hasselback paused a few yards back and looked up. We all did.

The building was a bit smaller than the main one, but was completely dark and unkempt. Hasselback turned around and smiled at us. It looked sinister in the shadows. That could have just been me being paranoid.

"This is it," he said, and placed the keys in Dex's hands. "Run these back to Roundtree when you're done."

He started to walk away.

"Wait, hold on," I called out, stopping the doctor. "That's it? Aren't you going to warn us about certain things? Tell us where we can go and can't go?"

The doctor smiled again. "You can go anywhere. And there's nothing to warn you about. I know you two are worried; it does look rather foreboding in the dark, but we still have our janitors clean in there once a week. They never report anything. It's empty, cleaned out, and absolutely free to explore."

I wasn't sure about that. This was the building where dangerous killers were housed for years.

He nodded at Dex. "Just bring your car around here; there's a small parking lot at the side. You can bring out your equipment, get set up, and go to it."

"You're sure? You don't want to give us a tour, maybe a small one on camera..." Dex said.

Hasselback laughed, pressing his hand against his abdomen. "You kids are not going to find anything. That's why I don't mind. Now, if you both will politely excuse me, I have to go home. Roundtree will be around if you need her, but I've got a cocktail party at the Four Seasons at eight, and I'm already running a bit behind."

He gave us a short salute and walked off into the night, his coat waving like a stiff flag.

"Well...that was..." Dex said, not finishing his sentence.

"Weird? I agree."

Dex rubbed his chin hair, making a scratchy noise that stood out against the vague and constant wind.

"I shouldn't complain though. Free rein of Block C. Let's see Spook Factory compete with that."

It didn't really matter if this was about our competition or not. It was unnerving to have access to an abandoned part of a mental hospital, even if the administrator was sure we wouldn't find anything. Actually, it was that fact that was the most unnerving of all. This was the perfect set-up for a horror movie.

I looked at Dex. He stood there gazing up at the building, hands in his pockets, his shaggy hair spiking up in the breeze.

"Are you thinking about backing out again?" I asked.

"Of course. You?"

I walked over to him and looked up. The place was scary as fuck and seemed to radiate an intense paranormal energy that I had rarely come across. D'Arcy Island, the dead heart of it, had something very similar.

I told Dex that and he agreed.

"I know, kiddo. And I don't think any amount of drugs is going to save me tonight."

My heart started beating a bit faster at that admission. I placed my hand at his back and leaned in, "It's not too late to back out."

"It kind of is," he said sadly. Then he exhaled, rolled his shoulders up and down. He pasted a cheesy grin on his face. "OK, let's do this, get it done, and get out."

It was moments like this I wish we had some theme song. I just nodded and we went back to the car, driving it down the slight winding driveway and parking at the side of Block C.

We spent the next ten minutes gathering up all of our equipment, including the EVP gadget that we hadn't even listened to yet. Sometimes I wondered if we were the absolute worst ghost hunters on earth. We were at least close.

We entered the building after trying the key several times in the old lock. The doors were just as heavy as the main building and though there was a tiny hint of Lemon Pledge in the air, it had a terribly musty and damp smell that flew out from the depths and hit me in the face.

"Pleasant," I said, coughing a bit at the dust that our movement scattered in the air.

"It's probably more pleasant now than it was back in the day," he said. The door slammed behind us, causing more particles to fly forward. It was surprisingly colder inside and I had this gross feeling of dampness that clung to my skin. Immediate clamminess. I shuddered and Dex nodded.

"Yeah. Fucking gross," he agreed, reading my expression. He flicked on a flashlight and handed it to me. Though we needed it to see, it made everything even eerier.

"Let's start on the top floor and work our way down," he said, gesturing to the nearest stairwell. I nodded. Slowly. Not wanting to at all. He handed me the EVP recorder and told me to have it running the whole time.

Then he attached a small wireless mic to my leather jacket collar, tested the sound quickly with his ear buds, and we were ready.

Of course, I had to walk first, being the host and all. It helped to have the flashlight and that Dex had the green night vision running on his camera, but it didn't make me feel any less like shitting myself.

The stairwell was cold. Ice cold. I shivered uncontrollably and jumped a bit as the door shut behind us, sealing us in this freezer.

"Now this is a cold spot," Dex muttered, aiming the camera at me. I knew he wanted me to do most of the talking.

"It's like being in a walk-in freezer," I said, trying to speak clearly for the microphone. "At least a few degrees colder in here than it is outside."

I pointed my flashlight up the stairwell and walked up, carefully, my boots sliding a bit at the strange dampness on the steps. It was gross and grimy and I had a feeling that the janitors never cleaned this place at all.

I breathed a sigh of relief when I saw the door to the third level. I opened it up and was immediately blasted by an Arctic breeze that rushed past me from behind. It was enough to knock me over slightly and cause me to let go of the door. It shut in our face.

I turned to see Dex on the step below me, trying not to blind him with the flashlight. "Did you feel that?"

"I did," he replied uneasily.

I took in a few deep breaths. "That was like...the wind was racing us up the stairs." Wind. Or a ghost.

Dex nodded, knowing what I was saying. "Time to keep going."

I swallowed and let out a sharp breath through my cold nose. I opened the door again, expecting the weird wind spirit to brush past me again. But when nothing did, I pushed it further and we both stepped out onto the top level.

"So, we'll just walk to the end and back," he said.

"Just like last time." I could handle routine.

"Just like."

I aimed the light down the long hallway. The dust here was rampant and obscured most of the light, like it was eating it alive. The thought made me shiver. It felt very wrong to be there. The dust itself was like some sort of entity, pushing us back.

"I don't like this," I said, trying to keep my voice from quivering. "I can feel something here...something that wasn't in the other building."

"Good," he said. "Keep saying what's on your mind."

Ah, Dex was already just thinking about what sounded best for the show. I wish I had the ability to shut down the fear and let my logic take over. Then again, his voice didn't sound as steady as it usually did.

I felt him take a step toward me, his presence more than comforting.

"I'll be right here. A few feet behind. You can do this."

I let out another deep breath and started slowly walking. The dust swirled and danced, creating weird shapes and clouds in the vague light. The floor was clean but greasy and stuck to the bottom of my feet.

Occasionally I would shine the light to the sides to show the rooms that were there and I could hear Dex craning the camera to follow. The doors were all closed like the other building but there was one major, and spooky, difference. Each door here had several deadbolts on it as well as a little window slot that you slid open from the outside. Just like you'd see in prison. In solitary confinement. I wondered if the insides were padded cells but I didn't want to open the slot to find out. I had a feeling if I pointed it out, Dex would ask me to do it.

We were near the end of the hall when I heard something. I stopped and froze and Dex stopped with me. I listened hard, trying to quiet my breath.

A giggle.

The sound grasped my chest.

The giggle again. From right in front of me.

Then a pause. Silence, and after a beat or two, the quiet noise of our breath coming out slowly. The camera motor whirred.

The giggle appeared again, now from the other end of the hall.

"Are you recording this?" Dex whispered, meaning the EVP.

"Uh huh." We both kept still. The giggle floated in and out. It sounded a lot like the one I had heard in the bathroom, the one belonging to Abby, but I couldn't be sure. Did it matter in the end? I thought in this case, it might.

There was a bit more of a pause. Enough for me to straighten up and exhale loudly, not caring if it rattled the mic. I was feeling faint and dizzy and getting water seemed to be the most important thing.

"I think I need some-" I started to say but was cut off by a howling, deafening peal of laughter that came from the dark end of the hall and rushed toward us until it was coming from every direction, surrounding Dex and me. It was like we were trapped inside a cell of noise.

I waved my flashlight around wildly, trying to pinpoint something, anything, but there was nothing. Just Dex, looking more scared than usual, and the dust that was swallowing us.

"Are you getting anything?" I yelled above the laughter. It penetrated my ears and agitated the insides of my head.

He shook his head and fiddled with the camera.

And then as abruptly as it began, the laughter stopped. The silence sounded strange.

"Holy shit," I breathed out.

Dex didn't say anything, just continued to flip through his settings. I was about to ask him what he was doing when...

RATTLE.

At the end of the hall, a clanking, rattling sound, like someone was sliding a chain lock across. It was loud, metallic, echoing ominously in the depths.

Then it stopped and was followed by the slow CREAK of a door opening. Someone was coming out of one of the cells.

Once again, I felt nothing but fear and total, paralyzing terror. Self-defense wouldn't make a lick of difference. I wanted to run, run away now. And fast.

I turned around to do so but Dex actually took a step toward the sound. I flashed the light on him.

"What are you doing?" I cried. "Let's go!"

"Put that light away!" he hissed.

I couldn't believe that after all he feared, he was walking toward the sound. And he thought I was the brave one.

He walked slowly down the hallway, eyes on the camera screen, which I could now see was in infrared mode.

I felt torn. I wanted to run but I didn't want to leave him. I sighed, gathered up what little rope of courage I had, and followed him.

I looked at the screen. It showed way more of the hallway than my flashlight did. The infrared technology was adept at cutting through the atmospheric disturbances. It was grainy but you could still see most of the hall and the doors. They all looked closed, thank God.

Dex stopped walking and I did too. I was behind him now and felt the unknown nipping at my back. I put my hand to his waist and held it there, hoping it would bring relief to both of us.

I wanted to whisper in his ear that we should go but I couldn't bring myself to talk. Something was showing up on the infrared.

At the very top of the screen, two faint yellow marks appeared. Two more appeared a bit below it. And two more below that. They were footprints. The outline of heels and toes.

Bare footprints.

Coming toward us.

I looked forward and was about to shine the light on whatever it was but Dex sensed this, held out his arm and pushed me behind him. We were both too afraid to speak but I knew what he was thinking. Either the direct light would scare whatever it was away.

Or it would show us what it was.

The footsteps continued and then stopped about a yard away. A strange, thick hush of air and silence enveloped us. It felt like my ears needed to pop. We both waited, crushed by the atmospheric pressure, disoriented and eyeing the screen for the footsteps to continue.

A cold, pointy finger touched the back of my neck and trailed down my spine.

I screamed. So loud.

I jumped on spot, away from the wayward hand and leaped forward into Dex.

He instinctively put his arms around me, camera in hand and all, and I buried myself into him as much as I could, trying to control my screams and the urge to vomit.

"What happened?" he cried out. I couldn't answer. I couldn't find my breath. "OK, come on."

He took me under his arm and toward the door to the stairwell, putting me inside and shutting us in. It was ice cold again. He walked us into the corner of the landing, just beside the door and held me for a few minutes while I tried my hardest to gain some control of my lungs and my heart.

"Something just touched me," I mumbled into him. "Ran its finger down my spine. From my neck to my lower back."

Dex sighed loudly. He didn't say anything and neither did I. This went on for a very long minute. I just kept myself huddled into his body, afraid for my life.

Finally he said, "You know what. There's no reason I can't do this episode by myself. You don't need to be on camera for this. I think you should call it a day."

I pulled back and looked up at him. I could barely see his outline in the dark hallway, the only light from the camera and flashlight.

"You want me to leave?"

"Yeah," he said softly. "I don't like this. Don't like how vulnerable you are. I'll walk you out. Leave you with Ratchett. Or in the car. Then I'll finish up and –

"No, Dex," I told him. "Forget it. I'm not leaving you here with...her. And I am definitely not hanging out with Roundtree or in the car by myself."

"But-"

"I said no. That's not how this works and you know it. Either we do this together or we leave together. There is either us...or nothing at all."

I was actually quite surprised I said that. But it was true. We were no good on our own. Only together did things make any sense.

He took one of his hands away from my side and slowly, deliberately scratched his chin. The sound of the hairs bristled in the space. I could tell he was licking his lips, maybe chewing on them. Thinking it all over.

Then he placed his hand on my face. It was gentle but the touch startled me in the dark. He rubbed his thumb lightly on my cheekbone. Back and forth, smoothly. Softly. He moved back in, closer to me, so my chest was against his chest. His arm around my back tightened, squeezing me. I sensed his face coming closer.

I was out of breath again.

CHAPTER SEVENTEEN

"Perry," he murmured, his voice coming out low, rough and vibrant in the echoes of the dark stairwell. It was delicious and dark, burrowing pleasantly in my ear, making me shiver again. I couldn't quite tell where his face was but I knew it was somewhere close. Very close. Like if I leaned in one inch more, my lips would meet his lips. That kind of close.

It was unbearable.

The thumb on my cheekbone slowed down in its gentle caress. The tension between us began to spark and stiffen, like whatever was keeping us apart was going to finally bring us together.

"Perry," he said again, slowly, smoothly. He was so close. One inch. Just one inch. "I don't think you have any idea about the way I-"

SLAM!

A door below us slammed shut, causing a billow of cold air to come rising up in between the stairs. We both jumped and pulled back.

Great fucking timing!

Dex kept his arm around me and his warm hand at my face but turned his head and yelled, "Hello? Doctor Hasselback?"

We listened hard but couldn't hear anything. I could hear my heart whooshing loudly though. More from the way it had seemed like Dex was about to kiss me than from whoever just came into or left the stairwell. The way you what, Dex!?

The moment was gone, though. Dex let go of me completely and then shone the flashlight down the middle of the stairwell.

"See anything?" I asked, my voiced coming out all squeaky like a pubescent boy.

"No," he said, drawing the word out. "But I think we should still check it out."

I let out the air I had been holding inside me for the last few minutes. It floated away in the frigid air.

He turned around and placed one hand on my shoulder and said, "I'm serious about taking you out of here."

I put my hand on top of his hand and gave it a squeeze. So we were just going to forget about what just almost happened. What else was new? Back to the damn ghosts.

"I know. I'm staying. Staying until we both go."

He didn't say anything for a few beats and began to move toward me again. My heart held still.

But then he hesitated, took my hand into his and led me to the stairs. He gave me the flashlight and told me to light our way.

We both made our way down carefully until we were at the second level. The door here was shut like it was before.

"Time to try floor number two. Same deal. OK, kiddo?"

I let out a small sound that sounded like a "yes" and we stepped into the next hallway.

This hallway was exactly like the one above. The same locked rooms. The same dust in the air. At least now I didn't have to be a host in any way. Dex filmed with one arm, while he kept his other arm around me, holding me snuggly into his side the whole time. I was grateful for his protectiveness even though every other second I was worried some creature was going to touch me from behind.

Everything went more or less smoothly (considering the circumstances) until he stopped in front of one of the doors to a patient's room. It was hard to tell from the light my flashlight was splashing on it, but it looked to be a different color from the other doors. A green instead of a white. The bolts also looked shiny and new. And the little slot window that you slid across? Well, that was open half an inch. You couldn't see anything but…

"What do you think?" he asked me. He wanted to know if we should open the slot.

"I don't think so," I said softly, my voice barely registering.

"You don't have to open it. I will. Just film me." He took his arm off me and placed the camera in my free hand. I took it clumsily and tried to aim it in his direction. It was hard. I was shaking so much from the fear. I knew he was going to do this no matter what I said.

He stepped up to the door and first tried the deadbolt. It was locked from the inside like the others. Strange, when you thought about it, but I was relieved we wouldn't have to be exploring a padded cell in the dark.

I kept the camera on his face, on close-up, as he looked at the slot inquisitively. Even through the grainy green light of night vision, he looked great on camera, better than I did. I wanted to think about that instead of what he was about to do.

"Give me the flashlight," he said, with his hand extended. I placed it in it.

He raised it up to the slot, put his fingers on the small knob and slowly slid the window across.

I waited with bated breath for something to come jumping out, like a hand or something, but nothing happened.

We waited a few moments. Dex eyed the camera and gave it a little wink. Then he leaned in closer to the slot and aimed the flashlight in there to get a better look inside.

I kept the camera on him, the focus coming in and out, trying to catch him, but took my eyes away from it and watched in real life. I leaned forward for a better view. Part of me wanted to see what was inside, no matter how scared I was.

We both huddled around the slot as Dex illuminated a dark corner of the room.

We couldn't see too much, but what we could see was in fact a padded cell. The walls looked like a fresh, clean mattress under the concentrated light. It faded and fuzzed out into a heavy mask of blackness on the sides where the light wouldn't reach.

We exchanged a look and I leaned in even closer. This was as creepy as anything. A pristine-looking padded cell. He nodded, understanding what I was thinking. Then he shone the light over to the other corner of the room.

A small, bald man was standing there. Still as death. His back to us. Staring at the wall.

I felt an immense flow of evil seep out of the window and take hold of my body in a paralyzing grip. I couldn't look away. Couldn't look at Dex or check if I was aiming the camera correctly. I was stuck, my eyes locked onto this man in the straightjacket in the murky depths of the locked padded cell.

The man turned, slowly, to look at us. His face was one of the most disturbing things I have ever seen. It burned itself in my memory. He had only a wide, black mouth filled with bloody, wet teeth. No eyes and no nose. Essentially...no face.

Then the spell was over.

The man moved so fast toward us that he almost disappeared, until his gleaming, gaping mouth appeared at the slot, snapping and yelping horribly in our faces.

Dex and I both screamed in unison and turned to run for our fucking lives. Dex held me up as I almost went down; I dropped the flashlight but couldn't care. We booked it down the hallway, moving as fast as humanly possible, our screams still emanating from our lungs, following us as we went.

We piled into the stairwell and ran down the steps two at a time, running and jumping until the stairs stopped and we slammed into a door.

Dex quickly flung it open and we burst inside a large, dark space, both collapsing onto a concrete floor. It scraped up my knees but I didn't care. I rolled onto my back, whimpering, unable to think, to breathe, to talk. The terror was taking hold of me and bringing tears to my eyes. I kept seeing the faceless face of the man in the cell, those bloodied, slightly pointed teeth. The smoothness where the eyes and nose should have been.

"Perry?" I heard Dex spit out. I opened my eyes and looked up at the ceiling. It was dim in here, wherever we were, but my eyes were quickly adjusting to some type of light. Natural light.

Dex laid his hand on my stomach causing me to jump.

"Sorry," he said between gasps. "I didn't know where you were."

I grabbed hold of his hand and held it. Held it so tight that it must have hurt him, at least a little bit.

He grunted and I felt him adjust himself beside me.

"Can you sit up?" he asked.

I did so, feeling lightheaded from the lack of oxygen. I looked around me, slowly and carefully. We were thankfully not in a padded cell but what looked to be the basement. We had overshot the whole first floor entirely and ran all the way to the very bottom.

I turned my head and looked at the source of the light. The basement was huge, taking up almost the entire square footage of the building. There was a line of four rectangular windows placed very high up against the ceiling. They looked out onto the parking lot and the light that was being filtered in was coming from the lampposts outside the building. A twinge of comfort came from the fact that we could see the Highlander parked just a few feet away. Our way out of here.

I sat up straighter and moved myself backward toward Dex. He was sitting beside me, knees up, breathing heavily and staring at the ground. When he noticed my eyes on him, he looked up. I was happy I could read his face. I wasn't happy to see he looked just as terrified as I must have.

"What..." I said slowly. But it's all I could say.

"The...fuck? I thought we were going to die," he admitted, his voice quiet and slightly amazed. "I thought...that was it."

"Who was that... *what* was that?"

"I don't think we want to know."

I shivered. I thought about that man/teeth thing opening the door and chasing us down into the basement. He would just need to open the door and we would most likely be trapped in here.

"Did you get it on the camera?" he asked, looking over at it beside me.

"Honestly, Dex, if you think I'm going to turn it on and look over the footage right now, you've got another thing coming."

He smiled quickly and eased himself to his feet. He stretched up and looked around him. "Well ain't this nice. Creepiest basement ever."

I got up beside him and took a proper scan of the place. It was creepy. Not as creepy as what was upstairs but it was in the running. Boilers here and there, pipes, weird shapes and shadows, the occasional chains hanging from the ceiling (nice added touch) plus a lot of other weird crap and storage boxes.

"How about we take a quick look around here and call it a night?"

I turned to look at him and raised my brow. Was he serious? After everything that just happened?

He shrugged and held his hand out for the camera. Of course he was serious.

I sighed and placed the camera in his hands. He took the EVP out of his pocket and gave it to me. "I guess you dropped the flashlight."

"Do you want me to go upstairs and get it?" I asked angrily.

He stepped toward me and said, "Perry, you are not going anywhere. We are filming this. Two minutes. And then we are gone. Into that car." He pointed out the window to the Highlander.

"What happens after two minutes?"

"In two minutes my heart rate will have slowed enough that I'll be able to think clearly. And I do not want to be here when my brain starts going over exactly what we saw upstairs. I couldn't handle it. Not here. Not now."

I agreed with him. The image of the man, the fright it gave us, the unknown of where he could be, what he was...it all kept trying to enter my mind every other second and I was so far doing an adequate job of keeping it all at bay. If Dex was going to lose it in two minutes, I was probably close as well.

"OK then," I said and together we walked, carefully and side by side, down the length of the basement. It was cold but not as cold as the stairwell. And aside from a dripping noise that I could have sworn was blood dripping off of Abby (it was a leaky pipe), there was nothing too ghoulish or terrifying. Not that there needed to be. We were both so on the edge that we were literally attached at the hip and jumping at every little creak that the building made.

We got to the very end of the floor area and poked our heads around a slight corner. Through the night vision on the camera we saw a bunch of boxes that were filled with straightjackets. How lovely.

"Want to try one on?" Dex joked, picking one out of the box and holding it like it was poisoned. I pinched his side hard, hard enough that he dropped it onto the box with a thump.

"That's not funny," I hissed. "Don't touch anything."

It boggled my mind how he was able to still make jokes after what happened upstairs and the whole history of him being in a mental institute. But I guess a lot of him was always a defense mechanism. He was tricking himself into thinking none of this was a big deal.

A strange scratching noise from the side of the boxes brought me out of my thoughts. Once again I wanted to run but Dex just moved the camera over and searched for the cause of the noise.

In the corner, between a box and the moldy, concrete wall there was a frenzied movement on the ground. It was a bunch of bugs, spiders or ants or I don't know what, and they were scurrying angrily over a small mound of something. Something dead.

"Oh God," I said, putting my hand to my mouth, feeling sick at the sight and terrified of the feeding insects.

Dex leaned down closer, trying to get a better look.

"It must be a dead rat or something," he said, adjusting the camera settings. "These things are going fucking-"

It jumped. The mound of writhing, consuming bugs suddenly flinched, moving closer to us. We both let out a small shriek and jumped backward. It stopped moving, but the fact that it moved to begin with was enough.

"OK, Dex, that's the sign we get the fuck out of here. Before the zombie rats come after us with bugs on their backs."

He nodded quickly, his eyes wide and round, freaked again.

We stepped away from the "dead" rat and walked back around the corner.

At that moment the entire basement was alight with an artificial, cutting glow that came searing through the small basement windows. Headlights were pulling into the driveway outside. A sedan parked a few spots down from the Highlander, closer to the main door.

"What the hell?" I said out loud, but Dex was already running toward the window, trying to see out. It was too tall for him, even after a few leaps, so he waved me over.

"Come on, quickly," he whispered urgently.

I went to his side as fast as I could, only bumping into one pipe on the way. Once I was underneath the windows he put his hands around my waist. They felt so firm around me.

"I'm going to lift you up, tell me what you see."

I wanted to protest at this arrangement since I was not exactly a lightweight but I knew he wouldn't have any of it and I also knew he was freakishly strong for his size.

I relaxed and he propped me up. He swayed slightly and grunted at the effort while moving one hand down to get better leverage on my ass but managed to keep me upright. I grabbed the edge of the window to keep some of the load off of him and peered through it.

I couldn't believe what I was seeing.

"It's Spook Factory," I cried out as I watched the unmistakable form of Annie and G.J. disappear into our building, while the rest of the crew exited the car and followed them, extravagant gear in hand. A faint sound of doors closing reached down into our murky basement.

"Are you shitting me!?" Dex exclaimed.

"No, they went inside. Put me down."

He lowered me awkwardly and we looked at each other, unsure of what to do.

"Really?" he asked again. I nodded vigorously and held up my finger to shush him. We listened. The front doors from above us made another sound, probably Little Joe and Waldo coming inside after them.

"Those fuckers!" Dex growled, and he took off toward the basement door like a shot.

"Dex!" I yelled and scampered after him, nearly clotheslining myself on more wayward plumbing. If he got his hands on them, he was going to rip them to shreds. And though I was sure Dex could hold his own, G.J. did give up a career in Mixed Martial Arts, after all.

But Dex was stopped at the basement door. It wouldn't open no matter how many times he yanked and twisted the handle. We were locked in. I suddenly wished I had brought my bobby pin and tweezers like I did the other day.

We started pounding on the door and yelling for help, hoping they would hear us. At this point we didn't have a choice.

After a few minutes, we saw a light appear in the stairwell outside the door window, and G.J.'s stupid smug face appeared on the other side. It was too bad the glass was seven layers thick and layered with wire, otherwise I was pretty sure Dex would have punched right through it and grabbed the douchebag's face. He looked angry enough to do it.

"Hey!" Dex yelled, pounding on the window. "The door's locked. Let us out!"

G.J. laughed, the sound dim through the door. Then he shook his head. "This is just perfect. Why would I let you out?"

"G.J?" Annie's muffled but still annoying voice came from the top of the stairs, and she joined him at the door window, peering at us through the glass.

"What are you doing?" she asked.

"We're locked in here and your fuckfaced partner won't let us out," I said, hoping that Annie was the reasonable one.

Annie and G.J. exchanged a look and smiled at each other. Annie fixed her attention back on me and crossed her arms.

"You know, it's not very nice to have a monopoly on everything ghostly in Seattle."

"What?" Dex sneered. "We don't have a monopoly. This is the first fucking thing we've shot in this city."

"Yeah, it's not very nice. All bragging about this institute the other day," G.J. said. "You shouldn't have said anything at all but you couldn't help it."

"And now we've got your scoop," she added.

"Did you follow us here?" I asked incredulously.

She shrugged in such a casual way that I was afraid I was going to try blasting a hole through the window.

"We might have. Doesn't matter though. We would have shared this place with you but since you're being difficult and you seem to be stuck, well, perhaps not."

"The doctor, Doctor Hasselback, he'll find out," Dex said through gritted teeth.

"Oh, of course he will. He'll see it when it airs tomorrow. Yeah, tomorrow. We work fast. But he doesn't know us and if anyone is going to get in deep shit, it's you. For telling other shows where you are filming. Maybe even inviting us? How else would you explain all the footage we are going to get, uninterrupted."

"You bitch," I scowled.

"Whatever. This is the big leagues now," she said, and turned around, heading back up the stairs.

I pounded on the window again and yelled, "You can't leave us in here! We are seriously locked in! This is…this is…"

"Unfair?" G.J. filled in. "Maybe for you. Not for us. All is fair in television. Oh wait, I forgot you two are on the internet. Good luck with that."

And then he turned and headed up the stairs as well, taking the light with him.

Dex and I took to bellowing and hitting the door again to no avail. The last thing we heard before the fuckface disappeared into the darkness was, "Keep on screaming. It'll add to the atmosphere."

I pounded even harder, flinging my fists hard into the glass like a kid throwing a cartoon tantrum on the ground. My wrists were growing numb, the fleshy side of my fists felt bruised but I couldn't stop. It was all the fear, all the adrenaline coming out, and the door was taking the brunt of it.

Finally Dex stopped pounding himself and he grabbed both my arms, holding me still. "Come on, stop that."

"Dex," I said breathlessly. "We're locked in here. They're going to steal our show…they…"

"I know," he said gruffly. "But they aren't letting us out. I should have known we weren't done with them."

He exhaled long and hard and walked over to the middle of the room where the most light from the windows was. He eyed a clear spot on the ground and sat down with a groan, leaning against the wall. He patted the ground next to him.

My shoulders slumped. I felt so defeated. From everything we had just gone through, nearly being scared to death, finding untold horrors upstairs, and now we were just giving up while some other team was going to get all the credit for it.

"Sit," he said, more sternly this time.

I did so, sitting beside him, shoulder to shoulder and leaned back against the cold wall, which luckily wasn't as gross as it was near the boxes and the zombie rat.

I looked up at the windows to the outside. So close but so far. "What if we try to break out through there." I pointed at them. "I might be able to squeeze through, if my boobs let me."

"It's not so much your boobs but your ass that won't let you."

I shot him a terrible glare. "Thanks, asshole."

He rolled his eyes. "I'm not saying that's a bad thing. That's a small window. I don't even think your head could fit through it and besides, that glass is unbreakable."

"Are you sure?"

"Do you want to waste your time trying to hurtle things through it?"

"Kind of. Do you have a better idea?"

He didn't answer me but he brought out his phone. I frowned at it, his brows almost touching. "Oh, of fucking course. That's just great."

I peered over at it. "No service?"

He shook his head. "What about you?"

I pulled my phone out. There was half a bar, which was something, but the batteries were almost dead. I hadn't charged it in a couple of days. Aside from texting my family, there was no real need to use it.

I gave it to him and he dialed on the keypad.

"Phoning Jenn?" I asked, trying not to sound funny about it. She was our lifeline now, like it or lump it.

He nodded, holding the phone to his ear. "She should be at home."

Or she might be humping Bradley, I thought viciously.

"Won't she be mad about having to come all the way out here to rescue us?"

"Oh yes," he said with a fake smile. "There will be hell to pay later. But I'll pay it."

He let it ring a few times and then left a voicemail telling her to call us back and that it was an emergency.

He gave me back my phone. We both leaned against the wall again and sighed in unison.

"Well, this really sucks," I said, trying to make some sort of small talk so I didn't have to really think about the situation we were in. "At least we've got some footage."

He reached into his pocket and stuck some gum in his mouth. He chewed it a few times, the smacking noise reverberating in the room.

"What good is the footage," he said, "if they are running their episode tomorrow?"

"Well…"

He leaned his head back against the wall with a thump that made me wince. In the dimness I could make out the waves of frustration and anger swarming his eyes and brow.

"I should have worked more on the stuff we had. I should have…uploaded the EVP, at least listened to it. I should have done the score, I should edited what we had, I should have at least uploaded the interview with the doctor and-"

"Dex," I interrupted him, laying my hand on his knee. "It's been a distracting week. You didn't have time to do any of that. It's my fault. I'm the one in your office, messing up your routine."

He rolled his head to the side to look at me. "I invited you."

"Not really. Jenn invited me," I pointed out. "You were smart. You wanted me to stay in the hotel."

He stopped chewing for a few moments, keeping his eyes on me. From the angle, I couldn't see them properly. They looked like mysterious, fathomless holes, which wasn't much different from how they looked half the time anyway.

"I'm glad you're with me. Messing up my routine," he admitted. "I don't know what I'd do without you."

The way he said it, the gentle sincerity in the words, tickled little pleasure spots inside my skull but I couldn't let myself dwell on it.

"You probably wouldn't have to contend with your ex-girlfriend haunting your place." I gave his knee a little rub.

He moved his head over, his attention now on my hand.

I should probably stop rubbing him like this, I thought. But I didn't listen.

"What are we going to do if this is the end of us?" he asked in a small, tired voice, watching my hand curiously.

I stopped massaging him. "What do you mean?"

"If people like those fucks are going to beat us at our own game. What chance do we have?"

"That is not a very Dex-like thing to say," I muttered, feeling strangely upset at his admission.

"I know. But I'm serious."

I sighed and took my hand back, crossing my arms. I didn't want to think about life without Dex, without the series. It meant so much more to me than I'd even admit to myself. "I don't know. I guess I'd have to get a proper job."

"You wouldn't want to do anything with me?" he asked, sounding surprised.

"What? Of course I would. But what?"

"We could have our own music show," he mused. "Act really pretentious and talk about bands that nobody likes."

I smiled at that. "Yes, we certainly could. Though we wouldn't have to act pretentious...just be ourselves."

"Or," he said with a higher tone of voice, "we could form a band!"

This time my smile broke wide open. "You want to start a band?"

He looked at me. It was hard to tell if he was joking. His features were stern but his eyes twinkled like shiny coffee beans. "Only if you'll be in the band with me."

"My guitar skills are pretty sucky," I confessed.

"I know. You'd be the singer."

"Me?" I exclaimed. Dex was the one with the voice. "I can't sing."

"I bet you can."

"Well I guess I can do a wicked Chris Cornell impression," I conceded.

"Oh really? Let's hear it."

I shook my head. "Maybe one day, if you're lucky."

"Tease," he said.

I ignored that. "So if I'm the singer, what are you?"

"Drummer."

"Let me guess...you can play the drums too."

"I can play everything, kiddo," he stated. Somehow it didn't come across as boasting when it came out of his mouth. It was just fact and I believed it. "Actually, I always wanted to be a drummer. Played in high school. I mean, I tried to. A friend of mine had a set so I learned on that. Of course we had no money after my dad left, so having my own set was out of the question. But yeah, that was my goal. It just never worked out that way. Even when I joined Sing Sin I tried it out but...something about my rhythm being off. This was before mathcore got huge, mind you."

"I don't see mathcore drumming and a lounge act band really melding together."

"See, that's where people go wrong with their thinking. If there are things you don't think will mesh, you should at least try to see if they do. You might end up with something...life-altering."

"Or something you regret," I said, thinking of Jenn.

"True," he said with a sigh. I guess he knew what I was hinting at because he motioned for my phone again. I handed it to him and he dialed her number. Once again, it rang and rang and went straight to voicemail. He left another message, this one more demanding and explained our situation in full.

It was strange that she wasn't picking up, but I didn't know her habits and didn't want to say anything about them.

"Looks like we're just going to have to wait this one out," he said, putting the phone down between his legs.

"You could try calling Dean...or 911?"

"I'd rather keep the attention as minimal as possible," he said.

Hmmpf. He and his stupid pride again. He looked at me and raised his arm hopefully. "Want to try to sleep?"

"Here? Now?" I asked. Like hell I'd fall asleep with ghosts, goblins and G.J. flouncing around upstairs.

He shrugged and his arm started to lower. But I couldn't pass that up. I moved in as close as I could and placed his arm around my shoulder and snuggled in close. I breathed in the faint smell of cigarettes, minty gum and aftershave, a combination that was all Dex and as equally alluring. I placed my hand on his chest, feeling his heart beat beneath his jacket. The rhythm soothed me and despite the odds, I quickly fell asleep.

CHAPTER EIGHTEEN

I awoke with a start. A giant, blinding flash of light ripped beneath my eyelids and prompted me awake.

I sat up quickly, still in Dex's arms. The sedan's headlights from outside the basement windows were on and flooding the room.

"Oh fuck," Dex murmured, flinching awake and leaning forward, still keeping his arm around me. We watched as the Spook Factory's car backed out of the parking spot and roared away into the night, leaving us in the dark, dank basement once again.

"Guess they got what they wanted," I said groggily. "What time is it?"

Dex picked up the phone. It was 1 p.m. My phone had died, thankfully, but now the reception was suddenly non-existent.

"I can't believe it...were you sleeping?" I asked him.

He nodded and a yawn shortly followed. "I guess so. Wow, we must have been out for at least three hours."

"Jenn didn't call back."

He let out a short snort of air through his nose. It reminded me of an impatient horse I used to ride when I was young. "Well, she might have now that the phone's out of service."

"Dex..." I started, unsure of what I was going to say and how I was going to say it.

He shook his head. "I don't want to hear it."

He took his arm off me and sort of huddled himself against the wall.

I stared at him, unable to let it go. "Don't want to hear what?"

"I know what you're going to say."

"What am I going to say?" I would much rather he said it.

His hand flew up to his head and he tugged a bit at the ends of his hair. His left leg started to shake a bit.

"Dex..." I tried again. "Don't you think it's strange that we've been sitting here, in the basement of a haunted mental hospital for a few hours. And your girlfriend hasn't come to get us yet?"

"I don't want to get into it now."

I inched back from him and grabbed his wrist, taking his hand away from his hair. I leaned in so he could see my face. He was avoiding my eyes but I could see them just the same. They were panicked, glossy and all over the place.

"This, of all times, is probably the best time to get into it," I said. "There's no one here. At least, no one alive."

He didn't say anything to that. So I decided to step up to the plate.

"Do you think Jenn is having an affair?" I asked point blank.

He closed his eyes. He didn't look exactly pained, more that he was searching for which route to take. Let it all come out? Get defensive? Play ignorant? I sat back a bit and patiently waited for the story to come, whatever version it was going to be.

He opened his eyes and they slowly slid over to meet mine. "What makes you say that?"

His voice was blank, unreadable.

"Well..." I looked down at the phone. I picked it up and flipped it over in my hands nervously. "I just think...look, Rebecca, at lunch, told me she had a theory about Jenn and Bradley. And she wouldn't say what it was but then when we were at the club the other night..."

"Yes?" And now a tiny bit of panic came through his voice. He bit his lip.

"Well. The reason I left is because Bradley showed up and then they went off on their own and..."

I looked back at him. His eyes widened. "And?"

"I don't know. But they went upstairs; he said he had friends she had to meet or something, and I guess it might be nothing, but when they went upstairs, I saw him slip his arm around her waist and it...looked a bit too...natural. If you know what I mean."

He kept staring at me wide-eyed. His brows were raised creating a ledge of lines between them and his hairline.

"So the reason you left the club was because Jenn basically ditched you to hang out with Bradley?"

"Pretty much."

"Perry. Why did you lie to me? Why didn't you tell me?" He asked this so sincerely, his tone so soft and vulnerable that I started to feel a pinch of guilt at my heart for not being honest about it.

"Because," I stammered. "She's your girlfriend. I was afraid...that you'd think I made it up. That you wouldn't believe me."

"I always believe you," he said, sharply with a look that matched. That wasn't exactly true but I ignored it.

"OK," I said. "But honestly, what do I know? Maybe this was normal."

"You were protecting her. Why the hell would you do that?"

I shrugged. I guess I kind of was. "Maybe I wanted to give her the benefit of the doubt. Sometimes, she really is quite nice to me and I feel sorry for her in some ways. I know you guys are together and if anything was going to mess that up, I didn't want it to fall on my shoulders."

He looked away. I watched him chew on his lip till I was pretty sure he was going to draw blood.

"And I still know nothing," I added. "I mean, forget I said anything. So she's friends with Bradley. She was friends with you before..."

I trailed off. He gave me a wry look.

I looked away and sighed. "Oh man...seriously. Ignore me."

"It's too late for that. So you think Bradley and Jenn are boning?"

"No," I lied. "I just...you know what, I'm wrong. Wrong idea. Jenn's not like that, I'm sorry."

"You think Jenn's not like that?" he asked. He said it in such a way that I had to glance at him. He looked like he was on the verge of laughing but there was real conflict behind his eyes. Pain, almost, like some brutal battle was going on inside. But the pain...it wasn't related to Jenn. I knew that much.

"I'd like to think she's a pretty decent girl," I said. Truthfully, too.

A smirked tugged at his lips. "You know all those Anonymous comments you've been getting..."

My heart crackled in mid-thump. The air went out of me. I couldn't find the words to follow up. I knew where this was going and it throttled me.

He continued, "It was Jenn. She's been leaving them this whole time."

I was stunned. Floored. I could only blink hard, as if that would help me process what he had just told me: The truth.

He clamped his mouth shut, perhaps a bit afraid of my reaction. I couldn't blame him. I wasn't sure what to get angry over first. And angry was putting it lightly. I wanted to explode.

I got to my feet quickly and walked down the length of the basement, not feeling the boxes and crates that I bumped into in the dim light. I sucked in my breath and let it out in a vigorous fashion, needing to keep my emotions in check.

"Are you sure? How do you know that?" I eked out, trying hard to keep my voice low and calm. I faced the wall, not wanting to look at him.

I heard him get up and take a few steps forward, his footsteps echoing coldly. He stopped some feet behind me. I could feel the hesitation rolling off of him. He was unsure whether to come forward. I waited for him to explain himself.

"Well?" I repeated, louder now.

"I caught her," he mumbled. It made my blood boil beneath my cheeks. "Not in the act, but afterward. On the computer. I accidently hit the back button on the browser and it took me to one of her comments."

"How long ago was this?"

"Since the beginning," he answered, quiet and worried. "Maybe the second asinine comment you got. Then I checked into the IP addresses and they were all coming from my computer. I haven't told her about it, yet."

Holy shit. I closed my eyes and balled my hands up into tight little fists. There was so much wrong with all of this. I was furious toward Jenn, feeling like I had been duped by her stupid veneers and false sincerity, and I was even more furious that Dex knew all this time. All those times I was pouring my heart over the comments, about the way they made me feel. He knew and he didn't tell me. No wonder he was so mad about them.

"Why the hell didn't you tell me?" I tried to keep my voice at the same controlled level, but I failed. The last word croaked and rose above the rest.

I heard him come closer. He hovered behind me. He put his hand on my shoulder.

I whipped around at his touch and shrank back from him. "Don't you fucking touch me!"

He didn't listen. He reached out and grabbed my wrists, forcing my palms to uncurl. My fingernails had cut into my skin and stung at the open air.

He held me, his shadowy face looking tormented where the pale streetlights hit it.

"I'm sorry," he said.

"Let go of me!" I yelled. I wasn't afraid of him, I just didn't want him anywhere near me. I'd give him another broken nose, if that's what it took.

"Fine, punch me!" he yelled back, knowing my thoughts. "But you have to listen to me first!"

"You're a fucking liar!"

His grip tightened on my wrists. Not painful, but very firm. I could feel his arms shaking from the strain. He pulled me closer to him and I went, feeling that struggling would be useless.

"Put yourself in my shoes, Perry, please," he pleaded. The torment on his face turned into something short of desperation. "She's my girlfriend. You're my partner. What was I supposed to do? Who was I supposed to protect?"

Me, I thought. *You were supposed to protect me.*

I closed my eyes, feeling stupid. Of course he was right. He had to choose one of us. It would be her. Why on earth would it ever be me?

His grasp on me loosened, perhaps at seeing my face in all its downtrodden glory. I took the opportunity to wrangle myself away from him and walked off toward the corner where the straightjackets and the zombie rat were. I preferred both of those hideous things to him.

"Baby..." he called out after me.

"Don't you fucking call me that," I shrieked, leaning against a cold pipe, staring absently at the dark shadows in the corner. "You don't get to. Not after what you just said."

"Why is this bothering you?" he asked. I felt him closer again. Was he just going to slowly follow me all over the basement? Like a mosquito that wouldn't go away, no matter how many times you swatted at it?

I chuckled viciously. "Heaven forbid this should bother me."

"Did you want me to tell you?" he asked quietly.

"What the hell do you think?"

"Did you think I owed it to you?"

His questions were strange. I didn't know what he was getting at.

"I guess," I admitted with a sigh. "I would have told you."

"Why?"

"Because," I turned around slowly to look at him. I could barely see him here, I could only make out his faint outline, which was tall and tense. "You're…"

I couldn't finish the sentence. I didn't know how.

I swallowed hard and looked at the ground, trying to see the white rubber outline of my shoes in the dark.

"Perry," he said carefully. His tone made me look up.

"What?"

He hesitated. The air between was heavy, laden with anticipation.

"Are you in love with me?"

My eyes widened until it felt like they might fall out.

"Excuse me?" I managed to say.

He walked up to me but his face still remained hidden in the shadows.

"Do you love me?"

Whether I could see him or not, the honesty, the, dare I say, vulnerability, in his words were apparent. He was serious.

And suddenly I saw my life branching into two separate paths, depending on what my answer was. I could play it safe and lie. Protect my heart and protect my pride. Protect my relationship with him and the future of us working together.

Or I could be honest. I could finally admit to him how I really felt. Tell him and hope for the best. For the small chance that he happened to feel the same. Or for the larger chance that he didn't. I'd be humiliated and hurt. But I would do what Uncle Al wanted for me. For that giant knife to go into my heart, bleed myself dry. And get over it.

"Perry," he repeated. "Do you love me?"

I sucked in my breath, wishing I could see him better. Wishing he could see I was looking him right in the eyes.

"No," I told him, my voice calm and steady. "I don't."

It was the biggest lie I had ever told.

His shoulders deflated an inch.

"Oh," he said simply. Was that disappointment I heard? Or is that just what I wanted to hear.

"Why?" I asked. I found myself taking a step closer to him. I peered up at his dark face. "Do you want me to?"

I could tell he smiled.

"Well, kiddo…what man wouldn't want that?"

My heart melted, swirling in thick confusion. Was he serious? I couldn't tell without looking at him. I fished out my phone from my pocket and turned the light on.

I shone it at his face.

I barely had time to read it. A shimmer rippled through the air, like a wave of heat.

Abby's disfigured, broken head was right behind him, those eye sockets of grey goo peering at us over his shoulder.

A scream escaped my lips and I dropped the phone as I turned to run. I didn't know where to run, though, and I was quickly met with pipes and boxes that brought me to the ground in a heap. I heard Dex scream too, a terrible inhuman sound, and I struggled to my feet. I crashed through the basement until I was in the light of the main hall and ran toward the door.

Then I stopped myself in the middle of the room and looked for Dex to be right behind me like he usually was.

But he wasn't there. I was alone.

"Dex?" I cried out, wringing my hands nervously. My words fell short in the large space. "Dex, are you OK?"

Are you alive? I thought.

I listened hard for a sign of him, of anything. I couldn't hear anything except the occasional gust of wind from outside and the creaks and groans of the pipes. There was nothing else. The silence was terrifying. Nausea crept up my throat and held me paralyzed.

"Please Dex," I said under my breath and started to quietly ease back down the middle of the room. My eyes flitted from side to side, examining the shadows, fearing any movement.

As I got close to the corner where I had last seen him, a thick fuzzy noise wriggled into my ears. It was like static. A drone that made my insides feel like they were being brushed with steel wool.

I paused and listened. The drone got louder until I heard individual sounds more clearly. It was the collective noise of buzzing wings. Insects.

Wasps.

And to make a point, something landed on my outstretched, shaking hand.

I swatted at it but my movement caused the insect to drill its stinger into my hand. I cried out at the pain and connected with the scaly, winged creature with force. I felt it fly somewhere across the room.

I grasped my hand and raised it to the pale light from the windows. It was already swollen and an angry red color. I was grateful I wasn't allergic to bees, not like Dex was.

Oh, God. Dex.

The feeling came back into my feet and I hurried toward the buzzing noise in the corner. I was too horrified of what I might find but I couldn't hide and let it happen.

"Dex?" I looked around the boxes. It was too damn dark in here. I stepped carefully. My foot landed on a limb.

I shrieked and dropped to my knees, feeling around me like a blind person. It was a leg. Dex's. And it was still. I felt down his shin to where his boots were and felt the leg hair underneath his cargo pants.

Heart in my throat, I felt up his leg, adjusting myself on my knees. My foot nudged something metallic sounding. I quickly reached back and found my phone under my hands.

I whipped it forward and pressed the on button. It hadn't cracked, miraculously, and I aimed it at Dex.

I was not prepared for what I saw.

Dex was lying on his back, still as anything, except his hands were twitching at his sides.

His face. Oh God, his face.

He had no face. It was just a moving, writhing blanket of wasps that covered him from the neck up.

I cried out but no sound came from my lips. My chest constricted, squeezing the air out of me, lacing my heart until it couldn't beat anymore.

Dex was deathly allergic to just one wasp sting. He had at least 100 of them on his face. Just one sting and he would be dead. Dead and dead fast. The only antidote, the EpiPen, was in the car. The car that was so close but so far. And though his hands were twitching, those glorious long fingers of his, I couldn't tell if it was because he was alive or slowly dying.

I didn't want to spook or startle the insects, even though a few of them were losing interest in him and started to fly around my head like winged demons. I let them land on me, let them sting me. I reached, ever so slowly, inch by inch, for one of Dex's hands and covered it with my own. It was cold and clammy. But after a few seconds, it opened and he grasped my hand.

He was alive. My heart sang but the joy was short lived. The reality set in. Just because he was alive right now, it didn't mean he would be in a minute. I mean, what the hell was I supposed to do? He was covered in wasps. His face. His mouth, his nose, his neck. They were even going in his ears. I shivered at the image, the light wavering, and tried to keep calm. I had to think. I had to save him.

"Dex," I said with soft deliberation. "I'm here. I'm going to figure out what to do. You'll be OK."

That sounded so hopeless and ridiculous coming out of my mouth. But he squeezed my hand back, holding on for dear life. I was so close to losing it and bursting into tears.

I took in a deep breath and with the phone, gently swatted at another wasp that had landed on my shoulder. Luckily the thickness of my leather jacket was keeping most the stingers at bay.

What could I do? How did you get rid of wasps? There was no water down here. Not unless I found out a way to break open one of the pipes.

I sat back on my haunches and eyed the pipes by the walls. Though they had dripped from time to time, I doubted there was any water in the place. Why would there be?

If I couldn't douse them, what could I do? What worked at home during those late summer days in the back yard?

Smoke. My dad would light the open fireplace and it would keep the bees away during the day and the mosquitoes at night.

I could smoke them out.

"Dex," I said, projecting a calmness I didn't feel. "I'm going to smoke them out. OK? Just stay still, no matter what. Stay with me."

I placed the phone in my mouth and gripped it between my teeth. With one hand I searched his pants pocket for his trusty lighter; with the other I very carefully opened up the front flap of his cargo jacket and pulled out the bag of weed and the package of rollies.

I wasn't sure if this would work, but I didn't have a choice. I placed both of them on his chest, as close to his neck and face without disturbing the vile wasps. I pulled out the gold lighter and held up the rollie packet. I spun the wheel but the flame wouldn't light.

I brought my thumb down again and again against the hard, ragged edge but it sparked hopelessly.

"Oh shit," I cried out softly. This couldn't be it.

Trying harder, I spun and spun the knob until my thumb was painfully raw. Now a wasp made a go for my own neck and started crawling around it to the base of my skull.

I felt the painful pinch of a stinger where my spine started. At the same time, the lighter's wheel latched and a flamed sprung up. The sight of it, the minor triumph, erased the pain and the nasty spreading heat at my neck.

The flame caught the end of the rollie packet with ease. I waited before it was good and going and then I placed it on the Ziploc bag of weed, my fingers lightly singed.

I breathed in as much fresh air as I could, while I could, and watched as the plastic bag began to curl and smolder, giving off a sick, thick smell as the purple, blue toxic flames danced. A poisonous cloud of dark smoke rose, a potent mix of pot and chemicals.

I sat back on my heels, still gripping his hand and covered my mouth with my arm. I coughed uncontrollably at the smoke as the flames really started to spread; then, before it could catch hold of his jacket, I quickly knocked off the burning bag so it was on the ground near his head.

Now his jacket was on fire. I let go of his hand and took my own jacket off, throwing it on Dex's chest to put it out.

The wasps buzzed angrily around his head. They weren't doing anything but circling in a crazy motion up toward the ceiling and bit by bit, through the hazy smoke, I could make out Dex's face. His eyes were shut. I feared he was dead.

Then he coughed, his mouth opening, trying to suck in air but only getting smoke. I held his shoulder down with one arm, waiting for the last two wasps to leave his neck.

Once they did, flying groggily above him and then off to join the others, I quickly stuck my arms around his shoulders and pulled him forward to get out of the smoke.

"Come on," I coughed and got him on his knees. Down low by the floor, the smoke was thin. I kept one arm around him and urged him forward out of the corner and into the rest of the room. As we reached the more open area where the smoke hadn't reached yet, I stopped and he collapsed on the ground next to me, aching for air.

"Did they sting you?" I asked between chokeholds of air.

He shook his head violently, unable to speak.

I looked back at the cloud of smoke. It was spreading. The pot and bag were all burned up but now flames were jumping onto the boxes of straightjackets. That wasn't exactly good.

"Uh," I said, pointing at the new fire. When Dex was able to get enough air, he looked up, his face contorted and a scary shade of blue in the darkness.

Just then, the zombie rat came screaming out of the darkness toward us, on fire, with insects popping off its back and scattering on the concrete floor like wayward sparks.

I scampered to my feet, hoisted up Dex, and without thinking, I half ran, half dragged him toward the basement door. When we couldn't go any further and my lungs burned, we stopped and watched. The rat had run straight into the wall beneath the windows and was lying on the ground twitching as its own fire died down. A terrible, sick smell, like someone was roasting bad meat, filled the air along with the smoke from the boxes, which were now totally on fire. The flames leaped out from around the corner and into the basement, illuminating the space around us.

I leaned against the door after trying to open it one last time. Dex was hunched over, leaning forward with one arm propping him up against the wall. He was spitting on the ground and trying to compose himself.

"What are the chances of this place going up in flames with us stuck down here?" I asked uneasily.

Before he could look at me and answer, a deafening ringing sound broke out, blasting through my eardrums. It was the fire alarm. One second later, we were being doused with water.

I looked up and through drops of icy water, saw a never-ending spray spewing from the ceiling. The sprinklers had gone off.

Dex suddenly sprang into action and ran over to the camera and EVP, which he had left against the wall where we had slept. He scooped them up and buried them deep beneath his singed jacket in order to protect them from the water.

I wiped my face and looked back at the corner of the room. The flames were dying quickly under the deluge.

Dex watched the light die, holding his stomach to prevent the equipment from falling out beneath his jacket. He looked like a drowned, pregnant rat.

"What are the chances of this place flooding while we are stuck down here?" I asked about our brand new predicament and for some reason, I started laughing.

Dex looked up at me sharply. I couldn't help it. The situation, everything that had just happened, was so absolutely ludicrous.

He shook his head, droplets of water flying everywhere. Then, as if on cue, the sprinklers and the alarm stopped. We were left soaking wet. I was impossibly cold. But at least the fire was out. The wasps were gone. And both of us were alive.

When I gathered my wits up enough to keep the inane giggles at bay, I reached over and brushed his wet hair off his forehead. He looked extremely sexy when wet. A part of me wanted to physically attack him. Not out of anger, and not really out of lust, but just out of still having him standing beside me. I was so close to losing him. The reality of that made my nerves feel like they were still lit with flames.

He hadn't said anything yet. I wondered if he was shell-shocked.

"Dex?" I said, letting my hand slip down to his neck. I traced his wet skin with my fingers, feeling for any signs that the wasps had been there at all. It felt smooth and slick and the blood pumped furiously along his jugular.

"Are you OK?"

He nodded quickly and eyed my hand uneasily.

I took it back. I wanted to say so many things to him but I wasn't sure how.

And I didn't have to. Through the leftover drips from the sprinkler system, we heard the pitter patter of feet from the pavement outside, a flash of a shadow as it passed in front of the lights and the sound of the main door opening.

I looked behind me at the door's window. Roundtree was running down the stairs with a large spotlight and a security guard in tow.

She flung the door open and gasped when she saw us standing there like waterlogged ghouls.

"What on earth?" she cried out. The security guard raised his own flashlight on us and brought out his walkie talkie.

"We had an accident," I said as lightly as possible, feeling like the master of the understatement. She growled under her breath and pointed to the top of the stairs like she was my mother or something. We were more than ready to comply. We ran up the stairs, into the hospital foyer and out into the fresh night air.

We were going home.

CHAPTER NINETEEN

When I came to, I was in an unfamiliar bedroom. There was a poster of Ryan Reynolds on the wall, a collage of photos and some arty framed works of Parisian landscapes. The wallpaper was yellow with tiny roses.

I blinked hard at the overhead light and slowly eased myself onto my elbows. I was lying on a single bed and was alone. I looked around the room again. The dull thud of music reverberated throughout the walls. It matched the pounding in my head. I wasn't in pain but I could feel my heart hammering away upstairs in the thin space between my forehead and my skull.

What the hell had just happened? One minute I was talking to Jacob outside by the side of the house and the next I was in Adrianna's bedroom. At least, that's what it looked like from the mass of pictures on the wall, her tanned, smiling face with a gaggle of different kids I went to school with.

I rubbed at my forehead to get the pounding to stop. What had we been talking about anyway? Why had I just fainted?

Seriously, I'm quitting drugs tomorrow, I thought. *At least cutting back.*

I got off of the bed and vigorously rubbed my face up and down, stretching my jaw open and shaking my arms back and forth. A beer would put me right. Maybe a line if I happened to run into someone I knew.

Of course, it was more than likely that Jacob had a bit of coke somewhere. But I wasn't sure if it was worth it. He had been creepy, he had been talking about...demons? Was it demons? And then I ended up here. No, the coke wasn't worth it, not from him.

I opened the door and poked my head out into the hall. The sounds of the party came at me. At the end of the hallway, a couple was making out against a door. Pretty hardcore from the looks of it. The guy was getting a handjob at least; the blonde girl's hand was well into his pants and working him back and forth. I wanted to tell them the bedroom was free if he didn't want to make a mess in his pants but I kept it to myself and crept past them. They didn't notice anyway.

I reached the stairs and was met with a party that showed no sign of slowing down. If anything, people were more wild than before. Someone was sitting on top of the television, the beer bong had made its way into the kitchen, everyone seemed to be dirty dancing with anything and everyone. The girls' tops were all yanked down lower, their makeup smudged beneath their eyes. The guys were all ridiculously loud and I could see every single one of them had a boner in one form or another. Booze was spilled, smoke from pot and cigarettes filled the air. And by the door, a couple was getting into a yelling match that was eclipsed only by the music. People walked past them and took no notice. Everyone had other things on their mind. Mainly, getting fucked; in more ways than one.

I didn't recognize anyone I knew. Not Jacob. Not Tara. Not even Adrianna or her boyfriend Angus.

I sighed and continued to walk down. I was almost at the bottom step when a strange sound caught the tip of my ear. It had come from behind me.

I turned and looked. The couple that had been heavy petting had stopped and was standing at the top of the stairs. The guy with his Linkin Park T-shirt seemed frozen on the spot, like he was in mid-embrace. But the girl, the girl with her long blonde hair, she was…growling. And unlike the guy, she was moving. She pushed him backward toward the room I came out of, and he walked backward, as if on autopilot or under a spell.

Then she changed before my eyes. Her skin fizzed like acid was poured on it. Her eyes and her nose disappeared until she was just all mouth, with jagged teeth, her skin suddenly the smooth alabaster of fine porcelain. And then she dissolved before my eyes. All that was left was this sickening growl and the guy who was being shoved backward into the bedroom by some invisible force.

This had nothing to do with drugs. This was actually happening.

I whirled around to look at the party, expecting them to all be watching what I was watching. But everyone was carrying on as usual.

I looked back at the stairs. The door was shut. I had to know what was going on. If what I saw was correct…was real. I didn't care if I interrupted their sex session.

I walked back up the stairs and paused at the door. I couldn't hear anything except a strange sucking sound, like a vacuum was running on high power.

I took in a deep breath and was about to enter the room when something touched my shoulder.

Before I could scream a hand was around my mouth, squelching the sound.

I was turned around to see Jacob standing there. He had a gas can in his hand.

Do you see now? he whispered. But his mouth didn't mouth. The words just entered my head, as if he was in there.

I told you that's where I came from. That others would be here.

"What are you?" I asked, though my voice was muffled by his hand, my lips tasting the strange, sickly sweet flavor of his hand. It was a ridiculous question to ask. But suddenly, nothing seemed ridiculous. I saw a girl disappear in front of my eyes.

I'm a ghost, he projected, the words shooting into my head as clear as day. *I died a long time ago. I don't know what happened. I killed myself and now I'm stuck. Between here and the other world. The other world is much worse. Black and white.*

It was too much. I wanted to run, to flee, but he kept his hand at my mouth.

You're not going anywhere, Perry. You're special. I knew it from the start. You're the only one who can see me. And the only one who can help me stop them.

Stop who? I thought.

Stop the demons, he answered and I realized my thoughts were being read. *We aren't the same.*

Overwhelmed, I shut my eyes hard until all I saw were sparks of light behind them. I wanted to be somewhere else, anywhere else, with anyone else. I concentrated really hard, wishing I had the power to just change things. I felt the ground rumble lightly under my feet and the pictures on the hallway wall rattled. An eerie cry shot out from behind the door.

"Stop it!" Jacob yelled out loud. "You're attracting them!"

My eyes flew open and I glared at him. I reached up with my hand, grabbed his disgusting scarred wrist and yanked it away from my mouth.

"Attracting who!?" I yelled back.

Suddenly the door opened and the blonde girl stuck her head out. She looked like a normal teenage girl again except a trail of blood dripped out of the corner of her mouth. She scanned the hall before her eyes settled on Jacob and me.

She made a move for us, but Jacob quickly threw the can of gas toward her, a gush of acrid liquid flowing out of the spout and onto her, the walls and the floor.

She screamed, more in shock than in pain or anything else.

"Perry!" Jacob yelled. "Send her back!"

He reached into his pocket and tossed a lighter at me. I caught it somehow but I wasn't about to follow his orders.

The girl was writhing on the spot, the gasoline flowing off her toned body and staining the plush beige carpet beneath us. But she was normal. Aside from the blood, which could have been a result of rough, drunk sex or whatever, there was nothing strange about her anymore. She had eyes, heavily made up with green eye shadow, a pert nose and a normal mouth. I could see the traces of auburn lip liner beneath her lower lip.

Send her back? Did he seriously think I would light some random chick on fire?

I looked at Jacob to tell him he was crazy, that he wasn't a ghost, that this girl wasn't a demon, and that the beer I had earlier was probably spiked with acid, but the girl lunged forward and wrapped her hands around my neck. Her fingers felt like icy knives and they sank into my skin with startling precision. The feeling made me sick. And I couldn't breathe.

"Do it!" Jacob yelled again and made a go for the girl. I couldn't see what happened but her hands eventually let go and I was left breathless. I looked down to see him tackle her to the ground. He pinned her wrists down and she wriggled beneath them, hissing.

"They don't let us leave!" he cried out. "The keep us here!"

The girl made a swift kick to Jacob's groin. Ghost or not, it made him double over in pain. Then she fizzled again, skin bubbling, facial features disappearing until she was a hazy image above the carpet. The only thing that remained was that open, fathomless hole that was her mouth. And it came for me.

Without thinking, I flicked the lighter on and held it out in front of me as the shape collided into me.

I kept the flame going as the back of my head smashed against the wall behind me. Paintings rattled to the floor.

The girl, whatever was left of her, was suddenly outlined by the glow of the flames, like she was traced by some giant pen of golden ink. Her shape came into my vision, then turned into an actual girl again. Normal looking. She cried out in pain and fell to the ground as the sick, hungry flames consumed her, skin first.

I felt sick but couldn't look away. The girl wriggled on the floor until she was no more. She just vanished, leaving only ash, while the fire began to move along the upstairs carpet toward the stairs, licking at the wet walls.

I looked at Jacob, who was struggling to his feet. He nodded at me, the spiky tips of his Mohawk glowing in the flames' light.

Suddenly the door to the bedroom opened and the guy in the Linkin Park T-shirt wandered out. He froze at the sight of me, standing in the hallway, lighter in hand, gas can at my side, and the fire, which quickly ate up the crunchy carpet.

"Holy shit!" the guy cried out. I guess I should have been relieved that he was alive and that girl hadn't killed him, but any sense of relief was taken away when he yelled. "Fire! There's a girl up here, she started a fire!"

Then he burst past me in the hallway, leaping over the flames while screaming at the same time and ran down the stairs. I could hear the panic and commotion that resulted downstairs. People screaming, yelling, glasses breaking, drunks colliding with each other, falling down.

I looked at Jacob and then down at the lighter. The guy hadn't seen Jacob. He didn't know anything about the girl. It just looked like I, Perry Palomino, the fat sophomore, had tried to light Adrianna Gee's house on fire.

It was one hell of an accident.

~~

I woke up to something licking my face.

I sat up straight, expecting to fight something. But it was just Fat Rabbit, standing on top of my chest and wriggling around. His nails sank into my abdomen and I winced at the pressure.

"Aw, come on," I groaned and pushed him lightly off of me. He gave me a look and then darted out the door, which had been open a crack.

I looked down at myself in the light that came from the living room. I was back in Dex's den. I didn't know where I expected to wake up, but I had a feeling that my dreams had been exceedingly epic. I was covered in sweat again.

I held my hands out in front of me. The back of my left one was swollen and tight, a pale pink shade from the wasp sting. I grimaced at the sight as the memories of last night came flooding into my brain:

The man in the cell. Something about his featureless face was suddenly so familiar. Had I seen him before somewhere? Was he in my dream? I felt like I had dreamt about high school again, so that didn't make much sense. But when did my dreams ever make sense.

Then there was the Spook Factory, essentially sabotaging us and not letting us out of the basement. Had they gotten everything they wanted? Did they see the footprints, the man in the cell? Did Annie get a cold finger down her spine?

And Miss Anonymous ended up being Jenn. Good ol' Jennifer Rodriguez. Rebecca was certainly right about her. I wondered if she also knew about the comments. Or maybe it was just Dex. Dex trying to be a loyal boyfriend despite how disloyal he sometimes was. The idea that she had been sitting here in this room and giggling away at the computer as she told me I was fat and worthless...it caused my heart to thump hard in my chest. I was angry again, so very angry.

And finally there was the question. Dex had asked if I loved him. And I lied to save face. Why did he ask that to begin with? Did he suspect? Did he want me to have said yes, and if so, why? Either because he felt the same way or he wanted to have something else to lord over me.

I sighed long and hard, blowing out every last bit of air in an attempt to release the vibrant frustration that was building up inside of me. I was usually one of those people who woke up feeling calm after a hectic night, but suddenly I was just angry all over again. And I knew just who was getting the brunt of it.

I slipped my pajama pants on and padded my way across the room, opening the door and stepping out into the sun-soaked apartment. For once I wished it was raining; it would have suited my mood better.

Dex was sitting at the bar, his back to me, slurping back on a bowl of cereal. He was still in his blue plaid pajama pants but was shirtless. His hair was all ruffled and messy.

I stopped and watched him for a beat, gathering my thoughts. He turned around to look at me and jumped a little on his stool.

"Jesus!" he cried out and leaped off, his spoon clattering loudly into the bowl.

He rushed over to me, looking me up and down in horror, and then picked up my hand to examine the sting on the back of it.

"It's fine," I assured him. It wasn't killing me, at least.

He shook his head and then moved on to my other arm, where another welt had formed just below the elbow. He touched it gently with his finger. I winced. It started to itch again.

He sucked in his lip and then placed both his warm hands on the side of my face. I didn't like him being so up close first thing in the morning. I probably had sleep in my eyes and my teeth needed a good brushing. I knew I was too tired to do it last night; we had come straight home, got into dry clothes and went to bed.

"Nothing on your face," he said, still eyeing every crevice of it.

I smiled, tight-lipped and went to move away but he wasn't done yet. I closed my eyes as one of his hands went to the back of neck and settled on the large sting I had there. That one hurt and itched worst of all and he wasn't making it any better.

"Oh, Perry, I'm sorry," he said over a soft breath. Then he let go of me and walked off to the bathroom. I opened my eyes and let out the air I was holding.

"Where's Jenn?" I asked tentatively.

"Out," he replied from the bathroom. He returned with a tube of prescription cream, probably hydrocortisone.

He put a bit on his finger. I was distracted by his bare chest. His tattoo, *And with madness comes the light*. Like hell that was a song lyric. That meant something more than that to him, just as his "mark of a criminal" fleur-de-lis did.

He reached back behind my neck and gently dabbed the cream on, swirling it around in a massaging motion. I felt my eyes closing again at the caress of his fingers.

No. I'm still mad at you, I thought. My eyes flew open and I stepped back. I took the cream from his hands.

"I'm fine, Dex; I can put the cream on myself. I'm not a cripple." It probably came out a bit ungrateful, so I shot him a weak smile. He looked hurt and confused.

"OK," he said and nodded. He still stood there. "I'm really sorry."

I frowned at him and began to rub the cream on my hand. "Sorry for what?"

"Everything."

Oh, well, I guess that covers it.

"I mean," he started and pointed at his body. I eyed his arms and chest awkwardly, not wanting to give it too much of my time. "Look at me. I've got nothing on me. One sting Perry, and I would have died."

"I know," I said softly, keeping my attention on the meticulous way I was applying the cream.

"And you saved my life. You could have died too, allergic or not, if a lot of those wasps had got you..."

"But I didn't. And neither did you." I started now on the welt on my other arm. I didn't want to get into such a serious topic. I was still mad about the Anonymous thing and I didn't want to be distracted.

"Please, look at me." He placed two fingers underneath my chin and tilted my head up. I met his eyes and immediately felt exposed.

"What?" I said underneath my breath.

His eyes looked wet and shiny, a layer of sadness and regret over them. I didn't like to see him that way. I wanted the hard, flippant, uncaring Dex. Looking into these eyes made my nerves crumble.

"I'm sorry about Jenn," he said. "I'm sorry I didn't tell you she was leaving the comments."

I tried to look away but he wouldn't let me. He stuck his face closer to mine in an effort to express himself. The anger I felt throttling through me moments earlier was quickly subsiding, leaving me exhausted. I just wanted to forget about it now.

"I should have told you, I see that now. But I was protecting her and I thought I was protecting you in a weird way. It's better to think it's a bunch of sad, anonymous losers instead of the girlfriend of your partner. And I was...embarrassed. I still am. Really fucking embarrassed."

I raised my brow at him. He took his fingers away from my face and walked back toward the bar top. I watched his hips shake with each step, the way the sides of his back disappeared smoothly into the flannel band of his pants. No love handles there, not like me.

He raised his face to the ceiling, still keeping his back to me.

"I just hoped Jenn wasn't like that," he added. "I knew she was a bitch, and that was fine because I'm an ass, but I didn't know she could be that bad."

"But she is," I said. "And you have to live with that."

He leaned against the bar in silence, then sat back on the stool and resumed eating his cereal, which was probably all mushy by now.

I went over and pulled up the stool next to him, my bare feet cold against the metal rungs at the bottom.

Dex stared down at his bowl and pushed the soggy Fruit Loops around and around, creating a mini whirlpool of milk. "I just don't know what to do."

Dump her ass, you moron. That's what I wanted to say. But I could see Dex was opening up here and tormented by the situation. I kept silent. I wanted to comfort him but at the same time, I wanted him to see the truth of the matter. That their relationship was dead. It had been disintegrating all week, probably long before I got here, and it was on its final legs. There was no point beating around the bush, no point in keeping it going. It was sick, destroyed by the selfishness of both of them, and because I was on the outside, I was the only one in this apartment who could see it.

Perhaps the dog knew, too.

Dex turned his head to the side, his eyes darting at my face sheepishly. "You must think I'm an idiot."

I smiled despite myself. "I'm an idiot too."

"No," he said with a sigh. "You're not, Perry. You're sweet, honest and a very good friend."

Ah, the damn friend word again. The term made a flush bloom on my cheeks and was glad he took that moment to reach over for the box of cereal and pour more into his bowl.

I cleared my throat. "Well. I know what I would do but I'm not you and I can't tell you what to do. Did you talk to her last night?" She had been asleep when we came in.

"Briefly," he said shoveling cereal into his mouth. "She said she had been out with some girlfriends and that her phone had died."

Likely story, I thought.

He eyed me. "Of course, my phone didn't work either so I can't exactly accuse her of lying. Not that I think she was. She may be a bitch, but she does care about me and I know she wouldn't have just left me in a mental hospital basement, especially not alone with you."

I spied his cup of coffee, picked it up and took a sip of it. It was lukewarm but it worked. "She really thinks something is going on between us, doesn't she?"

He nodded grimly. "I guess if she's been stepping out then it's easy for her to imagine I'm guilty as well."

I stared at him, dumbly. He was kind of guilty. Unless I imagined the whole tryst we had on the island, and I knew my imagination wasn't that good.

He caught my eyes and looked away quickly. "Fine. I'm guilty too. Goddamn it, this whole situation is fucked."

It certainly was.

We both exhaled in unison. We sat there in silence for a bit, both of us side-by-side in our pajamas, he eating mushy cereal and me drinking his coffee, both consumed by our thoughts. I couldn't pretend that my motives for him dumping Jenn weren't at least a bit selfish. With her out of the picture, it opened up a whole realm of possibilities. At least, I hoped it did. But even if Jenn weren't an issue anymore...did he feel the same way I felt about him? I didn't think so.

"You need to break up with her," I suddenly blurted out.

He flinched. He placed his spoon down and shot me an inquisitive look. "Yeah?"

"Yeah."

"I know. But it's not that easy," he said carefully. I watched his eyes and understood what he meant. The apartment. The dog. Ending a long-term relationship. No, it definitely wasn't going to be easy.

"I don't...like change," he added, adding weight to his words.

I could help with the transition, I thought. I wanted to put my arm around his bare shoulders and hold him, pull him close to me.

"And then what happens after that?" he continued.

"You'd be single," I told him. My voice had automatically dropped in volume.

He pushed the bowl away from him and started chewing on his lip. Finally he looked at me and asked, "Would I be?"

That glowing cord of tension between us was suddenly visible and sparking again. My lungs felt heavy and the air around us felt static and alive. The hairs on my arms stood up and the area around my neck bite was pleasantly cool.

I shrugged carefully, wanting to break away from his intrusive eyes but I couldn't. They held me in place.

"Could you see yourself with someone else?" I asked softly. There was so much ridiculous hope in the question, and I know he could see it on my face.

He turned in his chair by an inch, facing me. He looked tired, with faint bags under his eyes. But they were so feverish and sparkling, so intense and alive, that it lit up his face and made even his five o' clock shadow look youthful.

"I could," he said with conviction. "If she'd have me."

My eyes widened at that. I couldn't help it.

"But I can't chance it," he added quickly. "And I don't think it would be a very smart choice. It would be too much of a risk and I've had too much of that in my life."

And at that he abruptly got off the stool, taking the bowl of cereal and my half-drank coffee out of my hand, walking around the bar and placing them in the sink. He avoided my eyes.

I sat frozen in shock, my heart thudding loudly.

"I'm going to give Doctor Hasselback a call and see what the damage is," he said casually, picking his cell phone up off the table. He walked past me and disappeared into his bedroom, shutting the door behind him.

"What the hell?" I said quietly and to no one in particular. Fat Rabbit was sitting on the couch and he looked over. I could almost see him rolling his eyes at me.

He had been talking about me, right? I mean...shit, he was vague but it had to be me. I was a risk? How the hell was I risk? Didn't he know how I felt?

No, you retard, I thought, cutting myself off. *You just told him point blank that you were not in love with him. Now he is taking that as the truth.*

Yup. The situation definitely was fucked and now I was partially to blame.

~~

After I had taken a shower and got ready for the day (blow-drying my hair extra straight just in case I wanted to wear it down for the Christmas party tonight), Dex came into the den with good news.

"Doctor Hasselback said we could still air everything," he announced, walking across the room and sitting down at the computer. I was on the bed trying to re-stick the toe pads into the balls of my devil shoes.

"Oh yeah," I said mildly. Since our conversation earlier, I was feeling a bit swirly about that still. The show didn't seem to matter, though I knew in the long run it did.

He spun in the seat and gave me a funny look.

"You OK, kiddo?" he asked earnestly.

I managed to prevent my eyes from rolling.

"Yeah, I'm fine," I said. Then added, "What about the Spook Factory?"

"That's just what I'm looking up," he said, turning back to the screen and clacking away on the keyboard. "He didn't seem too pissed off about the other show; I guess in the end any publicity is good publicity, but we know for sure that they didn't get any interviews with the doctor, so maybe we still have a chance of standing out against them."

"You're really worried about this, aren't you?"

He paused. "As I should be."

He went back to typing and the Fantasy Network website came up on the screen. He scrolled along until he got to the Spook Factory tab.

"No," he said with relief. "It's the same old episode as last time. They haven't uploaded theirs yet. They were bluffing."

"Or they never found anything."

"But we did. And we're going to do this now."

I pulled my phone out of my purse. It was almost noon.

"Are we going to have enough time before the Christmas party?"

"Christ," he swore, and focused his attention on the wall. "I totally forgot about that."

Had he really? I had been thinking about it on and off all day. About how damn awkward it was going to be. Me and Dex. Jenn and Bradley. The rest of the Shownet peeps. I had a feeling something major was going to go down.

"Yeah, well Rebecca texted me a little while ago," I told him. "She and Emily are going to come over here at six to get ready together."

He looked at me. "Are you serious?"

"I'm always serious," I mimicked him with a smile.

"Rebecca, Emily, you...Jenn. All in my apartment?"

"Better get used to the awkwardness now because it's only going to get worse tonight," I pointed out.

He chewed on his lip. "God, I hope Rebecca brings some more pot."

"Yeah, sorry that the wasps got most of yours," I said.

He tilted his head to the side and a fleeting smile graced his lips. "I can only hope I was worth it."

"You know you were," I said.

He nodded, not believing it, and turned back to the computer. "Well, we better haul some ass. I'll get everything connected. I'm thinking I can run this episode without a score, or perhaps just use a bit from another episode. I could see this using the same stuff I wrote for the Darkhouse."

"What can I do?" I asked, getting up off the bed and joining him by his side.

His eyes darted to the bookshelf and back. "For one, you can hand me my pills and get me a glass of water."

I was glad he wasn't looking at me. The flash of terror would have been totally visible on my face.

"Why, uh, why are you still bothering to take the pills if they aren't working?" I prodded as innocently as possible.

He shrugged. "I don't know. I think it could be dangerous if I stopped cold turkey. I'll just go back to the doctor next week or something and discuss my options or something."

"Next week," I repeated slowly.

"Yeah. You'll be back home by then."

"Right." Suddenly not spending every waking minute with Dex was a terrifying thought. I didn't want to go home now.

"Don't you have a date with that 'roid monkey, too?"

Oh man, Brock. He completely slipped my mind, and rightfully so.

"Maybe," I said.

"Hell, maybe this time next week, you'll be the one in the relationship and I won't be. We'll switch places. Role reversal."

And at that he looked up at me. His eyes were soft and playful. He didn't seem bothered at all by the concept of me being in a relationship with Brock.

"Please, the pills, Perry," he said again.

I nodded, snapped myself into action and handed the book to him. While he opened the cover, I went out to the kitchen to get a glass of water.

As I was filling it up, I heard a familiar buzzing noise. I turned around, the water splashing out of the glass and into the sink. A wasp landed on the fridge and was climbing up it, its little yellow and black body bright against the chrome steel. I looked behind me and grabbed the nearest suitable smashing device, which happened to be the box of Fruit Loops that Dex had left out. I put the glass down and crept closer to the wasp, not wanting to scare it.

"Die, you little bitch," I muttered before slamming the box into the fridge. The wasp fell onto the floor in a wriggling heap. I picked up a hanging saucepan and brought the flat end down on top of it with a resounding

SMASH. I carefully lifted it up. The bugger was squished beyond recognition.

"What the hell are you doing in there?" Dex cried out from the den.

"Just a minute," I yelled back, and scraped the remains of the wasp into the sink, washing it down the drain. I wondered how it got in the apartment. There didn't seem to be any other wasps. It was probably the wasp that stung my neck. It must have hitched a ride in my clothes or hair.

I shivered at that thought while I filled up his glass again and brought it to him.

He looked up at me curiously. "What happened?"

I didn't want to scare him so I just shrugged. "Killed a spider."

"You know it's going to rain now," he said, taking the glass from my hands. He threw the pills back into his mouth all at once and swallowed them with ease.

"I'll take my chances," I replied, and focused back on the screen. His editing software was all open and the footage from last night was quickly being downloaded through a USB.

"Can I do anything?" I asked, feeling useless when it came to this part of the show.

"Sure," he said and handed me the EVP and a pair of headphones. "If you don't mind spooking yourself out a little bit, you can listen to what we recorded and make notes of anything interesting."

He reached into a drawer and pulled out a pen and paper. "Note if the wavelengths on the front monitor change, and if you hear anything, record the time so we can find it easily."

I was already feeling spooked at my new task, even though the lights in the den were on and the door was open, letting the winter sun filter in through the gauzy curtains of the living room.

I gingerly placed the headphones on my head and before I hit play I told him I was going to listen to it while in the room with him.

I sat back on the bed, getting cozy and making sure there was nothing but the wall behind me. I pressed play and began to listen to what we recorded on Tuesday night. That felt like eons ago.

For most of the recording it was just sounds of us working. It was us talking, our footsteps, the camera. There was nothing on the EVP that wouldn't show up on the audio from the footage he shot.

But then, after I had told him I was going to go use the washroom, the sound in the hallway abruptly changed. I heard the door close behind me and Dex's footsteps as we roamed down the hallway away from the monitor, which had been propped up against the wall. But everything else went dead silent. No background fuzz. Not his breath going in and out. Soon the footsteps stopped, too, and it was the blank, unnerving silence that you get when your ears suddenly stop ringing.

I looked down at the monitor to make a note of the time of the recording but the wavelength on the screen started to jump sporadically. I turned the volume up, straining to hear something.

It was very faint. But I heard it.

A voice calling, "Declan. Declan."

I froze and hit pause. I looked to Dex, who was working at the computer, his back to me, his outline glowing against the monitor. Had Dex heard someone when he was there alone?

I hit play and listened harder, the volume going up to maximum level.

"Declan," the voice continued. The familiar accent of an elderly woman. Creepy Clown Lady.

My eyes bugged out.

"Declan, can you hear me? You should hear me now. You should see me soon. Your medication no longer works. She switched it on you."

I let out a yelp and hit pause again.

Dex turned in his chair and stared at me. "What is it, kiddo? You hear something?"

"I...I'm not sure yet," I said, my voice shaking. "I'll have to keep listening."

He frowned at me and pursed his lips. "You look like you've seen...or heard...a ghost. Is it...her? Abby?" He said her name warily as if saying it out loud would conjure up her spirit.

I shook my head, not wanting him to hear it quite yet. Freaking clown lady was going to rat me out!

"I'll let you listen in a bit, OK?"

"OK," he said hesitantly and turned back to his screen.

I breathed out slowly, readied myself and hit play again.

Clown Lady's voice continued. "It is for the best. You need to be yourself. That's the only way we connect again. You need to remember me. Remember your Pippa. I know it's hard, you don't want to remember the past. Neither of you do. But it's time to accept what happened. What happened to both of you. I wish my family had let me stay with you, Declan. You needed someone to take care of you. Someone who loved you like I did."

I was so engrossed in what I was hearing, I wasn't aware that Dex had stopped working and was watching me. My hands had been covering my face in fascination and some strange pain as Clown Lady...or Pippa...had been talking. Dex knew something was up.

I glanced at him quickly and bit my lip hard.

Pippa kept talking, her voice pausing every so often as if to listen for Dex's reaction. But on the recording, he never made any sound in return. "Remember the days we used to spend down in Central Park? The ghosts that walked among us? I'm one of them now. But I'm different. Because I was different before. Just like you. I can cross over when I choose. But I have to be careful. I'm being watched, we all are. By the soulless ones who keep us here. The demons."

Suddenly the ring of Dex's phone blasted across the earphones and I had to pluck them off my head with a cry. I had forgotten the volume was turned way up.

I waited, holding them away from my ears, able to hear the phone and Dex answering it. It had been me calling from the floor below, just before Abby attacked me.

When the noise died down, I put the headphones back on.

Pippa said, "Go to her Declan. Whatever you do, don't let that Abby get a hold of her. The effects will last longer than you think. She's in real danger, especially when you think she's fine. When you think she's safe, the damage will be done."

There was a pause.

Then, "I don't suppose you will hear this until later since you don't seem to hear me now. But when you hear this, know that I'll be around if I can and when I can. It's getting trickier to see you. I'm being watched, as I said. So I need you to stop all your medication Declan. It's time to face what you are. And what Perry is. And who I am to you. To both of you. Perry, if you're listening...ask your parents who Declan O'Shea is. And watch them carefully. You'll get the truth that I am not allowed to reveal."

Then she stopped and the recorder went back to being fuzzy. I waited a few beats and then heard the door to the hall open and Dex and I walking back inside, ready to shoot the hallway scene, totally unaware of the magnitude of what was just recorded on the EVP.

That was more than enough for now. I took the headphones off and placed them gently on the bed. I hit stop on the recorder and tried to think.

Dex was still watching me. I met his eyes. I knew he had to hear this. I just didn't want him to hear it now. It was totally, completely selfish of me but...I didn't want him to know what I had done. Not till tonight was over.

"What happened?" he asked carefully. "You look like you're about to cry."

I shook my head. "There's something on this tape, Dex, that you need to hear. But...it's nothing we can use for the show. I need you to promise me that you won't listen to it until tomorrow."

He was confused. He scratched at his sideburns, wincing a bit at what I was asking him. "I can't listen to it?"

"You can. And you need to. And you will. I just...don't think it would be smart if you did so before tonight. It's...personal."

"I don't know what that means, kiddo," he admitted.

"I know it doesn't make sense. But it will. Maybe. It makes no sense to me. But I think it will to you."

"Oh, well thanks for making it less vague."

"Please, Dex," I pleaded. I got off the bed and stooped in front of him so my face was right up in his. He looked surprised. "Promise me. Don't lie."

I held out my pinky finger for him to take. He nodded, conceding, and took my finger in his, shaking on it.

"OK, I won't listen to it," he said earnestly. "I mean it, too."

"Thank you," I said. And I kissed him gently on the forehead, his skin tasting lightly salted. I was so worried about what he would think of me when he found out I switched the pills. And I was worried about everything else she had said. It felt like it had the potential to change everything and I didn't know in what way.

I pulled my lips away and sat back down on the bed, unsure of what to do with myself and the buttload of information I was given.

I eyed Dex. He was even more confused now, and gently touched his forehead where my lips had been.

"Perry, I've got to ask, should I be worried? Because I am really fucking worried now."

I shook my head back and forth and managed to give him just the tiniest smile. "You have nothing to worry about."

"I'm worried about *you*. You just kissed me, like you were saying goodbye. For a long time."

"I'm not going anywhere," I assured him. Not on my own accord, anyway.

Suddenly, Fat Rabbit's bark erupted from the living room and his form bounded off the couch and clattered all the way to the door. The sound of keys in it. The rustle of grocery bags. High heels walking on hardwood.

Jenn was home.

Dex and I both tensed in unison and waited as she walked down the apartment toward the den. We exchanged a nervous glance. She was so going to know something was up, not that we were doing anything wrong.

She stopped at the door and looked in at us. She was wearing a denim mini-skirt that was way too inappropriate for both her age and the weather.

"What are you guys up to?" she asked suspiciously.

Oh man, I just wanted to go up to pull her damn curly hair out of her head. I wanted to tell her I knew everything, about Bradley, about Miss Anonymous. But I pasted on a fake smile and said, "Just creeping ourselves out with the footage we shot last night. You know, when we were locked in the basement of the mental hospital."

She sighed and fixed her hazel eyes on me and said, "Look, I'm sorry about that. I told Dex this morning, my phone honestly died the minute I got in the cab. And I did call you, Dex, from Patricia's phone, but you never answered. Anyway, I didn't think it was a big deal, just another night shoot."

Sorry my ass.

"Well, obviously it wasn't," Dex said. I noticed he sat rigid in his seat, not getting up to go greet her.

"So I was wrong," she said defensively. "How was I to know? You obviously had no clue that your stupid rivals would be following you around. Though maybe you should have…"

"Jenn…" he warned her in a tone I wouldn't question.

She raised up her hand as a peace offering. "I stopped by the store and got some appetizers and wine and whatever. I figured we could have a bit to eat here before we left for the party. Who knows if Jimmy has sprung for actual food or not."

"I hope you bought enough food for five of us," I said.

Dex shot me a look. He looked scared.

"What? Five of us?" Jenn repeated.

"Oh yeah, I forgot to tell you. Rebecca and Emily are coming over at six so we can all get ready together," I said cheerfully.

Jenn's nose wrinkled. "What?" She looked at Dex, who shrugged.

"You get along with your Wine Babe, don't you?" I asked innocently.

"Of course," Jenn said. I knew she wouldn't let me think that someone didn't like her precious, gorgeous self. "I was just surprised, that's all. I would have gotten some more goat cheese and crackers."

She gave us a quick smile and then disappeared back into the apartment and into her room. I could hear her sighing in annoyance as she went.

Dex eyed me with a twinkle, shaking his head but smiling. "You just ruined her whole night, you know."

"I know," I said, returning the smile. And I was just getting started.

CHAPTER TWENTY

At six o' clock on the dot, the buzzer from downstairs sounded. Dex had been working for the last six hours getting the episode ready and it seemed like it was good to go and ready to be uploaded.

"I still would have preferred to have done an original soundtrack," he said as he crossed the apartment, stretching his arms out at his side, shaking off the cramps from sitting before pressing the buzzer for Rebecca and Emily to come in.

Jenn was standing in the kitchen, hastily (and begrudgingly) pasting goat cheese on a bunch of organic crackers that had the look and appeal of cardboard. I had thought about helping her with stuff but decided against it. Instead I drank a glass of the wine she bought and watched her as she worked. She was uncomfortable as anything, all fidgety and nervous, probably from my watchful eyes and the fact that she was going to be surrounded by a bunch of women she didn't like.

Focusing my attention on Jenn and watching Dex work his magic in the editing studio kept my mind blissfully occupied for the day. The questions that arose on the tape (who was Declan O'Shea? Dex? And why would my parents know him? And how did Dex know Creepy Clown Lady, or Pippa?) were kept in the corner of my mind for the most part and the more of the wine I drank, the more I wasn't dwelling on it. The only thing on my radar was the evening. That was it. I was going to have fun at the party, that was the goal, and watching Jenn squirm already was putting the night on the right path.

Something was missing though...

"We need music!" I exclaimed and booted it over to the stereo.

"No Lady Gaga!" Jenn called out. I actually wanted to put it on out of spite but instead I put on *Peeping Tom*. I thought some of the songs were acerbically appropriate. But she still sneered as the first song came on.

"This weird crap, figures. You're just like Dex, you know," she said, finishing off the last cracker and washing her hands in the sink.

Dex and I exchanged a smirk.

"So I've been told," I said, joining him at the door.

There was a quick knock at the door and some giggles followed from the other side. Dex flung it open, revealing Rebecca and a cute, small blonde girl who must have been Emily. They both smiled at us and Rebecca let out a holler, holding a bottle of Jagermeister high in the air. Oh, God.

"Are you ready to party!?" she yelped, and then threw her arms around Dex, giving him a quick hug. She turned to me and did the same, smelling like all sorts of heavenly things.

She released me and looked over my shoulder at Jenn.

"Hey Jenny Jenn," she greeted her with the slightest trace of amusement.

Jenn smiled, close-lipped. "Becky. Emily. I made some appies."

She gestured to the plate on the bar counter but made no move to bring it over to us.

"So domestic, Jenn," Rebecca said humorously. Dex took her and Emily's coats from them (of course Rebecca's was a luxurious black velvet that matched her hair) while Rebecca put her arm around Emily and brought her up to me.

"Perry, I'd like you to meet my partner Emily," she said. I looked at Emily and offered my hand. She was about my height, maybe an inch or two higher, had a sweet round face and very pale blonde hair. Her eyes were an eerie shade of robin's egg blue that seized your attention. I couldn't make out if they were contacts or not, but they were mesmerizing.

She took my hand politely, but then pulled me into her and gave me a quick hug.

"I think we're on hugging terms already," she said in an angelic, breathy voice.

I looked the couple over. Rebecca was wearing a sequined red shift dress and fishnets while Emily was dressed a little plainer in a black skirt and patterned blouse.

"Are you guys dressed all ready? I thought we were going to get ready together?" I asked.

"Don't you worry," Rebecca said, picking up a huge pebbled leather bag from the floor. "I've got my clothes in here and I just need to convince Emily to put on something else."

Emily rolled her eyes but smiled. "I like this."

"For a job interview, sure," Rebecca said, kissing her on the cheek. I noticed her maroon lips didn't leave a mark. "But this is the party of the year!"

"OK, Rebecca," Dex said with a chuckle as he walked over to the fridge and pulled a beer out of it. "I think you're overselling this party just a bit. Don't you remember last year?"

"What happened last year?" Jenn asked.

"Well of course you don't remember, you passed out in the bathroom an hour into the party," Dex said.

Rebecca laughed sharply and Jenn glared at them both.

"Like you guys were any better," she sniveled. "I just remember it being boring."

"It was boring," Rebecca said. "Until Dean brought out the 151 he snuck in the restaurant. We didn't have to pay for any drinks after that."

I grimaced at the idea of drinking 151 under the table. Even the bottle of Jagermeister looked sinister. I couldn't let myself get too drunk tonight. I felt like I needed my wits about me.

"Don't worry," Emily said, noticing my expression. "We'll both be Shownet party virgins."

"Good," I said. "Because I have no idea what to expect."

"Don't expect much," Dex advised us, eying us both. "Jimmy is cheap as hell. I guess you already know that, kiddo."

"Kiddo," Jenn repeated. "Why do you always call her that? She's not that young."

Dex slowly turned his head to look at her. She was leaning back against the stove, sipping daintily from her glass of red wine. She raised her thin brows at him.

"It's a term of endearment," he said deliberately. "Jennifer."

While Dex and Jenn had a weird little staring match, I looked over at Rebecca and Emily. They looked as awkward as I felt. Rebecca bit her lip briefly and raised her eyes in a "yikes" gesture. Then she lifted up her heavy bag and said, "OK then, how about we start getting ready. That way we don't have to rush later."

"Sounds good," I said, and the three of us went over to the den as Rebecca added, "Let's see what you have planned to wear, Perry."

I could feel Jenn and Dex's eyes on us and as I closed the door to shut them out, I heard Jenn mutter under her breath to him, "I bet they're all going in there to make out."

I rolled my eyes in annoyance and shut the door. Honestly, I didn't know how Rebecca was still a Wine Babe after all of that.

In the room, Emily was staring up at the posters on the wall while Rebecca was already perched on the bed and staring at me expectantly.

"What the hell is going on out there?" she cried out in a hush.

"I..." I started; then wasn't sure what to say. Did I want to tell Rebecca that I told Dex about her theory? "It's a long story."

"You can cut that tension with a butter knife," she said. "It *better* be a long story."

I leaned against the door and sighed until my body was more relaxed. "Dex knows about Jenn and Bradley."

Her eyes narrowed suspiciously. "What about Jenn and Bradley?"

"Well, I kind of told him you had a theory about them."

"I never told you what the theory was."

"I guessed. I'm not dumb."

"No, darling, you're not dumb." She didn't look mad. I explained to them what happened when I went clubbing with Jenn on Wednesday.

"And last night when we were locked in the basement," I continued, "she wasn't answering the phone. And it all kind of came out. Verbal diarrhea."

"Oh boy," Rebecca said. She exchanged a look with Emily then looked back at me expectantly. "Do you know what he's going to do? I mean, he has to break up with her now if he knows."

I shrugged. "That...that I have no freaking idea. I wish I did. I told him he should but..."

"He's a scared little boy," she put in. "Honestly, I don't know how you're dealing with this. It can't be easy."

I eyed Emily nervously. She caught it and smiled reassuringly. "Bex told me about...your crush. It's cool. I only just met you, but for what it's worth, I think he's an idiot if he doesn't feel the same way back."

I blushed at her kind words.

"OK, Ems, you're turning her into an awkward pile of mush," Rebecca said, getting off the bed and rifling through her overflowing bag. "And we can't have mushy Perry tonight. We're getting sexy Perry, isn't that right, darling?"

I nodded slowly, feeling a bit on the spot. About an hour earlier, Ada had texted me with last-minute advice about tonight. Mainly to "just work the shit out of the dress."

"So what are you wearing?" Rebecca asked with her hands on her hips and a carrying kit of makeup in front of her.

I walked over to a stack of boxes where I had laid out the dress so it wouldn't get wrinkled. I picked it up and showed it to her, the teal color catching the light, making it look inviting enough to swim in.

"Ooh, that is gorgeous. And with the shoes, too! Good choice."

I beamed at that. Finally, it seemed I had fashion sense.

She touched Emily's arm and pointed at the door. "We're going to go into the bathroom and get that all ready with hair tools and makeup. The gorgeous station, we'll call it. Come out, shoes and all, when you're done and we'll finish you off."

They both left the room, and I was alone for the first time today.

I locked the door behind them in case Dex decided to mosey on in, and I stripped down until I was totally naked. I couldn't wear a bra with the dress but thankfully there was enough support in the corset that I didn't need one (a first) and the material was that shiny, thin kind that picked up every bump. I was very (and surprisingly) fortunate that I didn't have a lick of cellulite anywhere on my body but it did mean I wouldn't be wearing any underwear. Oh well, no one had to know I was going commando.

I slipped the dress over my head and to my surprise, it fit even better than when I first tried it on. I guess it came from not eating much this whole week. I had originally feared I would have gained weight from not working out but that didn't seem to be the case at all. I was able to reach behind and do up the zipper on my own and without holding my breath.

Next came the shoes. Unfortunately, I knew they weren't going to get more comfortable, unlike the dress. But I managed to stand in them now without wobbling and I made sure to stash a bunch of Band-Aids in my evening bag in case I got a bunch of blisters.

I walked to the door and poked my head out, not wanting Jenn or Dex to see me until I was absolutely ready. The door to their bedroom was closed and no one was in the apartment. The idea that they could be having sex in there made me feel momentarily sick. Rebecca had said that was what their relationship often came down to, just sex.

"Perry," Rebecca said from the bathroom, opening the door a crack and peering at me. I could see Emily behind her also trying to get glimpse.

"Oh my fucking goodness," she exclaimed, her eyes focusing on my rack. I guess I'd have to get used to that. I eyed the bedroom door nervously and she waved her hand at me quickly.

"Get that fine arse over here," she said, opening the bathroom door and ushering me inside.

She closed the door behind me, locked it, and clapped her hands together excitedly.

"Lesbian orgy in the bathroom!" she cried out, then quickly squeezed my shoulder with her hand. "Kidding! Seriously, you look amazing."

"You really do," Emily added from the other side of her, giving me the thumbs up in approval while fiddling with a curling iron.

"What the hell happened here?" Rebecca asked suddenly, grabbing my arm and flipping it over to show the welt. She eyed my hand too. "I noticed the hand before but I thought it was the lighting. What happened?"

"Wasps," I said, turning around, flipping up my hair so she could see the one on my neck. They both gasped dramatically.

"Where the hell did you find wasps at this time of year? Did you feel how cold it is outside? It's supposed to snow tonight," she informed me.

"Again, it's a long story. Let's just focus on making me look hot," I said, not wanting to talk about it.

"Darling, you are already hot. We're going to push you over the edge. Now sit up on the counter here," she said, patting the space between the two sinks.

I did as she asked, making sure to keep my legs together (commando, you know). Rebecca got the large makeup kit out and started to attack my face with it. I relaxed and put my trust in her hands. After all, she looked amazing herself.

I eyed Emily without moving my head. "Does she do this to you too?"

Emily laughed. "Well she tries. I'm not a makeup wearer."

"Ems is lucky she has those eyes of hers. They are just like yours, Perry. Except Emily does need some mascara from time to time."

"She doesn't like me looking too butchy," Emily spoke up and frowned at the awkward curl the iron produced.

"I don't think you could ever look butchy," I told her, trying not to move my lips as Rebecca rubbed foundation on them (for some reason). "Not that there's anything wrong with looking butchy. I mean, I don't know what you..um, lesbians are looking for but I mean..."

"Perry," Rebecca said sternly, interrupting my mindless stammering. "Stop talking. It's OK, we aren't easily offended. I like feminine women. So does Emily. It doesn't always work out that way but it does with us."

"OK, I-"

"No, seriously, stop talking. You're messing me all up."

I clamped my mouth shut and closed my eyes. I sat still for the next few minutes while Rebecca and Emily talked about some new vampire show on HBO they had started watching together. Eventually I heard the bedroom door open and Jenn's heels on the floor heading to the kitchen.

"Guess they are done making up in there," Emily said. My eyes opened and fixed on her.

"Emily," Rebecca admonished. She looked at me apologetically, her poreless nose just inches away from mine as she brushed powder on my cheeks. She lowered her voice. "Sorry Perry, could be old habits die hard in there. Or perhaps Dex has grown a pair and cut Jenn off for good. You never know. I don't know how he'd even want to touch her after learning she's been with Bradley."

"No kidding," Emily shot in, making a disgusting face. I noticed her hair was all done and she was pinning it to the top of her head.

"Well you're all done...kiddo...as Dex would say," Rebecca said. "But before we turn you around, I'm going to do something with your hair." She picked it off of my shoulders and tossed it back. "Very nice hair too, very soft. Usually Italian hair is quite wiry."

"Must be my Swedish side," I said, my lips moving slowly from the heavy applications of gloss.

She frowned at my locks, pursing her perfect mouth and drumming her long fingers against her cheek. Then she took a few bobby pins from beside her, brought out a small comb and did something to my bangs and sides of my hair.

"Half up, half down. Shows off your face, hides the bite on your neck."

"Can I look now?"

She and Emily looked at each other and smiled. "Yes!"

I hopped off the counter, my ass having gone to sleep, and rubbed at it while I turned around.

I couldn't believe the person who was looking back at me.

It was me, of course, but had I not put on the dress beforehand, I would have really been thrown for a loop because I had never looked like this in my entire life. And probably wouldn't ever again.

It wasn't a ton of makeup, but it was enough to make me look, well, a million times better than normal. My eyes looked huge but for once they weren't too cutesy. They were almost...sexy. I think it was the copious amounts of mascara and liquid liner that winged out on the sides. The shadow above it was a smoky blue that matched the dress but didn't look garish. My cheekbones were well defined; my cheeks had a natural pink flush, thanks to different types of blush swirled together, and my lips were a rosy-nude color that made them look a full size bigger.

"Holy..." I trailed off, unable to form words. "I look...weird."

Rebecca laughed and shook me lightly. "You don't look weird, Perry; you look gorgeous and like you're going to a party. I wish I could do the same to Ems here."

"Ha," Ems said. "Let's let the night belong to Perry. Not everyone has to be your Doolittle."

"Point taken," Rebecca said. "Now if you'll excuse me Perry, I think I need to use the loo and get ready myself."

She unlocked the bathroom door and poked her head out. Jenn was in the kitchen drinking her wine again. She had changed too, but from where we were I couldn't see what she was wearing.

"OK go, I'll join you soon," Rebecca said, and I cautiously stepped out into the apartment. I noted Dex's door was still shut.

I slowly walked toward Jenn, my heels clicking on the floor. At the sound, she looked up at me and spurted wine out of her mouth. That was probably the best reaction I could have hoped for.

"Oh my God," she said, and muffled into the cloth as she wiped her face and hands of the wine.

"What?" I asked naïvely, standing beside her and looking her over. She looked good, of course. When didn't she? She was wearing a very tight black, body-con

Lycra dress with strategic cut-outs down the side. Her shoes were high and a patent nude color, which naturally made her skinny legs look amazing. Her hair was down and on the frizzy side and she didn't have her makeup on yet. For the first time ever, I felt like I might be a bit of competition.

"Nothing," she sputtered. "You just took me by surprise. Are you sure you should be showing so much cleavage, though? I mean, it is a work party, after all."

And this was coming from someone who looked like her dress was painted on.

I just smiled at her, hoping my gloss didn't catch on my teeth. "Well, I always say, if you've got it, flaunt it. Now, where's my wine?"

I brushed past her and picked up my glass and filled it half-way with the wine that was out beside her. I took a huge gulp, careful not to choke like she did. Though I may have sounded brazenly confident, I was still shaking slightly from the altercation.

"Fair enough," she said, slowly, and shot me a suspicious look. She was probably wondering where I had stashed Perry Palomino. Then she shook her head and let out an annoyed sigh, her eyes shooting daggers at the bathroom door. "How long are they planning to hog the bathroom? I should have known two extra girls over would put me out."

"I'm sure they'll give you your de-frizz cream and anti-frizz iron if you ask," I said smoothly, trying to hide my smile behind the glass. I just had to throw the word frizz in there twice.

She patted at her hair anxiously and made a sound that sounded like a "harrumph."

"What was that?" I asked, leaning in closer to her.

She frowned at me, utterly confused. I loved knowing something that she didn't know. And she could tell. That upper hand kept me from taking her frizzy head in my hands and bashing it against the kitchen counter.

I noticed the *Peeping Tom* album was over and the CD player had switched onto something autotuney. I took another quick sip of wine, being careful with my gloss, and went over to the player. I scoured the stack of CDs lined up alongside it. Only Dex (and I) would still have a lot of CDs.

"Please, nothing weird," Jenn muttered. I decided to indulge her for now. I selected Beastie Boys *Ill Communication* and stuck it in the player. I pressed play, the barking dog of "Sure Shot" shooting out from the speakers.

As I did so, I heard the bedroom door open and the sound of dress shoes walking across the floor.

"Tie or no tie?" Dex asked.

I straightened up, turned around and stared.

Dex was standing in front of the bar counter facing Jenn. He was wearing a sharp black suit, shiny dress shoes, a white-collared shirt that wasn't buttoned all the way up and had a black tie in his hand. His shiny, ebony hair was lightly spiked up at the sides and off of his expressive forehead. His face was smooth, his moustache and chin scruff trimmed down to an inch of their existence. He looked...beautiful.

He noticed me staring at him and turned his body over to look. Our eyes met. They sparkled more than ever. Now he just looked insanely, devilishly handsome. He took my breath away.

And apparently the feeling was mutual. Because he didn't say anything either.

His eyes fixed on me in absolute surprise. He looked at my chest first, then my waist, my hips, my legs and then back at my face. And when he saw my face, his look intensified. I thought he'd look at me and laugh, considering how different I felt I looked. But he didn't.

"God, Dex, take a picture, it'll last longer," Jenn sneered, placing her wine glass down on the counter with a clank. He barely paid attention as she stormed past him and started pounding on the bathroom door, demanding Rebecca and Emily vacate immediately.

"Perry," he croaked out. "I didn't..."

"Recognize me?" I filled in. "I didn't either."

I walked over to him so he could get a better look and stopped a foot away. He looked even better close up.

My hormones were on fire and making me feel funny all over. I made another mental note to not drink too much.

"Yeah," he breathed out. "You look...nice."

I smiled at that. "As long as I don't look as ridiculous as I feel."

He was still awestruck. "You don't look ridiculous. You look...beautiful."

I blushed on command. I noticed the pounding on the door had stopped and the bedroom door slammed. Jenn was probably attacking her hair in there, defrizzing the crap out of it even though she didn't *really* need to.

"I'm serious," he added, wiping at his chin and giving me the once-over again. The way his eyes glued to my form, they caused goosebumps to pop on my arms. I hoped he wouldn't notice. I wanted nothing more than to be beautiful enough that he'd pick me up in his arms, carry me into the den, throw me on the bed and have his damn way with me.

"Well, give Rebecca credit," I said nervously, waving my hands all over my face. "This was all her magic."

"It's not magic, Perry. You're the most beautiful woman I've ever known and before you say anything, you've always been that way to me."

My mouth dropped open a little bit.

"And I've been with a lot of women, Perry, so I know. Believe me. And you have to learn how to accept a compliment, you got it?"

He reached for my shoulder in a rather awkward manner, then ended up sliding it down my arm, reaching for my hand and holding it in his, his thumb caressing around the welt on it.

I was still speechless but I nodded because I could see how sincere he was. That was maybe the most romantic thing anyone had ever said to me. Aside from the "and I've been with a lot of women" part.

"What do you think?" Rebecca's voice interrupted my thoughts. Dex dropped my hand and turned to look at her. She and Emily were both changed and dolled up. Emily looked cute, albeit slightly uncomfortable with her empire-waisted grey dress, but Rebecca looked wonderful. Her dress was a deep red, to her ankles and slit quite low between her breasts.

She looked down at them and smiled at Dex and me. "I couldn't let Perry be the only one on display."

I was grateful for that. What Jenn has said earlier about it being a work party had been gnawing at my esteem a bit. Rebecca was ensuring I wouldn't be the sluttiest-looking one there.

When I found my voice, I said, "You both look amazing."

"Good enough," Rebecca said, flashing her white teeth at us. "As do both of you."

She walked over to Dex, her heels stomping across the floor. She took the tie from his other hand and said, "No tie. It doesn't suit you."

Then she undid another button his shirt. "You don't have too much chest hair; you can get away with this."

If it wasn't Rebecca up in Dex's face like that, I would have felt a pang of jealousy.

She peered down at me from the lofty perch of her heels, her hands still around Dex's collar as she straightened it out. "What do you think of Perry here?"

The question was obviously for Dex.

"I might prefer the way she normally is," he said to my surprise. "But I think she looks stunning."

"Damn right," she said, giving his collar a final tug. "She doesn't need the makeup, really, but goodness she needs to show off that body more."

I glanced down at my boobs and the rest of me. From my angle, I looked huge, as always.

I looked back up and saw Rebecca, Dex and Emily all looking at me rather rapturously. I smiled cheesily at them, the awkwardness just flooding my pores, and said, "I think now is the time to do shots."

Rebecca let out a hoot and she and Emily ran behind the counter, pulling out the Jager, which ended up in the freezer where it belonged.

Dex patted me lightly on the back as we walked over to join them.

"Relax, kiddo," he said, his voice low and gruff.

I shot him a quick smile. I just felt totally out of my element, yet I was enjoying the novelty of being "hot" at the same time.

Rebecca fished out four glasses from the cupboards and poured us each a shot. We raised them to each other and clinked.

"Wait!" Emily cried out and quickly brought out a tiny camera from her purse. "Pictures!"

"Ems is a mad photo taker," Rebecca explained.

"And pure evil when it comes to tagging photos on Facebook," Dex said, half-glaring at the blonde-haired cherub.

She paid no attention, but held the camera out and attempted to get a picture of us all in mid-shot. The flash flared out blindingly.

We all finished the shots, the Jager burning only a little. Emily flipped the camera around and squeeled.

"It worked," she said, and showed us all. Though Rebecca's head was half cut-out, it was Dex and me with the shot glasses to our lips and Emily at the corner. It was a rather cute picture considering the subject matter, but that said I unfortunately realized it was the only picture that had ever been taken of Dex and me together. I know I had been called "Paparazzi Perry" in high school, but for some reason taking pictures of Dex and me seemed...weird. I guess because we always had the video camera out. I made a mental note to get a photo of just the two of us later.

Jenn burst out of the bedroom and looked us all over with disdain, her hair piled high on top of her head. "Seriously? Jagermeister? How old are we here?"

I raised my hand. "I'm twenty three!"

I could have sworn a little vein in her head was about to pop. I tried not to smile at that.

"OK," she said, picking up the cordless phone. "I think we should call a cab now and head over. They did say to be there by 8 and we're pushing it now."

Probably promised to meet Bradley at a certain time, I thought. And from the look I caught on Rebecca's face, I could see she was thinking the same thing. As for Dex, though, I couldn't tell. He was trying hard not to look in my direction and winning at it.

I grabbed my leather jacket from the coat rack and hustled into the den to grab my little evening purse that Ada had lent me. When I came back out, everyone was at the balcony window and staring outside.

"What is it?" I asked, coming over without tripping over my heels.

"It's snowing," Rebecca said incredulously. I guessed it was as rare in Seattle as it was in Portland.

I poked my head out to join them at the fogged-up window pane. Dark clouds, lit up orange from the city glow, had rolled in over the past few hours. Little, miniscule flakes of white were falling from them. So it was snowing after all. Another thing that made me think tonight was going to be different from any other night. This was going to be memorable.

It already was.

CHAPTER TWENTY-ONE

With five of us, we had to take two separate cabs to the party. There was a slightly weird moment where I wasn't sure who to ride with, Dex and Jenn or Emily and Rebecca. I really was the fifth wheel in this case, the singleton. But luckily Rebecca was the first one to speak up and insist that I was riding with her and Emily. Fine by me.

I got in our cab (the first to arrive), which smelled like incense and was filled with the sounds of Bhangra music.

As the cab pulled away from Dex and Jenn's apartment, Emily started making small talk with the driver about the impending snowfall, while Rebecca picked up my non-welted hand and gave it squeeze.

"So," she said, leaning in close, her voice dancing. "That couldn't have gone better."

"I don't know what you mean."

"Oh, come on, Perry. You saw the way Dex was looking at you. We ambushed you guys. He was holding your hand; I saw it."

I shrugged, not wanting to think too much into it lest my heart start eating away at my logic. "Think nothing of it."

"I know what you're doing," she whispered.

"Do you?" I asked, fixing my eyes on her to show I meant business.

She wasn't fazed. "Yes."

Then she brought out the bottle of Jager from her purse. "Pardon me, good sir," she said, tapping the cabbie on the shoulder. "Do you mind if we quickly imbibe from this? We will be neat and tidy."

The cabbie eyed the bottle quickly, then eyed Rebecca's chest. "If you're quick. Don't spill, you'll pay the fine," he said, pointing at the sign on the door that indicated we'd be paying for any wayward liquids or vomit.

She nodded. "Don't worry."

She took a shot straight out of the bottle, then handed it to Emily and me. We exchanged a worried glance between each other, though I suppose the Shownet virgins of the bunch needed it the most, and followed through. The shot burned less the second time, but I was already feeling saucy and lightheaded, which was typically a bad combination.

"I wonder how awkward Jenn and Dex's car ride is," I mused out loud.

"Well, if I know them," Rebecca offered, "one of them is giving the other the silent treatment. Though at this stage, I couldn't say who. They definitely aren't acting normal, that's for certain."

"You think you'll make a move tonight?" Emily asked, leaning forward on the other side of her partner.

"Me?"

"Yes darling, you," Rebecca said. She drummed her long manicured nails on her knees along to the music. The snow outside was starting to stick to the windshield. "If you don't make a move on him tonight, Perry, I think you're missing out. You are so bloody alike."

I let what she said stew in my mind. We were alike. I was seeing this more and more each day. Either we always were, or it was a byproduct of spending too much time together. Maybe he was becoming more like me, as I was becoming more like him. I was certainly adapting to the fearlessness he seemed to possess, at least on the surface. But that didn't mean anything. It happened all the time with people who were together a lot.

Soon we were pulling up to the restaurant just outside of the downtown area, down by the waterfront where the ferries and cruise ships were. It looked like a normal restaurant in a brick building, nothing fancy, and certainly not indicating there was a party inside.

But as soon as we all stepped out of the cab, after squabbling over who was paying the cab fare (Emily won because she had an actual "real" job), I recognized Dean and Seb standing outside the doorway sharing a cigarillo. The light snow fell lightly around us and was sticking to the ground in bits. To quote a song, it was beginning to feel a lot like Christmas.

I held my jacket close to me and Emily and I both hovered nearby as Rebecca went to hug both of the gamers. They extended the same courtesy to us. When Dean pulled back from our embrace he got the same look on his face that Dex had earlier.

"Wow," he stuttered.

"Thank you," I replied with a smile, remembering Dex's words about taking a compliment. I'd take "wow" as a compliment, wouldn't you?

"You look great," he said, and jerked his thumb at me while glancing at Rebecca. "You talk to Bradley about her? Maybe you guys need a third babe in Wine Babes."

I laughed. "Aw, hell no."

He grinned at me. "Well, you just went up a few more points in my book."

"Score for me," I said with a wink. I don't know why I winked; I never winked at anyone before, but out it came. The dress, the makeup, the Jager...it was all very dangerous. And suddenly making a "move" on Dex seemed to be not only possible but not the most important thing this evening either. There was a chance I could catch the eyes of other men. Dean was a bit too nerdy to be my type, and Seb seemed to be a bit of a thirty-something slacker, but who knew who else was inside?

"How's the party?" Rebecca asked.

"Lame. It's too early, though you guys are some of the last ones to arrive," he said, taking a puff of the cigarillo and passing it to Seb, who had so far remained quiet. Judging from the red glaze to his eyes, he was just probably very baked.

"Are Jenn and Dex here yet?" I asked.

"Yeah," he thumbed now at the door. "They got here a few minutes ago."

"I don't know how they beat our cab," Rebecca said, shaking her head. "What about Bradley?"

"Not yet," Dean said. "But Jimmy is here and he's in a good mood, buying drinks for people. It's not an open bar but at least the drinks are cheap and the food is free. As is the karaoke. But man, I wish they had a rule that you didn't have to listen to it until you were good and drunk."

He reached out and tapped me lightly on my shoulder. I was shaking in my spot, feeling the cold flakes land on my bare legs. Tights would have been smart.

"He's looking forward to meeting you again," he said to me.

I bet, I thought. "Shall we go inside? I'm dying a bit."

Dean nodded and Seb tossed the smoke out onto a patch of snow that had just formed.

We walked into the restaurant, which was filled with patrons. It was somewhat fancy in that modern way, which meant white tablecloths, black napkins, weird fountains and artwork and lots of mirrors and glass. The waitresses were all dressed like hookers in black.

"We've got the room in the back," Dean said over his shoulder, and we followed him past the main dining room, down a narrow corridor past the bathrooms and into a smaller, cozier space.

The design was the same but there were only about eight round tables with about two to six people at each one. There was an open buffet of appetizers; a small bar in the corner and in front of the room was a small stage where the karaoke machine was hooked up. The lyrics to "Don't Let the Sun Go Down on Me" were playing on a screen behind it and some middle-aged man in a Hawaiian shirt was doing his best Elton John and/or George Michael impression. It wasn't very good.

We all cringed in unison at the off-key wails and looked around the party. We spotted Dex and Jenn at the table near the back of the room. It was empty, which was sign enough that we should make our way over.

As we did so, every single head in the room turned to look at us. Most of the people I didn't recognize at all, but they seemed to know me. They leaned in close to each other and whispered. I didn't want to know what they were saying.

I stopped in front of Dex and Jenn. They were watching the guy perform and laughing at him, but Dex immediately stood up and pulled out a chair for me beside him.

I smiled quickly at him and sat down as neatly as possible, with Rebecca and Emily going beside me. Dean and Seb went and sat at the table next to us, beside Jimmy Kwan and his very pretty, very petite half-Asian wife. At least, that's who I assumed it was. Jimmy was Korean-American and I knew he was married, despite the odds (not because he's Korean, but because he's a jerk).

I managed to stop staring at them before they looked over.

"How did you guys beat us here?" I asked, leaning closer to Dex.

"We bribed our cabbie. Like hell I'd let you drink the bar clean before I got here."

"Right," I said, and turned my attention back to the karaoke singer, who was almost – mercifully – done. "Who is that guy?"

"That's Rick. He hosts a handyman show. There's the whole home design and handy fucks table down by the stage there."

He pointed at the table next to them, "That's the whole Amanda Panda's Animal Friends sector."

He moved his finger over to the other side of the stage, where a bunch of long-haired dudes were. Despite the festive dress code, most were still wearing band T-shirts. They were all cheering and doing shots of dark booze.

"Crucial Taught?" I asked. "The Shitty Beatles?"

"Close. That's Riff Raff. The show. That tall guy with the blonde mullet, he's actually an awesome guitar player. Mick Stevens. Look him up. He could teach you a thing or two, if not just by watching the show."

"I bet he could," I said. "But so could you."

Dex grinned at me and I felt my insides pulse.

"I could. But while I'm good, he's one of the best."

"Dex," I heard a familiar voice say from behind us. I swiveled and looked up to Jimmy Kwan standing there, staring down at me expectantly.

"Jimmy," Dex said and got up. I followed his lead and got up alongside him. I stuck my hand out for Jimmy. He just eyed it and frowned at me from underneath his spectacles.

"Perry Palomino?" he asked in a tight voice.

I raised my brows at Dex, who did the same in return as he sipped his Jack and Coke. Who else would I be?

"You look a lot different from our first meeting," Jimmy continued. "And on the show."

He stroked his chin, seeming to think while eyeing me up and down. OK, I looked different but I still looked like the same girl.

"She got all gussied up for you," Dex said with his charming grin on display. He leaned in close to Jimmy and whispered in his ear. "Just don't tell your wife."

Jimmy chuckled, the first time I'd seen actual harmless amusement on his face. "Well I'm flattered."

Great, can I sit down now? I thought. I felt awkward and I didn't need to turn my head to know that other people in the room were looking at us.

"It's nice to see you again, Jimmy," I said, taking my hand back and looking him straight through his glasses. "I hope the way you're ogling me means you're going to start paying me more."

Dex burst out in shocked laughter, choking on his drink while Jenn and Rebecca let out a low gasp. I watched Jimmy carefully, wondering if he was going to fire me on the spot for being a smartass.

Instead he smiled, broadly, showing misshapen teeth, and reached over and patted me hard on the arm.

"I like you better already," he said with a laugh as looked over at Dex, who was trying to get his cough under control. "Good job with her, Dex. You're corrupting bright young women everywhere."

"That's not my doing," Dex managed to say, setting his drink down and wiping his mouth with the sleeve of his suit jacket. "That's the real her coming out."

I shrugged and tried to look nonplussed, though I was also kicking myself for being so risky with my words. Just because it worked with Dex, it didn't mean it worked with me. Though perhaps this really was me. And it had worked.

"Well, whatever it is," Jimmy said. "I'm glad to meet you again, Perry. Welcome to the Shownet family. We're lucky to have you."

I smiled graciously and shot Dex a shy smile. "And I'm lucky to have Dex here."

Believe it or not, Dex actually blushed for the first time ever. It was amazingly cute. I sensed Jenn shifting uncomfortably on the other side of him.

Jimmy gave us both an odd look, his attention shifting between us, as if he was trying to suss out our real relationship with each other. Good luck with that. Even I didn't know at this point.

"Well, we are lucky to have Dex, too," Jimmy said, and then fixed his eyes on him. "By the way, Dex, do you have a friend called Maximus?"

Both Dex and I perked up.

"Max?" Dex asked. "Yes, why?"

He shot me a nervous glance and I shrugged, just as intrigued as he was.

"He called me the other day, said you two were friends," Jimmy explained. "He said he was moving to Portland, God knows why, and was wondering if I needed his services."

"Portland?" I repeated at the same time Dex said "Services?"

Jimmy shrugged. "I think he had an idea for a show. He said you guys were at NYU, I don't know I couldn't really understand his accent. He mentioned something about helping you in Red Fox. I haven't called him back yet; I just wanted to make sure he's legit."

I watched Dex closely. He rubbed at his sideburn and smiled hesitantly. "Yeah, he's legit..."

Jimmy put his hand on Dex's shoulder and said, "We'll talk about this on Monday. By the way, I saw what you shot at the institute. Good stuff. Both of you."

He turned and went back to his table, leaving Dex and me staring at each other.

"Well, Maximus did mention he might move to the Pacific Northwest," I pointed out.

"True," Dex said slowly.

While we were thinking that over, the MC for the night took over the mic and told us the karaoke machine was going on a break and that a dance floor would be forming behind our table. Everyone got up and pushed the table in closer to the others. As we did so, and as a makeshift DJ started pumping out hits from a Mac, Bradley entered the room.

It was hard not to stare at him. He was so tall and handsome, especially with his fashionable five o' clock shadow and the way his golden highlighted hair set off his blue eyes. His pinstriped navy suit was snazzy too, and made him look a million times richer than anyone in the room, which was ultimately his point.

Everyone at our table was still standing up when he came over. He gave us a short wave and a jackass grin.

"Sorry I'm late," he said in his smooth voice. He pulled out his chair without hesitation and sat down right beside Jenn. I looked at Rebecca and Emily, who were as tense and wide-eyed as I was. I don't think any of us could believe his nerve, going straight for his fuck buddy.

Dex couldn't believe it either. I watched as his hands tightened over the top of his chair, his knuckles turning a bluish white. I waited for him to lift the chair above his head and ram it into Bradley's head.

To his credit though, he didn't, even though I saw his eyes sparking, projecting his patented death glare. I took my hand and gently poked him in the side. He jumped and looked down at me. I smiled sympathetically. He bit his lip, looked back at the two and then quickly muttered, "I'm going to get a shot."

I watched him walk off as Rebecca got out of her chair and hurried after him.

"Wait for me," she called.

I eyed Jenn, who had now sat back down beside Bradley. I wanted to flip the entire table over. I could see it all in my head, the drinks flying in the air and covering her from head to toe.

I felt a hand at my elbow, bringing me back to reality, and turned to see Dean standing there. He pushed his glasses up further on his nose.

"Care to dance, Perry?" he asked with the tiniest hint of trepidation.

"What?" I said, surprised. His face fell a tiny bit. "No, I mean, of course. I just can't dance too well in these heels. Or, like, ever."

Dean smiled and exhaled at the same time, his teeth white against his cocoa skin. "Good, I can't dance in general, so you're in good company."

I let him lead me to the dance floor, which was quickly filling up with people as a re-mixed version of Justin Timberlake's "Sexy Back" just started playing over the speakers. I think everyone was just grateful for something else to listen to than god-awful karaoke.

"Seriously, though," I whispered to Dean. "I'm going to dance like an idiot."

"Well, let's see it," he said. Then he started busting out some pretty impressive dance moves, darting back and forth with just the right head movements, singing along with the song. He was actually good, which meant I was going to look a million times sillier. Oh well. I'd just have to "get my sexy on."

I started moving and grooving, all the stupid things that I had tried out with Dex in his living room.

Halfway through the song, I was attracting a lot of attention. Well, Dean was too. He was the serious, talented half and I was the silly goof who was dancing like Elaine from *Seinfeld*. Rebecca and Emily appeared beside us, dancing too, as did Jimmy and his wife, who were off beside the DJ. I turned to see where Dex was and he was right behind me. He shook his head at my moves and grinned, but kept walking past me to go talk to Jimmy.

I kept dancing as the re-mixed beats pounded on, getting faster and faster near the end. I started putting some kicks into my moves.

"Not bad," Dean yelled above the music, giving me the thumbs up and then working the gesture into his moves seamlessly.

I smiled and kicked again.

This time my shoe came loose.

It left my foot and sailed through the air as if in slow motion and headed right toward Dex.

He turned just in time to see my raspberry platform soaring toward him like a heat-seeking missile. He ducked.

And it went straight into the person who was standing behind Dex: Jimmy Kwan. My shoe smacked him right on the head and bounced off of his dome and onto the DJ's table with a clunk.

Everyone went silent. I mean, *everyone*.

I gasped. My hands flew up to my mouth. I was frozen on the spot, mortified beyond belief.

Then the room erupted into peals of laughter. Dex was laughing the hardest of all, so hard he could barely stand back up straight. Jimmy shot me a wry look and slowly shook his head, not impressed. But one quick glance at his wife and she was snickering too.

I knew I was beet red. I felt flushed beyond belief.

Dean put his arm around me, trying to speak but laughing too hard. Finally he sputtered, "Oh man. You just made this the best Christmas party ever!"

I grinned back at him. Unsure at first but then I couldn't help but laugh either. Served Jimmy right, even though I needed my shoe back.

As if on cue, Jimmy's wife walked over to me, still giggling, my rogue shoe dangling from her fingers. She placed it in my hands. "I don't think we've been properly introduced. I'm Fae Kwan."

"Nice to meet you, Fae," I said. "Sorry about um...my aim."

She giggled and looked behind her at Jimmy. He was attempting to talk to Dex while rubbing at his head. Dex was trying to keep a straight face but kept on laughing every other second.

"I think my husband will be OK," she smiled, then noticed the blush on my face. "Do you need some cold water?"

I nodded quickly and Fae led the way out of the room and to the bathrooms.

We made small talk at the sinks, just a bit about the show and the network. I didn't have to go to the bathroom yet (and I wasn't about to break the seal this early in the game) so I just dabbed a bunch of cold water on my cheeks and neck, extra careful not to mess up Rebecca's makeup job.

As we left the restroom Fae told me she was going to talk to the waitress in the restaurant about getting some more food for us before everyone got too drunk. She was afraid my hit to Jimmy was spurring everyone to be more merry and festive than usual and that usually translated into more drinking.

I watched her leave, her tiny form weaving through the restaurant tables, then I took a deep breath and prepared myself to return to the party.

As I turned around I saw Jenn and Bradley appear in the corridor. I froze at the side of the hall. They both shot me nervous glances but kept walking. Past me and past the bathrooms.

"Where the hell do you think you're going?" I yelled after them. The words shocked me. I couldn't help it.

Jenn and Bradley came to a halt. Jenn slowly turned around and cocked her head at me, her eyes blazing.

"Excuse me?" she sneered loudly.

I took a more commanding stance in the middle of the hall and looked at them dead on. "I said, where are you going?"

"None of your business, shrimp," Bradley sniped. "Come on, Jenn, let's go." He touched her shoulder briefly in an effort to lead her out of the restaurant. But she wouldn't move. She just watched me for a few moments and then started walking toward me.

"Jenn!" Bradley hissed, making a grab for her.

She shrugged him off and stopped a couple of feet away.

"What the hell is your deal, Palomino?" she asked in an accusing tone, narrowing her eyes. She was trying to look intimidating. I wasn't about to have any of that.

"I have no deal, Jenn; I just think it's a bit, uh, uncouth of you to go sneaking off with your fuck buddy here in the middle of a party."

Her jaw dropped. Bradley made a surprised noise from behind her. I smiled, a grin of pure evil.

"Oh, that's right," I continued, noting their faces. "Everybody knows. I do. Rebecca does. Your boyfriend does."

"You don't know anything," she spat out through her gritted veneers. That vein in her forehead pulsed dangerously.

"Oh, but we do. You know what we also know? Why, that you're my Miss Anonymous. Which means you are nothing more than a sad, pathetic, insecure, cold-hearted...cunt. That's right. Cunt!"

I yelled that last word a lot louder than I should have. Fae caught it as she was coming back down the hallway. She looked at us in shock, afraid of what was going to happen next, and stopped a little way off to make sure nothing stupid happened.

Jenn's jaw dropped even lower and she let out a small, indignant cry. "How dare you?"

"How dare you!?" I countered, feeling years of anger, years of being bullied and ignored and picked on, all rising through me like an unstoppable volcano. "All this time you were being nice to me and I felt like I had to protect you while you went and diddled Bradley behind Dex's back. Meanwhile, you were the stupid fucking bitch who was leaving all those comments on the blog, calling me fat, calling me pathetic. You were just talking about yourself and projecting it on me. That's all. You're too selfish and stupid to realize it. And yes, Dex knows. He's the one who told me. He's the one who caught you using his computer!"

Jenn looked shocked into submission. Her eyes were almost frozen in anger or fear. Fear that we all knew about her. The truth about her.

Bradley took a tentative step toward her, his arm extended, and whispered, "Is that true, Jenn?"

She snapped out of it and whipped around to face him, her fists clenched at her sides. "No, it's not true! Perry is just a fucking psychopath!"

I looked over at Fae, who was inching down the hall, and gave her an apologetic smile. I know I had just shown an ugly and vulgar side of myself, but it had to happen. She returned the smile, perhaps knowing more about Jenn than I knew, and tapped me lightly on the shoulder to lead me back to the party.

"Forget about her," she said softly. I exhaled loudly, trying to release the building anger. I turned to follow her and saw Rebecca walking toward me, concerned.

"You go back to Dex!" I heard Jenn yell from behind me. "He's never going to love you, no matter how hard you try to slut it up for him!"

Oh, *that did it.*

I let out an unearthly scream and whirled around ready to tackle her to the ground and rip her hair out of her head. But just as I made the lunge, I felt hands around both of my arms. Rebecca and Fae had leaped forward and grabbed hold of me, holding me back. In fact, I think at one point I was weightless, my legs kicking out while Rebecca put her arms around me and attempted to pick me up.

Funnily enough, Jenn had also made a go at me but Bradley was right there and scooped her up by the waist.

So it was Jenn and I almost battling to the death outside the bathrooms, save for the people on either side of us, trying to keep the party from turning into a bloodbath.

Realizing how stupid it was to fight Jenn (even though I would win), I eventually relented and let Fae lead me backward away from Jenn's writhing, screaming form. She was almost foaming at the mouth. I glared at her one last time before turning around while Rebecca marched over to them. I heard her yell at Jenn, "You go for a walk, Jenn, and clear your head!" Then she yelled at Bradley, "And you, mister, don't you dare follow her. You are coming back to the party with us and sitting down at the table and acting like none of this ever happened!"

That seemed like a pretty tall order from Rebecca. Jenn and I almost got into a fight. How on earth do you pretend that didn't happen?

CHAPTER TWENTY-TWO

Fae gently, and with a hint of trepidation, led me back into the party room. I could hear Rebecca and Bradley following behind me. I would have thought everyone knew what was going on, but they all looked preoccupied, including Dex, who was in the corner and talking to Jimmy like nothing had happened. I let out a sigh of relief at that and looked down at Fae's kind face.

"I'm really sorry about that," I said.

"Don't worry about it. You think you're the first person Jenn has had a problem with? Believe me, you're not."

I smiled with relief and a touch of embarrassment. If it weren't for Rebecca and Fae, Jenn and I would be involved in the world's biggest and most disgraceful catfight. I would have kicked her ass and she would have fought dirty. But at least now it was all out in the open and done with. As much as she denied it, she knew we all knew the truth and that was all I needed.

I let out a huge breath and Fae gave me a quick hug before sauntering off to Jimmy. I wondered if she'd later fill him on to what happened. Probably. I just hoped it didn't damage my reputation any further. In one evening I would become known as a smartass, a shoe-kicker, and a brawler. This really was one hell of a Christmas party.

I was standing beside the small stage, gathering my thoughts and composure, as the MC came back out in his cheesy cheap suit.

"So," he bellowed into the mic. The DJ shut the house music off. "I think it's time for karaoke again. Now before you complain, I think it's safe to say that dancing has become a bit of a liability tonight."

The MC wiggled his bushy brows at me and I rolled my eyes, blushing once again. Everyone in the room laughed and one person hollered. Without turning to look, I was pretty sure it was Rebecca.

"OK then," I said underneath my breath, and stepped on to the stage. I held my hand out for the mic. "Well, if we're going to do this, let's do this."

I was still so angry and frustrated, the adrenaline coursing through my veins, that I needed something to distract me, even if that meant making another fool of myself in public.

The MC looked surprised but handed the mic to me. "All right, looks like she's going first. Just no kicking moves, OK?"

Everyone laughed again, and I smiled sarcastically at him until he got off the stage and walked over to the machine.

"What do you want to sing?" he asked, about to flip through the songs.

"Soundgarden!" Dex yelled from the back of the room. I looked over everyone's head and saw him giving me the OK sign and smiling cheekily. He had sat back down at the table beside Rebecca and Emily. Of course he would say that. He wanted to hear it ever since I told him I did a Chris Cornell impression. Actually it was more of a parody than an impression...

"Ah, a Seattle favorite," the MC said, and touched a few buttons on the machine. "You got it, Dex. We don't have much selection here, so it'll have to be this Pretty Noose."

Luckily "Pretty Noose" wasn't the hardest song to sing and I knew it by heart so I didn't need to look at the lyrics. I nodded, swallowed hard, my eyes avoiding the crowd, knowing that again everyone was looking at me. As the "wah-wah" guitar intro flowed in, I quickly kicked off my shoes beside me, not risking it. And I waited.

I nodded my head in time to the cymbal hits, my fingers dancing beside me to guitar. Then the drums and sound burst in and I put the mic to my lips, and sang (overdramatically) along.

By the time I was done with the first verse, my voice was warmed up and I was singing/imitating the shit out of the song. My voice was surprisingly powerful and clear, only cracking at certain bits. The Riff Raff crew at the front were clapping already and letting out little woos. I was too embarrassed to look at my table, so I kept my eyes closed and channeled as much energy into my "performance" as I could. I acted like I was being hung from a noose and headbanged along with the beat.

When I wasn't doing that, I was acting like I was at a drum set. When I imitated the noose for the second time I looked over at Dex. He was watching me, not smiling, just looking amazed. I took that as a good sign, then fell dramatically to my knees just in time for the guitar solo, which I pretended to play (even though I was never able to play it well in real life). I air-guitared and everyone cheered. I reached back and pulled the rest of my hair loose, so when I got back up to my feet, I was able to headbang with abandon, my black tresses flying everywhere.

Near the end of the song, everyone was singing along (like the true Seattleites they were) and I finished it off by giving a dramatic, "Yeah!"

The room erupted into applause. I stood up straight, my knees shaking against each other, and brushed my hair off my face. I beamed at the attention. I couldn't help it.

"Great job miss...miss..." the MC said as he came back on the stage and took the mic from me.

"Palomino!" someone yelled from one of the tables.

"Ah yes, round of applause for Miss Palomino. Now, who is next?"

I exited the stage, grabbing my shoes as I went, just as some forty-something woman from the animal show hopped up. I walked barefoot over to the bar and leaned against it while putting my dreaded shoes back on my feet.

"Fuck me," Dex exclaimed. I looked up and smiled at him. He was standing beside me, still looking awed.

"It was your song, Dex," I said.

"You...you..."

I gave him an expectant look.

"You're going to put me to shame when I go up there."

"Pffft," I said, and turned back to the bar to get the bartender's attention. I got it right away. He was tall, wiry and cute and grinned at me.

"What can I get for you, gorgeous?" he asked, his hand sliding over the glasses beneath the counter.

"I'm getting it," Dex said, leaning against the counter beside me, his shoulder pressed up against mine. He threw a fifty in front of the bartender.

I raised my brow at him, trying not to laugh. "High rolling, are we now?"

"Just keep it under ten bucks," Dex said with a wink.

I nudged him playfully and told the bartender to pour us both a Jack and Coke.

"Rubbing off on you again, am I?" Dex asked.

I rolled my eyes and turned around to survey the room. Jenn was back at the table now beside Bradley. Dex followed my eyes and sighed.

"I know," he said slowly.

I eyed him quizzically. "Did you hear about what happened?"

"What happened?" he asked. He seemed sincere.

"I'll tell you later," I said quickly, not wanting to get into it here. Not until after everyone had cooled down.

"Always with the later, Perry. What if there is no later?"

I gave him a strange look. "What do you mean?"

"I mean," he started, reaching across the bar and handing me my drink, "we really oughta start living in the now, don't you think?"

He raised his glass. I raised mine. We clinked. I was about to take a sip but he said, "Uh-uh, Perry. You have to look me in the eyes. Otherwise it's seven years bad sex. For both of us. And we can't have that, can we?"

I blushed again and looked deep into his eyes. He was looking at me like he never had before. His dark brown beautiful eyes that were so familiar to me had suddenly changed. There was another layer there, this one filled with things I didn't dare dream about. Longing, passion, lust and intensity. I wondered how sudden the change was. Maybe he had always looked at me like that and I was only just noticing.

We both took a slow sip of our drinks, not taking our eyes off each other. He smiled, his lips twitching in an almost predatory way. I couldn't say I wasn't returning the same look.

"Uh, sir, your change?" the bartender's voice penetrated the space between our interlocked eyes.

Dex tore his gaze off of me and smiled at the bartender, unamused. "Yes, thanks."

He swiped the change from him and tossed a ten dollar bill on the table as a tip.

I felt awkward and off guard so I straightened up, instinctively smoothing my hair behind my ears. "You *are* a high roller," I joked, my voice uneven.

He smirked at that but it couldn't dissipate the awkwardness and sudden tension between us.

"Guess we better join the others," he said, clearing his throat. He walked toward the table. I followed.

To their credit, Jenn and Bradley weren't talking to each other. Bradley was busy texting someone and Jenn was involved in small talk with a woman at the table next to them. As I took my seat, Rebecca and Emily broke out into little claps.

"Huzzah!" Rebecca said giddily. "You're a rock star, Perry!"

I waved at her bashfully. "Oh come on, that was a piss-poor impression."

"No, it was awesome," Emily shot in.

I took my seat as Dex took his and he whispered into my ear, "What did I tell you about taking a compliment?"

I nodded. I smiled gratefully at Rebecca and Emily. It was a hard thing to accept but I was learning. I don't think I had ever been complimented so much in my entire life. This evening had almost become the high point of my existence.

"Well, it's my turn now," Dex said and abruptly got out of his seat. The song had just ended (another person attempting to sing to Elton John) and the last singer was coming off the stage to polite golf claps.

I watched Dex saunter his way to the front of the stage, swaying a bit and bumping into the occasional chair. The booze was starting to kick in with him.

Rebecca placed her hand on mine and gave it a quick squeeze.

"How are you doing?" she asked sweetly, her eyes flitting to Jenn and back. I didn't bother following them. I was avoiding looking in Jenn's direction like I'd get some eye disease if I did.

"Good," I answered, then remembered the way Dex had looked at me only moments earlier. "I think. Maybe better than good."

She smiled quickly. "Good."

We turned our attention to Dex, who was now on the stage and whispering something to the MC. The MC nodded, looking impressed, and then plugged a few things on the machine.

"He's quite the singer," Rebecca said, loudly this time, so that Jenn and Bradley both looked at her. She nodded at the stage and suddenly Dex had everyone's attention.

The song he chose started to play. It took a while for me to recognize it. It was "This Guy's In Love With You" by Herb Alpert, written by Burt Bacharach. An old song and one I didn't know too well, but it somehow suited Dex and loungey/crooner act just fine.

More than fine, actually. The minute Dex got the mic, he was hamming it up to the extreme. His voice was flawless and better than Herb's. He was acting the song out, stepping off the stage and serenading all the women at the Amanda Panda table, telling them all that he needed and wanted their love.

I know I had a stupid smile on my face as I watched him. I couldn't help it and I didn't care who it saw it.

Then he left the table, the women's gazes following him adoringly. He walked over to our table. My heart pounded loudly in my head. He started singing to Rebecca and Emily first. They giggled in response.

Then he turned to Jenn. And, at the most dramatic part, he belted the song out...to her. His voice soared, his eyes fixed on her and she...she just looked away. She looked at Bradley. And as much as I hated the fact that Dex tried one last attempt to "woo" Jenn or make things right with her, it broke my heart to see his beautiful effort going to waste right in front of him.

But if it bothered him, he didn't show it. He just cruised back to the stage, giving a few high fives to the Riff Raff crew before he stepped back on.

He continued the song, but this time his attention was only in one place and in one place to the end.

It was straight ahead.

On me.

Every note he sang, every gesture he made to his heart, he made it without breaking eye contact with me. The rest of the room seemed to drift away, fizzling out at the corner of my vision. According to the lyrics, he needed me to say I was I love with him...this guy. And I beamed it back at him, unable to look away. Because...I was in love with that guy. It was a poignant moment between the two of us and it was a moment we would always have, no matter what happened tomorrow.

When the song wound down and he was swaying to the remaining beats, Jenn and Bradley both got up, walked around the tables and left the room. I don't know if anyone else besides Rebecca and Emily noticed. Maybe Fae. And definitely Dex. His eyes darted to the side and followed their forms as they left. And his posture shrank by at least a foot.

Dex took the mic and tossed it up at the MC, who caught it awkwardly. Then Dex casually leaped off the stage and went down the corridor as if to follow Jenn and Bradley.

I looked at Rebecca, unsure if I should do something.

"Go after him," she said determinedly. "And if looks like he's about to beat up Bradley, well then, for heaven's sake...let him!"

I nodded and got out of my seat. I walked quickly out of the room, hoping no one thought the mass of people who just left the room was a bit suspicious. Maybe no one would notice that half of Wine Babes and all of Experiment in Terror was missing.

I walked as fast as my killer pumps would allow, not dwelling on the blisters that had formed on top of my toes (thanks, stupid toe pads), past the washrooms and through the restaurant. It was getting late now and the place was only half-full with late-night revelers. They all eyed me as I hurried past.

I burst out of the front doors and into the absolute chill of the night. The front of building was deserted; only a taxi cab and a lone car were slowly cruising down the street. The snow was now at least two inches high and falling steadily. It was cold as hell but, for the moment, my drunk skin didn't feel it.

I looked around, up and down the streets that branched off. I didn't see anyone at all. It was like all of Seattle had shut down due to the miniscule amounts of white stuff.

A movement out of the corner of my eye made me turn to my left. At the corner of the brick building, a lone puff of smoke emerged.

I walked carefully, trying not to slip on the wet, icy ground beneath me, and poked my head around the corner.

Dex was there, leaning against the wall, watching the empty street in front of him and smoking a cigarette.

"Dex?" I said gently, afraid to startle him.

He looked over at me and gave me a quick, sheepish smile after he noticed me looking at the cigarette in his hand. "Sorry," he mumbled, taking another drag. "I had to. I bummed it off a...bum."

I gingerly made my way over to him, keeping one hand on the brick wall for support, and stopped right up next to him. I peered at his face, looking for signs of pain.

He glanced at me quickly, frowned and looked away. "What is it?"

"Are you OK?" I asked. I placed my hand on the crook of his elbow.

He looked down at my hand, bit his lip for a few seconds, then let out a large exhalation of smoke that floated up into the falling snowflakes. They had started to gather in his hair.

I waited patiently for his answer, even though I knew he wasn't OK. I tightened my grip around his arm, trying not to feel the snow that was gathering on my bare shoulders and legs.

"Where did Jenn and Bradley go?" I asked quietly.

He shrugged. "To fuck somewhere, I'm sure."

"I'm sorry," I said.

He smiled at me. There was sadness on his brow but an odd little twinkle in his eye. It was a strange combination.

"I'm sorry too," he said. "Hope you realize I really need this smoke."

"I wouldn't blame you if you started sticking it straight into your veins."

"Now that's a good idea," he said. He smiled but it quickly faded and he stared down at his dress shoes as they stood out against the white snow. He eyed me quickly. "You must be freezing."

"I'm not," I said, hoping my teeth wouldn't start chattering on cue.

He rolled his eyes and smirked. He stuck the cigarette in his mouth, hanging it loosely from his lips, took off his suit jacket and placed it around my shoulders. He pulled me in closer to him at the same time. I instinctively put my nose to the collar and breathed in.

"You're smelling it," he observed, sounding amused.

"I like the smell of you," I admitted shyly. I felt like we were rounding some home stretch and the finish line was in sight. It didn't matter anymore what I said. I was sending my pride and ego packing.

He swallowed hard and took in another drag of his smoke, not breaking our eye contact. "Is that all you like about me?"

I took in a deep breath and said, "I just...like you. I like everything about you."

And with that, I could almost hear dramatic drumming in my head, the swirls of disorienting guitar, like the turbulent ending of "Something." I could feel it pulsing through my veins, I could feel it in the snow-filled air around us, I could feel it vibrating off of both our bodies, like we were both attached to some electrical source, some furnace, and the switches were all being flipped on. The air in my lungs was becoming heavier and catching on the way out.

Dex came off of the wall and turned toward me. The energy between us intensified. He took the cigarette and flicked it out onto the road just as another cab cruised by, slowing down slightly as it drove past us. I paid no attention. The only thing I saw was Dex's face and his eyes as they gazed down at me more rapturously than before.

He took his hand and gently brushed the snow off my hair, tucking stray pieces between my ears. He let his hand drift down to the edge of my jaw and held it there, a surge of heat against the cold.

"You've always been there for me, Perry," he said with what sounded like velvet rocks in his voice. "Even from the very beginning, even if you never meant to be, even when you shouldn't have been. You're the light in all this madness. You're my light. I should have been with you..." The thought hit him as his face crumpled in amazement. "Oh God, why am I not with you?"

"Because you're an idiot," I said.

And then I kissed him.

CHAPTER TWENTY-THREE

I don't know what possessed me. I'd later play victim to ending the tension, for having to do the inevitable. For what had to happen. What I had wanted to happen for quite a long time.

But whatever the reason, I leaned into Dex. I grabbed the sides of his head with both of my hands, his hair slightly slippery from the snow and hair gel, and I pulled his face down to mine. I placed my lips flush on his and kissed him sweetly at first, not caring if he returned the favor. Then, when his lips parted slightly, I teased the inside of them lightly with my tongue. He let out a breath of hot air, maybe from surprise, and I pulled back. I kept my hands on his head and tried to catch my own breath before I got carried away.

We looked at each other, both of us a bit in shock, him more than I. There was only a split-second pause before Dex grunted, "Oh, fuck it."

Then I was in his arms. He lifted me up and twirled me around on the spot, placing me up against the cold brick wall. I wrapped my legs around him, hooking them at the ankles behind his ass. I was vaguely aware that I wasn't wearing underwear.

He kept one hand around my waist, propping me up, while the other was working its way to the side of my head, disappearing into my hair. He was breathing heavily and staring at my lips. The look in his eyes was utter madness.

"The things I want to do to you..." he whispered roughly.

I took my hand behind his head and brought his ear down to my mouth.

"Do them," I breathed back, and licked the rim of his ear. He let out a small moan and suddenly his lips were on mine. The sweet business was out of the way. His tongue was rampant and skilled and darted feverishly in and out of my mouth, leaving me panting and needing more, as if I couldn't be sustained by him. Then his mouth met my neck and started doing the same there, causing the heat to flare up between my legs. I knew we were in public, making out on the side of the road, but I was so close to just hiking my dress up and undoing the fly on his pants.

One of his hands made its way underneath my ass and started feeling up the back of my bare thighs, slowly searching underneath. There was a slight hesitation when he realized I was going commando and another small moan came out from his lips.

"Perry!"

Rebecca's English accent came through the air, knocking a scary sense of reality into me.

"Perry?" it called again.

Dex and I took our mouths off each other and stared into each other's eyes, bewildered yet enraptured by what had just happened. I quickly unhooked my legs and he placed me gently on the ground, just as Rebecca came around the corner.

She stopped and looked at us, taken aback and trying not to smile. Though we weren't in an embrace, Dex had both arms on either side of me, propped up against the wall. Both of us looked disheveled with messy hair, and Dex's white shirt was half-pulled out from where I must have grabbed at it.

We both stared at her, chests heaving, breathing hard, our breath meeting together in the frigid air.

"Uh, we're just getting the cab now for us," she said slowly. "Perry, you want to come and get your coat and purse?"

The way she said it, it wasn't a question but a command. She jerked her head toward the building and then walked back around the corner. I looked at Dex quickly, pulled his jacket off and handed it to him and then followed her. He reached out for my hand but let go as I kept moving.

I rounded the corner, smoothing out my dress and patting down the back of my head. I was shaking all over, a combination of the cold and the passion.

Rebecca was by the door, giving me a sympathetic look.

"Perry," she said in a tone I didn't like.

"Save it," I said to her and kept walking into the building. The warm air felt heavenly on my gooseflesh.

"All right," she conceded, following me as I walked through the restaurant. Though it wasn't true, I felt like everyone had known what I was doing out there.

We entered the party and I saw that the festivities were still in full swing. I turned at looked at her.

"Why are we leaving already?" I asked.

"I think you and Dex need some time to be alone," she said breezily and walked past me to the table where Emily was sitting with my coat and purse displayed.

I chewed on my lip anxiously. Was Rebecca approving of this whole thing or wasn't she?

She handed me my coat and bag and then put on her own, the black velvet catching the party lights. She noticed the expression I was giving her.

"What? It's true. Who knows where Jenn and Bradley went. It doesn't matter. This just..."

"Has to happen," I finished without thinking. We looked at each other and smiled, knowing it.

She nodded. "Come on."

Emily got up and we walked out of the room. I gave the room one last glance, looking at Dean and Seb, who were at the bar, and at Jimmy and Fae, who were talking to the Handyman table.

"Shouldn't we say goodbye?" I asked.

Rebecca put her arm around me and pushed me forward, gently. "You'll see them again. For now, it's best if we leave unnoticed. Trust me. People here talk. And I'm pretty sure Jenn and Bradley will be the talk of the network come Monday, once Fae starts flapping her mouth."

We walked out of the restaurant and into the cold. Dex was standing in front of a cab that was running, its exhaust filling the frigid air. His back was to us and he was puffing away on another cigarette. I started to question whether a bum had given them to him or not, or if he had a secret stash for moments just like this.

At the sound of the restaurant door closing, he turned around and eyed us briefly. Then he went back to taking a drag.

I was strangely hesitant around him now. I wasn't sure how to act. But Rebecca did. She marched right up to him, her heels handling the snow with ease, plucked the cigarette from his mouth and tossed it behind her shoulder and into the snow.

"Hey," Dex protested.

"No excuses," she said, wagging her finger in front of him. She reached into her giant bag and pulled out the bottle of Jager, which was still half-full. "Take this instead. It's medicinal."

"So are cigarettes," Dex protested. But he took the bottle anyway.

"For what...a broken heart?" she asked. There was almost a malicious edge to her voice, as if she had been down this road with him many times before. Maybe she had been.

"Very funny," he muttered, glaring at her.

"Oh come on, Dex," she said, throwing her arm around him and leading him to the cab. "We're on your side. Always have been. Now get in, pisshead."

She opened the cab door and pushed him lightly. Then Emily followed. Rebecca looked at me and said, "I'll take the front. Get in, Perry."

I did as she said. It was weird to have Emily between Dex and me, but at the same time it left a bit of needed distance. It gave me time to compose my thoughts. That was until Dex passed the bottle of Jager across Emily and straight to me.

I took it and downed a shot against my better judgment. It didn't even burn anymore. Either I was drunk or my whole body was on fire, inside and out. Maybe it was both.

"Trying to get her drunk, Dex?" Rebecca asked from the front seat, eyeing us briefly.

"Hey, no drinking in the cab," the driver admonished.

"Oh, relax, we're dropping them off first," she said, placing her smooth hand on the cabbie's shoulder.

I gave the bottle to Emily, sank back in my seat and turned my focus to the window. Seattle looked so different in the snowfall. The urban grit was replaced by a picture postcard scene. In the morning it would probably be all grey slush, but in the evening it was pristine. There was barely anyone around and the buildings looked like icicles rising from the ground. The orange glow that the streetlights scattered on the snow looked less garish and gave off almost a warm, homey feel. Maybe everything was looking better because I just had one of the best nights of my life. Maybe it looked pure because I could still taste the somehow inoffensive taste of Nicorette, Jack Daniels and cigarettes on my lips, could feel his hands on my thighs.

Everything had changed. Everything was going to change. This wasn't some sexual encounter in the woods. The whole week had been building up to this moment. As Rebecca hinted at, it had to happen. If not, just so I could get it over with. So I could stop wanting him every five minutes. So I could just let it all out.

I breathed out slowly, my breath fogging up the window. I felt Emily's small hand on my bare knee. I looked at her and smiled quickly, then looked at Dex. He was leaning against the cab window, holding the bottle now, looking like he was passed out.

As soon as the cab stopped in front of his apartment, though, he straightened up instinctively. He leaned forward, thanked the cabbie and handed over the cab fare before anyone could protest.

"Talk to you soon," he said, patting Rebecca on the shoulder and giving a quick wave to Emily, and exited the cab. I looked at the girls in surprise.

"Well, I guess…thank you for-"

"Perry," Rebecca said slowly. She eyed the cabbie. He sighed and put the car into park, knowing this could be a long girly convo.

"Perry," she resumed. "Let's do lunch tomorrow, OK? I think we'll have a lot to talk about. I assume we will. Am I right?"

"I hope so," I said quietly.

She gave me a quick smile. "I thought so. Go get 'em, tiger."

I laughed at that and said goodbye to Emily, too, giving her a quick hug.

I got out of the cab. Dex was already down by the main doors, waiting for me.

I joined his side. The cab honked twice and we both turned in unison to wave.

He produced his keycard and the door buzzed open. He held the door for me but didn't touch me as I passed him and strode into the tiled lobby.

I walked to the elevators. He pushed the button. We got in. Neither of us had said a word. As the elevator went up, we stood beside each other in awkward silence. I even stared at him, blatantly, hoping for something, anything. He just put his hands in his pockets and stared up at the ceiling, letting out his breath in slow stages.

When we reached the floor, we walked down the hall to the apartment.

He unlocked the door and I stepped in. I expected to hear Fat Rabbit scratching at the bathroom door but he must have been asleep. It was silent.

"Jenn?" Dex called out tentatively. There was no answer, though it sounded like the dog stirred a bit. As he locked the door behind him, I walked over to the kitchen counter and leaned against it, easing off both of my shoes.

I moved the shoes over with my feet. I could sense Dex behind me. The tension was unbearable. I could hear him kick off his own shoes and then take off his suit jacket. He flung the jacket forward so it ended up in the living room.

Then he walked toward me, the sound of his feet steady on the floor. I remained still, leaning forward against the counter, my breath caught in my throat. I was afraid to move, afraid to breathe.

He stopped right behind me. His presence, his energy, was overwhelming. He reached over and picked my hair off of my shoulders and pushed it to the side of me. I quivered a bit at his touch.

I felt him lean closer and lay his lips on the back of my neck where the welt was. I closed my eyes, enjoying the feel of his hot kiss. He moved a bit over, placing one hand gently on my right arm and moved his lips along the ridge of my shoulders. It sent actual shivers down my spine, shivers I couldn't contain. I kept my eyes tightly shut, trying to regain the slightest bit of composure while he was working away at unraveling my nerves.

His lips came down to my shoulder and then back up again. He reached over and tucked his fingers underneath the line of my jawbone and gently moved my head to the side in a slow, excruciating attempt to have me face him.

He leaned in closer, his chest pressed up against my back, and brought my face to the side, where his lips removed themselves from the curve of my neck and tickled at the side of my mouth.

I couldn't restrain myself anymore. I turned around to face him and his hands were in my hair and his lips and tongue were on my mouth. It was just as frantic and feverish as before, maybe even more so.

He put his hands around my waist and, in one smooth motion, he lifted me up and placed me on the kitchen counter. I wrapped my legs around him again and brought him as close into me as he would go.

As we made out his hands traveled up my dress, hiking it up around my waist. I throbbed at the idea of being bare in front of him and reached forward. I grabbed both sides of his white dress shirt and ripped it right open, buttons flying everywhere and landing on the kitchen floor like white rain. I had always wanted to do that.

I quickly tore the rest of his shirt off of him and threw it on the ground somewhere. Meanwhile, he had unzipped the back of my dress and his lips were on my breasts. I leaned back, torn between wanting to be in control and wanting to let go. In the end, he decided that for me. He gently pushed me back until my back was flat on the counter; then he worked his way down to my thighs. I shuddered in anticipation as his tongue worked its way up and met me inside with a languid wash of warmth and slickness.

I groaned, my back arching, and for once I didn't feel a bit self-conscious.

He worked his magic, much like he did on the island, only it was different now. More powerful. More inviting. More destructive.

Just before I felt myself going over the edge, I straightened up and grabbed the top of his head, pulling him up to look at me. He quickly wiped his mouth and asked, "Do you want me to stop?" Through the waves of desire on his face, he looked worried.

I shook my head, trying to find my voice.

"No," I said breathily. "I want you inside of me. Now."

Dex raised his eyebrow and stood up straight. He stared at me for a few beats, breathing hard, almost as if he couldn't believe what I had said. Then he said, "Yes ma'am."

He quickly undid his pants and I slipped my dress over my head. When we were both done, we were stark-ass naked.

Now, he had seen me naked before. More than once, somehow. But I'd never seen him. So I couldn't be blamed for taking my time and letting my eyes slide all over his body. I wasn't disappointed. Just as I thought, he was nothing but all man, more than enough size for his height.

I wrapped my legs around him again and brought him to me. I ran my nails against his chest, tracing his tattoo, then brought his lips to mine. He made sure I was ready again and then guided himself in. The fact that he wasn't wearing a condom briefly entered my mind but in the heat of the moment, it wasn't registering.

I put my hands around his shoulders and squeezed him hard as he entered me. It hurt. It had been a while.

"You OK?" he asked, breathing heavily in my ear between lazy moans and licks.

"Yeah," I answered, wincing only slightly. Soon the pain was gone and he had found his rhythm. We both had. It was seamless, effortless. When I wanted it faster, I dug my nails into the round of his ass and moved him faster. When he wanted it slower, he pulled back and trailed his tongue and lips all over my body.

Throughout all of it, he wanted eye contact. There was barely a moment where I wasn't looking into his eyes. It was unnerving, but if I looked away, he brought my gaze back to his.

"I need to see you," he whispered, looking deep into my eyes. It was so personal, and I felt so vulnerable; my first instinct was to keep him out. But in the end I relented. And I watched the range of emotions run across those fathomless irises, watched him battle so many inner demons. It made everything that much more intense, as if it wasn't already.

After awhile, when his fingers slid their way down to where I was swelling, I was on the verge of total collapse. He knew it too, biting at my lower lip and neck and working his fingertips as he slid in and out of me at a more vigorous pace.

Soon, there was no turning back, for either of us. His breath was shortening too, groaning more often than not.

"Dex," I cried out softly, trying to warn him. He kept his eyes on me but I had to break free. My head rolled back and my body burst open into a quivering mess of feelings and starshine. Unlike last time, a wave of emotions rode through me. I moaned and cried out his name over and over again, the occasional swear word thrown in there, and that brought him over the edge as well. Both of us were crying out, so loud that Fat Rabbit must have been traumatized in the bathroom, our nails digging into each other, our rocking motion slowing down.

I was left feeling like I was floating above us all. A shimmer seemed to envelope the apartment, bending and swaying at the corner of my eyes. The emotions gripped my throat and teased behind my eyes. I felt like crying. It was too much. *I love you*, I wanted to cry out. I wanted to let it all out, over and over again.

But I just lay back against the counter and held his head into my chest, trying to catch my breath, trying to return to the world. And despite having gotten it "over with," my first thought was that I wanted to do that again. Immediately.

After a few minutes, he lifted up his head and looked at me. And the expression on his face...it changed everything. He was looking at me in absolute fear. I thought I had caught that look before on the island, but it was different now. He and Jenn were over, weren't they? There was nothing left to fear.

He pulled back, straightening up and then pulled out of me.

I reached forward for his arm, to keep him beside me, but he shrugged it off and walked off to the bathroom. I sat up slowly, turning, and watched his naked form disappear.

What the hell was that? I didn't like that look at all. It gnawed at my heart and made me second-guess everything that had just happened.

Take it easy, I told myself. *Maybe he just realized he should have used a condom and is freaking out.*

I couldn't blame him for that. I hoped that was it. That was a pretty stupid move on both our behalves.

I hoped off the counter, my legs feeling like jelly, my breath and heart rate still erratic. I eyed the mess on the counter and contemplated leaving it there for Jenn to clean up. But that would be too mean and too trashy. I grabbed a paper towel and wiped it off, throwing the rest in the garbage.

Then I gathered up my shoes and my dress and hightailed it, naked, to the den just in case Jenn decided to come home early from her shenanigans.

It wasn't till I entered the room and shut the door behind me, that I realized the magnitude of what just happened.

I just had sex with Dex.

I wouldn't have believed it had it not been for the leftover throbbing between my legs, the funny way I walked, the wetness as it ran down me, the bruises he left on my neck from his overzealous sucking. The way his eyes looked as we had made love.

The way his eyes looked afterward.

I rubbed my face anxiously and looked around the den. I needed something to distract me before he came out. I didn't want to think too much into anything, not before I got a chance to talk to him.

I slipped on my pajama pants and shirt and decided to pack my bag, just in case Jenn came home and they had their long overdue massive blowout and I was suddenly sent home due to awkwardness.

I didn't have much to pack in the end and was done in a few minutes. I thought I heard the bathroom door open so I waited a few minutes, opened the door to the apartment and looked out. Dex was sitting on the couch in his pajama pants, his back to me and his head in his hands.

I cautiously stepped out and made my way over to him. I stopped by his side, feeling uneasy and self-conscious.

"Are you OK?" I asked softly, looking down at him.

He didn't answer me. He just kept his focus on the carpet. I noticed that Fat Rabbit had trotted out of the room and was sniffing around the front door.

I placed my hand on his shoulder. He jumped at my touch. This wasn't good.

"Dex," I said. I kept my hand there and crouched down beside him. "Talk to me."

There was still no answer. Now I was really starting to worry.

I reached up with my hand and grasped his wrist. I tried to pull it off his head but he resisted.

"Dex, please," I said loud enough that Fat Rabbit stopped his sniffing and slowly sulked over to us.

Finally he looked at me. His eyes were red like he had been crying. They were also angry.

"What is it?" I asked, leaning forward and searching them. "What happened?"

"Nothing happened," he said. "And I hope you remember it that way."

I was taken aback. My heart lurched uncomfortably. My nerves began to sizzle in the worst way. I couldn't think the worst, though. I took in a deep breath.

"What do you mean by that?" I asked carefully.

He whipped his wrist out of my grasp and looked at the blank TV. "What do you think I mean?"

I straightened up and crossed my arms uneasily. "Dex, just tell me what you're talking about. You owe me that much."

He chuckled. It was mean. "I don't owe you anything, Perry."

Now I really was starting to freak out. "Dex, what the hell is wrong with you? Why are you acting like this?"

"Why are you acting like this?" he countered, waving at me. "All in my face and bugging me every fucking second."

"Bugging you?" I repeated. "We just had sex and now you're freaking out about it like –"

"I'm not freaking out about it," he shot back.

"Well then what the hell is this?" I shouted. "Cuz we were all fine an hour ago before this happened."

"I knew this was a mistake," he muttered into his hands. "This changed everything."

I could barely speak. I felt like he had stabbed me with an ice pick. I wanted to throw up right on him. I brought my hand to my mouth, fearing it might happen. The tears rushed to my eyes but I didn't let them flow.

"This wasn't a mistake..." I said, trying hard not to sob the words out. "How...how could you say that?"

"You're just reading too much into this," he sniped. "Typical."

Another blow, this one chipping away at my pride. My other hand flew to my chest. I felt like my heart was being ripped out of my chest in slow increments. I was breathless, thoughtless. I waved around for something to lean on and found the corner of the couch.

I stared down at Dex as sparks came in and out of the corner of my vision. That was usually a sign that I was going to faint. He looked up at me, a wave of concern passing over him briefly. Maybe it was regret. It didn't matter. What he said was what he said. And it was killing me inside.

I leaned against the couch, trying to get oxygen, trying to prevent my face from crumbling hopelessly.

Eventually I heard him say, "Perry?"

I looked at him in disbelief. "What was this to you, Dex? A rebound? An itch you had to get out of your system? Another notch to add to your bedpost? Another person to screw around and fuck with? Mentally and physically!?"

He frowned and blinked a few times. He was unable to say anything.

"OK, then," I said, my voice shaking. "Guess it was all of the above. Glad I finally know how you really feel."

I turned and hurried off to the den. All I wanted to do was throw myself on the bed and cry my eyes out, but I had promised myself I would get out of the city without shedding a single tear. I shoved my boots on my feet, not caring that was only wearing pajamas, and put my jacket on top of my shirt. I hoisted the duffel bag and purse on my shoulders and marched out of the den toward the front door.

"Where are you going?" Dex cried out, getting to his feet and coming after me. He grabbed my arm and I wriggled free. Then I took my hands and pushed him hard against his chest so that he stumbled backward.

"You made your point, Dex," I spat out at him viciously. "You've now been very clear."

"Perry, wait," he said quickly, his voice uneasy, and rushed back to me. "You can't leave now. It's snowing, you're in your pajamas..."

"I am leaving. And I'm not coming back. Rebecca was right about you. You're nothing but a scared little boy!"

I turned and made my way to the door, feeling the build-up of emotion rifling through my body, feeling like I was on the verge of total emotional and physical destruction. It was all too much. Too much.

He grabbed me again, putting both his hands around my waist and pulling me up to him. His eyes were crazy, flying everywhere, the eyes of an utter madman.

"Why do you care so much?" he demanded, his grip tightening. His voice rose higher and cracked. "You told me you didn't love me!"

He shouted that last bit in absolute desperation.

I fought him off and stumbled backward into the door. I faced him and yelled, "You're not the only who knows how to lie, Dex!"

His face sank. It was the face of utter and total regret. A face of shame. And a face of supreme agony. He let go of me, dumbfounded.

I took the opportunity to open the door. I paused in the doorway and took the anchor bracelet off my wrist. I ripped it in half in front of his eyes and then threw it at his feet.

"You're not my anchor! You never were. You're nothing to me! Go find some other love-struck, spineless girl to host your stupid show!"

I stepped out in the hallway and gave him one final, vile glare.

"I quit!" I yelled at him, fully venomous and fully meaning it. I was done.

Forever.

Then I pulled the door shut. Only then did Dex make a move to stop me, a choked cry escaping from his lips. But it was too late. I ran down the hall and scampered down the stairs all the way to the parking garage.

I knew it was stupid and foolish to ride my motorbike in the snow, especially after a few drinks, but maybe I could find a cheap hotel on the outskirts of town. That plan kept me going, kept my brain occupied and kept my emotions from ruining me before I could escape.

In the cold garage, I frantically strapped my bag to the bike, mounted it and roared out onto the street. The wheels slipped a bit on the snow but the traction held. The snowfall had stopped, thankfully, and I was able to see clearly through my helmet as I made my way through the downtown area and onto the I-5.

It wasn't till I was outside of the city limits that my vision began to blur. There were too many tears running down my face.

Look for Experiment in Terror #5
On Demon Wings
to be published Spring 2012

For more information about the series, please visit:
www.experimentinterror.com

Follow the author on Twitter at
@MetalBlonde

Become a fan of the EIT Facebook Page by liking us at
www.facebook.com/experimentinterror

Made in the USA
Lexington, KY
25 June 2013